One of t... people is ...the root of evil in the...

GARDEN OF MALICE

Is it . . .

HUGH

Roz's employer and Lady Viola's notoriously ruthless son?

CEDRIC or FLORENCE NORTH

The aging pianist? Or his wife, whose secrets are buried deep?

HUGH or BEATRICE BADGETT

The "salt-of-the-earth" scientist? Or his wife, who is ashamed of his humble beginnings?

CORY or STELLA

The estate gardeners, who have access to *very* powerful insecticide?

FRANCESCA

The striking, mysterious guest who seems to terrify everyone?

ALAN

The handsome painter whom Roz would love to trust . . . if only she dared?

GARDEN
OF
MALICE

Susan Kenney

There are many beautiful country homes and gardens in England, but Montfort Abbey is not one of them and is not intended to bear any particular resemblance to any real place. All the characters in this book are fictitious and none of the events chronicled herein has ever taken place.

Library of Congress Catalog Card Number: 83-8929

ISBN: 0-345- 31712-2

This edition published by arrangement with Charles Scribner's Sons

Excerpts from "Burnt Norton" in Four Quartets *by T. S. Eliot are reprinted by permission of Harcourt Brace Jovanovich, Inc., and Faber & Faber Ltd; copyright 1943 by T. S. Eliot, renewed 1971 by Esme Valerie Eliot.*

Excerpts from "To the Rose Upon the Rood of Time" in Collected
~~~~~ ~~~~~ Butler Yeats *(New York: Macmillan, 1956) are*
~~~~~ ~~~~~ Publishing Co., Inc., New
~~~~~ ~~~~~ Anne Yeats, and*

For my mother,
Virginia Fuller Tucker McIlvaine Perkins,
who has always loved flowers, letters, and mysteries

1

ROSAMUND HOWARD GRABBED FOR THE ARM rest as the taxi careened around another curve of the ancient, winding street. Her head still droned from six hours on the jet plane, her spine still reverberated to the clack of the railroad train, and now she was being tossed and jerked from side to side of the beat-up, shabby vehicle like so much loose change on a roller coaster. *I'm going to be buzzed and rattled and jostled apart before I even get to Montfort Abbey,* she thought.

Then, inexplicably, the car stopped pitching and lurched upright. She peered ahead and saw that they had entered a long, straight stretch of roadway—almost an alley. On either side, the oatmeal-colored medieval houses leaned inward, forming a canyon down which the throbbing of the engine echoed strangely. Sitting up, Roz tugged the larger of her two suitcases onto the seat between her hip and the door and wedged herself in. She felt dazed, sore, gummy-mouthed, and frowsy. She wasn't even sure what day it was in England. Friday, Saturday—Sunday? It couldn't be Friday; she distinctly remembered being in New York Friday night. That was the last thing she distinctly remembered.

She looked at her reflection in the grimy window. Dark shadows around h⸱⸱⸱⸱⸱⸱⸱ hair pulling out ⸱⸱⸱⸱⸱⸱ of her n⸱⸱⸱⸱⸱

should have gotten more sleep on the plane, she thought, *instead of worrying so much about meeting Giles again.* After all, it had been nearly a year. She had gone over again and again her first words, the casual but crisp professional tone. *Oh hello, Giles. . . . Giles, how nice to see you.* That was a problem right there. She'd never even called him Giles to his face. It was still Mr. Montfort-Snow. *Oh hello, Mr. Montfort-Snow. . . . Hi there, Mr. Montfort-Snow, how are you?*

And then, after all that, when she arrived at the Framley Railway Station, instead of Giles Montfort-Snow by any name, there was only the rusty-coated person with Ralph's Hire-Car Service pasted across his jacket, calling her name off a crumpled piece of paper.

"You for the Abbey?" he had inquired suspiciously, squinting at her, and when she nodded, speechless with surprise at being sent for instead of met, he had grunted, "Well, come on, then," picked up her bags, and stalked off.

Oh well, she thought, resting her head on the back of the seat, *what difference does it make?* She was on her way, would be there soon, the meeting with Giles over, and work begun on the definitive edition of the posthumous papers of Lady Viola Montfort-Snow. Roz sighed. Even now, she could hardly believe it. An obscure assistant professor of English at Vassar—publications, yes, but nothing major—chosen from numerous excellent scholars on both sides of the Atlantic breathless for the chance to get at these papers. This was the opportunity of a lifetime, her chance to make a mark in her profession, to make herself secure. The ivory tower had long since acquired revolving doors and ⸻ll but the most distinguished and ⸻ng scholars. One ⸻ reputa-

would come up for tenure and promotion after this year's leave of absence to do the papers, and if she could do the job well, her future would be assured. She hadn't felt secure in a long time, not since her parents had died while she was still in graduate school. She had no one to look after her. Sighing, she shut her eyes tight for a moment. On the other hand, she had only herself to worry about, no ties to keep her, no one really to miss her if she stayed. An unhappy love affair had died. It was a good time to go. Things had a way of turning out for the best—or at least better than one thought.

Roz opened her eyes, aware that the hysterical whine of the car's engine had subsided. They had left the town and were on a highway. She looked out the window at the countryside. Flat marshland stretched as far as the eye could see in all directions. Fen country, reaching from just north of Cambridge beyond Ely to the west, and east past Bury to the sea. She knew it only from maps. East Anglia, England's out-thrust left hip. She imagined herself high above the little car, and saw it beetling north along a narrow black line drawn across land as flat and sectioned as a chessboard. Roz rolled down the window; heavy, mud-scented air rushed in, smelling of dark, damp earth and vegetation. Above the expanse of meadow grass, a building or grove of trees loomed eerily out of the haze, then vanished as abruptly as a mirage. A light wind flattened and rippled the grass in waves. To the west, on the horizon, an irregular blue smudge appeared faintly, a clenched fist with finger pointing upward. Roz sat forward, interested, but just then they passed through a deep road cut, and the high mound of earth obscured her view.

There wa

sent her, but she still had only a hazy mental picture of the Abbey Tower so often mentioned by Lady Viola, rising tall and stark out of a foundation of smoky mist, shrouded in its curtain of fencloud, remote and mysterious, austere and inaccessible. Very much like Lady Viola herself. Roz loved Lady Viola's poems, her garden books, her essays, the two odd, mystical novels—all the products of a long and prolific life as a writer and gardener—but she did not have a very clear idea of Lady Viola herself, even after spending the last several months saturating herself in all the published works by and about her. None of them had taken into account the contents of the large brown leather trunk discovered the year before by her son Giles in the attic of a small chapel on the grounds, four years after Lady Viola's death. There Roz hoped to find the key—in the stacks of personal papers, diaries, and letters that were going to be her task to edit for publication. Roz shook her head at the small, suspicious voice that even now whispered nervously, *Why me? Why you, indeed,* she chided herself. *Why ask?* She was the one on her way to the Abbey to do the job, and, nervous or not, she was going to do it well.

Her defense of herself was jolted by a renewal of the lurch and bump. They had turned off the main highway and were now skittering down a road narrowed to one lane by tall hedges on either side. The bases of some of the bushes were as big as tree trunks. Roz wondered if these were Montfort Abbey hedges, planted by the monks years before the Dissolution, before Gilbert Fotheringay had acquired the Abbey from King Henry VIII, appropriated first the name and then the stones to build his Tudor manor, leaving only a few of the original buildings intact as ~~what had once been the most~~ ~~this part of En-~~ ~~now Gil-~~

her husband, Herbert Snow, into the most famous garden in England.

The car bumped off the paved lane onto gravel. A sign read TO MONTFORT ABBEY GARDENS. Roz sat forward. The view was clear for an instant, looking out over gently sloping flat land to a stand of cedars whose long feathery branches seemed to float on air, smaller trees and foliage surrounding what appeared to be one sprawling, massive building of honey-colored stone. Roz blinked. That couldn't be right. Where were the ruins, the fallen masonry, the separate buildings?

She leaned back. Of course it had to be an illusion. She looked again, but her vision was suddenly obscured by a stand of trees. She moved back and forth, trying to get another glimpse of the Abbey as the car proceeded up a long, winding drive. Sure enough, like some elaborate pastoral stage setting, spaces appeared along the stone facade as they drew closer. The whole structure seemed to fall apart before Roz's eyes, until she thought she could distinguish at least five separate buildings among the trees and shrubs. The most imposing was the tall, square, battlemented tower three stories high with round turrets pointed upward like fat pencils on either side, set slightly off-center between two lower flanking wings as though a giant hand had slid it to one side. Underneath the tower was an arch, and what looked like a gatehouse. Roz glanced to the right and was startled to see a large car park with several cars in it. She had forgotten the Abbey Gardens were now open to the public.

The car jerked to a halt in front of the gatehouse. Roz opened the door and stepped out with a peculiar floating sensation on to the gravel drive. As though from far away, the driver's voice said, "I'll get your bags, miss."

She nod

dark tunnel under the tower. She walked into its shadow. On her left was a door, on her right a large plate glass window and another doorway into what appeared to be a small room. In the corner of the window was a square placard reading: "Gardens open the year round 10 A.M. to dusk, Tuesdays to Sundays. Closed Mondays and holidays excepting Bank holidays. Admission 75p. No dogs or other pets. Bath chairs allowed with prior permission."

Roz edged closer and peered through the glass into the space beyond the sign; behind her own reflection she could just make out a square room with a desk, a chair, an ancient filigreed cash register, and a book stand full of folders and books. Other than that, the room was empty. She stared at the little counter, wondering if Giles himself ever sat there and sold tickets.

"You're wondering if I ever sit there and sell tickets," a deep voice remarked behind her.

Roz turned quickly. Giles Montfort-Snow stood silhouetted in the opening, his tall, lean figure framed in the precise center of the arch, his blond hair gleaming, his deep-set hazel eyes and long nose, sharply etched in the oblique sunlight. "Everyone always does," he said gravely.

Instantly she forgave him everything—her lack of reception at the station, the hair-raising taxi ride, her confusion and uneasiness. She had never seen anyone look more at home. The Lord of the Manor. After the briefest of hesitations, he came through the arch, extending both his hands to grasp hers.

"Welcome to Montfort, my dear Rosamund. I'm so

skirt. "Hello, ah . . . Mr. Montfort-Snow," she stammered.

Still smiling, Giles released her hands and took a step past her. "Where are your bags? Oh, the driver has them. Let me just attend to that, and then we'll go right inside. You must be simply exhausted."

And I must look it, Roz thought as she watched Giles stride quickly over to the driver, speak to him, nod, and wave him off. As the car drove away, Giles picked up a suitcase in either hand and walked back toward her. "Let me show you where you'll be staying. Your digs, as we say in Britain."

Obediently, Roz followed Giles around the corner into a large open space consisting mostly of lawn surrounded by crushed gravel paths edged with brick. Beyond the paths grew thick borders of flowers in shades of violet, blue, magenta, and burgundy, arranged in tiers that increased in height until they merged with great thickets of climbing roses. The space was enclosed on all four sides by buildings and walls, but everything was so obscured by flowers and vines that Roz could hardly tell which was which. She was so busy looking all around that she almost ran straight into Giles as he stopped to shift both suitcases under one arm so he had a hand free to lift the latch of a great wooden door. It looked centuries old, brass-bound with hinges the size of encyclopedias, but it swung back easily once Giles tipped the latch. He stood aside and let Roz pass first into the dark space beyond.

After the bright slanting sunlight of the courtyard, the interior loomed obscurely, and Roz instinctively ducked her head.

"This is the Refectory." Giles's voice came from behind her as he shut the door. "It was once the monks' dining hall and . . . recreation area, you might say. It was in frightful shape when my parents took over. Quite sound, though. The walls are twenty-two inches thick, built of the same stone

7

used at Ely. This is where I live, and where you will stay."

As her eyes adjusted to the dim light, Roz saw they were in a hallway separated from another larger room by an intricately carved screen, beyond which she could just make out the shapes of some chairs and a sofa, as well as a large, shadowed fireplace flanked by doors at the far end. Light filtered in through the leaded glass windows; the smell of flowers was everywhere. She followed Giles down the hall to a stairway.

"Let me show you your room," he said, pausing at the bottom of the stairs. "I'll leave you to yourself for a bit, and then I thought you might like to take a turn around the garden. It's still quite early; I'll have to clear the rest of the tourists out so we can have some privacy. I'd like you to see it as it would have been when Mother was alive, not swarming with day-trippers and cameras snapping away in the air like death-watch beetles."

There was an awkward silence. Then Roz realized that Giles was watching her with a politely inquiring look on his face. In spite of her slightly dazed condition—no sleep for over eighteen hours, now—she said quickly, "Oh yes, I'd like that."

Giles nodded, then turned and went up the stairs. Carefully fitting her feet into the bowl-like depressions worn into the middle of each stone step, Roz followed him up. They emerged into another hall. To the left, a single door stood ajar—"My room," Giles remarked as they passed—and to the right, a long corridor with windows on one side and several doors on the other. Giles pushed open the second door. "This will be your room," he said. "It overlooks the courtyard, and the lavatory is just in there." He leaned around the corner of the door, placing her bags inside. "I'll leave you for a moment, then, while I go shut up shop. Come down when you're ready." Giles smiled briefly. "Then you can meet my garden." He nodded and was gone.

Roz heard the downstairs door clank shut. She was alone. She took a deep breath and walked into her room. Coarsely woven rush carpeting rustled under her feet. The walls were rough white plaster, crisscrossed with thick black beams. The small casement windows flanked a large pier glass; the curtains and bed coverings were of red *toile* depicting a fairly gruesome boar hunt. Everywhere—on the delicate Sheraton dressing table, the small oak writing desk, the tiny bedside stands—were bouquets of flowers.

But it was the scent of roses that layered and filled the air, and as she moved closer to one of the windows, she saw it was almost completely covered over by a dense growth of climbing roses. She carefully pushed the window open farther, took a deep breath, and looked out over the garden.

It lay there in the sunlight, what she could see of it, the low sun now throwing into relief the walls and hedges that divided the various gardens from one another. Ruins were indistinguishable from buildings; there were openings and arches and doors and gates, gravel walks and brick walks, hedges rising beyond hedges. From this angle, it looked to Roz like a three-dimensional Chinese puzzle, a skittles box, a maze. She studied it for a full minute, trying to take it all in. Impossible. Oh well, there was plenty of time for that. Meanwhile, Giles was waiting to show her around. *Meet my garden,* he had said. Rather odd, come to think of it, as though the garden were a person.

Roz turned away from the window and went into the little bathroom. She splashed cold water on her face, brushed her teeth, then returned to the bedroom and contemplated herself in the large mirror. With her hair frowsing all over, those startled-looking, round blue eyes, her long-legged figure made even more adolescent-looking by the mussed-up traveling dress, she looked approximately half her age, which was thirty. She also

9

looked about as scholarly and professional as Snow White.

Sighing, she turned away from the mirror, pulled the dress up over her head, tossed it on the bed, and changed into jeans and a long-sleeved shirt. Not very scholarly-looking, either, but at least it was what she was used to wearing. She reached up and pinned her hair back tightly into its knot, smoothing away all the wisps and frays.

And then, as though the change of clothes had really made a difference, a feeling of excitement replaced her anxiety. She couldn't wait to see the papers. She picked up a sweater and hurried out into the hall. Glancing down through the large casement window, she saw the now-empty car park and, beyond that, the distant, low-lying fens hazy in the late afternoon light. For a moment Roz had the sensation that she and the Abbey were floating like an island in the clouds, sheltered and removed. There was not a soul in sight, not a sound to be heard.

She was just stepping back from the window when she heard a rustling noise behind her. She turned quickly and peered down the long passage. Again the sound, a scuffling and then a thump, but coming from Giles's room. She walked down the hall and pushed open the door. A flick of movement caught her eye, barely more than a disturbance of the air, a sense of something snatched away.

"Mr. Montfort-Snow?" she said tentatively.

At the far end of the room the wall swayed. Roz blinked in disbelief. The swaying stopped, and everything was still again.

Roz walked forward, her eyes on the wall. As she stared at it, the whole wall billowed out, then fell back with a thump. Roz smiled. It was a large, grayish tapestry almost the color of stone, across which faded and dusty figures paraded in some medieval pastime, moving ever so slightly in the breeze from an open window. She was just reaching out to run her hand over the stitching when she heard the

crunch of gravel underneath the window. She looked
down to see Giles, his tall figure oddly foreshortened,
striding under the arch. With one amused look over
her shoulder at the still swaying tapestry, she hurried out of Giles's room, down the stairs, and out into
the sunlit garden.

2

"OH, HERE YOU ARE, MY DEAR ROSAMUND,"
Giles said as she emerged from the Refectory. "Very prompt. You've changed your
clothes, I see. Come along, then; we'd best do
the garden right away, so you'll be able to get a sense
of the place."

Roz nodded, but Giles didn't see her; he was already walking away down the gravel path toward
the gatehouse tower. She would have preferred to
see the papers first, but obviously Giles thought seeing the garden was more important.

"Let's start here," he said, standing with his back
to the Tower. "This is the Courtyard, looking north.
Behind us is the Refectory, where we've just been,
and over there where the *Rosa Virginiana* tumbles
down is the room you're staying in," he said, waving
a hand in front of her.

"Behind that far wall are the Cloister and the
Maze, but never mind that now, we'll get to them in
due course. The Gatehouse Tower behind us is one of
the earlier buildings, formerly the kitchen entrance;
all the rest were once the stables and outbuildings. I
cobbled the little ticket office up out of an old sentry
box—rather clever, don't you think? The short path

11

there is all that remains of the old Abbey Dormitory. It's now the quarters of my housekeeper, Mrs. Farthing."

Roz blinked in surprise. She had not known Giles had a housekeeper, but of course he would have to, to keep this sprawling place in order.

"Now, Mrs. Farthing is what we call an old family retainer," Giles went on. "She's been here for donkeys' years—took care of me as a boy and adored my mother. She's never married; *Mrs.* is a courtesy title. She stays on, keeps house, and takes tickets, though I'm afraid she's not terribly efficient. Still, one has a responsibility . . ."

Giles paused. Roz waited for him to finish, but he did not go on. So much for Mrs. Farthing. Instead, he pointed directly across the Courtyard at a heavily cross-timbered building with a steep-pitched tile roof, four spindly chimney pots poking up along the peak. It looked at odds with the other low stone buildings.

"That long Tudor building over there is the Moat House. It's all that remains of Gilbert de Montfort's great manor—that and a bit of moat. Here I am, five centuries later, living in the old Abbey buildings, and almost everything he built is gone. And it's still called the Abbey." Giles was silent for a moment as he contemplated the Moat House. "Odd, isn't it?" he said finally.

"Yes, isn't it?" Roz said, and cursed herself. Even Snow White could do better than that.

Giles did not appear to have heard her. "I should have liked to live there myself," he said, "but my mother leased it to an old friend for forty years, and now the nephew has taken it over. Chap named Alan Stewart. He hasn't been here long—a year or so. He's something of an artist, keeps to himself. He's done a number of paintings and drawings for me, all of flowers. Sort of a hobby, I gather."

Roz looked again at the Moat House, mildly surprised at the thought of another resident. Where had

12

she gotten the impression that Giles lived here alone? Hadn't he said something to that effect in New York, when they were first discussing the edition? She was sure he had. She gazed at the Moat House for a moment longer, then let her eyes roam around the rest of the Courtyard. Was that another building tucked away among the vines and flowers? She thought she saw two large windows and a roof. But before she could ask, Giles had walked ahead of her through a small archway in the near corner of the wall. Another garden.

This one was small, crowded with flowers—red poppies, orange chrysanthemums, marigolds, daisies, yellow snapdragons poking upward indiscriminately, floundering onto the brick walks. Green fingerlike clematis with blossoms like bits of lemon peel covered the wall in front of her. Quite a contrast to the subdued, rather cool colors and martialed ranks of the Courtyard.

"This is the Cottage Plot, your typical English kitchen garden," Giles said. "Not a bit formal—planted mainly for color and bloom and the odd pot herb and medicinal. Some people think it's common and vulgar, but I quite like it. My mother re-created it when she converted the building there into a cottage."

As if anything Viola created could be vulgar, Roz thought as she looked at the wall in front of her. She could make out a small wooden door, and, farther up, a tiny, arched window. Then she realized she was looking at the side wall of the building that fronted on the Courtyard.

"It's been called the Granary for as long as I can remember," Giles went on. "It's now the home of Cedric North, the pianist, another old friend of Mother's. He's remarkably old, you know. Quite eighty, I should think. Lives there with his second wife."

"Oh, really?" Roz peered at the Granary with new interest. This name, at least, was familiar. Cedric

North. She remembered a record jacket—an old, round-faced man with white hair fringing his forehead, leaning over a piano. But she hadn't realized he lived here. And his wife. That made three more residents, not to mention Mrs. Farthing. But why hadn't Giles told her there were so many? She was beginning to feel at a disadvantage. She turned around just in time to see him disappear out the other side of the Cottage Plot.

When she caught up with him, he was standing in the middle of a long avenue of trees. On one side the trees grew dense and full, arching over, while on the walled side they were spread-eagled flat against the stone, as if driven there by an explosion.

"The Plum Tree Walk," Giles said. "On the other side of that wall is the Garden of Healthful Herbs, but we won't go in there now. I do want to get on." And off he went again, striding quickly down the alley of trees.

Feeling a little like Alice running after the White Rabbit, Roz hurried after him. "How many other people are there?" she asked somewhat breathlessly. "I mean . . . I didn't know . . ."

Giles stopped short and turned, an amused expression on his face. Then he began to tick off on his fingers. "In addition to the Norths and Alan Stewart, there are Cory and Stella, the gardeners—frightfully professional, you know, University and the Royal College of Horticulture and all that—they live in the converted stable just back over there. That bit of Victorian madness you glimpse over the poplars behind the Dormitory is the home of Hugh and Beatrice Badgett." As Roz stared at him in disbelief, he went on.

"Hugh's a rather well-known scientist. Quite remarkable, really, when you consider that he is the son of a farmer. His father, Humphrey, ran the Home Farm for my parents. The family had worked this land for generations. Good peasant stock, but hardly worth educating, one would have thought.

14

Sote, my mother called them, as you no doubt remember. S.O.T.E. Salt of the earth. She adored peasants. Hugh went off to University on scholarship—my parents helped, of course—and now he is a distinguished microbotanist. Still, I like to think he has remained a son of the land. He and his wife, Beatrice, manage the Home Farm for me now. I really think Hugh can't bear to leave the place."

Giles was silent for a moment, staring straight ahead, seemingly abstracted. Then he seemed to come to.

"That's the lot. Not so very many after all, now is it? Anyway, you'll meet them all soon. I've arranged a luncheon in your honor day after tomorrow." With that, Giles stuck his hands in his pockets and headed down the alley toward where the trees ended, leaving Roz with the feeling that she had run out of fingers on which to tick off people—not to mention gardens.

But there was Giles, waiting for her at the end of the walk. He took her arm as they crossed over a small stone bridge with a narrow rivulet of murky water flowing underneath.

"The moat, or what's left of it," Giles remarked. "But here's what I'm so anxious for you to see." He stepped to one side, turned, and swept an arm wide, as though introducing a roomful of guests.

"The pride of Montfort Abbey. The Rose Garden."

Roz looked in the direction of his outflung arm. And stared.

Bushes and trees and vines of roses in every imaginable color stretched out before her in geometrically precise patterns, spokes in a wheel, rays in a sunburst—easily an acre of roses, as high as her knee, her shoulder, taller than her head, blooms the size of teacups, of soup bowls, miniature blossoms no larger than a thimble, ruffles and pleats of dark red velvet, vermilion rose, pink, lavender, mauve, white, coral ivory, yellow, fawn, scarlet, all flaming upward, splashing against green, glossy leaves. The colors dashed and flared at her eyes, the fragrance surrounded her, and the sound of bees suddenly boomed in her ears as she saw them glistening in the shadows of the leaves, darting drunkenly in and out. Lines and verses and snatches of poetry and song jostled each other in her head, "Nor praise the deep vermilion" . . . "Red Rose, proud Rose, sad Rose of all my days" . . . "the door we never opened/Into the rose-garden."

"Rosamund?"

Roz jumped, startled. "What?" she said, then realized how abrupt she had sounded. "Oh, I'm so sorry, ah . . . Mr. Montfort-Snow," she began.

"Never mind," Giles interrupted in an amused tone. "Your reaction is typical. But see here. Don't you think it's about time you called me Giles? After all, we are going to be associates, aren't we?" He smiled at her.

"Fine," she said. "And you can call me Roz."

"Ah! I don't think I want to do that." Giles turned and marched down the nearest alley of roses, stopping near a short, straggly bush with small red and white striped blooms that looked as though they had been wound up out of peppermint ribbon candy. "Do you know the name of this rose?" Giles asked, resting his hand lightly on one of the small blooms.

Roz shook her head, her heart sinking. He must think she knew a lot more about roses than she did. It didn't look like much—small, scrawny, a poor relation of a rose. Giles plucked a blossom and handed it to her.

"Of all the hundreds of roses in this garden, this one is my particular favorite. I don't know quite why; perhaps because it is the oldest. It's a gallica, and its origin is lost in time. It's even older than York-Lancaster, with which it's sometimes confused. Older than 1485, if you can imagine. Probably as old as the Abbey itself. My mother found it here, growing wild." Giles picked another rose and held it up like a glass of wine. "Its name is *Rosamundi. Rose of the World*," he said, regarding her with an odd smile.

Roz stared at him, the back of her neck beginning to prickle.

"Do you believe that names are fate?"

Uh oh, Roz said to herself. She studied his face. He looked perfectly sincere.

"When I first met you and heard your name, I knew at once that you were fated to help me do my mother's papers."

Roz turned away. *How perfectly absurd,* she thought, lifting up a pale yellow rose the size of a bread-and-butter plate, heavy on its stem, and burying her nose in it. It smelled of tea and cream. She tried to collect her thoughts. No one had called her Rosamund in years. *I'll never get used to it,* she thought, breathing in the sweet odor of the rose. Maybe he would like to call her by her old nickname, Rozzie. Her father had called her that. Roz smiled at the recollection. But what did it matter? Whatever name he used, she would still be Roz Howard. She looked up.

"You can call me Rosamund if you want to," she said gravely.

To her relief, Giles threw his head back and laughed. "You don't sound as though you like the idea much! But I'm afraid I've embarrassed you with all this talk of names. Still, Roz is such a quick, abrupt-sounding name. Not like you at all. I know what you're thinking, though. What's in a name—all this fuss. But never mind. Sometimes I think the roses are all I have left for family. They do mean rather a lot to me. But I shall try to call you Roz, if that's what your friends call you. I doubt I'll succeed, though. I find it very hard to change. Unlike Lawrence Johnstone over there."

Roz looked behind her. Who was this, now? But there was no one to be seen.

17

"No, no," Giles chuckled. "The rose you were just admiring. Lawrence Johnstone, formerly Hidcote Yellow. Another member of the family," he said, a look of amusement on his face. He was making fun of her. Roz started to protest, but Giles casually took her arm and guided her along the long axis of the Rose Garden toward a far corner, where curtains of coral pink climbing roses completely covered the high wall.

"Another little friend of mine, Mme. Henri Buillot," Giles said. Roz realized he was perfectly serious. Well, never mind. If he wanted to think of these plants as his friends and relations, it was no concern of hers. She matched her stride to his, aware of the light pressure of his fingers on her elbow. Then suddenly he stopped, stiffening.

"Shh." He stood listening intently. A faint scrabbling teased at Roz's ears. She flinched as a rose branch pricked her sleeve from behind, like a hand plucking at her for attention.

Releasing her arm, Giles marched over to a high, dense thicket of rose bushes.

"Come out," he demanded.

With a flurry of thrashing and crackling of branches, a misshapen shadow burst out of the thicket and scuttled forward, head down. A small wizened face the color and texture of an old paper bag blinked apprehensively first at Giles, then Roz. One shoulder hunched higher than the other as the shape straightened up, wrung its hands, clutched at a soiled apron over a faded black dress.

"Begging your pardon, Mr. Giles," it croaked. "But sommun's here ter . . ."

"Farthing. What are you doing here?" Giles interrupted.

"Oh well, I er . . . I . . ." the little reedy voice stammered, but Giles went on impatiently.

"What ever possessed you to come here? Haven't I told you I don't want you wandering around when I have guests? Now get back to the kitchen and make

18

us a cold collation of some kind. I'm sure Miss Howard is famished after her long journey."

"But, sir, it's . . ." She gulped, and wrung her hands.

"That will be all, Farthing." With a wave of his hand, he dismissed her. *Beloved old family retainer?* Roz wondered, mildly shocked at his tone. With one distracted look at Roz, the little figure scuttled off. Giles watched her as though to make sure she didn't scoot back under the bushes.

"I can't bear the sight of that woman," he said when she was out of sight. "She reminds me of a weasel, or a hedgehog. But it can't be helped." He looked down at his watch, then up at the sky. "See here, it's getting on for dark, and there's one more garden you must see tonight." He marched off down the center aisle toward the far wall. And, with one last look over her shoulder at the Rose Garden, Roz followed.

There was a narrow opening in the wall, almost hidden behind the curtain of climbing roses. Giles stood aside and let her pass through first. Roz ducked, but still the leaves dragged softly over her face and hair, pulling loose some strands. She stood erect on the other side, pushing her hair out of her eyes.

In the fading light, her first impression was of ghostly masses of blue, white, gray, and green so dark it was almost black. And then the blues, all shades—sapphire, indigo, azure, blue-purple, lavender, sky blue—leapt out of the subdued background like jewels, intense, gleaming, scattered over the ground in beds of periwinkle, swaying on tall spikes of larkspur and dephinium, globes of whiskered allium like unblown dandelion heads. The paths of crushed white marble wound through, pristine and geometric, and what roses Roz could see were small, white, and perfect, as though made of china. In the center where the paths crossed grew a weeping willow tree, gnarled and misshapen, like a huge bonzai, its branches drooping down like icicles, its long, pointed leaves pale and transparent as tissue paper, a peculiar bluish-green in color. The dark, twisted shape stood out against the white-washed walls like the central image in a willow-pattern plate. Viola's last creation.

"The Chinese Porcelain Garden," she said softly.

Giles nodded.

They stood side by side, silent. The air of the garden seemed heavy, like mist. Yet all the flowers, the leaves, stood out in crisp relief.

"It's so beautiful," she said. Beautiful, but also frightening. It must have taken such concentration, such control to create all this.

"There's not another willow tree like that in the world," Giles said. "It took my mother fifteen years to breed it out of mutant stock. She destroyed hundreds of saplings before she got the color she wanted." Roz nodded, reached out and touched one of the delicate, bluish leaves. She turned to look at the rest of the garden. In the corner was a small, rumpled pagoda of a building, ancient and ramshackle, resembling more than anything else a blurred sugar-lump castle at the bottom of an aquarium. In fact, the whole place gave the effect of being underwater. It was eerie, particularly in this slanting light. Everything was so still. Even Giles's voice seemed to come from far away.

"That, of course, is the Abbot's Chapel, where my mother worked the last years of her life. It was here I found her papers, hidden behind the stonework in the belfry. My mother loved that little chapel, insisted it be left just as it was, as a *memento mori.* It's the only part of the old Abbey church that's left. Now I work there myself, doing all my little odd bits to keep the place going. I've put a plaque over the door."

Roz moved closer to read the bronze plaque. "Lady
20

Viola Montfort-Snow, 1900–1975. *Ave atque vale, mater.* Giles."

Roz stood with her eyes fixed on the Chapel. She could hear Giles behind her, restlessly pacing up and down the path, crunching chips of marble. Then suddenly the garden was still. She turned around. Giles was gone.

"Giles?" No answer. *Where had he gone off to now,* she wondered in exasperation. Why was he always wandering off and leaving her? Didn't he realize she didn't know her away around? But of course Giles hadn't left her on purpose. It had probably not even occurred to him, knowing the garden like the back of his hand, that she might not be able to follow him wherever he went. Obviously he'd started back to the Refectory, where Mrs. Farthing waited with her cold collation. But never mind; it had to be perfectly simple, or he wouldn't have just gone off.

She walked toward the exit—or was it the entrance?—at the end of the widest marble path next to the Abbot's Chapel and pushed through the opening; little corkscrew tendrils of ivy tugged at her hair, and a blue star-shaped flower flopped in her face. Impatiently, she pushed it away and stepped out into open space.

To one side ran a long wall, festooned with the looping scars of a former arcade. This must be the Cloister. Straight ahead of her, maybe a hundred yards off, loomed a high, dark mass of hedge. To her right was a low, flat meadow. Rising up out of the pasture grass were tall, hooded columns of stone cloaked in vines, looking like shaggy druids. The remains of the old church nave, no doubt. As she walked toward them, she piled up imaginary stones and ribs and vaults in proportion to what was left. The ghostly structure filled the space as far as the heavy thicket in front of her. How enormous it must have been, that old church, its vaulted interior soaring up, dwarfing the trees, the walls, even the Gatehouse Tower. And Gilbert had torn it down. She stopped, and stared past the columns of stone to the horizon, the sky a pale, washed gray barely tinged with a last glow of pink from the setting sun.

And as she watched, part of the stone column directly in front of her moved, shook itself free, resolved for an instant into a separate, moving shape, a hooded figure that, seeming to hear her indrawn breath, just as silently floated toward and became one with the next shaggy stone.

Roz stood still, blinking her eyes. "Who's there?" she called. "Giles?" There was no answer, only the faint rustle of the field grass under her feet. Mrs. Farthing? But no, she'd been sent back to the Refectory. Roz stared for a moment at the columns of stone, trying to recall some of the other names. She couldn't remember a single one. "Hello?" she called. Nothing. She shrugged, turned her back on the pillars of stone, and walked decisively toward a gap in the wall.

Seconds later she was back in the open space, having blundered back into the Porcelain Garden she thought she had just left. She stood once more in the Cloister, looking at the high, dense hedge far down the grass. She thought she saw a gap there. She walked toward it and peered inside, but saw nothing more than another row of hedge. A path went off to either side, then stopped, or appeared to. Of course. This was the Maze, copied by Gilbert from the one at Hampton Court, in the place of the monks' old devotional garden. *Ha,* Roz thought. A *sneaky trick.* From reverent solitudes to secular entertainment. Well, she could go no farther here; lost in the garden itself, she wasn't about to tackle a maze. She backed out of the opening and turned around.

And then she heard, muffled but still audible, the sound of voices coming from inside the Maze.

"She'll never sell to you, not in a million years. If it's to anybody . . ."

"Keep your voice down, you bloody idiot," another voice interrupted. Roz stood transfixed. "We'll see how the rest of you feel when the papers start coming out."

There was a low, shocked noise, almost a choking sound. Then a barely audible murmur of disbelief. Then the second voice snarled angrily:

"Yes, yes, the whole sordid story. Are you really willing to risk it? Everything you've all worked for?" The voice went on, cruelly, tauntingly. "You'd better see about it, tell him to think it over very carefully."

Roz stood there, appalled. Surely that was Giles speaking. But he sounded so threatening, so angry. Sordid story? Papers? Did they mean *the* papers?

Just then there was a scuffling noise very near; the hedge in front of her swayed. *Let me out of here,* she thought, and ran toward the Cloister wall—straight into a battered wooden door. She fumbled at the latch, pushed the door open, and saw to her relief the long, low silhouette of the Refectory. Shutting the door quietly behind her, she hurried across the Courtyard without looking back.

3

AND AFTER ALL, ROZ THOUGHT THE NEXT MORNing as she followed Giles through the Courtyard toward the Viola Room in the Gatehouse Tower, *it couldn't have been Giles talking in the Maze.* When she had let herself into the hall, breathless and a little shaken, he was just coming out of the sitting room. He had been there all the time, waiting for her.

"Oh, Rosamund," he had said, looking relieved. "You did find your way, after all. I thought you were right behind me, but when I got here, you were nowhere to be seen. I was about to send out a search party. But here you are, so that's all right." He had seemed breathless and mildly shaken himself, as though he really had been worried about her. They had gone into the kitchen and sat down to pots of tea, small florettes of sandwiches, bread, cheese, sausage, and fruit. When she said she preferred coffee to tea, Giles had immediately jumped up and made her a cup himself.

While they were eating, Roz considered whether she should say anything about the voices to him. He might think she had been deliberately eavesdropping. But the papers had been mentioned, so when they were finished, she reluctantly told him the whole story.

If she had expected him to be upset, he hardly seemed it. He just looked mildly surprised, and sat lost in thought for a moment. Then, abruptly, he seemed to come to, looking straight at her.

"Oh, Rosamund—Roz—how perfectly dreadful for you," he said. "I was afraid of this. That's just the sort of thing one can expect around here at the very mention of the papers. And all because . . ." He hesitated. "Still, the less said about that at this point, the better, I suppose."

Roz had stared at him, bewildered. Because what? Better than what? But obviously Giles wasn't talking—not now, anyway. She had watched him for a while, as he sat quietly looking out the window at the darkness. Then all at once the tension and fatigue of her long trip had overtaken her, and after a hasty good night, Roz had staggered up to her room and collapsed into the softness of her bed. She had slept heavily and dreamed of flowers, so vividly that in her dream the smell of roses lingered.

* * *

Now she stood at the very top of the Gatehouse Tower in the doorway of the Viola Room. Bookshelves lined the walls, file cabinets flanked the bookshelves, and there were two desks, each with a typewriter, underneath the deeply embedded, mullioned windows. A portable copy machine stood to one side; the stone floor was covered with a worn but colorful oriental carpet. And stacked in the middle of the carpet—all over the carpet, actually—were several dozen marbled green cardboard document boxes, a number of cardboard cartons, and a pile of accordian folders tied with elastic string.

"Well, here they are," Giles said, standing in the midst of them. "The Lady Viola papers. All jumbled every which way, letters, reading notes—the diaries are in the bookcase—what have you. You can see we have our work cut out for us."

But he made no move toward the boxes; instead, he walked over to the windows facing the car park and looked out.

Roz nodded, unable to suppress her impatience any longer. She took a step forward.

But Giles's voice halted her in mid-step. "Rosamund, I've been thinking about what you overheard yesterday. And before we start, I think it would be best if we agreed now to keep the contents of the papers secret until publication. I don't want you to tell a soul anything about them."

Roz looked at him in surprise.

"And," Giles went on, regarding her seriously, "if you should meet anyone here who wants to know who you are or what you are doing here, I don't want you to say anything. That way we can avoid a great deal of awkward questioning."

Roz stared at him. "What?" she said.

"I don't want you to tell anyone here what you are doing. I don't want you talking to any of the other residents. At least for the time being."

Roz continued to stare at him, hardly able to believe her ears.

"It's the others, you know," Giles said. "No telling what they might do. They simply mustn't know."

Roz took a deep breath. "I don't really think you can keep me and the papers a secret, Giles, or the fact that you and I are working on the papers together. I'm willing to be discreet—after all, I don't even know what's in the papers yet—but I don't think I can work that way. These 'others' you keep talking about—they've got to know I'm here, and why, and I've got to know about them. I hope you can understand the necessity for this, otherwise . . ." She stopped, not wanting to put the "otherwise" into words.

To her relief, Giles merely nodded. "My dear Rosamund. That's not what I meant at all. They know you're here, of course, though not why—not yet, anyway. My only thought was that they might try to interfere, to confuse you, influence you before we even get started. But I didn't mean to keep you under wraps indefinitely. Have you forgotten the luncheon party I've arranged in your honor tomorrow? So you shall meet them all, and they you. I want to make a formal announcement," he finished reasonably. "That's all."

Roz reddened. Was that all he had meant? She looked down at the floor, saying nothing.

"But you will let me wait until the luncheon to introduce you, won't you? And not say anything about yourself, or the papers, until one o'clock tomorrow?"

Roz considered, tracing out the geometric pattern of the rug underneath her feet. Oh, why not? The little secrecy seemed harmless enough. She looked up at Giles and nodded. "That will be fine." She paused briefly, then looked straight at him. "Now that we've got that cleared up, may I see the papers?"

But Giles did not appear to have heard her. He continued to stare out the window, his hands clasped behind his back. "Here they come," he said. "The tourists. How I hated to open the gardens to paying

26

visitors, but there was really no alternative, what with the confiscatory death duties—first father's, then mother's, and the rates always going up . . . Once upon a time, as far as the eye could see was Montfort land.

"But of course it gets worse all the time, more and more difficult to make ends meet. You can't imagine the overhead, with two highly paid full-time gardeners, not to mention the lads from the village, and the upkeep. Why, insect killer alone! I've had to open the gardens more and more, until now it's six days a week, 10 A.M. till dusk, and we've barely enough time to do the spading up and the weeding. And still we run so close to the bone that two days' rain in the week will put us in the red for a month. We're totally dependent on receipts from day-trippers and tours to keep us ahead of the game." Giles's face was impassive as he turned to face her, but there was tension in the restless scuffing of his feet over the worn surface of the ancient rug, in the set of his shoulders.

"The Britannia Trust wants it. They already hold the little village of Effam Priory, and most of the land around it that was once part of the estate. I suppose they'd like the Abbey to complete the set," he said bitterly. "Mother never got over losing the ancestral acreage, even though she was only eight at the time, so imagine how she felt when she got the Abbey back." Giles paused. "I don't want to lose everything she's gained." Giles fixed Roz with a glance so piercing that she recoiled involuntarily.

"That's why I'm quite counting on this edition of mother's papers, you know, to pull us out of the red once and for all. If the book sells well, it could mean the difference between . . ." Here Giles hesitated, becoming as abstracted as he had been last night. "I don't want to lose the Abbey," he said finally.

Roz did not know what to say. But what a forlorn hope. The papers would never make the best-seller list, even with their manifest literary value, barring some sensational, hitherto-unrevealed scandal,

27

some incredible revelation or lurid confession. But there would be nothing like that in Lady Viola's diaries and letters. She had been gentle, kind, loving, devoted to the earth. Unless . . . Roz suddenly recalled the conversation she had heard last night. Sordid story?

But her train of thought was interrupted as Giles suddenly moved across the room.

"Yes. Well. I rather think you ought to get a sense of what's here, before we go any further. For this, of course, is precisely why I have brought you here."

The "have brought you here" was not lost on Roz. She watched Giles as he sank down on his heels, opened one of the boxes, pulled out a sheet of paper, and handed it to her.

Roz reached out, anticipating her first sight of a Lady Viola holograph. The paper in her hand felt clammy; it was mottled gray, as if it had been dusted over with ash. She stared at it in astonishment.

"It's a photocopy!"

"Of course," Giles said calmly. "Does it matter?" He continued rummaging through the papers in the box he had opened. He glanced up at her, and stopped. "Oh dear," he said. "Is there something wrong?"

Roz did not answer. She turned and walked to the north window, holding the copy. Photocopies. Where were the originals? Didn't Giles trust her? She stared down at the shaggy skittleboard beneath her, bitterly disappointed. She wasn't even going to see the originals. Could she even work this way? She thought for a moment about packing up and going home.

But wait a minute. He hadn't said she couldn't consult the originals, had he? If she could make him see the importance . . . It was worth a try.

"Well," she said briskly, "there is always something to be learned from the different shades and strengths of ink, variations in hand pressure, slants, erasures, impressions on the page, that sort of thing.

28

They're invaluable in the process of dating, and you can't get them from a copy."

"My mother was always very careful about dating her letters," Giles said. "There's little question about that. It's really not a problem then, is it? But it's all very interesting, I'm sure." Giles paused and smiled. "You don't mind, really, do you?"

"No," she said slowly, turning to face him. "I don't mind, as long as we have access to the originals."

"Of course you will have access to the originals, my dear. They are safely housed in Duke's College Library, Cambridge. But won't these do for a start, and to go on with? Besides, I thought we could use these as working copies, pencil right on them, and so forth. Much more convenient, don't you think?"

Roz sighed. Maybe it was for the best. After all, scholars did work that way sometimes, to save wear and tear on the originals. Still, ordinarily the originals were there, available on request. She sat down at the desk by the window.

"Of course I'm only an amateur," Giles said. "But sometimes I think it's better, really, not to be so rigid. Professionals—by this I don't mean you—in fact you're rather different, I sense, and that is why I chose you—can get so wrapped up in the petty little details that they lose sight of the whole picture . . . that is why we must go carefully. Our first job is to arrange and annotate." Giles, who had been pacing back and forth, stopped now and looked down at her. "Are you listening?"

"Yes—yes, I am," Roz said quickly.

"Here, see what you can do with this," Giles said, handing her another letter. She looked at the date. June 11, 1915.

Dearest Grim-grumbles,
    Your silly foxkin has got herself in a fix this time. Last night as I was wandering around in a daze—you know the oasthouse at the back of the west stable block?—And in my shift, dream-

29

ing away (I'd been reading *Tess*) whom should I trip—no, positively stumble over but Langley the gatekeeper, fallen flat on his face and reeking of beer, in an alcoholic stupor . . .

Roz walked over to the box the letter had come from and began to pull out the rest of the letters.

"What are you doing?" Giles said sharply.

"I'm looking for the rest of the Godwin correspondence. I thought I'd read it all first to get a sense of the voice that Viola used, what their relationship was, how it changed over the years. . . ."

A stony silence filled the room. Roz looked over at Giles. He sat down, folded his hands over the papers in front of him, and stared at her.

"No," he said after a moment. "I'm afraid that's not the way we're going to do things."

Roz rocked back on her heels, a chill spreading over her.

"We will go year by year, starting at the beginning, and proceed chronologically. That way is the way I want to proceed. Will proceed." He stopped abruptly.

"I don't think it's a good idea to go barging on ahead," he went on. "Suppose you find something shocking out of context, so to speak. Put in perspective, it might have a completely different meaning. That's why it's so important that you reveal nothing as we go along, and that we go along chronologically, as things happened. And that is why you must not tell anyone—*anyone*—what we find in the papers at any time. I cannot stress this too strongly. Things can get so blown out of proportion and misunderstood. I'm sure you wouldn't want to make us the laughingstock of the literary world, not to mention the general public, by making revelations, speculations, and then having to take it all back at some future time. So we shall go carefully, year by year, and let the picture build."

So there it was, cards on the table. A matter of control. Giles wasn't looking for someone to work with;

he wanted someone he could tell exactly what to do. She should have known. All that business with her name, and Mrs. Farthing. He wasn't a bit like his mother, not really. Lady Viola had always appeared so tolerant, so gentle. But Giles was used to being in charge, and if Roz wanted to do this edition, she would just have to get used to it.

Of course, she could walk out now, pack her bags, and go. But she needed this job. It was as simple as that, and Giles seemed to know it.

"All right," she said to Giles. "We'll do it your way."

And as she watched, she saw the shuttered, wary, austere expression vanish into a look of cheerful openness. "Jolly good," he said. Then he leaned back, laced his long, elegant fingers behind his head, and closed his eyes.

"Why don't you just read off the first of those letters to me, and I'll see what I can do by way of annotation."

Roz picked up the first letter and began to read aloud, her voice even, her hands as steady as she could make them, pencil poised, ready to take down whatever Giles might say.

4

THE NEXT MORNING ROZ WOKE EARLY. SHE FELT exceptionally clear-headed; all traces of confusion and disorientation seemed finally to have lifted. She looked forward to beginning work in earnest. It had not gone so badly, after all. There was still plenty for her to do.

She went downstairs into the kitchen, and, somewhat to her surprise, came upon Mrs. Farthing, who, when she caught sight of Roz, cowered momentarily behind the gas stove and then made a dash for the door. But Roz was in her way.

"Hello there, Mrs. Farthing," Roz said pleasantly.

The little creature bobbed her head, grabbed up the hem of her apron, and began to twist it. Her high shoulder twitched, and her two feet, splayed flat as pancakes in run-over carpet slippers, shuffled indecisively back and forth over the brick floor. She turned her small, wizened face askew and squinted at Roz.

"Er. Hello, miss . . . Ah. Er . . . Mr. Giles has been and gone. I've left your breakfast makings just there," she said, obviously anxious to be gone herself.

"Thank you, Mrs. Farthing," Roz said as she moved aside to let the woman pass. "Oh, and Mrs. Farthing," she continued, "do let me know if there's anything I can do to help. With the luncheon, I mean. You must have a great deal of work to do already."

Halfway out the door, Mrs. Farthing jerked still, turned, and stared. "Luncheon, miss? Luncheon? I don't know nothin' about a luncheon. Oh no, miss, beggin' your pardon . . ." Mrs. Farthing's face unwrinkled itself in parody of sudden enlightenment. "Aha! *That* were why Mr. Giles went out so early to knock the others up." Mrs. Farthing licked her lips. "To tell 'em. And then to get ther fish. We allus has fish for his lunches."

"You mean you didn't know?" Roz asked incredulously.

Mrs. Farthing shook her head. "First I've heard of it. But that don't signify. Happens all the time. Mr. Giles never tells me nothin'." Mrs. Farthing nodded her head so vigorously that her wispy hair stood up all around her face like a worn-out feather duster. Then she looked curiously at Roz. "Is it for you then, miss?"

"Yes," Roz replied, and stopped short, remembering Giles's orders.

Mrs. Farthing stood there clutching her bunched-up apron in small, gnarled paws, regarding Roz suspiciously. Roz could almost hear the words forming in her mind. *And just who might you be, miss, when you're at home?* Roz found herself wishing that Mrs. Farthing would pull her vanishing trick after all.

"Is there sommat wrong, miss?" Mrs. Farthing squeaked, her face a lumpy cauliflower of curiosity.

"What? Oh, oh no, nothing's wrong, thanks," Roz said, turning vaguely toward the refrigerator. She had to get something to eat.

"Here, miss, let me do that," Mrs. Farthing said, heading Roz off at the stove. She bustled around, lighting a fire under the tea kettle, pulling out a chair. She stood goggling like a frog footman as Roz sat down at the scrubbed pine table to eat her cold cereal.

While she ate, Roz looked at her surroundings—anywhere but at Mrs. Farthing. The kitchen was both rustic and modern. Bunches of carrots, leeks, parsnips, onions, bundles of dried herbs and flowers hung from the low oak beams. So did several spectacular cobwebs. Roz looked down from the ceiling to find Mrs. Farthing still staring at her intently.

"Thank you very much, Mrs. Farthing," she began. At that moment, a shadow passed over the table—someone moving by the window at Roz's back.

Mrs. Farthing blinked and went pale. "I . . . I . . ." she mumbled, her apron a crumpled wad stuffed tightly against her midriff. Roz stared at her. "What is it, Mrs. Farthing?" she asked. "Is something wrong?"

But just as Mrs. Farthing took a great gulp of air and seemed about to speak, a figure loomed behind her in the doorway.

"Thank you very much, Farthing, that will be

33

all," Giles said. "Wait for me in the ticket house. I shall be along directly."

Mrs. Farthing seemed to shrink even smaller, scuttled sideways under Giles's elbow, and ran away. *She's terrified of him,* Roz thought.

Giles walked across the kitchen to the refrigerator. In his hand he held a large paper parcel, oozing slightly and smelling of salt water.

"Don't let me disturb you, Rosamund," he said. "I'll just put this away, and then I must have a word with Farthing about the arrangements. We won't be working today, of course."

Roz nodded, but Giles had already turned away. "See you at one o'clock sharp." With a quick wave of his hand, he went out of the kitchen, leaving the hanging bunches of vegetables and herbs rustling in his wake.

Oh well, thought Roz. *It will all be over soon. After today I can stop worrying about what to say to people, and just concentrate on the papers.* Putting her dishes in the sink, she left the kitchen and let herself out into the Courtyard.

It was still fairly early in the morning, and the sun cast shadows from behind the high walls to the east, drowning in pools of soft, indistinct color the bright iridescence of the Courtyard borders. Roz walked along the path beside the Refectory to the Gatehouse Tower, and stood for a moment in front of the arch. Behind her, she felt the solid, looming presence of the Tower, and saw its slanting, crenellated shadows thrown obliquely across the lawn. From inside the little ticket house, she heard murmurings. Giles and Mrs. Farthing, having words. She turned and walked in the opposite direction across the Courtyard toward the Granary. With its heavy slate roof and large windows projecting from the flat, stone walls, it looked as though it might slip forward any moment onto the gravel walk. A large PRIVATE

34

sign hung across the front door. *Intimidating enough,* Roz thought, and changed direction slightly, not really knowing where she was going. Without the prospect of working on the papers, she was really at a loss what to do with herself.

Maybe I should go look for one of the gardeners, she thought. Giles had spoken of the two gardeners, Cory and Stella, with respect. Real professionals, trained at the Royal College of Horticulture, and here at Montfort now for upwards of twenty years. Long enough to have known both Viola and Sir Herbert, and to have helped with the garden in its long transition from trash heap and ruin to one of the most intricately designed gardens in England. Roz wondered if the gardeners would mind her tagging along this morning to watch them work.

At that moment a lean, wiry figure with short, gingery hair like wet wood shavings and wire spectacles sliding down the tip of her nose came through a doorway in the angle of the wall next to the Moat House. Head down, the figure trudged toward Roz, bending over slightly against the weight of a bulging canvas carryall slung over one shoulder. Roots, leaves, vines, and twigs bristled untidily out of the edges of the canvas. The woman saw Roz's shadow and looked up quickly, slowed, but did not stop.

"Hullo, can I help you? I hope you're not a visitor, because the garden is closed Mondays," the woman said, not unpleasantly. One muddy finger came up and shoved the glasses back up her nose, leaving behind a streak of dirt. She peered at Roz, turning sideways as she trudged. Roz fell in and walked beside her.

"No, I'm not a visitor—that is, I am, but not the ordinary sort. That is . . ." Roz hesitated. "My name's Roz Howard, and I'm a friend of Giles's from America," she finished lamely. "Are you the head gardener?"

"One of them. I'm Cory Small." The woman lowered her bag to the ground and extended a smudged brown hand. "Pleased to meet you, I'm sure. Stella's the other one; she's about somewhere. Not sure exactly where, probably down by Giles's pond." Cory stood, one hand still gripping the bag. "Were you looking specifically for me?"

"Well, no. Not exactly. I mean, the place is empty today, so I thought it might be a good time to walk around and get an idea of the place, of how things are done . . ."

"Aha." Cory shifted both hands to the neck of the bag. "Ordinarily I'd say yes, but Giles has just been round to invite us to a luncheon today, so there's really not time. We always run about like mad things on Mondays, trying to catch up what we can't get around to during the week when we're being inconspicuous. Giles's orders. Wants everyone to think the garden runs itself." She paused, then peered at Roz more closely. "I say, has that luncheon been got up for you? Rather short notice, if I do say so."

Roz nodded, hoping Cory wouldn't ask any more questions.

"Typical," Cory said in a wry tone. "Oh well. That's one mystery solved." She bent over to take up the bundle of brush. "Giles and his secrets." She stood up and shrugged, but whether it was at Giles or as a way of getting the bundle into place, Roz couldn't tell. Cory settled the carryall expertly on her back; not even a leaf or clump of dirt had fallen on the grass. Then, unexpectedly, she smiled at Roz, her dusty face crinkling into myriad tiny weather lines. "You're welcome to follow me, if you like. Right now I'm going straight to the brush heap, so you won't find that very enlightening. But you're welcome to poke about on your own. The rest are here somewhere, so you never know whom you might run into." And with a crisp "Cheerio," she trudged off through the Gatehouse arch.

Roz watched her go. So that was Cory. And Stella down by Giles's pond, wherever that was. And the

36

rest, whoever they were. Roz stood for a moment, uncertain which way to go.

And all at once she did not want to meet, talk to, or have to explain herself to anyone. Turning on her heel, she walked swiftly back across the Courtyard toward the Refectory, let herself into the dark hall, marched into the sitting room, picked up a glossy picture book of stately homes from the large coffee table in front of the couch, and settled back in the gloom to wait for one o'clock.

At one o'clock Roz was standing alone by the huge stone fireplace in the sitting room, feeling distinctly out of place. She had not seen Giles all morning. She had been rousted out of her place in a corner of the sitting room by a frantic Mrs. Farthing muttering distractedly, "Oh, no bother, miss, stay where you are," and then whisking a dust rag over everything in sight, including Roz. Roz had closed the *Stately Homes Yearbook* and gone to her room, where she uncharacteristically spent an hour fussing over her hair and dress. She decided not to knot up her shoulder-length brown hair. Generally she pulled it back because it fell in her face as she bent over her books, but this was a party, so she unpinned it, fluffed it up, put on a softly gathered dress of pale India gauze tied with a rope belt that had small sea shells dangling from the ends. Then she went downstairs swishing and tinkling, her nerves twittering in unison with the clinking shells.

She had just stepped into the sitting room when a wedge of light shone through the reredos, expanded, and produced Cory Small, followed by another tanned, outdoorsy-looking woman. Cory strode around the screen and extended a scrubbed and calloused hand. The other arm was wrapped around a huge bouquet of pink snapdragons, purple asters, larkspur, bachelor buttons, marigolds, and baby's breath.

37

"Hullo again. Here's Stella," Cory said. "Stella Langsir, Roz Howard. A friend of Giles's from America." With her free hand she thrust Stella forward and began to prowl around the room, peering into the shadows.

Stella was short, slightly stocky, with straight dark hair cut like a cowl around an open, choirboy's face. She looked at Roz out of large, lozenge-shaped, violet eyes and smiled shyly.

"Where's my vase?" Cory said crossly. "Giles told me to bring flowers and promised me a vase; I can't carry this lot around all afternoon like a silly opera singer."

At that moment Giles strode into the room, took one look at Roz standing between Cory and Stella, blinked rapidly four times, turned on his heel, and stalked out.

"There he is," Roz said weakly. "Or was."

"Don't mind Giles," Cory said dismissively. "It's your hair, I expect. You don't generally wear it down, do you? It was pulled back this morning when I saw you."

"My hair?" said Roz.

"You've just startled him. He awfully minds sudden changes, you know. He's gone off just now to get used to the idea, I imagine. He'll be back."

Roz stared at her in disbelief.

"Oh, that's just Giles," Cory said. "He likes people and things to stay the same. We're up against it all the time in the garden. He gets so caught up in how things look. Can't abide ugliness or deformity, either." Roz blinked. "Not that that's the case with you," Cory added hastily. "But you've probably noticed how Elsie Farthing goes around as though she were trying to burrow underground. Giles can't abide her looks, so he just tries to keep her out of his sight by being as nasty as possible."

Roz looked from Cory to Stella and back again. A line from one of Viola's poems popped into her head: "Nor stain nor blot nor cankered bloom/The smell of

38

blight the rose's doom." She remembered Giles unconsciously snapping and plucking deformed leaves and barely wilted blossoms as he walked along the garden paths. "I can't stand the sight of that woman," he had said in the Rose Garden of poor Mrs. Farthing. But, she thought, my *hair?* She shifted impatiently. "Where do you suppose he's gone?" she asked Cory.

"Who cares?" Cory said. "But I'll go chase him down for you. I've got to find myself a vase, anyway. Stel, you stay here with Miss Howard." And with a shake of corkscrew curls, Cory was gone, leaving in her wake the sweet, carroty smell of flowers.

Roz stood next to Stella, wondering what to say next. Was she supposed to be the hostess or the guest of honor? Stella's stolid presence did not help matters. How silly they must look, ranged side by side at the fireplace, as talkative as a pair of andirons. She took a deep breath and was about to address the silent Stella when once more the wedge of light struck across the screen, and four more people entered the hallway.

Stella looked up with a smile of recognition and—no doubt—relief. At that moment Cory came back, holding a huge cut-glass vase filled with flowers. Suddenly there were six people in the room, all greeting one another, all strangers to Roz. And still no Giles.

Just then Roz was distracted by the sight of an elderly man bobbing in her direction. White hair as fine as dandelion fluff stood out around his kindly face as he moved toward her, head nodding with what she hoped was recognition. But no. She knew him, but he did not know her.

"Howja do, m'dear," he said, extending a long-fingered, very well-cared-for, oddly youthful-looking hand. He bowed slightly, and his shirtfront crackled like a cardboard box. "I'm Cedric North. And this is Florence, my wife."

A tiny, fragile-looking woman with skin like a

39

wilted rose petal and wispy white hair peered around his shoulder and extended icy fingers. The little woman did not lift her eyes, and the fingertips were withdrawn almost before Roz could touch them. Small and neat and trim, the two old people looked as though they belonged together, like fine Royal Doulton salt-and-pepper shakers. Although Roz had never seen her before, Florence North looked vaguely familiar.

"Hello, I'm Roz Howard," she said.

"How do you do?" Florence's eyes met Roz's briefly, then darted away.

"Who are *you?*" demanded a strident female voice at Roz's right shoulder. Roz almost leapt backward into the fireplace; she had thought that place was still occupied by Stella. She turned to find a man and a woman standing there. The man looked away instantaneously, but the woman continued to stare Roz up and down.

They were younger than the Norths—early forties, perhaps. The man was of medium height, barely taller than Roz, slightly stooped, with brown hair thinning at the crown, a large nose, prominent teeth, and a receding chin, so that his face bore an unfortunate resemblance to the cowcatcher of an old-fashioned locomotive.

The woman with the peremptory voice stood in exotic contrast not just to him, but to everything in the room. With sleek black hair braided and coiled around her ears muff-fashion, earrings the size of doorknobs; dark, discontented eyes; shiny, rouged cheeks; and a scarlet dress that flounced flamenco-like around her calves as she stood restlessly shifting from one foot to another, she looked like a dancer about to go on stage. The only thing missing was a rose between her teeth—to keep her from biting the person next to her.

"Who are you?" she repeated suspiciously, glaring at Roz.

"I'm Roz Howard, a friend of Giles's from America," Roz said, repeating her own litany. "Who are *you?*"

The gypsy woman opened her mouth to speak, but, before she could answer, the brown-haired man stuck his head between them and said quickly, "I'm Hugh Badgett, and this is my wife, Beatrice. So pleased to meet you, Miss Howard."

"What's Giles up to now?" Beatrice said loudly, yanking her arm away out of her husband's grasp so hard she almost punched Roz in the ribs. Roz was thinking that this woman was quite possibly the rudest person she'd ever met when there was a flurry of movement at the far end of the room. Giles marched in, smiling expansively, carrying another vase of flowers. His eyes rested momentarily on Roz as though nothing had happened.

"So glad to see you all, so glad you could come," he said genially. He put the vase down and went around greeting his guests, his tall figure leaning intimately toward each in turn. "Cory, Stella, how charming you look . . . Cedric, so good of you to come. Florence, Hugh, glad you could spare a moment . . . Beatrice, darling . . ." Giles brushed past Mrs. Badgett and came to stand beside Roz.

"You've met everyone, I take it," he said. He did not look at her, glancing around the room at the others instead. He frowned. "Where's Alan?"

"He said to go ahead without him," Stella said softly from the corner of the room. "He wanted to have the last of the morning light. He'll be along any time now, I should think."

"Ah, good," Giles said, rubbing his hands as though they were cold. "We'll all have a little sherry, then, shall we?"

They were standing around the room self-consciously sipping their sherry when the latch to the Courtyard door clattered loudly, and the door swung wide. A broad figure appeared, dressed in rumpled tan corduroys, shirt open at the neck, and a shapeless tweed hacking jacket. Shaggy, dark mahogany hair flecked with gray tumbled over a triangular face that was almost faunlike in its expression of ironic good humor.

"Hullo," he said cheerfully. "Am I awfully late?"

The others smiled at him as he crossed the room, and the tense atmosphere seemed to relax momentarily. Roz thought: *It's going to be all right. Everyone likes him. I like him. And I haven't even met him.*

"Oh, Alan, good. Have a drink, and come meet our guest," Giles said, thrusting a glass of sherry into Alan's hand almost before he could get it out of his pocket. Alan took the glass without looking, his gray eyes on Roz, openly curious. He stood next to Giles, and Roz was surprised to see that they were the same height, an inch or two over six feet. Alan had seemed shorter when he came into the room, perhaps because of his broader build or his rumpled clothes. He stretched out his free hand and gripped hers warmly.

Giles thrust his head between them. "Rosamund, this is our neighbor in the Moat House, Alan Stewart," he said. "Alan, Rosamund Howard, my friend from America."

"Roz," she corrected, smiling brilliantly at Alan Stewart, suppressing the urge to add, "I work here."

"Where . . . ?" Alan began, bending toward her, but just then a bell tinkled politely from the direction of the dining room across the hall, and Mrs. Farthing appeared in the doorway, looking stiff and miserable in a white starched apron and what appeared to be a white index card across her brow.

"Luncheon is served," she blurted, and disappeared.

The guests collected, once more oddly silent, and milled through the doorway into the hall, past the stairs, and into the dining room. Mrs. Farthing was nowhere to be seen, but the passthrough in the walnut paneling was open, and the clatter of

42

plates could be heard behind the wall. Giles gestured to Roz to go first. As she moved toward the long trestle table with its assembled multitude of crystal, china, silver, linen, and food, Roz looked back over her shoulder and saw Alan Stewart staring at her speculatively, but without the hostility or apprehension she sensed so inexplicably in everyone else. Then Giles was busily telling everyone where to sit, and amid the clink of glass and silver, Giles's luncheon began.

5

AFTER WHAT SEEMED TO ROZ MANY HOURS, BUT was in fact only two, the salmon had been hauled off to one side like a wrecked ship, the other courses had been duly produced and consumed, and at last the company was sitting around the long table at tea and biscuits.

Conversation had been sporadic, and Roz thought grimly that she had seldom heard such sustained banality as had gone the rounds during the long meal. Giles had not yet made his announcement, and she was the object of a number of covert stares and sizings-up. For her part, she had surreptitiously looked from face to face, trying to match any of them up with the voices she had overheard in the Maze two nights ago. But it was hopeless.

There had been one oddly tense exchange between Giles and Hugh, begun by Giles's whimsical retelling of his introduction to Rosamundi, and Roz's introduction to her namesake rose, which had led him and Cedric into an amusing disquisition on the pronunciation of certain old English names—Cholmondeley–Chumley, Featherstonehaugh–Foon, and so on.

"Did you know that Farthing is a corruption of Fotheringay?" Giles had said. "Quite gives one pause, doesn't it?"

While Roz was wondering why and to whom it should give pause, Giles had gone on, addressing Hugh directly. "Speaking of which, Hugh, why don't you change your name back to the original Bagehot? So much more appropriate for a man of your accomplishments, don't you think? And not without precedent"—Giles paused, looking significantly at Hugh—"in your family."

"Giles, really . . ." Hugh had murmured, looking all around him and going red-faced.

"Stuff it, Giles," said Beatrice.

Giles had laughed, and the conversation had passed on to something else, but Roz was left feeling that something veiled and nasty had transpired. She had felt sorry for Hugh, and friendlier—but not much—toward Beatrice.

The afternoon and conversation stretched on, and still Giles said nothing about Roz's reason for being at Montfort. She was beginning to wonder if she would finally be forced to say something herself, in spite of her promise to him. What was he waiting for? She sat stiffly at her end of the table, listening to Cedric drone on about American concert halls he had known, his sweetly imperturbable old baby's face dappled in the changing light. Out of the corner of her eye she could see Alan Stewart watching her, chin on hands, elbows planted firmly on the table. He seemed to be measuring her with his eyes, but oddly enough she didn't mind; he had a quality of quiet repose about him that Roz found reassuring. But so far they had hardly exchanged a word.

Of all the guests, only Alan and Cedric seemed at ease. On Giles's right, Florence North sat chewing on her underlip. Her hair had come almost completely undone, and she was very pale. Next to her, Hugh sat hunched, chin on his chest, shoulders up around his ears, a mild, scholarly man with as much personality as an empty garden hose. On Giles's left sat Beatrice Badgett, her flaming red cheeks and vivid hair a striking contrast to Hugh's and Florence's paleness, her basilisk glare evenly favoring Giles, Hugh, and Roz herself. Cory and Stella sat facing each other in the middle, and, in fact, generally looked only at each other, their faces impassive, their movements deliberate and controlled, as though they were afraid of knocking something over. Once during the course of the meal Roz had looked down to see the muscles of Cory's brown forearms working, and wondered if her hands were twisting together under the table.

And through it all Roz had the sense of everyone listening for something left unsaid, waiting tensely for something to happen. She found herself sitting ever more upright, ears perked, eyebrows lifted expectantly, straining forward, fingers twisting her napkin into a little turban around her finger, watching all the faces that surreptitiously watched hers, while Cedric droned on. Her mind wandered back over the few letters she had read so far, back over all she had read by and about Viola, about what these people had meant to Viola, to the Abbey . . .

Suddenly she was aware that the drone beside her had ceased. She turned to find Alan Stewart watching her. He nodded his head across the table. Cedric had fallen sound asleep, lulled by his own tune, his chin wedged firmly between the points of his old-fashioned, starched collar.

"Now we should all get up and move one place to the right," Alan said. "But not stuff poor Cedric in the teapot. It's Coalport, Viola's own, and excessively valuable."

Roz grinned appreciatively at him.

"Ah, good. I've been trying to catch your eye for hours. But you've been quite preoccupied." His voice was low, husky, with just a trace of a Scots accent. "Now that I've got your attention, there's not a moment to lose. When did you arrive, how do you like it here, and why has Giles been hiding you away?"

"I left New York Friday night, got here Saturday afternoon. Then Sunday, and today's Monday. I think." She stopped, suddenly bewildered. Only Monday? "It doesn't seem quite right, somehow."

"As long as that?" Alan replied, raising his eyebrows. "Look here, have you really been stuffed away in a tower somewhere? Hiding in a closet? I haven't seen you at all. I should have noticed."

"I've been here," Roz said. "But more or less incognito." *Whoops,* she thought, *that's done it.*

"Oh, really? As what?" Alan asked, his eyebrows peaked with curiosity.

Roz ignored his question. "I do like it here. It's so very quiet, and the garden is so beautiful." *Curse Giles and his secrets,* she thought. *I just haven't got the temperament for intrigue.*

"Ah yes," Alan said, looking at her oddly. "It's very quiet and peaceful here. Which is precisely what I—we—like about it. Things stay much the same. Same old gardens, same old plants, same old people. Or that's the illusion, anyway. Very comforting, I dare say."

"We?" Roz repeated, wondering if Alan were married. But Alan only waved a hand casually at the rest of the guests.

"Us. The residents. What Giles is pleased to call his little colony." He paused, then continued in a neutral tone. "Will you stop long?"

Oh no, Roz thought. *Here we go again. Giles!* she telegraphed. *Help!* To Alan she said: "No—I mean, yes. Not permanently, but in . . . indefinitely. All summer, anyway, and most of the fall. I have a leave of absence . . . ." She hesitated.

"Oh, really?" Alan asked innocently. "From where?"

Roz swallowed, and, hoping Giles would hear and help her out of her predicament by finally making his damned announcement, raised her voice.

"Yes. Well. The fact is I teach English literature at Vassar College, in Poughkeepsie, New York."

And after all her caution, all her attempts to be discreet, every person in the room jolted alert, as if this had been what they were waiting for.

"You're an English professor?" Beatrice screeched. "A *don?* You can't be serious." She whirled on Giles, glaring at him accusingly. "What is she doing here?"

But Giles said nothing. Beatrice looked back at Roz, as if expecting her to answer. All the others looked directly at Roz, clearly amazed.

She felt her cheeks flame. *Okay, Giles,* she thought, feeling their stares almost as a physical pressure. *There's your surprise. Whatever they expected, it wasn't this.* She looked down the table at him, past all the staring faces, pleading with him silently to tell all. He looked back at her, his eyes almost closed, his head tilted slightly backward so that his nose stood out sharply, his mouth turned downward and then up at the corners in a strange, archaic smile. *Why, he looks absolutely sinister,* Roz thought. She stared at him, appalled. *It must be a trick of the light.*

"It's those wretched papers, isn't it, Giles?" Beatrice demanded.

"Hush, Beatrice," Hugh said.

"Oh dear," Florence gasped, her hands flying to her mouth.

"A friend of Giles's from America," Cory murmured, looking speculatively at Roz, who flushed again.

And still Giles said nothing.

Roz could not stand it another moment. She didn't like evasions, stringing people along, keeping them in suspense, particularly when it seemed to be having this bizarre effect. She glanced at

47

Florence, worried that the little woman was about to faint.

"Well, the fact is, yes, I'm here to help Giles edit his mother's papers—the posthumous ones found in the chapel—for future publication. We've just begun."

Silence.

Roz was aware, although she had not taken her eyes off Giles's face, that she was the focus of everyone's completely thunderstruck attention. She felt strangely detached, as if on a speeding train she had just yelled "Fire!" into a corridor and now stood looking at the rows of startled faces peering out of slammed-back doors. Cedric snorted awake and blinked at the others, then at Roz. Florence had gone paper white, her face slack, her lips working; she looked as though she were going to turn to powder and blow away. Hugh sat rigid, his jaw clamped shut. Beatrice glared, and Cory and Stella stared blankly. Alan looked from one face to the next, bewildered. They all gazed open-mouthed at Roz, then, like a deck of cards being flipped over, one by one transferred their eyes to Giles. He sat calmly at the other end of the table, his elbows resting on either side of his plate, his fingers forming a bellows that breathed in and out in the exact rhythm of the clock ticking on the wall behind him.

Then everyone began to talk at once.

"But Viola promised . . ." quavered Florence.

"Giles, you mustn't do this," Hugh said plaintively.

"You absolute beast," Beatrice said in an ominously level voice. Her expression would have frozen a volcano in mid-eruption.

Cedric sat upright, yanked down his crumpled shirtfront, and looked around. "Goodness me! What's the rumpus! Just a silly lot of papers. Some old baggage to be left until called for. Doesn't mean there's anything in it. So the time's up. Nothing to fuss about, is there? Come, come!" He leaned forward and peered down the table to where Florence sat, pale and trembling. "Florrie, take a drink of water. You look as though you're going to faint." Florence reached forward for her water goblet, managing only to knock it over onto the tablecloth.

Hugh jerked upright, as though he had been kicked sharply under the table. Maybe he had. Beatrice looked thunderclaps first at him, then at Giles. "What are the dates of these papers?" he asked.

"1915–1975."

"Inclusive? You're sure?"

Giles nodded, his eyelids fluttering.

"But you can't . . . we'll all be . . ." Abruptly Hugh snapped his mouth shut, his face suffused with a sudden flush of panic. Roz stared at him.

Then Giles spoke. "But my dear Hugh. Aren't you rather jumping to conclusions? What do you suppose might concern you in the papers?"

Then Florence spoke, her voice as thin and insubstantial as skim milk. "Oh Giles, do you mean to say that there's nothing, after all, about . . ." She hesitated, then gave Giles a beseeching look.

Giles reached over and patted her hand. *Oh good,* Roz thought. *He's going to reassure her.* "Now Florence," he said. "I haven't said that. It all remains to be seen. You must be patient, just like everyone else." *Oh no,* Roz thought, watching Florence's face fall.

"The papers will be published," Giles said, his voice rising slightly, "in their entirety. This is not a decision I feel I must justify to any of you. They are of manifest literary value, and of great scholarly and general interest. And frankly, my dear friends, I need the money. Montfort and I cannot go on much longer on just the proceeds of admission. My mother's memory and Montfort Abbey must be preserved."

49

Silence. Then a thin sound, almost a whisper. "Miss Howard."

It was Florence addressing her in her careful, faded voice. "I ask you, as a fellow human being, a woman, perhaps a wife and mother, what if—if you thought the publication of Lady Viola's papers. . ." She paused, as if searching for words. "Of certain hidden diaries and letters would cause great distress to those still living. Might expose, tear down . . ." She took a trembling breath. ". . . Or otherwise do damage to people still alive. Do you believe that living people should be exposed, left open to ridicule . . ." Her thin voice quavered, then broke. Hugh leaned over and put his arm around her shoulders as she lifted a trembling hand to her eyes.

Roz did not know what to say. But it didn't matter. This had gone on long enough. Without looking at Giles, she began, "Why Mrs. North, of course there has to be some regard for the living—"

"The papers will be published in their entirety," Giles interrupted. His voice dropped clear and sharp with the finality of a guillotine. "History, my dear Florence. Lives of the great must take precedence over the lives of the obscure."

Florence let out a mewing cry of despair and sank her head in her hands. Hugh slammed both fists on the table and was about to rise, but whatever he was going to say was drowned out by a loud shriek from the kitchen, followed by the crash of breaking crockery. Mrs. Farthing's voice could be heard, squeaking hysterically.

Then the hall door banged open. Footsteps clacked down the hall. A tall, blond woman appeared in the doorway, dressed in a loosely fitting, highly fashionable suit of slate blue. Her blue eyes danced from face to face, and she smiled broadly, her wide, high-cheekboned face glowing with excitement.

"Surprise, everyone!" she called in a throaty,

thrilling voice, flinging arms out wide in a gesture of greeting. "Surprise! Francesca's back!"

Florence half rose with a strangled cry. Her high-backed chair caught on the uneven brick floor and fell over with a clatter. She stared at the tall figure in the doorway. "Oh my God," she gasped. Her eyes rolled up, and she slid to the floor between her chair and Hugh's feet. She had finally fainted, after all.

"Mother!" Hugh cried.

Cedric rose precipitously, and suddenly the whole room resounded with the thunder of chairs crashing to the floor, silver clanking, glassware tumbling, as people stood up, babbling in confusion.

Hugh knelt down and cradled Florence's head on one arm.

"Mother?" he said again.

Mother? Roz looked from one face to the next. All eyes were fixed on Florence. Hugh looked back over his shoulder and motioned Francesca back out of sight. Beatrice rounded the end of the table and knelt at Florence's other side, darting one cobra glance at the blond figure frozen in the doorway, another at Giles. Cory, Stella, and Cedric gathered around the three on the floor. Only Giles, Alan, and Roz remained seated. Francesca backed through the now-open kitchen door and bumped into a disheveled Mrs. Farthing, who stood in the middle of the floor with her mouth open, as if she had just been hatched by the mess of broken crockery.

"I seed her coming through the window, sir, but I couldn't stop her," she wailed. "Gave me such a turn." Mrs. Farthing fanned her brow with the index card, now unattached.

Giles glanced at Mrs. Farthing, but said nothing.

"I'll phone Dr. Neville," Cory said, pushing against Francesca and sidestepping large shards of crested dinnerware. "Stella, why don't you help Elsie with this mess?" Stella brushed past Francesca

51

into the kitchen, taking Mrs. Farthing with her. The kitchen door swung shut behind them.

"Is she dead?" Francesca said tensely. "I didn't mean to—"

"Not now," said Hugh.

Florence murmured something and twisted her head from side to side against Hugh's arm. Giles sat unmoving, staring enigmatically at Francesca. Alan got up quietly, briefly put his hand on Cedric's shoulder, then made his way around the table, righting the overturned chairs. Florence opened her eyes, looked around blankly, and burst into tears. The little group contracted around her.

Roz stared at the whole scene with the dazed detachment of the only unscathed passenger in a train wreck.

They she stood up, brushed off her skirt, said "Excuse me" to the empty air, and left.

6

WELL, WHAT NEXT? ROZ WONDERED AS SHE TOOK a deep breath of the clean, savory-smelling air. She was in a square, low-lying garden, mostly green, with uneven brick paths. Bending close, she read the names of the plants: oregano, lavender, marjoram. The Herb Garden. She looked around at the feathery blue cloves of onion and garlic flowers swaying like fragile minarets, the knotted thyme between the bricks. Though she walked with care, she couldn't help crushing some of the leaves beneath her feet, and a fresh, peppery odor filled the air. It was so calm and quiet here; she could feel her heart slow its hammering.

So what next, indeed? *Giles is some kind of monster, and you are about to become his accomplice. Those people in there are absolutely petrified at the thought of the letters being published, and Giles doesn't care one bit. So why don't you go back to your room, pack your bags, and take the next plane home?*

Because, my dear Rosamund, she answered herself, *then you will not only be out of this job, but out of a job, period. And besides, it's not that simple.* The news about the papers may have been a shock, but Francesca's abrupt arrival could hardly be considered her responsibility—or even Giles's, for that matter. Anyway, Francesca who? What was she doing here, besides making people scream and faint?

Roz put her hands up to her face and covered it for a moment, trying to think. What about Giles? He had been so rigid, so unbending, so insensitive. But was he entirely unjustified? He had made himself perfectly clear; there was something to be said for that. He would not be moved, even by hysteria. Yet, he was so . . . condescending. Lives of the great and lives of the obscure, indeed. But why rub it in? There was such a thing as tact.

She should have been prepared for this, she supposed. Since she'd met him, Giles had been—well, if not exactly condescending, then certainly formal. *"I have brought you here,"* he had said. *"We'll do it my way."* She had felt completely intimidated. That must be how Hugh and Florence felt.

She heard a step behind her and turned quickly toward the noise.

"Oh, here you are," Giles said. "I saw you slip out. Can't say I blame you. A bit thick, wasn't it?"

Smiling faintly, he sauntered past her, took a deep breath, and stretched. Roz noticed how square and angular his shoulders appeared under the fashionably tailored suit. She remembered Alan Stewart's rumpled appearance, his curious gray eyes, and his directness, which in a way had precipitated the disaster, or at least part of it.

"Is Florence . . . ?"

"Oh my, yes. Everything's quite all right now. Florence isn't nearly so frail as she appears; you should see her when she's being fierce. She'll recover nicely. Hugh and Cedric have taken her home. So everything's quite shipshape."

Was she imagining things, or did he seem a little rattled—distracted, even? She watched him pace restlessly around the bricks.

"And now they know, of course. So that's over and done with." Abruptly, he turned and ducked his head through another low archway. "Why don't we go along into the Rose Garden? It's so lovely this time of day."

His voice faded as he moved across the miniature stone bridge into the Rose Garden. Roz followed him. Below, the moat flowed darkly. He turned and waited for her.

"Poor Rosamund. I really haven't allowed you much time in the garden, have I? Especially in this garden, the most important of all."

Roz looked out over the Rose Garden. The heavy fragrance of old roses, the colors, the drowsing insects, the peace swept over her. Giles strolled along ahead of her, hands in his pockets, looking completely at ease. He didn't seem the least concerned, now, about what had happened at the luncheon. But she was. In fact, she hardly knew where to start.

"Giles? Who's Francesca?" she called after him.

Giles's back contracted as though she'd suddenly prodded him between the shoulder blades. Roz wished she could see his face. But when he turned around, both his face and his voice were completely expressionless.

"Well, it's really quite a complicated affair. Fran-
54

cesca is what you might call a relation of the Badgetts. She's a performer of sorts; Francesca Fotheringay is the name she goes by. She's been away quite some time. She took this moment—rather unfortunately, I might add—to make her surprise reappearance in the haunts of her youth. We all thought she was still in the States—when we thought of her at all, that is—and to have her pop up suddenly like that . . . well, it gave everyone quite a turn, as you saw."

Everyone except you and Alan Stewart, thought Roz.

Giles went on. "She'll be staying on with Farthing for a while, in the Dormitory wing. Rather a nuisance, but I shall see that she's not in our way at all." And with a quick, indefinable smile at Roz, h turned and strode away, plucking a wilted rose off its stem as he brushed by, shredding it to pieces and throwing the remains under a bush.

"Come along, Rosamund," he said over his shoulder. "I have something else to show you. Something we missed the other night."

She came up to Giles just as he was stepping past a coarse fringe of yew into another garden. Roz stopped and looked around her. She couldn't recall ever having been here before. On her left, the high-gabled, cross-timbered end of the Moat House rose starkly beyond the ivy-shrouded wall. Three-leaved, glossy, red-stemmed, the ivy looked familiar to Roz. But no, she must be mistaken. Who would want to cultivate poison ivy over a garden wall?

The garden was mostly lush, green vegetation of various shapes and hues: glossy stiff leaves, spotty ones like green elephant ears, pointed leaves, great stalks with leaves like swords, leaves with rosy veins, leaves mottled white and green. It was not particularly attractive, really. A musky, almost rank odor rose up from the plants.

"This was another of my mother's fancies," Giles

55

remarked casually. "A garden filled entirely with poisonous plants."

Roz stopped short, feeling as though she had suddenly stepped into a nest of snakes. Watching her, Giles smiled. "It's a great favorite with morbid creatures who fancy being the last of the Borgias. Are you interested? We can spare a moment." He marched down a crooked path toward the center. "False hellebore, daphne, foxglove, dumbcane, deadly nightshade, poison hemlock, oleander—it grows in pots here," he said, pointing to a tall, spiky plant with spidery, evil-looking yellow blossoms. "Henbane, thornapple, Christmas rose, castor bean. There are varieties here that are grown nowhere else in England. Not to mention the mushrooms."

As Roz stared at him in horrified fascination, Giles bent down and parted some of the dark green, ugly leaves that spread densely over the ground. Underneath was a nest of white mushrooms shaped like half-opened umbrellas. "Amanita, destroying angel," he said softly.

Roz wondered briefly how Alan Stewart felt about having deadly miasmas wafting through his windows. Then she noticed there were no windows on this side of the Moat House.

"Actually it's Alan who's made rather a study of these. He's quite the amateur botanist, among other things," Giles said. "Isn't it surprising how many have blue or white blossoms?"

Blue and white. Roz thought of the Porcelain Garden. And Viola had created *this* little horror, too?

"Of course, so do the herbs," Giles went on. "These are herbs as well. Merely deadly ones." Giles reached over and touched a tall, feathery-leaved plant with intensely blue snapdragonlike flowers. "This is my particular favorite—aconite, or monkshood. Rather clever for an Abbey garden, don't you

56

think? Also very deadly." He plucked one of the blossoms, then chuckled at Roz's reaction.

"Here now, don't look so appalled. I'm hardly Rappaccini's daughter; I'm not going to eat it. It's quite safe, really; one would have to crush or chew this to extract the poisonous principle. I say, is something wrong? There, don't breathe so quickly, you'll make yourself faint."

"I'm all right," Roz said. She glanced down at the little bronze cemetery plaques almost hidden in the foliage plants. "Warning! Poisonous Plants! Do Not Touch!" *I've got to get out of here,* she thought.

On the far side of the garden, opposite the Moat House wall, she saw an iron grille, and beyond it, open space. She walked rapidly through the garden toward the grille. A fresh breeze came through the bars, but the grille was latched. She looked back at Giles. He was still bent over among the poisonous plants, plucking withered blossoms and pulling up small weeds.

"Giles, I think I'd like to get back to work."

"Now?" He stood up, brushing off his trousers, and saw her standing against the grille. He looked down at his watch, then glanced at her, an odd expression on his face.

"Of course, Rosamund, lead the way," he said. Roz felt a stab of annoyance. He probably knew, damn him, that she didn't know where she was, or how to get to the Tower. She would have to learn how to get around the garden herself, so that he couldn't keep doing this to her.

"Just this way, then," he said, inclining his head through the archway. Roz noticed that it, too, was rounded, like the arch that led from the Courtyard into the Herb Garden. Matching gardens, blue and white.

And suddenly her sense of place wheeled around, and she knew exactly where she was, looking out over the Courtyard back toward the Refectory and the Gatehouse Tower. Giles began to stroll casually across the grass.

Roz caught up with him.

"Giles," she said, "why was Florence so upset at the prospect of the diaries and letters coming out?"

Giles stopped, turned, and looked at her, his face expressionless. "I thought we'd already discussed that. I really can't imagine."

"Do you think Florence is just making it all up, or is there really something in the papers that might do her injury?"

Giles continued to stare at her.

"Because if there is," she said slowly, "we're going to have to deal with it sooner or later, and I'd just as soon deal with it now."

There, she had gotten his attention, for better or for worse. She braced herself. But Giles's expression did not change, and when he spoke, his voice was calm and reasonable.

"My, you *are* persistent, aren't you? But Rosamund—Roz—how can I convince you that I really haven't the faintest notion what Florence—or anyone else, for that matter—fears? What I do know is that it is important that you and I go on with this, in spite of this little spot of bother."

You and I. He had said *you and I*. He hadn't given her the sack, in spite of her challenge to him.

Giles went on. "I don't think we can let what may be pure hysteria influence our work. Florence and Hugh do not control the papers. I do. I cannot let their fears dictate what will or will not come out." Giles sighed. "That's all I meant to make clear to them at lunch. Perhaps I was a bit too . . . stern. But whatever happens, I know that I can count on you, and you on me, to do what we think is right."

"Why didn't you make the announcement at lunch?"

"Why, my dear, you rather took that out of my hands, didn't you? I assure you, I was about to."

Roz glanced at him skeptically, but his sincerity seemed genuine. She hadn't realized until this moment how much she wanted to think the best of Giles. But that was her nature, really, to think that everyone acted from the best of motives. He had fulfilled his obligation to her so far; she must fulfill hers to him. And to Viola.

And the others? She would just have to see what happened when the time came. Don't anticipate, Giles had said. Avoid speculation. Everything remained to be seen. And what was to be seen was purely and simply the work she had come to do.

But Giles was waiting for her. She smiled at him, and together they started across the Courtyard toward the Tower Room.

7

ROZ WOKE LATER THAN USUAL TUESDAY MORNING. She yawned and stretched sleepily; she and Giles had worked until well past midnight on the letters, driven almost compulsively by the scene in the dining room. They had traced references, identified names, places, and incidents, had collated over twenty letters and put them in their correct order. In her absorption with this, Roz had forgotten everything except Viola. She had been almost mesmerized by the letters, and, as she read on, each word, each line, seemed to imprint itself in her memory. Already an image of Viola was building up, the young Viola of the early letters—bright, eager, going here and there, reading this, imploring friends to write, to call, to visit, asking what they thought of a poem, a line of prose. It was a Viola quite different from the woman in the published works, much more vulnerable, intimate, charming. It was all Giles could do to make her stop.

She dressed in jeans and a cotton shirt, pulled a sweater over her head—it was always cool in the Tower Room—and went downstairs. Mrs. Farthing was not in evidence, but the kitchen was swept clean of yesterday's debris. A window was open, and the dried plants rustled faintly against the dark rafters. Roz ate her breakfast quickly and hurried off across the Courtyard to the Tower Room.

She expected to see Mrs. Farthing's shadow behind the glass of the ticket booth, but the room was empty. Where was she? It had been almost ten when Roz left the Refectory; the tourists were probably already parking their cars, ready to come in the minute the gate opened.

She was just mounting the first flight of stairs when she heard murmuring on the far side of the wall. A door slammed faintly, and then the glass slide of the ticket booth rattled back. Elsie Farthing faithfully in attendance no doubt, and not a moment too soon. Then, through the small slit window overlooking the Courtyard, Roz caught a glimpse of color, a figure whirling by, a toss of long blond hair. No, it wasn't Elsie. Someone more interesting. Roz turned away from the window and walked back down the stairs.

Francesca was standing at the open ticket window adjusting the sign. She stood in the shadow of the arch, tall and blond, with the iridescence of an exotic bird of paradise, her hair curled in long, glossy tendrils around a strongly defined, broad-cheeked face. She wore a swirling gossamer pantsdress of sapphire blue, heels high enough to allow her to stare down at Roz, and makeup elaborate and colorful enough for a nightclub act.

60

"Hello," said Roz.

Francesca jerked around.

"Oh," she said. She cocked a peacock's eye at Roz. "Can I help you?" she inquired politely, her back to the ticket office window.

Roz, who had been about to ask her the same thing, said simply, "I'm Roz Howard."

Francesca rustled slightly, fluttering long eyelashes. Roz expected her blue draperies to come fanning around her like a great feathered ruff. "I'm Francesca Fotheringay. I don't believe we've met. Are you a tourist?" Her voice was deep and throaty, with an odd tremor in it. There was a kind of vibrant, restless energy about her that made her seem somehow larger and more vivid than an ordinary person.

"No, we haven't met," Roz replied. "That is, not formally. I'm here to work with Giles on his mother's papers."

Francesca's eyes opened wide. "You're Giles's American bluestocking?" She looked Roz up and down. "I must say, you don't look much like a don to me. You're much too young and pretty."

Roz flushed; she didn't like being patronized, particularly by someone like Francesca. Meanwhile, the blond woman continued to stare at her. Suddenly Francesca snapped her fingers, tossed back her hair, and smiled.

"Oh, I say. Weren't you at the luncheon yesterday? You do look familiar."

"I was there," Roz said stiffly. "But I left shortly after you arrived. Things were getting a bit confusing, and there didn't seem to be anything I could do, so I just got out of the way."

Francesca swirled her hair again, batted two brilliantly drawn, watchful eyes, and grinned. "Oh dear. Yes, I suppose I should have warned them, but I'd just got back from the States, and I wanted everyone to be surprised." She laughed, a low chuckle. "I rather did, didn't I? I had no idea poor"—Francesca hesitated, and looked away momentarily, as though searching for a name—"poor Florence would squiff like that, but everyone says she's been quite put about lately. Giles's latest scheme—the papers—I expect. It must have come as quite a shock, even though one could have guessed it was in the offing . . ."

Francesca trailed off and looked inquiringly at Roz, who was so busy keeping track of which schemes and shocks were which she could only stare blankly back.

"But of course you'd know ever so much more about that than I do," Francesca finished unexpectedly. "Wouldn't you?"

"Ah yes . . . well," Roz stammered. "I really had no idea that Florence—Mrs. North—would be so upset by the idea of the papers being published. Or anyone else, for that matter. It was quite a surprise to me. And to Giles, too, I imagine."

Francesca regarded her with eyes as bright as sequins. "Well, she'll have to get used to it sooner or later. We all will," she said, leaning back and spreading her winged arms out on the sill of the ticket window. Her pose was casual, but her tone was almost sardonic. "And sooner rather than later, it now appears." She stared off over the Courtyard, frowning. "Though it is rather odd, if I do say so, these papers turning up so suddenly after all these years. And Giles finding them. I could have sworn . . ." She stopped abruptly and narrowed her eyes at Roz. "I say, there really *are* papers, aren't there? I mean, you've actually *seen* them, have you? It's not just Giles's idea of a joke, is it?"

Roz felt her face flush with anger. "Of course it isn't," she said evenly. "There is quite an extensive and complete collection of letters and a full run of diaries." What were the dates Giles had given at lunch? She didn't want to contradict him. "From 1915 until Viola's death in 1975."

Francesca blinked at her once, twice. Then her

face drained of color completely, so that for a moment she looked grotesque, like a painted plaster mannequin, stiff-jawed and bleak-eyed.

As Roz stared at her in amazement, Francesca recovered herself.

"Oh, really," she said carefully. "That many. And have you been over them all?"

"Well, no, not exactly. We've only just gotten started. We're working chronologically; so far we've just been sorting and compiling, annotating, that kind of thing." And really, what business was it of hers, anyway? Roz took a step toward the stairwell. Francesca followed her.

"I see. And who are the letters from?"

"A number of different people." Roz took another step. "Now if you'll excuse me . . ."

Francesca leaned closer to Roz, pinioning her with a lancelike fingernail. "Badgetts? Any Badgetts? Humphrey Bagdett? Florence? Do you recognize those names?" Francesca was moving forward, closer and closer, so that Roz found herself backed up close to the door of the Tower stair.

"I really can't say," Roz answered.

"Have you seen them, actually seen them?" Francesca persisted.

"No," Roz admitted. "I haven't seen them. Only the ones to 1920."

Francesca stared into Roz's face, her eyes glittering. Roz felt suddenly overcome and shifted her eyes to the other side of the arch. A crowd of tourists was marching briskly in their direction from the car park.

"Excuse me, but there's someone coming," she said. "Isn't Mrs. Farthing here?"

Francesca whirled, her attention distracted. "Elsie? Oh . . . I really haven't the faintest idea." She gave herself a little shake, arranged her draperies, and looked enigmatically at Roz.

"Here, don't let me keep you," she said. "I'm sure you've piles of work to do. I'll just slip inside and mind the gate till Elsie shows up. I used to do this years ago; I'm quite used to it."

With that she turned and let herself into the ticket booth, fluttering down onto the high stool. Just before she shut the door, she looked slyly at Roz. "We'll have to talk again sometime."

You bet, Roz thought as she continued up the Tower stairs. *You talk, and I'll listen.*

Giles was already there when she appeared in the doorway of the Viola Room. "You're here at last," he said, waving a stack of papers at her. "I've come across more letters to Sir Herbert. From when they first met—quite charming. They fit right into our time scheme—no later than 1920—so you needn't scratch about today. Do sit down."

And before she could tell him about her encounter with Francesca, he was halfway through the first paragraph. She picked up her pencil to follow him, making notations wherever necessary.

They read and annotated until noon. The letters *were* charming, more restrained than the Grumbles letters, yet still lively, even girlish. As Giles read on, Roz let Lady Viola's voice sink into her brain, speak to her as though she were the one being addressed, so that Viola's spirit seemed to hover about her, talking, gesturing, joking, pleading, laughing—gay and generous and imperious, imaginative and practical by turns. Roz found herself growing fonder and fonder of Viola. And Giles knew so much about his mother's life; so far there had been no questions he couldn't answer.

Roz felt her mind taking it all in, filing it away, learning all she could about this woman who had written fifteen books, married, had a son, created an exquisite garden, and written a page of diary a day at the very least, as well as several thousand letters. She couldn't wait to get at the diary, that repository of the private self, as the letters were of the public. The contrast would be interesting. But she found herself wondering where Viola had found the time.

And why had she hidden all the papers? How had Giles come to find them? She sat there dreamily, letting her mind wander.

"I say." Giles's voice startled her. She looked up.

"What? Asleep at the helm? Poor Rosamund, is it really such a bore as that? Come, it's past noon; let's have some lunch. I'm starving."

Gratefully, Roz rose, stretching her cramped legs. Giles preceded her down the stairs, and Roz waited just outside the arch while he poked his head in the door of the ticket booth and spoke briefly to Mrs. Farthing. She looked out over the garden; it seemed rather empty. Behind her she heard Mrs. Farthing say, "I don't understand it, Mr. Giles. They should be pouring in a day like today. I don't know what's going on."

When he rejoined her, Giles was frowning. "No paying visitors today. That's very odd. I shall have to see to it after lunch."

They had just finished the plate of sandwiches Mrs. Farthing had left and Roz was fixing herself a cup of coffee when she heard the big oak door open. Steps sounded briskly in the hallway. Shades of yesterday's luncheon. She looked up expectantly. Hugh Badgett appeared in the kitchen doorway, flushed and breathless, his hair mussed, his brown suit rumpled. He looked as though he had just come a long distance. In fact, in his mild way he looked quite desperate.

"Giles, I must speak to you," he said. "In private."

"That's not really . . ." Giles began, but Roz had already picked up her coffee cup and was heading out the door.

"See you later," she said.

She had just settled herself down in the sitting room with her coffee and a back issue of *Country Life* when the sound of voices changed from low, discreetly indistinguishable murmuring to what was clearly a full-scale row. *Oh, oh, not another one,* she thought, recalling the nasty argument she had overheard in the garden her first night here. That hadn't been Giles and Hugh, though, because she had met Giles inside. Maybe one of them had been Hugh. Perhaps, for all his gentlemanly inconspicuousness, he was a secret hell-raiser. He would have to be at least a closet Tartar to stand up to Beatrice of the flagrant dress and gongs on her ears. But Hugh and who else?

Just then she heard his voice. "Giles, don't you understand? Mother is just frantic with worry that it will all come out after all these years!"

Giles murmured something short and unintelligible. Roz hoped it was a reassurance.

"No, no, Giles," Hugh said beseechingly. "You don't understand. It may even kill her. Cedric doesn't know a thing, and there's Beatrice's family." There was a painful pause. "Not to mention Frankie."

"Frankie is an abomination."

Silence.

"Then you won't reconsider."

"Will he?"

There was no response. The silence lengthened. Roz leaned forward, listening. Finally Hugh's voice sounded, wearily. "Then I can't answer for the consequences."

Suddenly there was a violent crashing sound. Roz jumped up. Hugh marched out past the screen, white-faced, fists clenched. She stared after him. He had seemed so gentle, even timid; she could hardly believe it was the same man she had met earlier. He did not look at her, just hurried down the hall and out the door without closing it behind him.

Giles appeared in the dining room doorway, looking quite undisturbed. He caught sight of Roz. "You heard?" he said.

Roz nodded.

"We shall run out of crockery at this rate. Hugh's rather upset, as you no doubt noticed. Thinks the papers coming out will kill his mother. And Beatrice has threatened to move out."

Roz said nothing. Giles stood there, tall, intimidating, his profile thrown into relief by the light from the open door. It occurred to her that it might just as well have been Giles who had tossed the dishes.

"Absolute rot, of course," he said. "They'll just have to make the best of it, along with everybody else. I do wonder sometimes who they think they are," he added, looking quizzically at Roz. "Don't you?" Then he walked forward and put a hand on the door. "I've got to go and see what's going on with the gate. We should have more visitors than we do; there may be something amiss. I shan't be a moment."

As Roz followed him out into the sunlit Courtyard, he turned to her and said, "Why don't you have a stroll around the garden? I'll come find you in a bit."

As she stood uncertainly by the door of the Refectory, she caught a glimpse of movement across the Courtyard. Florence North was bent over by the front door of the Granary, briskly sweeping a cloud of dust off the stone step. She was wearing a printed housedress and soft canvas shoes, obviously turning out the place. Roz walked across the lawn until she was within speaking distance.

"Hello," she said brightly.

Florence turned and stood up at the same time, losing her balance so that she fell back rather heavily on one of the great yew bushes that flanked the Granary door. Roz rushed over to rescue her, but the springy yews had held the woman nearly upright.

"Oh, oh," she gasped, deathly pale. "Oh, it's you, Miss Howard. For a moment I thought you were a tourist. What's happened to my dustpan?" She

67

turned and began to rummage in the bushes. "Sometimes they come right up here and peer in the windows, in spite of the sign." She waved vaguely at the large PRIVATE sign across the paneled door. Roz handed her the dustpan. Florence blinked, ducked her head, and brushed at the front of her housedress. *Where have I seen that before?* Roz wondered, feeling an odd sense of *déjà vu.*

"Ah," Florence went on. "Oh dear. Oh dear. So ridiculous and unnecessary. You have no idea what a nuisance they are," she went on in a conspiratorial tone. "Of course they come to see him—Cedric, my husband—you know. Why, one day, Cedric, my husband, was playing scales, rather complicated ones if I do say so, so that if you didn't really know, it might have been Bach, or Vivaldi, and he looked up and found an . . . an . . . *audience* all around the room—in the hall, down in the drawing room. All over the house. I chased them out, of course. He never would. He has no sense of his importance. Giles, too, I often think . . . but never mind." Florence frowned suddenly and dipped her head, avoiding Roz's eye. *Mrs. Farthing,* Roz thought. *That's who.* Though obviously there was a world of difference between the two women; there was nothing servile about Florence.

Then the little woman looked up.

"Ah, you're not working then, you and Giles? On the . . . on the . . ." Florence's voice drifted off. A fluttering movement caught Roz's eye. She looked down to see Florence's wispy hands wringing away at each other. In fact, her whole body was trembling. Roz reached out a hand, but just then Florence stepped backward into the doorway.

"Ah, Miss Howard," she said softly. "I really must talk to you. Could you come in right now? It's rather urgent."

"Of course," Roz said.

She was about to follow Florence inside when the woman's eyes lifted, then focused with a queer shuddering motion at a point somewhere beyond Roz's right shoulder.

"Oh yes. Oh yes," Florence repeated, her eyes sliding away down Roz's front to her feet. "Thank you very much, I'm sure, Miss Howard. Perhaps another time," she said loudly. Roz stared at her.

"Hello, Florence," said Giles.

Roz turned. He stood in the middle of the Courtyard lawn, hair tousled, hands in his pockets, beads of perspiration on his upper lip, but otherwise completely composed.

"And Rosamund," he said, nodding. He walked toward them.

Roz glanced at Florence. Her face was as blank as a shuttered window. She stood rigidly in front of the Granary door, staring at Giles. Trying to catch her eye, Roz said, "We'll have that talk you wanted sometime soon then, Mrs. North." Florence gave her a look of absolute horror. Then, without a word, she turned and went inside. The door clicked shut, and Roz heard the sound of a bolt being shot home.

"Well," said Giles.

"Well," said Roz. She went to stand beside him. "Did you find out if anything was wrong?" she asked.

"I did indeed. Someone had put up the *Closed* sign at the road. And in the ticket window. We've lost over half a day's take. All, really, since most of the tourists come early and plan to spend the day here."

"Any idea who?" They began to walk toward the Gatehouse.

"It could be any of them. No one here really likes having the tourists swarming all over, you know. I'm sure it was just a little joke, to get back at me for the other day. The luncheon, I mean." Giles paused. "What did Florence want?"

"Oh, she was just describing one of her little forays with the tourists," Roz said lightly. "I could

69

imagine her shooting them out just like the farmer's wife."

Unexpectedly, Giles grinned at her. " '. . . Who cut off their tails with a carving knife.' " He chuckled. "Oh, how very appropriate. Oh yes. Florence takes her job as Cedric's wife very seriously. The great artist must be protected."

"I can see that," Roz said.

"She's never quite managed to get over her nervousness at rising so high in life. She *was* the farmer's wife, you know."

"A farmer's wife—was she really?" Roz asked absently. She was thinking of Florence's hands wringing, wringing. What had Florence wanted to talk to her about? The papers, no doubt. And she hadn't wanted Giles to know. Roz wondered if it would be considered ethical, not to mention professional, if she were to consult some of the others without Giles's knowledge.

"No, *no,*" Giles was saying. "Not just any farmer's wife. *The* farmer's wife. She was Florence Badgett, the wife of Humphrey, who ran the Home Farm for my parents. Didn't you hear Hugh call her *Mother* yesterday? They were all peasants. Salt of the earth. She and Cedric knew each other for years, but not on the same social level, of course. Cedric admired my mother, and after Father died, he moved into the Granary. We all rather hoped that he and Mother might marry, but Mother had . . . other interests. Well, to make a long story short, Humphrey died, Florence was a widow for a year or so, and then one day they simply eloped. Such an uproar. Since then Florence has been hard at work being worthy of Cedric. Sometimes I wonder if Mother ever forgave her. For no longer being salt of the earth, of course."

"I see," Roz said thoughtfully. But she was not in fact sure that she did see. There was something indefinable in Giles's tone, his manner. Something unsympathetic, disapproving—or was it just amused? She remembered Cory's words, "He minds change so." Maybe that was it. But more important, could this be what Florence and the rest of them were worried about having revealed? Their lowly origins? Protecting Cedric? Beatrice? But surely it was common knowledge, and hardly worth getting so worked up over?

"Shall we return to the scene of the crime?" Giles said.

"What?" Roz looked up, startled.

Giles laughed.

"The papers, my dear Rosamund. The papers. We're already frightfully behind schedule, and there's not a moment to lose, is there?" With that, he marched off toward the Gatehouse Arch.

Roz stood watching his retreating figure. Not a moment to lose? This was the first she'd heard of any urgency, plodding along as they had been. She would just as soon get on with it, but Giles had insisted on working chronologically. They were years—decades, even—away from Viola's acquisition of Montfort Abbey, let alone the arrival of the present residents. Slowly she followed Giles into the shadow of the arch, then shrank back as she heard him shouting angrily:

"Didn't I tell you to get away from here? I don't want to see you near this place again! The absolute height of stupidity . . ." Up and down the voice thrashed, and Roz shut her eyes against the sight of Mrs. Farthing's pinched little face cringing and blinking. She walked forward.

"Giles," she said loudly.

Giles whirled and saw her. "Ah, Rosamund," he said in a perfectly normal tone. "I was just about to go upstairs. Do come along." It was as though nothing had happened. Giles disappeared into the stairwell. Roz heard his footsteps echoing up the stairs. She peered through the ticket window. "Are you all right, Mrs. Farthing?" she asked.

To her horror, Mrs. Farthing seemed to collapse

71

in on herself, head on her hands, arms on the windowsill. Tears welled out of her eyes and fell onto the stone floor. "Oh, miss, it weren't my fault, the sign was right there and I never thought to question Mr. Giles, he hates it so! Oh, oh . . ." Her wizened little face contracted even more, and she dug both gnarled paws into her eyes. Roz reached through the opening and patted a quivering, bony shoulder.

"Of course it's not your fault, Mrs. Farthing. I'm sure Giles understands that."

"You're too kind, miss, but it don't make no difference. He gets so angry sometimes it scares the stuffin' outer me. And now this on top o' eerything else. He'd like to get rid of me, if it weren't for—" Mrs. Farthing caught her breath, rolled her eyes around, and dropped her trembling chin on her chest. Roz stood, absently patting the woman's shoulder. Why was Giles so hard on poor Mrs. Farthing? Surely it hadn't been her fault, just a misunderstanding . . .

"Look here," Roz said. "Why don't you go inside and fix yourself a cup of tea? I'll stay here and watch the window. There's no one coming, anyway." Giles could wait; she was feeling quite cross with him at the moment.

Mrs. Farthing shuffled off. Roz watched her as she disappeared into the shadows, right shoulder raised so that she looked even more as though she were walking along a wall, trying to squeeze into it and disappear. *Servile,* Roz thought. *That's what servile looks like.* S.O.T.E. Salt of the earth, Viola had called her: Servile. "Peasants, servants, laborers, necessary condescension of the genes, sufficient unto themselves, aspiring to no heights greater than yonder hill, content with their simple rituals of the earth, their Maypoles and mummer's plays, their dialects so expressive of emotions they are hardly aware they feel, inarticulate, unconscious, yet so in touch with the earth, the seasons . . . how I envy them." Viola's words. She'd just read them. Different from Giles—more accepting, not so condescending, so angry. But then, she had never seen Viola in action.

But who could tell? As she sat in the little ticket office waiting for Mrs. Farthing to come back, she felt her mind being bounced back and forth, back and forth, between the past and present, between Viola and the present inhabitants of Montfort.

8

SOMEWHAT TO ROZ'S SURPRISE, AFTER THE series of tense encounters between Giles and the other residents of Montfort everything seemed to settle down, and their work went quite smoothly for the next several days. She and Giles worked steadily on the papers far into the evenings, stopping only for meals and an occasional walk in the garden. To her relief, Mrs. Farthing's continuing presence was attested to by the appearance of hot meals at regular intervals at the pass-through in the dining room, though not the appearance of Mrs. Farthing herself. In fact, Roz saw very little of the other residents, and only from a distance. It was almost as though they had been warned off.

But in spite of her earlier reservations, Roz found herself once again caught up in the immediacy of Viola's life, growing more and more familiar with its tempo and texture, with the names and dates and places now almost at her fingertips. Giles began to leave her to work on the letters by herself for longer and longer periods, going off to transact business of his own, and Roz welcomed this indication of trust and confidence on his part. She seldom met anyone she knew in the garden, and, when she did, the encounters were polite and perfunctory. Any uneasiness she felt, any sense of something hanging fire, she discounted as a consequence of the long hours spent hunched over the desk in the Tower moving along at what seemed a snail's pace, day by day, month by month, year by year in Viola's life. Later, when she had a better sense of what might or might not be coming, she could cut back. Meanwhile, there was something to be said for life settling down to a comfortable, if somewhat circumscribed, routine.

One morning a little over a week after the luncheon, Roz woke early, almost with the sun. She lay in bed and watched the spectral figures of mist withdraw from the rose leaves surrounding her window as the sun climbed above the lower walls. Finally, even though it was still early, she got up, propelled by a feeling of restlessness and suspense. Last night she and Giles had finally come to the point at which Viola and Sir Herbert were debating whether or not to buy the Abbey, and she wanted to get back to the papers as soon as possible.

When she came into the kitchen there was no sign of either Mrs. Farthing or Giles. She set the kettle on to boil and stood staring out the window over the Courtyard while she munched on a cold scone. The seried ranks of perennials that bordered the Courtyard were still in shadow, but the sun shone brightly on the dew on the grass, and Roz felt a sudden impulse to go outside. Turning the kettle off, she left the kitchen and let herself quietly into the Courtyard.

At first Roz thought she had been temporarily blinded by the glare of bright sunshine. But there was a rotten smell in the air, a sickly odor of decaying vegetation. As she shaded her eyes and squinted around her at the flowerbeds, she thought they seemed oddly flat, barren of color. She looked closer.

And stared, appalled.

The intricate masses of blooms and foliage that had softened the rough stone walls—spikes and globes and disks of purple, blue, mauve, lavender—had disappeared. All around the Courtyard plants lay uprooted, flung about in tangled heaps, clumps of drying dirt clinging to the pale exposed roots already wizening in the sun. The bigger, stronger plants—the hardier geraniums, foxglove, iris spears—lay trampled in the shade that still filled the area by the east wall near the Granary. The beds were churned and pockmarked, stamped on and trodden over, violently disrupted.

Roz felt as though she were in another place. Her eyes blurred, and the noises of the garden—bees humming, birds twittering—sounded far away, muffled, as though her ears were stuffed with cotton.

She shook her head to clear it, then looked up, suddenly aware of voices drifting faintly over the wall from beyond the Moat House. She ran across the ruined Courtyard into the Herb Garden, noticing with some relief that the low-growing herbs lay undisturbed in their beds. At least they were still intact. She inhaled deeply of the savory earth odor.

No.

Something else was wrong.

The soft aroma of the herbs was overpowered by a stench even worse than the odor of rotting plants in the Courtyard. Putting her hand over her nose and mouth, Roz stepped quickly through the hedgerow onto the bridge over the moat. Immediately she regretted it. Here the stink was so overpowering she almost choked.

Holding her breath, she looked down at the moat.

All the water was gone, leaving a six-foot-wide channel of oily ooze that stretched from one end of the Rose Garden to the other. The glistening ribbon of slime steamed, and a thin green line of scum dribbled down the middle, the soft mud making occasional popping sounds as more bubbles of gas boiled to the surface and burst, leaving behind little craters that quickly filled with more slime. Roz stared fascinated at the bubbling mess for a moment, then ran off the bridge into the middle of the Rose Garden, gasping for air.

She took a few deep breaths. Then, no longer in danger of being asphyxiated, she looked around. Cory and Stella were standing at the far end of the moat near the wall of the Porcelain Garden. Arms folded, faces impassive, they stood peering down into the remains of the moat. Roz hurried toward them.

"Hello," she said. "What's going on?"

Both gardeners glanced at her. "Not much," Cory said after a moment. "Somebody's gone and pulled the bloody plug, that's all." Stella walked away alongside the moat, hands on her hips, looking downward and shaking her head.

"What a mess," Roz said. "And the borders, too. Who—"

"What borders?" Cory interrupted.

"Why, the ones in the Courtyard. They're all pulled up all over the grass." She watched as Cory took off at a dead run through the nearest arch, with Stella right on her heels. After a moment Roz ran after them.

When she emerged into the Courtyard, Stella was on her knees holding up a wilted delphinium.

"Can you bloody well credit it?" she moaned. "The whole flaming lot of them." She tossed the limp flower onto the grass, rubbed her hands on her thighs, and sat back on her heels.

76

"I'm sorry," Roz said. She didn't know what else to say.

"Never mind. It's hardly your fault," Cory said.

"Vandals," Stella muttered. "Bloody vandals."

"Has anything like this ever happened before?"

"No," Stella replied. Cory had wandered off to pace restlessly around the Courtyard borders. "No, it hasn't, not ever. Oh there's always been the odd yank . . ." Stella glanced up, reddening, and added quickly, "I mean the odd theft; people have been known to lift a plant or two and smuggle it away in their handbags or coat pockets—a wild orchid or some other small rare plant. That's why we sell cuttings now, to discourage lifting." Stella shook her head. "If only we'd come through here this morning instead of going straight down the Plum Walk to the moat, we might have saved some."

"There was no mistaking the stink," Cory said from the far wall. "Who would have thought there was something else? Anyway, it wouldn't have mattered. These have been torn up for hours. They're long gone."

"If only he'd left well enough alone," Stella said. "If he'd just let it go to the Britannia Trust, it would have all been settled by now, and this . . ."

"Hush," Cory said, coming over to stand by Stella. *If only's* and *might-have-beens* don't plant plants. So we should get cracking. A day lost, and then some. His lordship will not be pleased."

She turned to Roz. "The situation is this. The dam's been plucked bango right out of the pond. There's not a stick left. Half a day to put it right, and then two days for the pond to fill up again and back up into the moat and cover the slime. We obviously can't have visitors coming in to pay and be overcome. The place smells like a bloody sewer."

"We could spend the time rebedding these two sides from what's in the greenhouses," Stella added. "Then we'd have to scour the nurseries round about, see what they have on hand that would go. We could

77

probably do that in a day's time, after we've taken care of the dam."

Cory rubbed her forehead with a smudged hand. "It's going to cost hundreds; Giles will have to authorize the expense. He's been crying so poor lately . . ."

The gardeners walked off together, not deliberately excluding Roz, but talking almost as if they were one mind trying to solve the problem at hand. She felt like an intruder.

"Is there something I can do?" she called after them. "Or shall I just make myself scarce?"

Cory and Stella looked back simultaneously, as if suddenly remembering she were there.

"Oh, thanks, but . . ." Cory began, then paused. "Hang on a sec, maybe there is." She frowned. "Was Giles there when you got up?"

"I don't know. I didn't hear him. We worked late last night, so maybe he's still asleep."

"Yes, we saw your light in the Tower." Cory ran a hand through her bronze curls. "Well, we can't do anything until the master wakes. Could you . . ."

At that moment the door of the Refectory banged back and Giles emerged, freshly shaven and dressed for town. Where was he off to now? Roz had thought they were going to work all day.

Giles took another step, then stopped dead in his tracks, sniffed, curled a lip, and stared around him. Then he resumed his progress across the lawn toward them, a quizzical look on his face.

"Gardeners move in mysterious ways their wonders to perform," he said with elaborate politeness. "I assume it will be back in shape by opening time?"

Stella stared glumly at the ground. Cory lifted her chin and said quietly, "You know it won't, Giles. It was done deliberately. Thoroughly. Someone must have got in in the night. There's not a hope of putting it right before the weekend."

78

Giles looked at the plants, piled up like so much garbage.

"You must be joking," he said.

"What's more," Cory continued, "presumably the same somebody has gone and yanked the dam apart. All the water's been let out of your pond and the moat's a stinking mess of rotten sludge. That's what you smell, in case you were wondering."

Everyone stood stock still for a moment, then Giles and Cory and Stella began to talk all at once, shaking their heads, gesticulating, exclaiming, Giles accusing, Cory and Stella defending themselves as best they could. Arguing heatedly, the three of them moved off in the direction of the moat.

Roz stood in the middle of the Courtyard, not sure what to do next. Then Giles's face reappeared in the entrance of the Herb Garden. "Oh, Rosamund!" he shouted. "I say, why don't you go along and get started on today's lot? I may be a while!"

Roz stared after him for a moment. Then she turned, and, trying not to look down, carefully picked her way through the piles of vegetation until she reached the Tower.

It was an hour later, just past nine, when Giles appeared in the Viola room. His cravat was askew, and the trousers of his elegant pin-striped suit were muddied and shapeless as far as the knee, obviously having been put to use as impromptu waders. Roz was oddly touched by this ruination; it confirmed her idea that Giles cared more for the garden than he did for almost anything else, including his own appearance.

He stood in the middle of the room, his face shiny with perspiration, streaked with mud, a loose strand of hair falling down over his forehead. He brushed the hair back impatiently, leaving a brownish-green streak diagonally above his brow.

"Well," he announced.

79

"You look as though you've been in the trenches."

"And so I have." Giles perched delicately on the edge of his desk. Crumbs of dirt pattered to the floor. He looked down. "Oh dear."

"Don't worry, I can clean it up."

"Sorry to have been so long. We've had a go at putting back the dam, and while the pond is filling up, I've decided to clean the moat, fish out all the chocolate wrappers and orange peels—people are such baboons, really," he said with a sneer of distaste. "I'll have to help, though. Cory and Stella can't do it alone. So I'll be swarming around in the muck for a day or so. I've had to close the garden, of course. There's no other way."

"What about the borders?"

"Cory and Stella have already gone along to Duck's Nursery in Newmarket. They'll get potted plants to replace as much as we can—though it won't look the same, not by any means—" Giles paused. "We can probably reopen in two days' time. We've got to. It's such a frightful expense." His shoulders slumped, and he stared at the floor. "This—along with the other brouhaha—will completely wipe out my reserve."

"Can you find out who did it? Could it have been one person?"

Giles sighed. "I'm afraid it hardly matters, at least not now."

Roz stared at him in disbelief. "Hardly matters?"

"What's done is done," he replied. "What does matter is putting it right as soon as possible. I won't reopen the place until everything is back to normal. All mother's work, the garden, the whole atmosphere of Montfort Abbey—" Giles stopped, becoming distant and thoughtful. Then abruptly he came to and turned back to Roz. "However, none of this really concerns you, my dear. What I came to tell you . . . I mean, ask you . . . is whether you'd mind awfully carrying on alone with the letters while I field-marshall the recovery operation. I'm afraid it can't be helped." He shrugged apologetically.

"Of course, Giles. You know I'll do whatever I can."

Giles stood up. "Thank you, my dear," he said softly, then turned, walked across the room without another word, and vanished down the stairs. Roz sat back, bouncing a pencil thoughtfully on her palm.

She did not like the implications of this new incident; it had to be one of the consequences Hugh had warned Giles about. Things were getting more and more out of hand, and she was going to have to decide on a course of action. She could leave right now—just pack up and go—or she could stay and work on the papers, on Giles's terms. She thought of Florence's pale, anxious face; of Hugh, arguing passionately with Giles in the kitchen. *They* were the ones who needed help, not Giles. If she stayed, perhaps she could intervene—not now, but when the time came. If it came at all. Maybe there was really nothing in the papers for Florence and Hugh to worry about; that was still a possibility, wasn't it? Oughtn't she to find out? And if there were, Giles might listen to her advice, especially if she had proved herself invaluable to him by then.

I'll stay, she decided. *I'll stay and see what I can do.* She would have to be more careful with him, of course, not to take too much for granted. She had been so busy since her arrival trying to make her way around the garden, around Viola, that she hadn't paid enough attention to making her way around Giles. But she had a better idea of what he was like now, particularly after seeing him with the others. She knew, too, how much the garden and the papers mattered to him. *That's it*, she thought. *I'll stay, and watch, and see what I can do to help.*

With some misgivings, she went back to work.

9

ROZ WAS JUST FINISHING UP A STACK OF LETTERS to "Bear"—Lady Ursula Drottingholm, a friend of Viola's from childhood—when she heard a light step on the stair. She looked up to see a dark mop of mussed, unruly hair appear at the turning, followed by a clever faun's face, a rumpled hacking jacket, and worn corduroy trousers. Alan Stewart paused in the doorway, looked back over his shoulder down the stairs, then smiled triumphantly at Roz.

"Cheers," he said, and jammed his hands farther into his pockets, squaring his wide shoulders into an unfinished shrug. Roz let go the breath she had been holding. In spite of the interruption, she was glad to see him; they hadn't met since the ill-fated luncheon. As he came closer, she saw that his jacket and shirt were spattered here and there with flecks of paint, some of them still fresh and shiny. There was a minuscule spot of blue just in front of his right ear, obviously missed in the washing.

"Hello," she said, smiling.

"I'm Alan Stewart. We met the other day."

"Yes, I know. You're the artist."

Alan blinked at her, looked down at his shirtfront and jacket, then smiled. "Right. That is, when I can get to it. But I've been driven right out of my digs, you know." He peered at her. "You *do* know, don't you? Smell of rotten Humpty-Dumpty had a great fall? Simply revolting."

Roz nodded sympathetically, wondering where he

had been all this time. Alan moved across the room, balanced himself teeter-totter fashion on the edge of Giles's desk, crossed his stretched-out legs at the ankles, and clasped his hands loosely in front of him. With his shapeless jacket thrust back away from his torso, he was still quite broad, but more slim-hipped and athletic-looking than he had seemed at first glance, and not nearly so rumpled. *It must be the painting that does it,* Roz thought. She pictured him as an expressionist—restless, all over the place, moving quickly, with that deceptive ease that made him seem so much more compact than he was. And yet with all his quick grace and energy of movement, there was that sense of repose about him that Roz had found so reassuring earlier.

"Seven hundred people—all the king's men, I expect—are slopping around in the moat, with Giles barking orders and reviving people with a little tube of *sal volatile.* The stench is truly remarkable, and it sucks right up the drains—clever system we have in England, the drains all on the outside so you can get at 'em, I suppose—and into my bathroom and kitchen, and thence into everything. The reek instantaneously tarnished the silver, rotted the book bindings, and curdled my egg tempera. And I can't open the windows because it's too noisy, what with all the shrieks and carryings-on. I never thought that drains could work the other way, but it does give some credit to the miasmal theory of disease, don't you think?"

He grinned at her briefly, then took a long, frankly appraising look around the room.

"So this is the mysterious Lady Viola room. Did you know none of us is allowed up here? We've all been warned off in no uncertain terms—particularly, I now realize with the marvelous aid of hindsight—since your arrival."

"Oh?" Roz said, watching Alan's face. If he knew he wasn't supposed to be up here, why had he come?

"Ah yes. It has not set well with everyone, some less well than others. I don't mind particularly, but"—Alan stopped, cocking his head in the direction of the door as though listening intently—"I must confess I feel slightly uncomfortable up here, as though I oughtn't to be caught. Silly, really. But this place has that effect, rather. Can't think why, unless it's . . ." He stopped, eying her narrowly.

Roz grinned suddenly. For it was clear that everything going on in Alan's head clearly communicated itself directly to his open, responsive face. He had been going to say "Giles," and he wanted to know if she knew. Roz sat back in her chair, smiling at him.

"Giles," she finished for him. "I'll bet you're terrible at chess and poker."

Alan stared at her in astonishment. "Why yes, I am. I invariably get trounced, even by my six-year-old nephew. But how did you know?"

"Your face."

"Oh, that. That's what Derek—my nephew—says." He shrugged, smiled apologetically. "Well, it can't be helped."

They were both silent.

"Well," said Alan after a moment.

"Well," Roz repeated. "What can I do for you?"

"What? Oh, you mean why am I here in spite of the terrible danger of incurring Giles's wrath? Curiosity, of course. After Florence swooned at lunch the other day, and you so tactfully cleared yourself out, Giles laid down the law and told everyone your work was strictly private. No others need apply, and he would be exceedingly furious if any of us bothered you. Can't help making one wonder, you know?"

"Do you have any idea why?"

"I gather he doesn't want anyone to scoop the scandal," Alan said matter-of-factly. "I imagine he's planned a big press build-up, prior publicity, interview with the author's son who cannot reveal et cetera et cetera, shocking revelations of aristocratic taradiddle, and so forth." Alan gestured broadly, sketching in the air a tabloid-sized newspaper, blocking in with finger and thumb huge blaring headlines, squinting his eyes and widening them in an expression of shocked and avid horror.

"Of course it will sell in boxcar lots," he finished, resuming his own relaxed posture.

"But what's the scandal?" Roz persisted, trying not to be distracted by Alan's good humor.

"Haven't the foggiest," he said simply. "Poor Florence and Hugh are convinced that there's something dreadful about them in those letters, and Giles refuses to deny it. They've been on about it for quite a while—since the papers turned up, as a matter of fact—but it's only lately, since things have gotten bad financially and Giles has begun to mutter about publishing the whole lot, that everyone has got the wind up. The place is getting to be an armed camp. But you already know that, from that marvelous rout of a luncheon last week."

"Do you know why Beatrice was so angry?" Roz asked.

Alan shifted, folded his arms, and smiled. "Ah, Beatrice. Beatrice is always angry; it's her nature. Besides that, she doesn't like it here. Her family thinks she married beneath her, and it doesn't help to have Giles lording it over Hugh. Giles has always treated him rather shabbily. You heard him at lunch taunting Hugh about the corruption of his family name. Beatrice is quite fed up, I suspect. Yet Hugh won't leave."

"Because his mother's here?"

Alan raised his eyebrows. "Oh, you got that bit? Generally they all keep it quiet, though I can't imagine why. Perhaps the habit of intrigue is catching—in the air or the walls. Like secret passages, only in the mind. I don't know. The familial relationships here at Montfort are quite beyond me, I'm afraid. I'm still trying to work them out

85

on both hands, what with intermarriages and re-marriages and deceased wife's sister's son and so on."

"What about Francesca?"

"Not a clue. She simply came out of nowhere."

"She certainly had an effect. People falling in faints, muttering and screaming . . ."

"Quite. But you know, I rather think Giles's attitude—all this hush-hush, wait-and-see—is responsible for a good deal of repressed hysteria. Everyone was wrought up anyway over the papers, and then Francesca's surprise appearance simply blew the lid off." Alan shrugged. "But that puts me solidly in what Eliot calls a world of speculation. Only Giles knows for sure."

"And you?"

"That's a good question. But I don't really come into it much, unless Viola had the second sight. I've only been here about two years. Purely by chance. An elderly relative—of mine, not theirs—had the lease, and I took it over. It was perfect for me."

Roz watched Alan speculatively. He appeared completely open and frank, disinterestedly sympathetic, but not particularly concerned himself. And certainly he didn't seem averse to telling her what he knew. So far.

"What do you think of Giles?" Roz asked.

Alan studiously scratched at a bit of dried paint on his left cuff. "I find Giles utterly fascinating, but according to . . ." He stopped dead.

For the first time since she had met him, Roz had the feeling he was holding something back. Then he looked up, meeting her glance matter-of-factly. "And what about you?" he asked. "What do you think of all this?" He waved a hand around the room.

"It's a scholar's dream," Roz said evenly.

"I see. The Chance of a Lifetime. Of course it would be. It's your job, isn't it? I mean, your profession?"

Roz nodded her head, but said nothing.

"Obviously you want to get back to it, and I've kept you from it long enough." Alan straightened up and shook his clothes down into their usual state of casual disarray. "However, the real reason I came here was not to get in your way, but to see if you mightn't come out for drinks and dinner with me one night. See a bit of the surrounding countryside. Cory tells me you haven't been out of the grounds yet."

Roz stared at him. So someone *was* keeping track. Maybe lots of someones.

"Well?" Alan persisted. "I don't like the thought of you cooped up in this gloomy tower day after day—and far into the night, if I'm not mistaken. You'll go all pasty white and breathless, like the Lady of Shalott. So what about it?" He grinned amiably. "That is, if it's permitted."

Roz smiled. "I'd like that very much, Alan," she said gravely.

"Good. Tomorrow, then?"

Roz hesitated. There were the papers, and with Giles gone . . . But—permitted, indeed. Who did Alan think would stop her? Impulsively, she nodded.

"Tomorrow will be fine," she said.

"That's settled, then. You clear it with Giles, if that's necessary. I'll come for you at five. And now I leave you to your work." And with one quick glance over his shoulder, Alan went out the door and down the stairs.

Roz stood up and moved over to the window. Directly below her she saw Alan walking across the swept and tidied Courtyard. He paused briefly and looked around all four borders to where the bare earth lay neatened and combed flat, decorated with little buttons and bows of color barely visible against the dirt. Shaking his head, he went on into the Moat House.

Roz stared thoughtfully at the blank facade of the Moat House for some time. Alan was an extremely attractive man, bright, matter-of-fact even about his own curiosity. She had agreed to have dinner with him, without consulting Giles. Yet for all his openness, his candor, the honesty of his face and manner, she could not get over the feeling that he had not, after all, told her all he knew. There was something indefinable . . . But that was nonsense. Had she told him all *she* knew? Of course not. But she knew so little and, in fact, had the feeling that every day she knew less and less.

She turned and glared at the piles of letters on her desk. They had got as far as 1930. Ten years. Five hundred letters. It was so very slow. There must be at least five thousand more.

She sighed. And somewhere in them lay a terrible secret. Or maybe not. Only Giles knew. Or did he? Did anyone? She tapped her foot impatiently.

The thought crossed her mind that perhaps the best way to deal with all this chaos of events and personalities was not to keep on stacking up letters year after year, but to go back outside into the garden and find out as much as she could from whomever she met about the people who were still alive, instead of burying herself in this literary dead-letter office.

She leaned on her desk, struggling with this new temptation to walk out the door, down the stairs, and start knocking on doors. Simply talk to the first person she met. Any of them probably knew more than she did.

She shook her head. No, that wasn't the way. The papers—everything was in the papers. The letters lay fixed and waiting, already written. The dead stayed put, did not talk back or change their lines. Somewhere in these piles had to be the answer. She was bound to get to it sooner or later—if, in fact, it existed.

Straightening up, Roz focused on the top letter of the stack in front of her.

"Dear Bear," it began. "I am so lonely here in this

trash heap of a former Abbey. Won't you join me for a weekend? Herbert has gone along to London for the session, and I've only Rasputin here for company. But I have the most marvelous news . . ."

Rasputin. Viola's borzoi, bought in 1927. Bertie in Parliament, staying at their London flat. Montfort in the early stages, Viola alone. Roz's pencil began to fly as she added notations in the margin of the copy. Viola, Bertie, Bear, dead these many years. And Rasputin, down under the ground of the farthest pasture with all the other pets. The chance of a lifetime, Alan had said.

And so it was—a lifetime, indeed. Concentrating her attention on the work before her, she read on quickly, wanting nothing more right now than to learn Viola's marvelous news.

10

THE NEXT MORNING, ROZ WOKE EARLY AGAIN with a pleasant sense of anticipation. She had made considerable progress with the letters on her own, pushing ahead through the thirties to the beginning of World War II. There had been references to the Badgetts and the Home Farm, to Giles and Hugh as little boys playing together, and Roz felt that finally she was getting close to finding out what—if anything—was the dark secret that made the idea of publication so abhorrent to Hugh and Florence. The immediacy of the life in the letters had almost erased from her mind the trouble in the garden yesterday.

And according to Giles, that was well on its way to being tidied away.

In Giles's continued absence she had been able to deviate slightly from their agreed-upon approach and read through the rest of the Lady Ursula letters. There had been only fifty more or so coming up as far as 1943, and Roz had marveled as she read them that so cultivated and witty an intelligence could write such gushy, emotional letters well into her thirties. With her dear Bear, Viola had never quite lost that worshipful, beseeching tone of an adolescent girl with a crush on a much-admired older woman, even though the tone of the later and less frequent letters was modified slightly by the respectful formality of someone addressing an old and cherished friend. It was that sort of change, Roz reflected as she lay in bed, that Giles's approach risked missing. She would have to talk to him about it after this garden business was cleared up. Meanwhile, she had a lot to look foward to today. More letters, and then dinner with Alan . . .

She sat up and stretched, taking a deep breath. The heavy scent of roses drifted through her window, sweet and pungent. She had always loved roses; in fact, they were her favorite flower. She took several more breaths, inhaling the strong fragrance. *The Rose Garden,* she thought. *Why not? The letters can wait. I'll go there first thing this morning, before anyone else is up, and just walk around and look.*

Walking lightly so as not to wake Giles as she passed his closed door at the end of the hall, she made her way downstairs and let herself out into the garden.

Even though the Abbey had been built on high ground some distance from the nearest fen, there was a persistent misty quality about the morning air. Layers of fog lingered in the shadows of the walled Courtyard, swam around the newly laid herbaceous borders, flowed through the arches and gates and doorways that led from one garden into another.

She had always felt drawn to the Rose Garden; of all the gardens here, it was the one she liked most just to be in, walking among the hundreds of roses, each with its own name and personality as well as color, all contained in the Celtic cross pattern Viola had so laboriously worked out—four paths leading out from a central rounded space. Many of the letters she had read yesterday were about the Rose Garden: "Scarlet Allen Chandler, somewhat formal but so precise," Viola had written. ". . . striped *Variegata di Bologna,* jaunty as a beach umbrella, gentle Roger Lambelin, dark mysterious *Deuil de Paul Fontaine,* aristocratic Prince Camille de Rohan." Name after name, like a long list of friends or correspondents: Zephyrine Drohin, Honorine de Brabant, La Reine Victoria, *Souvenir de Malmaison. It would make quite a garden party,* Roz thought, *if all the roses were guests. As perhaps they are.*

She shivered slightly as she walked through a knee-high layer of mist into the Herb Garden. The air was drying rapidly as the sun rose higher, but it still had the richness of early morning, diffused throughout the droplets of mist. As she took a few deep breaths, she noticed the fragrance of roses was oddly strong, almost overpowering, this morning. But of course they were coming into full bloom now, and their scent would permeate the whole garden. Lucky for us, she thought, considering how the place smelled yesterday.

Quickening her step, she went out the far side of the Herb Garden into the Plum Walk to avoid the still-empty moat. It would be nice to approach the Rose Garden from the far end, as she had seen it the first time, so she could once again see all the different shapes and hues and textures, the hundreds of blooms massed in their wreaths of foliage all at once, in one great splash of color.

She walked slowly along the wall, head down, eyes on the ground, until she thought that she must be standing precisely on the axis of the longest cruciform path. She took a deep breath of rose-scented air and looked up.

There was not a rose to be seen.

Roz caught her breath, blinked, and looked again. All the roses were gone.

The entire garden was bare. It was now no more than a mass of bushy green, with an occasional thorny spike sticking forlornly into the air. Roz stared, then slowly moved closer, searching with her eyes and then her fingers among the leaves, wondering if there were something wrong with her vision. Had she suddenly gone colorblind?

She reached out and touched the nearest bush, then bent to look underneath for the dropped petals. The ground was thick with them, as though all the roses had dropped their petals at once. But that couldn't be it; even she could tell that. There were no withered brown rose hips waiting to be deadheaded. Just stems ending abruptly, obviously cut.

A small bronze plaque almost buried in white petals, heads of roses, bits of buds and stem, caught her eye. "*Rosa f.* White Wings," it read. A snatch of a tune from her childhood ran in her head: *"White wings, you never grow weary, you carry me faithfully over the sea . . ."*

Tears stung her eyes as she looked around her. Everywhere the ground was littered with blossoms, petals, buds, leaves, stems cut off—roses in every stage of growth, even the littlest green buds as small as a pencil tip. She bent down and picked up one tiny, perfect bud. Not enough stem to put in water.

She straightened up, brushed impatiently at her eyes with the heel of her hand. The smell of decaying roses was growing stronger as the sun moved higher. The brick paths that separated the beds were covered with petals as thick as autumn leaves. Roz stepped carefully along the path toward the center, trying, absurdly, not to crush any more blossoms than she had to. She reached out to touch a small, pointed, glossy purple leaf. She knew it by name—it was one of the first names she had learned, *Rosa Rubrifolia:* Rosy-Red-Leaves, like something from a fairy tale. She could not even remember the color of its flower.

She turned and ran blindly back down the path out of the Rose Garden, down the Plum Tree Walk past the Herb Garden, the Granary, the Cottage Plot, past the corner of the Tower wing, straight for Cory's and Stella's flat in the converted stable.

The door was shut tight; Roz banged furiously on it. Stella came into view, dressed in tan hiking shorts and matching shirt, holding a coffee mug. She saw Roz, cocked her head curiously, and came down the narrow hallway to unlatch the door. A large Black Forest cuckoo clock overhead clattered open; the little cuckoo hooted seven times, punctuating the silence, then slammed itself back inside its little gingerbread chalet.

"Why, Roz, whatever's wrong? You're a sight." Stella put the cup down hard. "Cory!" Cory's head appeared around the corner, corkscrew curls still damp. Like Stella, she was dressed in khaki, ready for the day's work.

"The Rose Garden. I've just come from there and . . . it's gone."

Both gardeners stared at her open-mouthed for an instant. Then Cory shouldered past Roz without a word, Stella right behind her. The door banged back against the hinges; above it, the cuckoo clock wheezed in protest. The gardeners raced down the drive, and Roz followed after them.

By the time Roz reached the Rose Garden, Cory and Stella were standing in almost the exact spot from which Roz had first seen the devastated garden.

93

One of Stella's hands rested lightly on a denuded rose bush. The other shaded her eyes.

"Well," said Cory grimly. "How do you like this little spot of bother?"

"I don't a bit," Stella answered.

"This packs up the Rose Garden for the season, wouldn't you say?"

Stella nodded. "And for some time to come."

Cory turned away and stood, arms folded, her back to the wrecked garden. Dressed in her khaki riding breeches and shirt, her secateurs strapped to her leg in a leather holster, she looked like some sort of desert soldier. Roz stared at her. She appeared unmoved.

"But how could anyone do such a thing?" Roz asked desperately. "Who . . . ?"

"Anyone with a pair or two of razor-sharp secateurs, a pocket hone, and about three hours' free time—in the middle of the night, of course—could do it," Cory replied. "Snip-snap, and Bob's your uncle. It's the picking up that takes so long, and obviously they've left that to us. The moon was nearly full last night, and it was clear. Plenty of light to see by, needn't miss a thing, and good shadows to sneak into if anyone happened by." Grim-faced, Cory turned back to face the garden.

"Needn't miss a thing," she repeated. Roz thought of the tiny pencil-tip buds, like babies' fingers, the tiny, soft leaves just barely opened, not even hardened to the air.

Stella leaned forward to finger one of the spikes sticking up out of the leaves. "Snicked right off, clean as a whistle. Every last one. Simply beggars the imagination." She reached down and slowly sifted her hands through the soft petals under the bush. Roz watched the two women. Neither had shown any obvious emotion, not even anger, as they had over the moat and the borders. But what did she expect them to do—run around screaming and tearing their hair? They were professionals,

94

and took a detached, unsentimental pride in their work. No doubt they were already thinking of what to do to minimize the damage. Roz, on the other hand, rank sentimental amateur that she was, felt as though someone had snick-snacked her toes and fingers.

"Will it come back?" she asked.

Cory turned back, squinting. "This year? Not likely. One or two might try to bloom. Most will next season, if we're lucky. Some will have to be replaced." She sighed and shook her head. "Forty years' work. Oh well. It's not a total loss. But just wait till Giles gets wind of this. This will really finish us as far as the tourists are concerned. The Rose Garden has always been the main attraction, particularly this time of year."

"Someone will have to break the news to Giles," Stella said. "I shouldn't like to have to do it."

Roz ignored her for the moment, even though she knew she was the someone Stella meant. She was still thinking about the roses. "Why didn't anyone hear?" she asked. "Alan, or the Norths, or . . . well, someone?" She really didn't see how so much damage could have been done by one person in one brief night, no matter what Cory said.

In fact, Cory and Stella could very well have done it themselves. It didn't look like the work of amateurs. And they were so calm.

"Secateurs don't make any noise," Cory said patiently. "Especially if they're razor sharp." As if to prove it, she took out her own, opened them, and noiselessly snipped a barren stem in two. She replaced the secateurs in her belt. "See, the stems aren't even crushed. Whoever did it probably started at the far end, down by the Allen Chandler; it looks as though the climbers have been pulled down, as well. But a step ladder would do. The water rushing down into the moat would cover a lot of noise. Then they simply worked their way down, bush by bush. . ."

95

And Cory dashed a clenched fist against her thigh. "Damn," she muttered.

Stella turned away. "Don't," she said.

"Oh, never mind, Stel," Cory said. She clapped a hand awkwardly on Stella's shoulder. "Come on, now. We've got some cleaning up to do."

"No deadheading today," Stella said tremulously.

"Nor any day soon," Cory said. She withdrew her hand from Stella's shoulder. "Well then," she continued briskly. "About eight dustbins, wouldn't you say? Want to call in the jobbers?"

"No," said Stella. "I think we should do this ourselves."

They stood a moment longer, looking over the unnaturally still and colorless foliage of the Rose Garden. Even the bees had departed.

Cory turned to Roz.

"Could you roust Giles out and tell him what's happened? He'll probably want to see us, but meanwhile we can get started."

Roz nodded. "Of course. Anything," she added lamely, realizing her own incapacity to be anything other than a carrier of bad news. She walked beside the two gardeners as far as the entrance to the Herb Garden, then turned and watched them as they walked silently toward the greenhouses.

No, she thought, as she watched their slumped shoulders, their bent heads bobbing down the avenue of plum trees. Not Cory and Stella. The garden meant too much to them. They were at odds with Giles over it, but they would never take out their enmity on the garden itself. Particularly the Rose Garden.

Roz watched them out of sight, then turned and made her way through the Herb Garden and across the Courtyard into the Refectory.

* * *

Giles was sitting at the scrubbed kitchen table, eating a bowl of cornflakes. He looked up at her, spoon poised halfway to his mouth.

"What? Up and about already? I thought you were still sleeping."

"Giles, someone's been in the garden again. They've cut down all the roses. I've just left Cory and Stella."

Giles's spoon fell back down into the cornflakes and clattered off the side of the bowl. He blinked at her. "I beg your pardon?"

"All the roses are gone. Someone cut them all off during the night."

Giles stood up, threw down his damask napkin, swept the bowl of cornflakes onto the floor, and strode past her out of the kitchen. Roz heard the great oak door slam back and bang shut again, its iron latch clinking into place. Absurdly, she was reminded of the gardeners' cuckoo clock. Through the kitchen window, she saw Giles's tall figure running across the Courtyard. She bent down and picked up the pieces of broken faience bowl, mopped the milk up with the napkin, and put everything in the sink. Then, feeling slightly dazed, she fixed herself some cornflakes, toast, and coffee, and sat down.

She tried not to think about the Rose Garden while she was eating, turning her thoughts instead to the papers, but the one led inevitably back to the other, circling round and round and finally coalescing in her mind. She wished she knew whether any of the roses were likely to survive. All that work, all that devotion, even if it was only a certain kind of plant laid out in a certain kind of pattern. But it had been Viola's pattern, and Giles had carried it on, was trying to preserve it by whatever means he could, including publishing his mother's papers. Was that so reprehensible? Deserving of such revenge? For him, the garden was a living thing. He had loved his mother, and he loved the garden she had created.

These assaults on the garden had been made by someone who knew that. The question was not why, but who? Or worse yet, how many, if not all? What she had not realized until her conversation with Alan yesterday afternoon was the extent of the hostility even before her arrival. The air of Montfort was filled with the whine of axes being ground. But apparently it always had been. The projected publication of the papers had just brought it all into the open.

Roz sat there mulling over possibilities, getting nowhere. She didn't have enough information for even an educated guess. If she could only find the right place to start, the knot at the end of the string, she could untangle the whole skein. But there were so many knots—too many.

She was still sitting at the table some time later when Giles came into the kitchen, breathless and disheveled. He flopped down in the chair opposite her.

"Good morning, Rosamund."

Roz blinked. He was certainly one for preserving the civilized forms. But she was thankful for the chance to collect her thoughts.

"Good morning, Giles," she said.

"Not quite an ordinary morning, is it? Nor particularly good, on the face of it," Giles said, digging a fingernail into the soft pine tabletop. He looked at her, eyes glittering. But with what? Anger, excitement, tears? Surely not tears, not Giles . . . Roz scrutinized his face. Not a clue.

"No doubt you are asking yourself—and it's very tactful of you not to be asking me—what's to be done."

Roz nodded.

"Yes, quite." Giles looked down at the stick figure his thumbnail had indented in the tabletop. "The garden will be closed again today, of course. I couldn't, as you probably might guess, let anyone view the . . . remains."

Roz felt a stab of sympathy for him.

"As a matter of fact," he went on, his eyelids now drooping over the strangely brilliant eyes, but still, she saw, watching her intently, "the garden is now closed. Indefinitely."

11

ROZ STARED AT HIM. CLOSE THE GARDEN? HOW could he? What was he planning to live on? Giles grinned at her consternation. Reaching into the inside breast pocket of his jacket, he pulled out a long, fat, torn-open envelope. He pushed it across the table to Roz. She opened it and pulled out an impressive array of legal-looking documents.

"This came yesterday. The contract for publication of my mother's papers. With a check for an absolutely staggering amount of cash, which I've deposited in my account. Quite enough to go on with for quite some time, garden or no garden." He sat back, crossed his legs, and tapped his fingers smartly on the table, unable to keep the look of triumph out of his eyes.

"Oh Giles, how marvelous!" Roz said, but her own voice echoed hollowly in her ears. She wondered why she didn't share his sense of relief—triumph. His narrow, sculptured face—now so animated, even transformed by this good news—still reminded her of something seen in stone, or in a painting, something stretched over the surface, taut and fixed. A statue's smile, an ancient, slow, and glittering grin. What would happen to the garden now?

Roz tried to recall her earlier sense of his involvement with the garden as a personal, emotional investment, the preservation of a heritage, even a love. She couldn't have been wrong about that. *My* garden, *my mother's* garden, *my* house, the sight of him unconsciously picking, pruning, taking care, wading around in the muck, dirtying his clothes, when he was ordinarily such a fastidious man. But the papers, too—a sacred trust, demanding to be picked over, pruned, preserved. Had he chosen to let the garden go for the sake of the papers? Or had she mistaken his emotional involvement with the garden, projecting her own feelings of growing attachment onto him? She sighed. It was an old and sentimental error, to think a garden was any more than a piece of ground with plants in it. And as of now, the papers were money in the bank. Still, he could not mean to let the garden go completely. Close it down permanently?

"I don't want the public to know what has happened here, at least not at the moment. But as we get closer to publication of the first volume, I think we can let the story come out, for publicity's sake . . ." He broke off and sat silent for a moment. "But that's anticipating. For now, we'll simply put out the story that the garden is being revamped, that some of the plants must be rebedded because of the dry weather. The public knows that these large formal gardens are like houses; they have to be redecorated now and again. Plants don't live forever, and all that rot. The roses will have to be cut back further, to reshape the bushes, and give them a chance to grow properly next year. They will, of course. The loss is only temporary. Still . . ."

Giles leaned forward, cleared his throat, and put his fingertips together in their characteristic pointed gothic arch. The arch narrowed and widened, in and out, while he continued to gaze at her. It suddenly came to her, watching Giles's enigmatic, ironic smile, that she did not trust him. And never had. Was that why, in spite of his good looks, his air of mastery, she had felt no physical attraction to him at all?

She returned his glance, saying nothing. At last he dropped his eyes and slapped both hands down on the table. When he spoke, his tone was businesslike.

"The question is, what is the real object of this attack? It would appear to be the garden. Extraordinary idea, really, to go about murdering a garden. Why? The garden has done nothing; it simply is. Again: why? Jealousy? Revenge? Slashing the heads off hundreds of roses is an act of extreme savagery. But those emotions occur only in human relationships."

"You go to jail for attacking people," Roz offered.

"Precisely. Which curtails the freedom to act. One might be willing to let a few decapitated roses go by the board. Merely destroying property, and not even really destroying it at that, but only temporarily putting it out of commission, is not a really serious offense. Mere vandalism. Of course we realize that it is the *idea* of the garden that is so vulnerable, but that would be impossible to maintain in court. It would come down to dollars and cents, the cost of actual physical damage. What are a few plants? They grow back. Eventually."

Giles stood up, stretched, and walked over to the window overlooking the Courtyard. He stood very straight, his hair gilded by the sunlight. His face was now in shadow. "The idea is to force me to shut Montfort down, put me out of business so I shall have to sell up, let it go to the Britannia Trust. And if this were to go on, that is precisely what would happen." He paused, staring out over the garden. "Not to mention holding up indefinitely the publication of the papers.

"But of course the destruction cannot be allowed

101

to go on. It comes down to this: the continued exis-
tence of Montfort Abbey, my mother's garden, and
the publication of her diaries and letters—a most important addition to modern biography, versus the
feelings of a few nonentities over their petty reputations. These people must be made to see that we will
go on in spite of the recent attempts to stop us. That
is precisely why, when I leave here, I shall go round
to the gardeners, the Norths, Hugh and Beatrice,
Alan—all of them—to tell them of the contract. They
can't do anything to stop us now. Montfort and I are
free. I shall repair the garden, restore it to exactly
what it was before. And the papers will be published,
just as we had planned." Giles paused, regarding
her. "And you and I can get back to the business of
editing—which is, after all, what you are here for,"
he said.

He stood up and tucked away the contract in his
jacket pocket. He regarded her amiably. "Speaking
of which, how far have you got without me?"

"Oh, up to 1940 or so," Roz replied absently, studying the scars on the tabletop. Nonentities. Petty reputations. Still, unless she found out anything to the
contrary, reluctantly she had to agree. Life was
short, and art was long. And editing his mother's life
in words was, after all, what she was here for. If she
lasted.

And speaking of lasting, she considered whether
to tell him that she had deviated from their agreement. On the whole, she thought she'd better. She
took a deep breath. "I'll probably be up to 1943 by
the end of tomorrow or the next day." She looked
up.

Giled was staring down at her, his face pale.

"Are you all right?" she asked.

He didn't move, only stared down at her as though
seeing her for the first time. Roz felt distinctly un-
easy. She returned his glance as steadily as she
could.

Finally he spoke. "That far? How very enterprising of you." He continued to stare at her for several more moments. Then he smiled faintly, the lines around his nose and mouth sharply etched.

"Then you shan't mind going on a bit longer on your own, shall you?" His smile widened. Roz didn't like the looks of it. He was acting rather strange. But then, a lot had happened in the last few days. Who wouldn't be a little off-balance?

Giles went on. "I have some rather urgent business to attend to in my study at the Abbot's Chapel after I go the rounds. But it will be just today, I'm quite sure."

"No, I don't mind," Roz said, studying his face. He looked back at her impassively.

"Good. There is one thing, though. I want you to go back over what you've done and recheck it. Don't go any further without me."

Roz stared blankly at him.

"Agreed?"

"Well, to tell you the truth, Giles . . ." The words died in her throat. Giles no longer looked impassive. He looked downright sinister.

"I would prefer that you not go beyond 1940 without me. Is that clear?"

Roz nodded. "Whatever you say."

Suddenly he relaxed, his thin mouth angling up into a friendly smile. "That's set, then. Until tomorrow." He started for the door, then stopped and turned. "Oh, the key. I've been thinking. Would you be so kind as to take charge of my Viola key? We must be more careful now than ever, what with these . . . incidents. Not to mention the contract. I don't want too many of these lying around." He reached into his pocket, brought out a bunch of keys, and detached one. "Here you are," he said, handing it to her. "Just in case. Don't let it out of your sight. You never know what might happen next."

And with a flip of his hand he was off, striding away with all his old restless energy. And then some. Roz watched him cross the Courtyard. She'd forgotten to tell him she was going out with Alan later. Oh well, she could leave him a note. Stuffing Giles's key into her jeans pocket along with her own, she left the Refectory and went across the Courtyard to the Tower.

The two keys rattled uncomfortably in her pocket as she went up the stairs, so as soon as she entered the Viola Room she took Giles's key out and laid in on his desk. It would be safe enough there. She considered locking herself in, but decided not to. After all, it was the garden they were after, not her.

Hands in her pockets, reluctant to begin going back over old ground, she crossed to the window, cranked it open, and looked out the Tower window over the walls to the fields beyond. Small figures bent and labored with what appeared to be pitchforks and shovels, dredging and scooping in and around the half-filled pond. She could not distinguish Giles's tall, fair-haired figure among the group, which appeared to be made up of several others besides Cory and Stella. Help from the village, perhaps. A small puddle glistened in the afternoon sun; the rest of the pond looked naked and exposed, smooth and round, as though scooped out by a giant spoon.

What she could see of the rest of the garden seemed peaceful enough; she glanced quickly over the tops of walls and fronts of buildings, pausing to study the crisscrossed Tudor front of the Moat House, wondering if Alan Stewart had been able to resume his painting. A flash of color caught her eye, in the corner of the Courtyard just below her, near the Cottage Plot. Edging into the corner of the window, she craned her neck so that she could see down into the entrance of the garden.

And there were Florence and Francesca: Francesca with her back to Roz, her hair wound up like a turban of golden cotton candy, and Florence, with

104

her white hair sticking out in tufts, her small face straining upward at an awkward angle toward Francesca, who was at least a foot taller. And on that upturned face there was such a look of anguish that Roz involuntarily caught her breath.

Then Florence spoke, her words floating upward.

"I just can't bear it, after all these years. Oh please, why couldn't you just—"

Francesca interrupted her. "I have my rights, the same as he does. Giles won't get away with this if I can help it. You'll see. I still have the key. I don't really care about the other. Let it come out." Francesca turned away, and Roz almost called out to her, because she was certain Florence was going to faint. Her face went paper white, and her small hands scrabbled at her face.

"Oh no, you can't," she said faintly. "I couldn't . . ." And covering her face with her hands, she began to sob. Francesca put her arm around the older woman's shoulders and pulled her along into the shadow of the arch.

Quickly Roz crossed to the other side of the room and peered out the window overlooking the other side of the arch. Florence and Francesca emerged, walking along the driveway to the garage. A moment later, a car shot out. Roz stood by the window for a moment, an odd bit of nursery rhyme running through her head. *"She cut off their tails with a carving knife/Did you ever see such a sight in your life . . ."* She had never seen such a look of distress as the one she had seen on Florence's face just now.

Well, she thought, enough is enough. You never see a look like that staring at you from a piece of paper. Letters and papers and preservation may all be very well and good, but when it comes down to it, the living are more important. It was time to intervene.

Roz turned away from the window and surveyed the room. Boxes of correspondence lay in various corners, in various parts of the room. Viola's entire diary was lined up in volumes in the bookcase. She caught sight of Giles's key on his desk, and suddenly she knew exactly what she was going to do.

She crossed the room quickly, took her own key out, shut and locked the door. Now no one could get in, not even Giles. Especially not Giles. She glanced at her watch. Barely eight-thirty. If she worked quickly, she had plenty of time. What had he said? *Who do they think they are?* She didn't care what he had said. She was going to go through all the papers now, this moment, just as she had wanted to from the beginning, and find out once and for all what frightful secret Giles was counting on to sell books, the secret the others so clearly feared. Then she would know once and for all what to do next.

12

AT FIRST ROZ WORKED FEVERISHLY, LISTENING for Giles's step on the stair. It would be obvious to him—all the boxes open, the letters stacked neatly in order as she read through them one by one—that she had violated his orders. But after a while an odd feeling of confidence swept over her, allaying the guilty sense that she was doing something she mustn't be caught at. He had been insistent, even dictatorial, but her reasons transcended his demands. Even if it meant her job, she had to do this. So where should she go from here? She walked over to her desk. Two hundred letters to Bear already gone through, and a parallel correspondence with Grumbles, many of whose letters she and Giles had already read.

She searched out the rest of the Grumbles letters and was surprised to see that there were so few, only about a hundred and fifty, ending in 1965. Roz felt a pang of disappointment. When had Grace Godwin died? The Grumbles letters she had seen were quite different in tone and content from the Bear letters, adding a whole new dimension to Viola's personality. She wished there were more.

That left three more substantial correspondences to go through: Viola's three hundred-odd letters to her Cousin Hester, spanning the years 1915 to 1958, the largest group of letters to a single correspondent; and two hundred or so letters to Sir Herbert during their infrequent separations, from just before their marriage in 1920 to Sir Herbert's sudden death in 1965. Then there were one hundred and fifty letters to Giles, oddly distant and formal in tone, mostly while he was away at school and college, from 1940, when he was six, until 1955, when he had graduated from Cambridge and come back to live at Montfort with Viola.

Roz leafed through these, skimming them for names and places she might recognize. She found she could go quite rapidly, and, as the morning passed, she made her way through a number of the piles and boxes. There were other groups of letters, including thirty-five to Viola's mother, who had died when Viola was thirty, and intermittent correspondence written from abroad to the string of gardeners who had managed Montfort during the Snows' absences before the long tenure of Cory and Stella commenced in 1960.

These garden letters were surprisingly detailed and quite imperious in tone; Viola gave quite specific orders from abroad. She must have carried the garden around with her in her head. In fact, the gardens came into almost every letter she

107

wrote from 1934 on, the year she and Sir Herbert had finally acquired Montfort. Gardens, gardens, and almost nothing about Giles, who also had been born in 1934. Of course, these were letters to gardeners. Yet it was surprising how little Giles came into any of the letters—it was almost as though the garden and her books were her children, and not the little boy.

The day wore on, and no one approached the Tower Room. Roz decided to skip lunch; the excitement of discovery had suppressed her appetite, and, more important, she did not believe she would ever have this opportunity again. When Giles found out, he would probably send her packing anyway.

Generally speaking, she was beginning to feel better. The letters made interesting but hardly lurid reading. She had found nothing scandalous or threatening, or even particularly striking. In fact, there was little to be discovered except the life and times of kind, generous, intelligent, witty, democratic Lady Viola, and the life and times of Montfort Abbey Gardens, with an occasional bit of world news thrown in. No surprises. Many of the letters were entertaining, colorful, and valuable as a record of English country life spanning the two World Wars. Others, full of practical arrangements and servant problems, were remarkably dull.

But Viola was a gifted and beloved writer. There would be interest. And after all, it was Viola's voice, her perceptions, and her developing personality that held the attention, not any one event or group of letters in itself. It was the whole that mattered, and Roz, after half a day's work, felt she had a better—if still largely intuitive—understanding of this. But scandal? Hardly.

Still, her research so far had actually raised more questions than it laid to rest. Roz stopped to ponder what might have motivated Viola to hide the papers in the first place. And why should Florence and Hugh, Francesca and Beatrice, be so upset at the prospect of the papers being published? Had Giles actually told them the letters contained something damaging to their reputations? Threatened them, in fact? She hoped that wasn't true; Giles had maintained all along to her that he didn't know precisely what was in the letters and diaries himself, but he had been quick enough to say that day at lunch that they ran from 1915 until 1975. And here Roz paused. Nineteen fifteen to 1975.

She was quite sure that Giles had said the papers went up to 1975. Now she realized she could not remember seeing a single letter dated later than 1965, the year of Sir Herbert's death, ten years before Viola's own. Roz looked around. There was one box of correspondence left. Maybe letters from that last decade had been bunched together.

Roz wondered, as she started on this last box, about the haphazard way in which a person's letters were preserved. In Viola's case, it was amazing that there was such a full record, that so much had been preserved intact. And that it was in such an orderly state, correspondence by correspondence—hardly a letter out of place, all of them dated, almost as though someone had already worked on them. But maybe Viola herself had destroyed some, and not others. That could explain the lack of letters from 1965 on. But why just those ten years? Perhaps it was merely a relative lack of material, flagging energies, readier use of the telephone, a final giving up of the habitual notewriting, depression after Herbert's death, her own advancing age.

Roz hauled out another stack of letters. Typewritten. Letters to Cory and Stella, the latest dated 1965. At the bottom, a small sheaf—the name leapt out at her—Humphrey Badgett, father of Hugh, manager of the Home Farm. Postmarked London, where Viola and Herbert had spent a lot of their time during the war years. Francesca had asked about these. Quickly she leafed through them, then sat back on her heels in disappointment. There were so few. And none were dated later than 1965. A small group of twelve letters, all clearly dated, bracketed the year 1944—four at the beginning, and eight at the end.

Roz read through them one by one. Humphrey had been away with the Infantry in France, leaving Florence and her young son, Hugh, alone at Montfort. They were reassuring, noncommittal, and chatty, without being familiar. Florence was fine and Hugh was fine. The tone was not the least condescending, and Roz thought how kind it was for Viola to write these letters to a lonely soldier at the front missing his home and family.

But there were no letters at all between March and October 1944. And the last letter puzzled Roz completely; there was one reference to "the darling baby." Whose baby? A Badgett baby? Giles had been an only child, that she knew, and there seemed to be no suggestion that Hugh had a sibling. Hugh was Giles's age—ten in 1944. But perhaps the Badgetts had had another child? If so, what had happened to it? No other Badgetts besides Hugh had been in evidence that she could tell. But that didn't mean there wasn't one. Maybe there were references in other letters, say to Sir Herbert, or to one or another of her friends, Bear or Grumbles or Cousin Hester. Roz went back to the other piles, leafed through each in turn, then rummaged more thoroughly.

The Bear letters stopped in 1943, but there was nothing peculiar about that, for Lady Ursula Drottingholm, according to *Burke's Peerage,* had died that year. The Grumbles letters were patchy; for instance, there were almost no letters from the thirties, or after the Snows took over Montfort Abbey well into the forties, but then the letters continued, twice a year or so, up to 1965.

Except for the months between March and November 1944, the letters to Herbert were spotty, since they had been together more often than not, but 1944 had been a time of separation, and once again—Roz checked and rechecked the date of each letter—there was an absence of letters for the middle of 1944. She turned to the Cousin Hester letters.

Again, the letters between March and November 1944 were missing. So were any letters to gardeners that might have been written at that time, and there were no letters to publishers, editors, or anyone else. March to November 1944 was a complete blank in Viola's life, as far as her letters were concerned. And so were the years after 1965.

How strange, Roz thought. Had the letters ever existed? If so, why had they been taken out, possibly even destroyed? What had they been about? And more important, did Giles know they were missing? If so, why hadn't he told her? Why had he told her and everyone else the letters went to 1975?

But there were still the diaries. A diary was a much more likely repository for secrets, and Viola had kept hers faithfully.

Roz walked over to the shelf and studied the long line of sixty-five identically bound volumes. Like the letters, these diaries were copies—facsimiles, really, for Giles had gone to the trouble of having both sides copied and everything bound exactly like the originals.

Roz took down the volume dated 1944. It was slimmer than many, but then, it had been war time—a busy time, hectic and distracting. She opened the volume and began to leaf through, glancing at the pages, noting dates, skimming the contents. January. February. War notes, garden notes. Florence ill. Humphrey and Sir Herbert away. Viola at Montfort. The end of February, spring already a promise. Roz flipped over a page, and read on.

Late autumn in the garden. Trouble in Greece. Roz skipped a few more pages. The Battle of the Bulge. Herbert back from Europe. The war beginning to go better. Then it was Christmas.

111

The gap in the 1944 volume exactly matched the gaps in all the letters. March through November 1944. The copied pages were continuous, and, without seeing the original volumes, Roz had no idea whether the pages had been cut out or had never existed. There were no page numbers, only dates. She searched her memory for an answer. Had Viola had a breakdown of some kind? But wouldn't there have been some acknowledgment, some reference to recovery? Not just this sudden ellipsis, dropping over a cliff into thin air, and then finding oneself standing on the ground unharmed, not a hair out of place?

No, she did not think Viola had stopped writing. In fact, she recalled, much of the second draft of *The Rose and the Thorn* had been completed that summer of 1944. Viola had definitely been well and writing during that year, and she had never let her books interfere with either her correspondence or her journal-keeping.

Roz bent down and looked at the run of diaries. Three rows, with twenty-two volumes in the top two, twenty-one in the lowest. She sighed with relief. The volumes were clearly marked 1955–1975. She took out the volume for 1966, walked over to her desk, and sat down to read.

As she put back the last volume of diary some time later, Roz was more perplexed than ever. In the earlier diaries, except for 1944, Viola had made an entry, however short, for every day. The later volumes had great gaps between dates, and the copies, like the 1944 volume, were not paged. Months at a time had dropped out, and the entries had a discontinuous, fragmentary quality that was totally uncharacteristic of Viola's rather orderly mind.

Roz stood in the middle of the room, chewing her thumbnail, and reflected on the possibilities.

Viola had been intermittently sick, too sick to

write her diaries or letters? Nothing scandalous about that. News, but no sensation. Certainly not worthy of being excised. But Roz, recalling the chronology of Viola's life, knew of no illness that could account for such large stretches of silence. Besides, those years had been among her most productive. At least five books in ten years—three volumes of poetry, *A Lovesome Thing, Of Oaks and Oleanders, The Cloister Garth;* a novel, *Sheba's Lament;* and a garden-essay book, *Montfort Month by Month.* Not to mention *Lady Viola's Books of Days.* Not much of a falling off there. So where were the letters and diary entries?

Roz went to her desk and sat down. She could ask Giles whether his mother had an intermittent, debilitating illness. He might just stare at her and say, "Of course, I thought you knew." Still, it would be just his word, for there was no other indication anywhere in Viola's books, in her letters, in local legend, reminiscence, or memoirs that such a possibility existed.

The other possibility, and the more perplexing and problematic one, was that either Viola or Giles or someone else had systematically abstracted parts of the diary, certain letters they didn't want read or published. This suggested there was something to be hidden—though Roz could not imagine what could be so shocking and unacceptable in this day and age that anyone could think it worth suppressing. Not Viola, because why abstract the shocking parts and hide the perfectly innocent? Not Giles, because he was looking for something lurid to sell books and carry him through his financial crisis. He would welcome a scandal, particularly if it didn't concern him or his mother directly—preferably one so sensational that people would knock each other down in the street getting to the bookstore.

How was she going to find out? If she asked Giles, then he would know she had gone against his specific

113

orders and read ahead. On the other hand, if he walked in right now . . .

She turned and surveyed the piles of letters, the diaries, all carefully replaced. No one need know that she'd gone ahead on her own hook. And that's exactly where she was right now—on the hook. *I've either got to keep my mouth shut, or tell him what I've found. Which is nothing. Or rather, the absence of something.*

Roz considered. On the whole, she thought she would probably tell him. She did not like deception. After all, she was a scholar, dedicated to finding the truth at all costs; she could justify herself in that way. The question was, was it worth her job, this nicety of principle? Did she have a choice?

She stood up and crossed over restlessly to the door. It was past three o'clock. She stood with her back to the door, thinking furiously.

There was only one way to tell if the diaries had been tampered with, and that was to see the originals. She could tell if the pages had been cut, substituted, the numbers erased. The other journals were numbered; the ones for 1965–1975 must have been, as well. She had to get Giles to show her the originals. And then, when she was sure . . .

She jumped, startled by the sound of someone stomping hurriedly up the stairs.

Giles, she thought, taking a last look around. Everything was shipshape. She twisted the key in the lock and opened the door to find Stella standing on the top step, huffing distractedly, two bright spots of pink shining on her cheeks.

"Where's Giles?" she demanded. "I've got to talk to him."

"He's not here. He wanted a chance to catch his breath and think things over. Is there something wrong?"

Stella leaned forward, hands on her hips, chest heaving. "I found the storage shed in the greenhouse unlocked when I went for a wheelbarrow. A five-gallon tin of insecticide, a brand new one we hadn't opened yet, is missing. And so is one of the sprayers."

"Are you sure Cory isn't using it?"

"No, no. You don't understand. The stuff's deadly poison. We use it on a precise schedule, once a week early in the morning before the breeze comes up. It's a selective nerve poison—Allothane 4-x-d. —a paralytic that attacks only crawling insects like larvae and scale, and leaves the bees and other necessary ones alone. But it's dangerous to humans. We wear protective suits and masks when we use it, and make sure the windows are all closed. It's *always* kept locked up. Oh . . ." Stella flung her hands away from her body and curled her fingers suddenly into fists.

"The point is, Cory's gone too, but not her suit, and she wouldn't have gone without telling me, and . . . oh, why are we standing here? Where *is* Giles?" She spun around helplessly. "Just tell me where he is. And I've got to find Cory . . ."

"Giles went to be by himself in the Abbot's Chapel . . ." Roz began, but almost before she had gotten the words out, Stella turned and was rattling down the stairs.

"Close all the windows!" her voice echoed back. "If the stuff blows into the living quarters, we'll have to evacuate the place."

As Roz wound the windows shut she could see Stella sprinting diagonally across the Courtyard toward the Cloister Lawn. She slammed the door behind her, locked it securely, then hurried down the steps and across the garden after Stella's retreating figure. As she passed the Refectory, she looked up; all the windows were shut tight. She sniffed the air suspiciously. She looked up at her own window, which she distinctly remembered having left open. It, too, was shut tight.

Roz turned as she ran, looking around at the windows of the other buildings—all closed, all blankly

115

reflecting the sun. She ran on past the loops of stone linked with ivy that formed what was left of the old Cloister until she reached the entrance of the Porcelain Garden.

Stella was moving away from the door of the Abbot's Chapel with the tentative fastidiousness of a cat backing out of a wet drainpipe. Roz pushed through the clematis, ran down the path, and stopped beside her. Stella had her hand over her mouth and nose. She rolled her eyes back at Roz. "Don't breathe!" she said in a muffled voice. "Roll down your sleeves and pull your shirt over your head to cover up as much as possible. I'm going to break the windows. Then you must go in and pull him out."

Oh no, Roz thought. *He's dead.*

"Roz! Listen to me!" Stella shouted. "I'd go in, but I can't risk it. The stuff absorbs through the skin." She gestured at her bare arms and legs. "After I break out the window, wait a moment, and then go in. And get out as quickly as possible. But don't *breathe.*" With that, she dashed around the side of the Chapel, and Roz heard the crash of breaking glass. Through the open door she saw the small, diamond-shaped mullions collapse inward in a sudden cascade of glass. Then she saw Stella whacking at the remaining fragments with a large terracotta pot, head averted.

"Let it dissipate a moment, then go in!" Stella called from the side.

Roz hesitated briefly, then took a deep breath and pushed open the door.

Giles lay slumped over his typewriter, breathing slowly and irregularly. Too slowly. Roz scurried over to him, holding her breath. How was she going to get him out? Putting one hand under his head and another around his chest, she pulled him upright. Whatever he had been typing caught between her hand and his neck. Impatiently she shook the pages loose; they floated aimlessly to the floor. Giles flopped back against the chair, and, before she could stop him, sprawled full-length on the floor. Roz grabbed his feet, hoisted them around her waist, straightened, and threw all her weight against his, dragging him across the irregular stones.

In spite of his slimness, he was remarkably heavy; she struggled backward, lurching against his limp weight, her lungs bursting as though she were underwater, until she was nearly to the door. Then Stella was next to her, and together they wrenched and dragged Giles through the door and outside, away from the Chapel. Roz let her breath out with a great whoosh like a swimmer breaking the surface, and breathed deeply of the clean, fresh air.

"You stay here," Stella said, and ran off.

Roz stood staring down at Giles's pale, angular face. Slackness brought out all the sharpness of his bone structure; his face looked haggard and sunken like an old man's. Then Stella was back. Roz flinched as Stella aimed a gushing hose full blast at Giles's body. Giles groaned, but his eyes didn't open.

"Get as many of his clothes off as you can," Stella ordered. "Jolly good thing he was so well covered."

Roz bent over and yanked at Giles's jacket and shirt, rolling him from side to side while Stella splashed water over him. She was vaguely and uncomfortably aware that she, too, was being drenched with icy water. Giles coughed, spluttered, and let out a choked yelp. Stella held the hose away and looked at him intently. Giles opened his eyes and blinked. The lids fluttered independently of one another. His eyes crossed, straightened, crossed again, struggling to focus. Then they closed again.

"Giles, can you hear me?" Roz shouted.

"Yesh, course I can. Not deaf. No need . . . shout . . ." he mumbled. His speech was slow and slurred, and his eyelids quivered. "Can't see you, though. Three, four, shut the door."

117

Stella stood behind his head, running the hose water over her own bare arms and legs, looking relieved. "He'll be all right. If he'd gotten a lethal dose he wouldn't be able to talk at all now, let alone open his eyes. Or even breathe. You stay here; I'll go call an ambulance."

"And the police," Roz added, bending close to Giles.

Giles's eyelids snapped open. "No. No. No ambulance, no police. Silly accident," he mumbled, as his eyes drifted closed.

"Giles! Giles!" Roz shouted in his ear. "Tell us what happened!"

Giles rolled his head from side to side. "Cory," he said quite clearly. "Cory."

Roz stared. Surely it hadn't been Cory? But where *was* Cory? Stella stood as though paralyzed, staring down at Giles, a look of horror on her face. Roz stepped between her and Giles's semiconscious form. Cory or no Cory, there wasn't a moment to lose.

"Where's your car?"

Stella jumped. "What?" she said in a dazed voice.

"I think we'd better get him to the hospital. No time to call the ambulance. We can worry about the police later."

"Right," said Stella, coming to. "You stay here." She whirled and ran off down the path, scattering water drops. The plants shuddered as she passed.

Roz sat down abruptly on a small stone bench under the blue willow tree and took a deep breath. At her feet, Giles snored gently, his eyes disconcertingly half-open and gleaming through the slits, one more open than the other. *Odd,* Roz thought, *you'd think that sleepers would look peaceful, childlike, innocent, all their cares momentarily resolved, but Giles looks worn, and haggard, and . . . corrupt.* Roz closed her eyes against the vision, and let her thoughts whirl away through the branches of the willow, its leaves beckoning transparent fingers in the light afternoon breeze. She and Giles had guessed wrong. They were not above attacking people.

She suddenly felt very tired. She wondered if there were still enough odorless, colorless deadly poison in the air to damage her own nervous system. The garden was deathly quiet. Where was everybody? She felt so alone.

She was still sitting on the stone bench taking small, shallow breaths when Stella appeared at a small gate in the far wall that had once been part of the old Cathedral. She inserted an old iron key in the grating, and swung the gate back, its hinges shrieking. It opened onto the meadows and pastures that rolled down to the flat fens beyond.

"I've driven the car up along the old farm track. Do you think together we can get him into it? I haven't told anyone else; it might cause a panic."

Or make things worse for Cory, Roz thought. But it was just as well. The two of them could deal with this. Stella had changed her clothes and was wearing a long-sleeved green coverall. She looked perfectly calm now. "One of us should drive him to the hospital: they'll know what to do. If we can just get him to the car." Stella gestured to a dark green Austin Marina parked in the grass just beyond the gate, its engine running. The passenger door on the left was open.

"Okay, let's try it," Roz said, standing up. Stella came and stood next to her, looking down at Giles's lank and recumbent frame. Then she looked Roz up and down, as if appraising her slender figure, compared to Stella's own short, sturdy one. "I'll take the head and shoulders, you take the legs," she said finally. Together they bent down, grabbed, heaved, and trotted through the gate with less difficulty than Roz had anticipated. They maneuvered Giles over to the open passenger door, and Roz stuffed his legs in as best she could, then shifted her grip upward toward his bare chest, easing him into the seat. He lolled raggedly and mumbled:

"No poleesh. Private mat . . . ter, stupid. Windows open, acshident . . . don't tell . . ." His head rolled. Roz leaned closer, alarmed. He seemed to be getting worse. Then, right in her face, his eyes snapped open suddenly, focused directly on her. Quite distinctly he said. "Don't forget what I said about the papers."

As Roz watched dumbfounded, his pupils rolled back, his eyelids drifted closed, and his mouth dropped open, slack. He snored. Stella had gone around to the other side and was getting into the driver's seat.

"Do you want me to come along?" Roz asked. "I'm afraid I can't drive him myself, but I'll come if you want."

Stella hesitated, looking uncertain. Clearly she wanted to stay and find Cory, make sure she was safe, or . . . safely occupied. But that was impossible. Roz had never driven a right-hand-drive car, and she didn't know the way. Stella stared at her bleakly, then sighed.

"No, I'll go. I can manage. It's about twenty kilometers to the hospital in Dorting. Say half an hour. You stay here, look after Giles's precious papers, if that's what he wants," she said, her mouth twisting to one side. "But please see if you can't find Cory first, and round up that insecticide. It oughtn't to be left about, accident or not. And when you find her, tell her to ring me up at the hospital to let me know she's all right, will you?" With that, Stella ducked into the car and slammed the door. Before she put the car in gear, she leaned across the unconscious Giles.

"If you need help, ask Alan Stewart," she said. "He's as reliable as anybody, and strong as an ox."

Giles groaned. Stella put the car in gear; it shot forward, leaving two liquid green streaks of mashed grass behind.

"Try not to worry," Roz shouted after her, too late. She watched the car as it bumped down the old track and out of sight through the tall grass: then she turned and made her way back through the garden to find Cory. And anyone else along the way.

13

ON THE FAR SIDE OF THE TOWER BEHIND THE stable there were two large greenhouses side by side, and, as she approached the first greenhouse, Roz heard a faint rhythmic tapping on the glass that increased in intensity until it sounded like a frantic drumming of fingers. As she drew closer, she saw that it was only the sprinkler going inside, spattering the glass, then subsiding into a light tip-tap as the sprinkler rotated to the other side. The door was open, and the long bedding frames had the freshly dug look of plants recently removed.

Roz looked inside. There was Cory, standing in the middle aisle as though nothing had happened, dressed in a tan coverall, her feet planted firmly on the trampled-down earth floor, curly hair tied up in a red kerchief, sorting clay pots according to size. Sweat glistened on her upper lip. She glanced at Roz, but shook her head, her lips still moving over the numbers. *She can't know anything has happened,* Roz thought. *She's obviously been here minding her own business right along. But then why couldn't Stella find her?*

Roz stood silently by while Cory stacked and put

away each size of earthenware pot. Then she turned to Roz.

"Sorry. Didn't want to lose count. I've got to order more of the number two." She pointed to a short stack of small, inverted pots. Then she leaned back against the bedding table, folded her arms, and smiled. "Not more bad news, I hope."

Roz took a deep breath. "Stella found some insecticide missing from . . ." From where? Had Stella said? ". . . from wherever it was kept, and she couldn't find you, so she came upstairs looking for Giles, but he was gone, so we both went to the Abbot's Chapel to look for him, and found him passed out cold, and Stella took him to the hospital in . . . in . . ." Roz passed a hand over her forehead, puzzled and embarrassed by her apparently incomplete grasp of the facts of the matter, not to mention the sudden collapse of her vocabulary. Had she gotten a whiff of bug spray after all?

Cory stood upright, taut and expressionless. "Did Stella say what insecticide it was? And how much was gone?"

"Allo something. After we pulled Giles out, Stella washed him down with a hose. Me, too." Roz gestured vaguely at her soaked clothing.

Cory nodded. "Allothane-4-x-d. It's mainly a contact poison, but water-soluble. Quite nasty if it settles on the skin and is absorbed, but it does wash off. I say, Stella washed herself off too, didn't she? Right away?"

Roz nodded. "She hosed herself off, and then changed her clothes before she left for the hospital. And she wouldn't go inside the chapel because she was wearing shorts. I pulled him out." Under the baggy coverall Roz saw Cory's shoulders relax. But her concern had been for Stella. She hadn't even asked about Giles.

Cory turned and began to rummage in a drawer for something. "Breathing it's not so bad; a lot gets

122

exhaled back out in water droplets. But you should change, too, you know."

As Roz stared at her, stricken, Cory calmly added, "Not because of the poison, of course. I meant because you're damp. You'll catch your death."

Dangling a set of keys, she beckoned to Roz. "We keep the stuff stored in a locked shed in the other greenhouse. Tools in here," she said, nodding at the impressive set of graduated bone-handled pruning knives, razor sharp and gleaming, ranged along the wall along with the hoes, spades, forks, and hand trowels. "Sprays and fertilizers and such in there. We just got a new tin last Friday. I put it away myself."

So much for fingerprints, Roz thought, plucking at her shirt as she followed Cory into the next greenhouse. She dodged around the sprinkler in an effort not to get any wetter than she was, and failed. She noticed she was shivering.

Cory had gone straight to the far end and was undoing a huge padlock. She pulled it away, then slid back a long steel bar that held a heavy, reinforced metal door. She stood in the doorway as Cory yanked on the single bare light bulb.

"Well, you're right. It isn't here," she said, standing with her hands on her hips just inside the doorway of the shed. A complicated array of tin cans, drums, brown bottles, spraying apparatus, and labeled watering cans lined the shelves of the windowless room. Cory took one more long look at the rows of shelves, then jerked out the light and came back out, carefully barring and padlocking the door behind her. As she stuffed the ring of keys back in the pocket of her coverall, Roz wondered who else had a key. But before she could ask, Cory had walked briskly back down the aisle and was shrugging herself out of the brown coverall by the door. "The next question is, where is it? We can't just leave it lying about. I suppose I'd better have a look." She hung the coverall on a peg just inside the greenhouse door,

123

then, after a moment's hesitation, turned and looked inquiringly at Roz.

"You did say that Giles seemed all right, didn't you?"

Roz looked at the other woman. *It's about time you asked,* she thought to herself. To Cory she said simply, "He was out cold when we found him, but he came to before too long. He was very woozy, but Stella seemed to think he'd be all right," she said, watching Cory's face.

"That's all right, then," Cory murmured, but there was no relief in her voice; it remained noncommittal. "Wouldn't want Giles pegging out just now that things are starting to go his way." Roz could not tell from her tone whether or not she was being ironic. From what little she knew of Giles's relations with the two gardeners, it could be either.

"I suppose," said Cory after a moment, "that Giles was sitting there clacking away as usual. He'd not hear a thing, not even if he had the windows open."

"He didn't," Roz said. "Stella smashed the window in before we got him out."

"Well, that's not so strange," Cory said. "These old window casements are the very devil to get open. He probably didn't bother. Besides, Giles likes his privacy. We never know what he's up to in there. I imagine the door was shut, as well?"

"Yes." Roz remembered pushing it open slowly, seeing Giles's figure stretched out on the floor. "Shut, but not locked."

"Hm, that's odd. He usually locks it," Cory mused. "Giles can't stand anybody sneaking up on him. Knock first is his motto. Doesn't always follow it himself, though. Jolly good thing it wasn't locked this time. Oh well, never mind. We can always ask him what happened when he gets back. Provided he can talk. Double vision and slurred speech are the most common effects of this stuff, and they tend to go on for a bit."

124

Cory stood thoughtfully for a moment. "I suppose I'll have to board those windows up—after I locate the can of insecticide, of course. Beats me why they had to lug the whole tin out of here. Either they didn't have time to fill the quart sprayer at the greenhouse, or they thought one quart might not do the job. As it obviously didn't."

There was an awkward pause. Finally Roz spoke. "Cory?"

"Yes?" Her brown, sinewy arm flexed and un-flexed; the keys jingled. Roz took a deep breath.

"Could Giles have been killed?"

Cory considered. "I expect so. But it depends on how familiar the . . . er . . . the perpetrator was with the poison. I should think he'd more likely have been killed by someone who didn't know what he was doing than someone who did."

"Which do you think?"

"Oh. Well." Cory barely hesitated. "I rather think the latter, don't you? Someone who did know, and gave Giles just enough to make sure he'd feel absolutely ghastly for a while, and scare him silly."

"But why?"

"I haven't the faintest idea. I'm not particularly fond of Giles myself; he's always messing about where he's not wanted in the garden, and this business of having to run everything himself drives both Stella and me quite mad. We've hoped for some time he'd just go Britannia Trust and be done with it. After all, what does he think will happen when *he* goes?" Cory paused, then looked Roz square in the eye. "But take a chance like that? Not on your life. We can wait him out," she said with a note of final-ity.

Roz looked at the keys in Cory's hand. "Who else has a key to the locked cupboard?"

"Stella, Giles, and me. Three keys. But that won't get you anywhere, I'm afraid. Giles has a silly habit of leaving his keys around where anyone can pick them up. Considering how suspicious he's been of

125

late, particularly about those precious papers of Viola's, it's pretty damned stupid. But maybe this will cure him of it."

Reaching behind her, Cory opened a small tool drawer, picked out a bunch of keys on a silver chain with a large crest attached, and tossed them onto the bedding frame next to Roz. "I was going to return them to him as soon as I finished counting the pots and putting in the nursery order. I found them in here when I got back from taking down the tourist sign up at the main road. Which, in case you're wondering, is where I was from midday on. Beast of a job; I had to dig up the cedar posts myself. They were halfway to China. But Rufus Salt from the village will remember; he stopped to help. I went off right after Giles gave me the word about closing down the garden. I've only just got back."

Roz shifted from one numb foot to the other. So Cory was now providing herself with an alibi. She knew Roz had suspected her—unjustly, as it turned out. "Stella was worried about you," she said by way of apology. But then why hadn't Stella known where to find her? Why hadn't Cory told her where she'd be? Was Stella lying? Had she known all along?

Cory was studying the wooden rafters of the greenhouse. "Yes, I'm sorry about that. Poor Stella. I told Giles to let her know where I'd be. Obviously, he didn't. Of course, I had no idea something like this would happen. Though I suppose it was inevitable, given the circumstances." Uncharacteristically, Cory sighed.

Roz watched her carefully, still suspicious. It sounded as if Cory was covering for Stella. And what circumstances? She was about to ask when Cory went on briskly:

"If that's all, I'll just go along and find the evidence." She dusted her hands down the khaki shorts, then picked up Giles's keys. "I'll keep these, then, unless you want to take charge of them. They're nearly all garden keys," she said, turning them over.

Roz shook her head. She didn't care about the other keys as long as the keys to the Viola Room were safe. "No, that's all right," she said.

Nodding formally, Cory stood back and waited for her to go out of the greenhouse, then came out and shut the door behind her. "I'll have Stella let you know how Giles is when she get home. And don't forget to change. Cheerio." And with that Cory strode away down the drive toward the garden.

Roz stood in the middle of the drive, wondering what to do next.

She could find out who else was here, that's what. The keys had been lying around loose for who knew how long; anybody could have picked them up. They all had motives, evidently; who had had the opportunity? She walked up the path from the greenhouse to the garage. She had seen Francesca and Florence leave early this morning. Had they come back?

The garage with its five stalls was wide open. Two of the stalls were empty. One had to be for the car Stella had driven to the hospital. The other was probably Francesca's; that meant she and Florence had been gone all day. One of the cars left had to be Giles's; so what about the other two? Hugh and Alan? Alan was supposed to pick her up at five. What time was it now? She glanced down at her watch. The dial was clouded over with moisture. Still, it couldn't be that late.

She looked up. The Poor Farm house stood before her in all it shabby gimcrack Victorian glory behind a hedge of yews just down from the garage. She started down the drive. She could stop in on her way back to the Refectory and tell the Badgetts what had happened and, incidentally, find out if Hugh were home. And Beatrice. She took a deep breath and

127

marched resolutely up the path to the gingerbread house.

The door was wide open; there wasn't even a screen door to separate the interior of the Badgetts' house from the rest of the world. What about the bugs? Then she remembered there didn't seem to be many insects at Montfort, aside from bumblebees. A testimony to the effectiveness of the bug killer that had just sent Giles to the hospital. She shuddered. *Easy does it,* she told herself. She tried to think of some way to announce herself, short of shouting "Anybody home?"

Just then Beatrice Badgett materialized in the doorway, as intimidating as ever in a black linen trouser suit with miniature crystal chandeliers dangling from her earlobes. She looked dressed to go, and there was a large suitcase standing just inside the doorway. She glared at Roz.

"What do you want?"

Not about to be stared down, Roz said evenly, "I came to tell you and your husband that Giles has been taken to the hospital."

Beatrice's opaque, stony glare turned to the flinty glitter of curiosity. "Oh really? What happened?" Her voice was not exactly cordial, but it had lost some of its earlier hostility.

"I'm not sure. There was apparently an accident with some insecticide. Stella's driven him to the hospital. We think he's going to be all right." Roz paused. She had almost expected Beatrice to say "Worse luck," but a flicker passed over the woman's face, and that was all. "Still you can't be too careful."

"Oh yes," Beatrice said pointedly. "You can't be too careful." She remained framed in the doorway, as impassive as a limner's portrait, blocking Roz's view of the interior of the Poor Farm.

"Is your husband at home?" Roz ventured.

"No. Will that be all?"

And before Roz could say another word, Beatrice

128

shut the door in her face with a firm "Good-bye, then."

Well, Roz thought to herself as she marched down the steps and back out onto the gravel drive, *that got me exactly nowhere.* She felt a little like Alice, running as fast as she could to stay in one place. How long had it been since Stella had left with Giles? The sun was slanting oblique shadows down the drive in front of her. Roz stopped and turned, hands on hips, and stared back at the house. It seemed to be staring out the corner of its eye at her. Lace curtains obscured the long Victorian windows, so that if someone stood watching her, Roz could not tell unless a curtain were to twitch before her very eyes. Resisting the urge to thumb her nose at it, she turned away and made her way down the path that branched away from the driveway toward the Refectory.

14

SHIVERING NOW, SHE WENT INTO THE GATE-house Arch, passing by the empty ticket office. Its large plate glass window reflected her figure walking by. *I'm a mess,* she thought distractedly. *What a lot of glass there is in this place.* Shading the glass to blot out her own reflection, she paused a moment to look inside the little room.

The space behind the glass was just a faint shadow of a room. She felt as though she were peering into looking-glass land, suddenly aware there was a room behind that was not just a reflection of the one she was in. Roz stared into the shadows. Suddenly her stomach contracted, and she remembered that she had entirely missed lunch. And her clothes were still damp and clammy against her skin. She was going to have to go back to the empty Refectory to change her clothes.

Trying not to shiver, she walked along the path toward the great door.

"Hi! Roz!"

Startled, she looked around. Alan Stewart stood in the door of the Moat House, hands in his pockets, grinning cheerfully at her. She had never been so glad to see anyone in her life. She turned and walked to meet him in the middle of the Courtyard.

"Hullo," said Alan, looking her up and down. "You're a bit damp around the edges. Been for a swim?"

"Not exactly." Roz took a deep breath, and, remembering Stella's assessment of Alan, proceeded to tell him the whole story, from Stella's appearance at the door of the Viola Room to the recovery of Giles's keys in the greenhouse. Or almost the whole story. She kept her suspicions about who had done it—or could have—to herself.

Alan stood silently listening, and, when she was finished, simply kicked an invisible clod of dirt across the lawn, his face for once expressionless.

Roz glared at him. Damn it, wasn't it worth even a raised eyebrow? But after the briefest hesitation, Alan put a hand on her shoulder—it felt warm, very warm, almost burning through the thin cloth of her shirt; for the first time she realized how cold she was—and gently turned her toward the Refectory, his arm falling naturally across her shoulders as they started across the grass.

"What did you want me to say?" he said after a moment. "It's perfectly dreadful, and I'd say you've held up very well, under the circumstances. I've been in my studio all day working."

Oh no, Roz thought, *you don't have to give me your alibi, or even an excuse. No,* she wanted to say. *I trust*

you. I've got to trust someone. But she said nothing.
"I keep the windows shut when I'm painting," Alan
was saying, "because if I don't, they catch the sun—
all those little leaded bits—and throw light daggers
all over everything. So I'm afraid I didn't hear or see
a thing. I'm sorry, I wish I had; it must have been
beastly for you. And poor Stella. At least Giles
doesn't seem too bad, given the circumstances. But
our garden vandal is starting to play a little rough,
wouldn't you say?"

He reached around her, pulled the Refectory door
open, and propelled her inside. "You're sure to catch
a chill if you don't get out of those clothes straightaway. Here, what's this?" Alan bent down and picked
up a white envelope from the flagstone floor.
"Slipped under the door." He looked at the inscrip-
tion. "It's for you," he said, handing her the envelope.

Roz took it absently. She went a step or two into
the dark hallway, then, hesitating, turned back
to face Alan standing in the doorway. She wanted to
ask him to stay, but she didn't want him to know
that she was afraid to be by herself, didn't want him
thinking she was hysterical. She held out her hand,
smiling stupidly, near collapse.

"See you later," she said.

Alan grasped her extended fingers. He looked
down quickly, rolled her fingers gently between
his, then picked up her other hand and squeezed it.
His flesh seemed to scald hers. He turned both her
palms upward. In spite of herself, she shivered violently.

"Your hands are like ice, you know." His eyes
traveled upward to her face. He looked mildly
alarmed. "Your lips are mauve. Here, this is absurd.
You've had a bad fright. I'm coming in while you
change. No, don't argue. It will make me feel better,
so there's an end to it. I do have a stake in your reappearance, you know."

With that, he let go her hands, pushed past her,

131

and went to lean against the wall at the bottom of the monks' stairs, arms folded, looking completely immovable. "I'll stay right here," he said, and grinned at her. "Unless, of course, I hear a crash from above—you falling on your face—in which case I shall immediately rush to your rescue."

With a grateful look, Roz wobbled past him and up the stairs.

"Take a nice hot bath while you're up there. We've heaps of time. And give a shout if there's any trouble."

Roz smiled to herself all the way down the hall. How sensitive of him to know without even being asked that she wanted him to stay. But when she glanced in the mirror of the bathroom, it didn't seem so remarkable, after all—her hair hung about her face in tangled wisps and tag ends going every which way, and her eyes were as big and round as English pennies plunked in a pool, ringed with eddies of fatigue and alarm. She looked scared out of her wits.

She looked down at the envelope in her hand. "Miss Howard, Refectory, personal," it said. She ripped it open. Inside was a folded notecard from "Mrs. Cedric North" and scrawled shakily across it, "Please, I must see you before it's too late. Come to the Granary tomorrow at four P.M. for tea. I beg you not to tell Giles or anyone until we've talked. Yours in haste, Florence North."

Florence's pale face and nervous, twisting fingers came back to her. Of course Roz would come for tea. She put the card down on the little Sheraton writing stand next to her bed and undressed quickly, then ran herself a bath as hot as she could stand.

Feeling much better after a ten-minute soak, Roz rubbed herself down with a large, soft towel whose embroidered crest and initials identified it as one left over from the Viola days. As she dressed, she thought how oddly secure she felt with Alan posted

132

at the bottom of the stairs, the only way up or down in the Refectory. That was surprising, considering how little, really, she knew about him and how little they had in common. She thought of Alan's tall, sturdy frame, and tried to visualize him dressed in anything but a rumpled hacking jacket, shirt open at the neck, corduroy jeans, all paint-bespattered, mildly redolent of turpentine. She wondered if he were going to change his clothes for their outing, and in a sudden panic that he might take it into his head after all to go away and leave her, she snatched up her pocketbook and hurried downstairs.

And there he was, right where she had left him, slouching casually against the wall at the foot of the stairs. He looked solid and substantial and thoroughly dependable. He glanced upward appreciatively, and, with a powerful flex of his shoulders, pushed away from the wall and stood straight, hands still in his pockets.

"Better now?" he asked. Pulling one hand out of his pocket, he grasped one of hers and gave it a lingering squeeze, almost as though he were a doctor taking her pulse. He let go gently. "That's all right, then. You'll do. Now, what do you say we start our little rendezvous early? It's half-past four; we can walk around the garden for a bit and then go back to my place for a drink. According to my Scots kirk-dweller forebears, it's indecent to have a drink before five." He shrugged at her. "Not before five, if *ever*. Old habits die hard."

He followed her out the door, shut it behind them, and stood waiting expectantly.

"Aren't you going to lock up?"

Roz stopped short. "I don't have a key," she said, surprised by the sudden revelation. She hadn't ever needed one before. She thought of the bunch of keys that she had left with Cory. *I should have taken them,* she thought. "The only keys I have are to the Viola Room."

She stood uncertainly, wondering if she should go

133

get Giles's keys after all and lock up. But no, the keys to the Viola Room were what mattered, and they were safe—one in her bag, the other locked inside the room itself. She didn't want to bother Cory again, make it seem as though she didn't trust her. "It doesn't matter," she said to Alan.

Alan raised his eyebrows at her. "Bit of an oversight on old Giles's part, wasn't it? Of course you need a key to lock up with, especially now with all these nasty goings-on." Alan shoved his hands back in his pockets, sighed, and shook his head. "Ay me. There's nothing to be done about it now, is there? I'll just have to escort you everywhere. Obviously you can't be left alone. It's clear you have an underdeveloped sense of danger."

Roz looked at Alan, trying to discern whether he was serious beneath the tone of mild irony. He gazed back at her mildly, his wide mouth slightly lifted at the corners, his dark, blue-gray eyes serious. For the time being, until she could feel her feet solidly back under her, she decided to take him at his word.

"Let's walk," she said simply.

Alan turned to his left and began to walk along the path along the wall that backed on the Cloister.

She followed him quietly, thinking of what a contrast it was to be walking in the garden with Alan instead of Giles. Alan, for all his casual amiability, did not seem compelled to fill the air with a running line of instructive chit-chat. With Alan, she had the feeling she could just be quiet, settle her thoughts.

It occurred to her, strolling along, that he was giving her this time. That, not old habits, was what they were walking for. She could ask questions later. The important question was, how far were *they* prepared to go to stop the papers from being published? And with Giles out of commission, she was the only one left to find out. Involuntarily, she shivered. Alan moved closer.

Walking next to him, his shoulder brushing hers,

she tried to concentrate on the others. Where had everyone been when Giles was being overcome? Francesca and Florence off somewhere, Alan upstairs painting in the Moat House. Beatrice at home packing. Cedric practicing; she had heard him pounding away when she went to look for Cory. Cory struggling with the sign up by the main road. Stella a question mark, but it was hard to believe she would gas Giles and then run around madly rescuing him at some risk to herself. That left only Hugh unaccounted for.

"Alan, have you seen Hugh at all this afternoon?"

Alan thought a moment, then shook his head. "No, but he's here, I think. I saw him this afternoon from my upstairs hall, coming into the Courtyard so fast his hair nearly blew off. Not since then, though. Nor anyone else, for that matter. Does it?" he inquired.

"Does it what?"

"Matter, silly. Of course it does—forgive me. I'm afraid I'm no help."

"What about Francesca? Or Mrs. Farthing?"

"Oh well, now. Francesca. She's a different story. Anyone would notice her if she were about."

"She's quite something, isn't she?" Roz said dryly, looking sideways at Alan's profile. One hand came out of his pocket, sketched the air.

"Ah yes. That marvelous, broad, androgynous face, and all those wisps and screws and tendrils of coin-colored hair." His other hand swept up as if of its own volition, describing with uncanny accuracy a complete outline of Francesca's long, lithe form. "I think of having her sit. She seems to go with the garden. I'd wind her up with a vine or two, some veils, and a garland of primroses, a basket of assorted flowers . . ." His voice grew distant.

"Though of course it's been done, now that I think of it. Proserpine on the vine," he mused.

"Who?"

He looked over at her, startled. "Oh, sorry.

135

Botticelli, I mean. *Primavera,* it's called Campanion to Venus on the half-shell, the one with Venus all done up in seaweed, stepping out of a scallop. I'm sorry, you're so quick that I forgot you couldn't read minds." His apologetic look was sincere. "I mean, Francesca's just like that—same incredibly long-legged, quirky-hipped stance, same whispy hair all over, same vapid boiled-gooseberry stare, same broad, flat, strong-boned face, os that you can't really tell from the face right away if it's a man or a woman. Come to think of it, it's almost as though she were a deliberate copy, as though she'd walked up to whoever does these things and handed up a picture postcard from the Uffizi and said, 'Here, I want to look like that.' "

He grinned at Roz. "Not that I don't like the painting, you understand. I just don't take much to Francesca. She's very striking, but not my type Botticelli, yes; Alan Stewart, no. You, on the other hand . . ."

He backed off slightly, squinted at her, and framed her face in a square of fingers. "Corot, perhaps or Renoir—no, too dark, and not enough freckles. Not Blowsy, either. Too quiet, I suppose, You have that quality of stillness, of things gathering in; Renoirs always seem to be shouting. American, I think. Cassatt? No, too pale, too yallery-greenery pastel. Whistler, perhaps. Yes, Whistler. Or Sargent. Dark, exact, direct, rather shy and thus a bit mysterious . . ."

Once more his voice trailed off. What was it she had just been thinking about Alan's silence? She had a feeling she was not listening to idle chatter, but to his thoughts, the workings-out of his mind in pictures, in images. With difficulty, she forced her thoughts back from Alan's image of her to the question of who had gassed Giles.

They had walked through an archway on the far side of the Courtyard, but it was not until Alan's hand brushed hers, flashing a little shock along the

136

sensitive inner skin of her arm, that she looked up and saw where they were. She pulled up short.

"What?" Alan said, putting his arm around her, a look of concern on his face. "Still got the wind up? Well, I can understand that. But it's perfectly safe, you know."

"I do know. I've been through all that with Giles. It's just . . . it's just that I'm put off by the thought of all these pretty flowers looking so lovely and innocent and being so deadly. Monkshood and nightshade and hellebore and dumbcane . . ."

Alan nodded. "What a memory," he remarked, moving away from her farther into the Garden of Poisonous Plants. "But of course it's eerie, isn't it? All the ones you never think of—'I'm called little buttercup,' and 'Daffydowndilly has gone up to town,' and 'little Jumping Joan,' not to mention 'Johnny-over-the-ground.' 'Silver bells and cockle shells/And pretty maids all in a row.' All the children's pets. It's terrifying, really. I've often wondered if that rhyme mightn't be ironic, 'Mistress Mary qui et contrary/How does your poison grow?' Silver bells—lily-of-the-valley—is one of the sweetest-smelling, and the deadliest. Pretty maids all in a row in their little coffins. And there's Mary, standing by rubbing her hands with an evil grin on her face. It doesn't bear much looking into. Fair gives you the creeps, doesn't it?"

Roz nodded vigorously. "Yes, it does. It's all so sinister, but even worse than that. It's so . . . oh, I don't know, hypocritical. And maliciously ambugious. A secret language, like that plague rhyme, 'Ring a ring of rosies/Pocket full of posies/Ashes ashes/We all fall down.' We all fall down dead from bubonic plague. Pretty plants, pretty-sounding names, but everything a euphemism. Like that one." She pointed to a tall, spiked plant with large yellow crepe-paperlike blossoms. "Be-still tree. As though people thought it would be better to pretend, not to say the real names. There's something so pathetically propitiatory, so evasive . . . I don't know." Involuntarily, she shuddered, lost her balance, and fell against Alan. He grasped her elbow, but did not let it go, instead continuing to walk along holding her against him.

"Like calling the Furies the Eumenides, the well-disposed. As if they didn't know what you were thinking all the time, the old bats. Oh yes, I know just what you mean. Beautiful and inviting and succulent and deadly. And you've had enough of noxious vapors for one day, I expect. But," he went on, carefully matching his step to hers, "there are no vapors to speak of, as I'm sure Giles has told you. The smell's not the thing; you have to chew or stew or squeeze, at the very least, to get the full effect."

Alan's tone, Roz noticed, was informal—light, but precise, almost professorial without being pedantic. He was not being ironic or sinister. It was a tone she had heard and used many times before. It occurred to her that he had effectively—and deliberately?—distracted her attention away from the day's events by steering the conversation into a more abstract, theoretical, even scholarly direction. But still Roz felt cold inside. How did he know so much about these poisonous plants? Was everyone in this place some sort of enthusiast? Was that what attracted them—him—any of them? Attracted and kept them here, under Giles's thumb? She looked curiously at Alan as he went on.

"Most of them in small doses are the basis of our modern medicines; I expect you know that. Nicotinic acid for vertigo, digitalis for the heart, reserpine, thorazine, atropine, stimulants and sedatives, tranquilizers, stomach panaceas, and the like. All known to the ancients. Of course, there was rather an appalling lot of trial and error—feeding shredded rhubarb leaves to children for the colic cured them of more than a bellyache, I'm afraid. But that's enough of

138

that," he said, tucking her arm close to his side. "This way."

As they walked, Roz tried to focus her thoughts on the Herb Garden, far away at the other end of the Moat House. She could almost smell it—the flat brick paths intersticed with mother-of-thyme and creeping marjoram, the tall garlic minarets, the musky tansy looking like spilled coins, the purple flowering borage, lavender, pennyroyal, the names she had learned most quickly, because she liked the look of them, the smell. Roz murmured their mes under her breath, almost like an incantation, an antidote to those around her that seemed to darken her mind with their hint of death . . .

Again she stopped abruptly as she saw where Alan was leading her. He let go of her arm and looked at her curiously.

"I'm sorry. I really don't want to go in there, either."

"The Rose Garden? Dear me, you really have got the wind up, haven't you? I expected you'd fight shy of the Porcelain Garden, but I forgot about the roses." He turned and surveyed the monotonous greenery of the defoliated Rose Garden. "Dear me, yes. How depressing. Narrows the possibilities for wandering quite a bit, doesn't it? Which is, I suppose, precisely what the malefactor had in mind. You can hardly wander pleasantly through a garden of bright images if someone's gone and nipped them all, can you?"

Roz nodded, feeling miserable again. She stood still, unable to move.

"Well," said Alan cheerily, "I suppose there's nothing for it but to have a drink. Unless you'd like to take a turn around the Wilderness Garden? The orchard? Oh, stuff it, Alan. Pub hours be damned. Come on." And once more taking her arm, he quickly marched her back through the Garden of Poisonous Plants, veered left along the front of the

Moat House, and, with a flourish, pushed open his front door.

"Not locked?" Roz asked as they moved inside.

"Who would bother with me? Gossip goes through my mind like ditch water through a culvert. I don't own any family treasures, have no disgusting habits, and my thumb is black as Beelzebub's. When it's not covered with paint, of course. I am a threat to no one that I know of. Come in, come in."

" 'Said the spider to the fly,' " Roz said without thinking.

Alan gave her a startled look, then laughed. But his voice was serious when he spoke.

"No, just come in. You're safe with me."

Feeling slightly ill at ease, Roz followed Alan into a small, dark foyer, up a short flight of stairs that led upward into light, and into a large room that dazzled her eyes with brilliance. They were on the first floor, and the whole north wall, the one that overlooked the Moat and the Rose Garden, was tier upon tier of small-paned, leaded windows through which opalescent shafts of late afternoon sun slanted, gleamed, and shot in ripples across the stark, white plaster walls.

"Oh, it's lovely," Roz murmured.

"Gilbert de Monfort plagiarized the whole thing from Bess of Hardwick. You may have heard the old jingle 'Hardwick Hall, more glass than wall'? Gilbert—the old reprobate—pinched the clerestory windows from the Abbey Church and bunged them in here. Then he went and wrapped a moat all round to keep his enemies out, the silly idiot, when they could have knocked out the whole front with a slingshot." Alan shook his head. "Which they never did, oddly enough. It's marvelous for me, of course. The north light, nice and indirect. I paint upstairs, in a room just like this one."

Alan moved to the far end of the room and stood in front of a large, gray sandstone fireplace, its chimney piece chiseled with an intricate but largely unintelligible coat of arms—de Montfort, no doubt—which rose to the ceiling between dark sections of linen-fold paneling. Alan opened a square section of the paneling to reveal a small bar. An ice bucket stood to one side. Roz heard the tinkle of ice cubes. "No, scratch the ice," Alan muttered, and dumped it out into a sink no bigger than a cereal bowl. "Warm gin for medicinal purposes, as my grandmother used to say back home in Pittenweem. That's in Fife; I dare say you've never heard of it. It's every bit as fascinatingly euphonious as Poughkeepsie, don't you think?" He brought her a gin and tonic, mostly gin, Roz realized as she sipped it cautiously.

"Do sit down. Let's see what else I have." Setting down his own drink? he shut the door of the little bar. "That closet's just for drink. I'll have to go elsewhere for the *hors d'oeuvres.*"

Passing in front of her, he went through another door concealed in the paneling. Roz heard him clanking around in what was presumably the kitchen. Presently he reemerged with a plate of cheese and a jar of pickles. Under one arm he had wedged a mauled-looking box of Carr's Water Biscuits. "Here we are. Warm gin, cheese, and pickles. Maiden's delight." He put everything down on a large, embossed copper tray table in front of Roz, and dropped down next to her on the couch.

"Now then, how do you like my house? It's tumbledown Tudor, of course." He stretched back comfortably, put his arms along the back of the couch, and gazed upward. Roz sank back into the overstuffed couch and looked up at the rough textured plaster, the great black beams that crisscrossed the ceiling.

"Interesting effect, don't you think?" Alan said. "As if they laid the plaster on with a push broom and smoothed it out with the rear end of a dead chicken."

Roz smiled at the thought of many small dwarflike

141

medieval men swarming over the walls pushing brooms and swinging dead chickens. She giggled, then laughed, and suddenly found herself unable to stop. She laughed and laughed; tears ran down her face; she rocked back and forth helplessly, clutching her stomach, trying to get her breath. Her drink sloshed into her lap, ran down her bare legs and into her sandals. Finally she got control of herself, gulped the last of her drink, and looked, breathless and embarrassed, at Alan. He was watching her sympathetically.

"Did you know a good belly laugh can bring a person's blood pressure down thirty points in a matter of seconds? I've often wondered if that were the basis of comic relief in tragedy, or the reason why people invariably giggle at horror shows. It's a much nicer way of letting go than screeching hysterics, but then I suspect you're about as hysterical as Whistler's mother. I'm quite sure you never screech."

Roz stared at him. His quick—and remarkably accurate—analysis of her character had made her realize how little she actually knew about him. And that was just the trouble. He seemed to know much more about her than she about him. She felt suddenly vulnerable, uncertain.

"You really are an artist, aren't you?" she blurted.

Alan watched her face for a moment. "Would you be disappointed if I weren't?"

"No, that's not what I meant," Roz said quickly, feeling awkward. "I meant . . . you're not a doctor, are you?"

"If you mean a physician, no, I'm not. Not at all. But obscure herbal medicines and plant poisons are an interest of mine. Is that what you were wondering?"

"Well, yes. I guess so. I . . ." As she had with Cory, she felt embarrassed that her suspicion had been so transparent. "I . . . I know a lot of academics and other professionals . . . doctors, lawyers —my father was a lawyer—but not many artists.

142

I . . ." Roz stopped, not sure what she wanted to say next.

Alan took her glass and got up to refill it. On the way back, he took down a small, leather-bound volume from the bookcase on th e side wall. He handed it to her. "Nicander. *Theriaca*. It's a discursive poem about poisons—plants and other kinds. One of many. The ancient jreeks appear to have had a fixation on pharmacopoeia."

Roz stared at the book in her hands, then opened it. She flipped to the title page. Translated and illustrated by Alan Stewart, B. Litt. Oxon. Longmans, 1975. She opened the body of the text. It was Greek on the left, English on the right, and every dozen or so pages there was a fine colored lithograph of whole plants—roots, leaves, and flower—all in detail. She leafed through the whole book, then closed it and held it in her lap. She looked up at Alan, who waa standing by the fireplace watching her.

"The benefits of a classical education. In my spare moments, I translate out-of-the-way botanical and zoological tracts and do the drawings myself. It's rather a specialty of the house. The odd medicinal, you know—Aescalapius, Appollodorus, Dioscorides are the famous ones, of course. This is a bit more obscure, but very useful." He flashed his ironic smile, handed her her drink, took the little volume from her, and replaced it. "I find it interesting, on occasion consuming. I can beat both my hobby horses with one stick. And I couldn't ask for a better place to do it," he said, inclining his head toward the far wall. Roz turned to look, puzzled. All she saw was a rather large painting of leaves and flowers in complex interwoven patterns, sharp-edged, textured, brightly colored, vaguely reminiscent of Gauguin.

"No, not that. I meant the Poison Plant Garden out there. That little lot is just right for me—my cup of tea, do forgive the pun. I've got what amounts to my own private herbarium. It will be even better

143

now that Giles has done away with the paying visitors for the duration. Not that I minded them; I used to just fade into the crowd." He moved to the couch and plunked down beside her.

Looking at his quite distinctive profile, his mussed-up hair, his large frame in the rumpled, comfortable clothes, Roz considered the possibility of his fading into the crowd. Not very likely. He leaned forward, plucked a pickle out of the jar, and began to munch it.

"Speaking of pickles, Alan . . . ," she said, and hesitated.

He turned to her with a quick flash of amusement. "The one I'm eating or the one we're in?"

"Which do you think?"

"The latter, as your countryman Henry James would say. Who did in Giles, and how and why? Does that about cover it? And speaking of being covered, do you know that you've got a lapful of gin? It's all over your skirt."

Roz glanced down; the whole front of her skirt was soaked.

"You've had quite a day of it, haven't you, what with one thing and another? Exposed to deadly insecticide, doused with cold water, glared at by our very own version of Medusa, insulted, frightened, confused. And now nearly drowned in gin. Poor Roz . . ." Alan leaned over and put his arm gently across her shoulders. "I'm sorry. I didn't mean to upset you," he said softly.

Looking into his face, Roz noticed how extraordinarily open and ingenuous it was. Honest, trustworthy, above suspicion. Had she really ever sensed a reserve, felt he was holding something back? She could hardly believe it, now. She closed her eyes. Detachment. Maybe that was it. He was curiously detached from the present circumstances, with an almost academic objectivity (but Alan was the last person she would think of as academic), a disinterested curiosity in what was going on. That should be her role, yet she was becoming increasingly engaged. Suddenly she felt pulled every which way, stretched thin, taut. She was so tired. And all at once her mind seemed to let go, like a well-used slingshot that has finally worn out its elastic. She slumped back against Alan's arm and shut her eyes, completely exhausted.

"I think maybe we should leave it alone for a while," Alan said after a moment. He hugged her briefly, then stood up. "I suggest we get away from here right now. The Horse and Groom on the Fenmarket Road has perfectly elegant pork pies, and there's a hope—today's Friday, isn't it?—of Cornish pasties, if we get there before six. Or bangers and mash, if you like."

He extended a hand, helped Roz to her feet, took their two glasses and stuffed them inside the little drink closet. "I'll fix you up with another skirt; it'll save us going all the way back to the Refectory." Without giving her time to protest, he went out the door they had entered, and Roz heard him thumping up some stairs. She wondered with a startled twinge of curiosity whose skirt it had been. Or still was.

Alan came back waving a denim-wrap-skirt as rumpled as his own clothing. He stopped short in the doorway, regarding her with raised eyebrows, then smiled. "Here." He handed her the skirt. "This should do. One size fits all, I understand, and it goes well enough. The loo's at the other end, in the corner behind the farthest panel. Amazing how they clobbered everything up and then hid it away in all those little squares, isn't it?" He smiled, then studied her face with interest.

Roz took the skirt without a word and walked across the room to the corner panel. The bathroom was small, very tidy, and wallpapered in lush, red velvet stripes, the kind of decor her mother had always referred to as Viennese bordello. She fluffed her hair, put on lipstick, looked at herself in the antique curlicue mirror, then wrapped the denim skirt around her waist. It fit perfectly. She rolled her own up in a wad and stuffed it into her pocketbook. She felt oddly irritated by the idea of wearing someone else's skirt.

When she emerged, Alan smiled his approval. "Very nice."

"Thanks," she said curtly.

"I thought you were about my sister's size," Alan said, grinning at her.

Roz turned away, startled into a blush.

"Neither large nor small, but somewhere in between. Very nice, very neat. You shall have to meet her someday; you really are of a size. Her name is Elspeth." He paused. "Whose skirt did you think it was?"

Roz turned back to him. "Thanks," she said. She smiled apologetically. It was the least she could do. "For the drinks, the skirt, the compliment, and the understanding," she added. "And I do think it would be a good idea to get away from here for a while."

Alan nodded. Then he offered her his crooked elbow as he had in the Courtyard. She took it gratefully. *I've got to get back to work,* she thought. *Back to the knot on the end of the piece of string that will unravel the tangled skein. Even Alan can't help with that. I've got to do it myself.*

"Roz?"

"What? Oh, sorry, Alan. I was thinking."

"That was perfectly clear. You looked miles away. Right, you're back. Let's make like a crumbling battlement and fall away."

Minutes later, they were on their way down the drive in Alan's cozy, rattletrap, stepped-on soup can of a car, sitting in companionable silence, thinking their own thoughts.

Abruptly she found her thoughts shifting back to Giles. She had never gotten a chance to ask him about the missing papers.

146

15

"GILES IS PROBABLY THE MOST THOROUGHLY hated man I know," Alan said casually as they were eating dinner by the light of a single fat, squashed-looking candle in a booth of the private bar at the Horse and Groom. It was the first time the subject of Giles and the Abbey had come up since they had left Montfort some two hours before. The rest of the time they had spent talking about themselves—or herself, Roz realized, having answered Alan's questions by delivering quite a detailed biography of her life and times as a girl growing up in Marcellus, New York, and later a student, first at Smith, then at Berkeley, and as a young professor at Vassar. These, at least, were questions she could answer. Brought up short by his remark about Giles, she looked at him in surprise.

"Didn't you know that?" he said. "Oh, but how could you? I keep forgetting you haven't been here very long. Still, I'd have thought you could tell."

"Oh, Alan, I don't know what I can or can't tell anymore. Sometimes I think I'm suffering from a permanent case of jet lag. Most of the time I feel as though I'm hearing only half the conversation, and the rest is going on by mental telepathy or osmosis or something, and I'm the only one who's missing the right equipment. The auditory equivalent of trying to read between the lines."

"Oh, I don't know," Alan said. "Your equipment seems perfectly in order to me."

Roz frowned at him, but he went right on. "Giles is

probably the most naturally arrogant and imperious man I've ever met. I think he was born that way—probably inherited it from Viola." He acknowledged Roz's surprised look. "Oh, I know Viola was supposed to be a combination of Saint Theresa, George Eliot, and Louis Agassiz—simple, visionary, direct, humble, and formidably wise—and everyone adored her. Still, I wonder. She always got her way. And that garden . . . has anyone ever shown you Viola's morgue?"

"Her morgue?"

"Yes. It's a plant mortuary, complete with little tombstones. Or at least those little sticker things that come on plants to tell you what they are. There's a special section behind the greenhouses where she put all the names and varieties of the plants that didn't work out. Weren't what she expected, or didn't fit in, somehow. She was quite ruthless, you know. You'd have to be, to create the kind of garden she did. That blue willow, for instance. Years of crossbreeding and mutations. Forcing plants . . ." Alan broke off and studied the tablecloth. Roz watched him for a while. But he did not go on.

"Speaking of the garden," she said finally, "what about Cory and Stella? Do they hate Giles?"

Alan lifted his head. "Ah, Cory and Stella. The good soldiers. They just carry on, fighting Giles every step of the way, trying to make a go of it. It's become their joint mission to thwart as much as they can his compulsion to keep the garden exactly as it was when Viola died. It's a terrible lot of work to keep a garden the same, because it wants to grow and change, you know, like everything else. They're always pulling out and putting back small, running as hard as they can to stay in one place. I don't think they like it one bit—Stella particularly; she's the creative one. She's the one who convinced Giles to put in a pond to drain the swamp down below the old church. But they both would have sold out to Britannia Trust long ago. No more doing it on the cheap, no more being overruled by Giles."

"If it's so horrible, why don't they leave?"

"Loyalties aside?" Alan stared at his plate, considering. "I suppose you've wondered if they are lovers, two women living together like that." Alan picked up his spoon and began to make little dents in the soft, padded tablecloth. "Well, I can assure you that they are not. But they are inseparable friends and associates; each supplies what the other hasn't. Stella's the mystic, and Cory's the practical one. Anyway, a couple of years ago Giles took it into his head that Montfort could get on with just one gardener, and he tried to fire Stella. They both stood up to him, and refused to be separated. Brought out their contract, and threatened to sue him. He had to back down, but he made it quite clear that he'd never give them a good reference, and that effectively canned their chances to get a job together elsewhere. Then Giles made them take a cut in pay for the privilege of staying on. They work for one salary and a bit, and he's got the upper hand. So of course there's no love lost there."

"But do they hate him enough to sabotage his garden and fill his study full of bug killer?"

Alan considered a moment. "I don't think Cory and Stella would hurt the garden for anything. They've got their loyalty to Viola and the place they helped to create. I think they'd want to protect the garden at all costs. But Giles is rather a different story. Still, I doubt it. They have other ways of getting back at him." Alan looked at her apologetically and shrugged. "But I really can't say."

Roz wondered if he were truly at a loss; once again she felt the disturbing wall of his reserve, the sense that he was not saying everything he thought. Or knew. She sighed.

"It all sounded so pastoral and harmonious," she

149

said. "Everyone and everything in its place, all cooperating, all liking each other, all working for the greater glory of the garden, the garden going on, and Viola's poetry . . ."

"You got that from Giles, no doubt. And Viola before him, of course. I don't know about the rest, but I believe the part about everything in its place. One of the frictions between Giles and the Badgetts is his obvious feeling that they have somehow got above themselves. I don't know any other explanation for his treatment of them. Hugh's quite a distinguished scientist. Absolutely at the top of his profession. Beatrice is the daughter of a bart—excuse me, a baronet—and hates it here. Thinks Giles lords it over her, as well as Hugh. She'd like to leave; it's hardly any life for her, stuck out here in the middle of the fens, and she thinks Hugh could go on to better things. After all, he goes off to his cozy little lab at Cambridge and is Dr. Professor Badgett, but when he comes home he's still the farmer's son, old Hughie the humble servant. Have you ever heard Giles taunt him about his lower-class accent? I'm sure he thinks Hugh speaks that way only to annoy him. All that education, and he still talks the way his ancestors did out in the fields. It all goes back to appearances; somehow, to have Hugh go on talking that way offends Giles's sense of decorum. But it also gives Giles a way of reminding Hugh who he really is, and where he belongs. Giles is a snob, and possibly a prig as well. There's an element of punishment in his treatment of Cory and Stella, in his relations with all of them, really, that's meant to be corrective. Or even coercive."

"But Viola wasn't a snob, or a prig," Roz protested. "If her books are any indication . . ."

Uncharacteristically, Alan interrupted her. "Ah, fair Rosamund. Books. I doubt whether anything most of us write should be taken precisely as read.

150

Viola was a romantic, and she took a sanguine view of the class struggle. Salt of the earth, and all that. The simple annals of the poor. She got away with it because everyone loved her. Shouting penury when she was down to her last half-dozen servants. Still, she was absurdly generous. But in these days of rampant *noblesse désoblige,* it's all relative, I'm afraid.

"No, the question is not who hates Giles enough to wreck his means of livelihood and endanger his person, but who wants to be first. Giles has always taken the line that he inherited everybody from his parents, like some feudal baron, but all of us pay good rents. Giles could never come even close to keeping this place up without the lot of us; the income from the paying visitors barely covers the upkeep of the garden, not to mention the rates, and the drains, and stones and mortar. Keeping the garden going is a frightful expense, especially where he's so insistent that the garden—and everything else—remain exactly as it was in Viola's time. The dead past burying the living, to paraphrase Aeschylus. The others want change, or want change acknowledged, and Giles wants things to stay the same. Yet everyone stays. It's a mutual stranglehold society."

Roz pondered this a moment. "So Giles can't really afford to lose anyone, can he? Then if the rest of them have this power, why don't they use it? Confront him directly? Why all this beating around the bush?" But she knew what Alan was saying; it was literally a vicious circle. And it had gone on long before her arrival, maybe even before the papers had become an issue. Still, the papers were now obviously a part of it all. Perhaps the most important part.

Alan tapped the spoon gently on the padded tabletop. "I really don't know. When I first came, I thought it might be loyalty and dedication, with a little inertia thrown in, a sort of *folie à tous,* if there is such a thing. But now, with the papers . . ."

Alan's voice trailed off, his eyes on the indentations he had made in the tablecloth. They resembled the outline of a woman's face.

"You know," Roz said, "even though Giles knows it's somebody here, he simply refuses to discuss who. He says it doesn't matter who, that it can't be helped, and that we'll just go on."

"Giles is a past master at seeming to ignore the obvious," Alan said. "Particularly if it suits his purpose. What better way to keep people in line than never even to notice they've got out of it? The ultimate in dismissiveness."

"But why would he be that way with me? If he does know who it is for certain, why not tell me? He doesn't have to keep me in line." *Or does he?* she added to herself. She remembered Giles their first day at the papers, quietly but unequivocally putting her in her place about how they were to proceed. And this morning, the same thing.

"I'm not sure, but I suspect you're rather quicker than he expected." Alan sat back, a speculative look on his face. "Just suppose everyone at Montfort has known all along that the papers are full of incredibly juicy bits—scandal and sensation. And suppose he's been putting the screws on all of them since the papers turned up, until finally they've reached the sticking point, and won't go round one more time. So he trots out his threat of publication, his ace in the hole, and announces he will tell all, make a bundle all at once, and to hell with them. But with 'or else' implied. Leaving them to choose between going on as before, helping Giles to keep up Montfort as a monument to Viola's memory, or seeing their lives ripped to tatters in public. And then he finds that he enjoys the sense of absolute control over people's lives, wants to draw it out as long as possible. So everything must be kept under wraps, except the threat.

What he knows, he knows, but no one else does. Meanwhile he's brought you in as a kind of prod, a stalking horse, to show he means business. And then he bides his time, waiting for all of them to reconsider, to come up with whatever it is that he requires."

Roz stared at Alan, horrified. She a prod, a stalking horse? The papers used as a kind of flail? It couldn't be. She shook her head emphatically. "I just can't believe that. I think Giles is perfectly sincere about publishing the papers. There's the contract to prove it, and the advance." No, it wasn't right; it couldn't be. To hire her, go through all the motions, and then not publish? She went on, aware that she was trying to convince herself as well as Alan. "I . . . I simply can't believe that Giles is like that. I think it's far more likely that it's a simple case of conflicting interests. Right now public curiosity about Viola and women like her is high—he's right about that—and he can make a killing, so to speak. It's crass, but hardly a monstrous motive. The others don't want him to, because they feel it will invade their privacy in some intolerable way."

"As simple as that?"

"As simple as that," Roz repeated.

"Occam's razor, in fact."

Roz nodded, surprised. She had forgotten Alan's classical education. It was nice to have someone who spoke her language, at least on occasion. It was also nice to have another point of view. Still, she hoped he was wrong. It was too cynical, too . . .

"What's the drill for publishing papers that contain unflattering or scandalous references to people still alive?" Alan asked suddenly.

"There are a number of approaches," Roz replied, grateful to be back on more familiar and academic ground. "You can publish and be damned, let the chips fall where they may. You can substitute A, B,

153

C, and X, and so on. You can delete the worst passages."

"Rows of dots and asterisks? Rather hard on the reader. Quite annoying, really. Not to mention coy. What the reader imagines is infinitely more scandalous."

"It beats a suit for libel."

"I dare say," Alan said dryly. "The problem, of course, being whether in fact the editee spake the truth."

"Exactly. It happens. But from the way Florence and Hugh and the rest of them have been behaving, I guess that whatever they think is in the papers must be quite shocking, as well as true. But I don't have any idea what it could be: I've been over all the letters—quickly, of course—and the diaries, and there's nothing that could affront anyone. Of course . . ." She stopped, uncertain whether she should tell Alan about the gaps.

"Well," said Alan, after it became clear she was not going to continue, "whatever Giles is up to, he's taking an awful chance. Trying to force people to go along with what he wants, what is best for him and Montfort—never mind what's best for them." He paused, then went on, almost as though he were talking to himself. "Forcing souls, just like forcing plants . . ."

Roz sat back in her chair. "I still can't believe it," she murmured. "Tell me about Florence. What has she got to lose or gain?"

"Ah, Florence," Alan said. "There's a story. She married Cedric about ten years ago. I suspect she still can't quite believe her luck. Hugh a terrific success, in line for an OBE, married to the daughter of a nobleman. She must feel that she's finally left her peasant roots behind. No more S.O.T.E. for her. But of course that's left poor Elsie behind to be the char. You did know Florence and Elsie are sisters, didn't you?"

154

Roz blinked at Alan, astonished at this latest revelation. But of course that was whom fragile, birdlike Florence had reminded her of—timid, scuttling to get out of sight. Florence had the same kind of sliding-away look in her eyes. But how strange. One sister a lady, sitting at table amidst the silver and crested china, the other washing crockery in the kitchen, still a char. Roz felt a surge of sympathy for Elsie, for Florence.

"Small gains hardly won," she murmured. "You make Giles sound like not a very nice person, to put it mildly."

"That's the least of it. Aside from his treatment of Elsie, Giles never lets Florence forget, in small mean ways, that she was once the farmer's wife. Hums 'Three Blind Mice' when she's standing by, and so on. The odd thing is that Cedric is completely oblivious to it all. Even immune. He doesn't care. His position is secure; he's an artist of world renown, and he loves Florence. But Florence is very protective of her position, very protective indeed."

"No wonder they all hate him," Roz said. Yet in the midst of all these revelations of his disordered relations with his neighbors, she felt a perverse sympathy for Giles. Or was it Viola? She found it hard to believe that they couldn't be what they seemed.

Yet what could Alan have at stake, not telling her the truth? She looked at him, the candlelight shining upward on his face, bringing into relief the planes and angles, so that he looked like an elegant, carved Elizabethan comedy mask. Yet the truth was, he had told her very little more than she already knew—had only cast it in a different light. And he was obviously not at all concerned with Giles's point of view. No one seemed to be concerned for Giles, in fact. Maybe that was why he was so self- and past-obsessed.

"And now Giles knocked out with bug stuff," she

155

mused aloud. "Cory thinks it was just a warning, you know. Not attempted murder."

"I agree. It fits in with the other incidents, then. Each a little stiffer than the last, but stopping short of real disaster."

"And the message?"

" 'Stop now, or who knows what we'll do next to ruin you.' " Alan's face in the candlelight took on a deliberately sinister cast. Then he smiled. "Rather an obscure way of getting across one's drift, but quite Giles's style, and therefore ironic, I think. Witty, oblique, and, as you said, quite between the lines. A bit of his own medicine."

They sat in silence for a moment. Roz gazed at Alan. He gazed back at her, serious now, apparently deep in thought. After a while she said: "The business with the garden has come up just since Giles announced his intentions to publish, hasn't it? Since I arrived?"

"Oh yes. It all dates from Giles's announcement; you're right about that. Oh, and the other arrival—Francesca's, I mean. Just to complicate matters further."

"What about Francesca? Where does she fit in?"

"Sorry, but once again I haven't the faintest idea. She came out of nowhere, as far as I can see." Alan drew one leg up and rested it on the bench, draped an arm over his knee, and stared blankly into the dark space of the little bar. Apparently still lost in thought, he began to hum quietly to himself. The tune was familiar; Roz recognized it as "She'll be Comin' round the Mountain."

" 'And we'll all sleep with Grandma'?" she said, smiling.

Alan blinked and turned his attention back to her. "Or words to that effect. Actually I was thinking more along the lines of 'We shall kill the old red rooster.' But there is a certain 'Move over, I'm here' quality to Francesca. Certainly everyone has crowded in to accommodate her. Except Giles, of course. He seems to ignore her completely. She's some obscure relation of the Badgetts, I gather. Obscure, and not quite on the up and up. They've stashed her with Elsie Farthing, whatever that means." Once more he was silent.

"And you have no idea what might be in the papers?"

"Not a clue," Alan said, without a change in expression. "Everyone was thunderstruck when they turned up in the first place. Viola was supposed to have burned the lot." Alan looked at her curiously. "But isn't that your turf? I thought you said you'd seen them all, and they are innocent?"

"I've looked, and there's nothing I can see that would hurt or threaten anybody . . ." She stopped short; she had been about to add, "At least so far."

Alan sat forward, a concerned look on his face. "I think you should make that known right away. Yourself." He reached over and covered her hand with his warm one. "And I think you know why, even with your underdeveloped sense of danger. Someone, we don't know exactly who, or why, wants desperately to keep those papers from being published. Ever. Mucking about in the garden bought some time, but now that Giles has gone around waving his contract and his check everyone knows he can go on, garden or no garden. He can't be stopped merely by shutting the place down. So Giles is sprayed with insecticide, and temporarily put out of commission."

He gripped her fingers hard, almost painfully. "But, fair Rosamund, that still leaves you. Anyone who wants to stop publication of those papers is going to figure out sooner or later he's got to stop you, too. We've all seen you march up to the Viola Room day after day, ploughing along no matter what the distractions, working faster than anyone might expect, even Giles. Certainly they must assume that

157

whatever there is to know, you will find out soon . . . if you haven't already. You just keep on, professional, objective, cool, competent . . . no, don't snatch your hand away, I'm not flattering you, *or* being ironic. You do give that impression, you know, whatever may go on inside, however icy your fingers may be. You, in fact, are the real threat, because you are the professional. Your name is on the contract too, isn't it? If Giles died tonight, you'd go right on, wouldn't you?"

"Of course."

"With A's and B's and dotted lines?"

"I don't know. It would depend."

"You see? Professional. Objective. Principled. Obviously incorruptible. And possibly—excuse me, but I'm as skeptical as you—dedicated to the truth at all costs. You said as much at lunch in front of the whole crowd, remember?"

Alan released her hand, and she sat back, digesting this view of herself. The whole truth, no matter what the cost. Had she said that? A life in words preserved forever. Short time's endless monument. Alan was right. The dotted line was an abomination. Truth had to transcend the ephemerality of personal feelings. The past and future were unavoidably separated by the present. But the papers—the words—held in them the possibility to link them all.

Abruptly, Roz was struck with an anxiety for the papers. Suddenly they seemed so vulnerable, the web of words so fragile. She had the key to the Viola Room. No one could get at the papers. But could she be absolutely sure of that? All along she had been so casual, believing that Giles's secrecy was unwarranted, arbitrary. She should never have left Giles's keys with Cory.

"Alan," she said, standing up. "Let's go back. I want to get Giles's keys from Cory and check on the papers, make sure they're all right."

"Right." Alan stood up briskly.

A moment later, as they got in the car, she turned to him.

"And you?"

He smiled at her. "I'm safe enough, can't you tell? I live and let live. I don't care for Giles, but he interests me. I have a great fondness for Montfort Abbey. And gardens. And . . ."

"And Giles could never force you to do anything," she said quietly.

Alan paused with the key in the ignition. "There's quite a bit more to you than meets the eye, isn't there? When I first saw you, I thought, Very nice, but so young and inexperienced, hardly a match for Giles. But you don't miss a thing, you really don't. You seem to gather everything in, digest it all, and come out right. You're the young lady James talked about on whom nothing is lost." He contemplated her. "Does it happen bit by bit, or all at once?"

Roz glared at him, not sure whether or not to be offended. "Oh, Alan, don't be condescending," she said finally. "I've been trained to ask the right questions, or keep on asking the wrong ones until the right one comes along. 'The unexamined life is not worth living.' That's the first thing they taught us in graduate school."

"Now who's being condescending?" Alan remarked cheerfully as he turned the key. The Mini coughed and choked and shuddered into life. "I'm familiar with Socrates's line. Now there's an interesting case of herbal poisoning, *conium maculata,* or poison hemlock, containing coniine, an allotrope of aconite. Paralyzes the central nervous system, starting in the extremities. And there he lay, the old man, noting down his own sensations of creeping death. That's my idea of the true intellectual." He glanced at her apologetically. "Sorry, I got carried away. I think it's time we talked of other things for a while." He jammed the car in gear. And all the long way back to Montfort Abbey, they talked of other things.

16

IT WAS QUITE DARK AS THEY PULLED UP IN THE drive, but the moonlight cast an eerie glow over the stones and shrubbery, making them appear almost skeletal. Alan coasted to a stop outside the arch and looked inquiringly at Roz.

"Would you mind pulling around to Cory and Stella's?" she said. "I want to get the rest of Giles's keys back."

"Right." Alan let in the clutch, and the car putted softly around the turn by the Poor Farm. All the lights were out; the Badgetts were either gone for the evening, or asleep. Roz wondered if Beatrice had actually left. "I'll just pull in the garage, and we can walk back," Alan said. "Stella's car is here; perhaps she'll have some news of Giles."

They stopped at the door to the gardeners' apartment. Roz waited while Alan knocked and went inside. She hoped he wouldn't stay too long; she was anxious to check on the papers.

After a minute or so Alan came back out and shut the door firmly behind him. Behind the glass Roz saw a curly-haired shadow waving at her. Then the lock clicked from inside. Cory locking the door, probably on Alan's orders.

Alan handed her the bunch of keys. "Cory's had them locked up all day. Stella says Giles is out of the woods, but as mad as a cross-eyed cat. He's allowed to go home tomorrow, and I've said I'd go fetch him. Want to come?"

"I'll see in the morning," Roz said absently, her mind still on the papers. She was surprised and a little disappointed that Giles was coming back so soon. She had been planning to spend the whole day turning the place upside down in search of the missing papers.

"As far as the doctors can tell, he didn't get much of a dose. Just enough to make him cock-eyed for a while. It could have been much worse," Alan said. "Cory found the can of insecticide and a long black hose stuffed up the waste pipe behind the Abbot's Chapel. There was quite a bit gone."

Without warning, Roz began to shiver violently again. Alan reached out and put his arm around her.

"Here now, what's this? He'll be all right. Perhaps this will bring the mad havoc-wreaker to his senses. We can put it about that the dose nearly took Giles off, that it was a much closer thing than it actually was. Don't you think?" With his arm still around her shoulders they began to walk down the drive toward the Refectory.

Giles coming home tomorrow. There wouldn't be time to do anything on her own. Not to mention tea with Florence . . . poor Florence. Perhaps she should just ask her straight out what she was afraid of. *But no,* she reflected. *I really have to see the missing papers first, see what's actually there, before I make any promises.* She sighed, and, without thinking, burrowed closer into the warmth of Alan's body. Well, she'd just have to do the best she could. Probably Giles wouldn't feel up to much; while he was resting she could . . . Alan hugged her close, so close she felt enveloped in the faintly resinous smell of his jacket.

She lifted her head and moved away.

Alan peered down at her in the dim light. "All right now?"

"Yes. I'm fine." She stood away from him and

161

smiled. "Really. Forewarned is forearmed, and I can lock the doors now." She held up the keys.

"Yes, well, Nevertheless, I am going to escort you back and have a look around, just to . . . now, now, don't bristle up like a hedgehog . . . just to set my own mind at ease."

Roz looked at his face. The amused expression was gone; he looked quite serious. But she really didn't want him along when she went up to the Viola Room.

"All right, Alan. But really, I'm not afraid."

They walked under the arch and across the grass to the door of the Refectory. Alan held the door for her, then followed her inside. He snapped on the lights in the hallway and peered into the sitting room through the ancient pierce-work choir screen. "Stand aside, fair Rosamund," he ordered. He went into the sitting room and looked behind the stuffed chairs, into all the shadowy nooks and crannies, even up the chimney. He returned to the hall, turning on lights as he went, walked past the stairs and into the dining room. Roz heard the sound of chairs being scraped back, one after another. It reminded her of the chaotic luncheon—how long ago? Last Monday, not even two weeks. It seemed like ages ago. She heard cupboards being opened in the kitchen, the rattling of latches, a door slamming. *The broom closet,* she thought in amusement. *Skinny midgets?* Alan came back into the hall.

"Nothing so far. I've latched the windows in the kitchen and dining room. The ones in the sitting room won't open. I'll just lock the door before we go upstairs." And, taking the keys from her, Alan twisted home the great dead bolt on the hall door. Then, motioning her to follow, he went up the worn, scooped stairs three at a time.

When Roz rounded the turn of the stair landing, he was just going down the long, dark passage toward her bedroom. He went into her room. Roz watched, her back to the door of Giles's room. Alan

162

came out, looking preoccupied, then went into the bathroom. There were two more bedrooms and another bath opening off the hall. Impatient to get to the Viola Room, Roz turned and pushed open the door to Giles's room. *I can look in here myself,* she thought.

Giles's room took up all the space over the dining room and kitchen below, abutting the Tower at the far end. The end wall was covered by the large and rather moldy-looking tapestry whose billowing in the breeze had startled Roz her first day there. Although the stair to the Viola Room ran up this side of the Tower, there was no entry into the Refectory; the only doors were the one at the bottom, opening onto the arch, and the one at the top, opening into the Viola Room. That was odd, of course, but this had been a fortification of sorts, and who knew what medieval monks had had in mind by way of siege.

Roz flicked on the light switch, throwing the large, walnut tester bedstead and ornately carved furniture into relief. She peered under the bed and opened the floor-to-ceiling oak armoire. She turned and surveyed the rest of the room. She had not been inside it since the day of her arrival; it was one of their tacit proprieties. The room was surprisingly neat and rather opulent for a single man, she thought. The heavy furniture, the huge black beams, and especially the tapestry gave it a medieval look. She walked toward the tapestry; it was a faded forest scene with castles in the background, tall, high-foreheaded ladies haughty in their swaybacked postures, dressed in flowing robes and improbable headdresses, accompanied by greyhounds, their complexions green with age. Roz ran her hand along the rough, woolly texture that from farther away had seemed as smooth as stone.

And then, quite distinctly, she heard a thud on the other side.

Now, where did that come from? she thought. Reaching down, Roz quickly lifted up the bottom of the tapestry and rested it on her shoulder, then ducked underneath. In the middle of the stone was a door.

And behind the door, on the other side of the stone wall, once again she heard a muffled thud.

Roz put her ear to the door. The tapestry fell about her like a cloak, cutting off most of the light and air. Dust tickled her nose, and she suppressed an urge to sneeze. She held her breath, listening. A faint rustling—bu. /here, and how far away? Silence. Then the sound of something being dragged above her head.

She looked down, found the latch in the murky shadow, and pressed it. The latch gave, but the door did not open. Short of breath now, she pushed back against the tapestry to give herself more air and light, tried to hold the heavy fabric out tentlike with her back while she put both hands on the latch, and pushed down hard.

"Roz?" Alan's voice came through the swimming air. "What! . . . Roz? What the devil are you doing?"

Cool, fresh air swept over her as Alan lifted the tapestry that had blanketed her like a shroud, and then folded it back.

"Look here, you gave me quite a turn, struggling around behind this old thing like a cat in a sack. And you're white as a sheet. What's going on?"

Roz put a finger to her lips and pointed to the door.

"Where does that go?" he whispered, letting down the tapestry as though it were a stage curtain.

"I don't know. I've never been in here before. But I heard a noise, and then I found the door. I think someone's in there."

"Is it locked?" Alan pressed the lock, then pushed with his whole weight. The door sprang open. Another distinct thud resounded in the darkness beyond. But it was still muffled, still far away.

164

"Whew," said Alan softly. "Is there such a thing as a light?"

Roz felt for a light switch just inside the door and snapped it on. This was no disused medieval monk's hole, not with electric lights and a modern paneled door. It was, in fact, something between a passage and a closet—about ten feet across, but very narrow. On their left, the stone wall was oddly rounded off from floor to ceiling; on the right, in a kind of alcove, there were several racks of sheet-enshrouded clothes; the middle was obviously kept clear as a passage to the door directly across from the one they had just come through.

"Where the devil are we?" said Alan.

"I think that must be the back of the stair," Roz said, gesturing toward the rounded wall. "We're in the turret behind the stair leading up to the Viola Room. But there's no opening off it . . ." Roz stopped, totally bewildered.

"What's in there, do you suppose?" Alan went over to the door across from them and pressed the latch; the door swung open easily. The space beyond was totally dark. The light from the closet passage fell across the floor, casting their shadows in front of them.

"I know where we are. Look."

Roz ducked through the door, stood to one side, and peered around. An odd pattern of light showed in the darkness to her left; slits—peepholes not big enough for windows—let in what moonlight there was and pricked the floor with thin slivers of light.

"We're over the arch directly under the Viola Room," Alan said in a normal voice. "I never thought of it, but of course there's space. That funny bit there is the coat of arms carved in the lintel. Little spy holes all around; you can see out, but no one can see in. In a pinch, you could send out an arrow or two, no doubt."

Carefully, they picked their way among the shapes and obstacles that seemed to litter the whole

165

space: dusty hooded pieces of furniture, an old wooden mantelpiece, a rusted child's bicycle, a collapsed bedstead, trunks and boxes. In the dim light, Roz made out yet another door. *It's like being on a train,* she thought, *going from one car to the next.* The room seemed to sway, lurch slightly as though it were moving on a track. From above she heard a rhythmic clicking sound.

"Alan," she whispered tensely.

". . . little low place, but perfectly good for a lumber room," Alan was saying. "Some of Giles's childish playthings, and—look here, a monk's outfit . . ."

Roz turned her head and suppressed a gasp. Swaying slightly on a peg right next to her was a dusty-looking, brown monk's habit. It resembled a hanging corpse.

And then, quite clearly, they heard the sound of scraping, a thud, and the sound of someone walking overhead.

"All right." Quickly, he crossed over and tried the door. It held fast. "This one really is locked, probably from the other side," Alan said as he jiggled the latch.

They looked at each other speculatively. Then Alan stood back and aimed a heavy kick at the door. The wood splintered into toothpicks, leaving the latch hanging loose from the door jamb.

"I've always wanted to do that," he remarked, and moved past the ruined door into the space beyond. He turned all around, a surprised look on his face. "Why, these are Elsie's digs," he said.

Roz said nothing. She had walked directly over to where a stairway emerged from the floor, spiraled upward, and ended against a flat wooden door. There was no stairway going down. Not anymore. The only way in was either the way they had come, or through Elsie's rooms.

She ran lightly up the stair, with Alan at her heels. From the other side of the door she heard the sound of heavy objects striking the floor, then footsteps. The rattle of metal on metal, then a slamming door.

"Giles's key," Roz whispered. "I left it inside. Now they've got it."

"Must have heard me smash the door in. Well, that's torn it." Alan braced his back against the wall of the stair, put one leg up, and heaved. The door scraped, groaned, and sprung open. They stood in the doorway, looking at the Viola Room.

Before Roz's eyes the scene tilted, swerved, then righted itself. The room was a total wreck. A jumbled pile of books blocked their path like fallen brick. Alan leapt over it, skidded across the piles of papers, and flung himself through the open doorway and toward the stairs, calling over his shoulder, "Back in a sec." And he was gone, like a terrier down a rabbit hole.

Roz moved through the center of the room, kicking away a pile of letters leaning against her overturned chair. She picked the chair up, sat down on it, and surveyed the room.

The place was a shambles. Boxes of papers were overturned, papers strewn everywhere, the whole floor carpeted with letters and pages, layer upon layer, like the litter of petals in the ruined Rose Garden. Empty manila folders stood like little peaked roofs blown off in a hurricane. Roz looked behind her to where they had broken in. An empty bookcase slanted outward on the open door, its books thrown into a heap on the floor. The door had been behind the bookcase all the time. Why hadn't Giles told her? A secret entrance. She should have guessed. She sighed wearily and gazed around at the ruin of days and days of work. Every folder, with the letters dated, collated, arranged, and filed, was empty. She glanced at her typewriter, wondering why whoever it was hadn't hurled that to the floor, as well.

There was a half-sheet of paper just barely showing above the carriage. She leaned forward.

And there neatly typed in block letters were the words:

YOU'RE NEXT

Roz stood up abruptly, knocking the chair over, and was nearly overcome by a wave of dizziness. She stood still until the dizziness passed, then carefully righted the chair, picked up the note by one corner, and started down the stairs, where Alan found her moments later, sitting on the bottom step, staring at the piece of paper as if in a trance.

"What's that?"

"I found it on my desk, in the typewriter."

He looked at it quickly, then sat down and put his arm around her, pulling her face against his chest. "Now are you convinced of what they're after?"

"The papers, and Giles." Roz hesitated. "And me." She looked up. "Did you see anyone?"

"Of course not. Whoever it was had long gone. I even went back through the other way, as far as the door into Elsie's apartment. Then I came back, locking everything on *your* side. These keys fit, by the way, except for the last two doors, of course. They're both a dead loss, I'm afraid." He handed the keys to her.

"What next?" Roz murmured, as much to herself as to Alan.

"I don't know," Alan answered thoughtfully. "But this nifty little warning, and the papers strewn all over, gives us a rough idea, don't you think? Whoever it is is wild to know what's in them. That's hardly a surprise; no one could ever tell if you'd found anything shocking just from looking at you, with that elfin poker face of yours. No, it looks as though we've interrupted a frantic search . . . which is odd, considering whoever it was probably had

168

most of the day and half the night." He paused, looked at her speculatively. "And there's something else odd here. If, as you say, there's nothing in the papers, why isn't the person reassured? Why the new threat?"

Roz said nothing. But she knew. The gaps. The searcher had found out there were letters missing, diaries with pages cut out. What they were looking for wasn't here. But she couldn't tell Alan that. Meanwhile, he was still watching her, waiting. After a while he went on.

"And why haven't they approached you, tried to enlist your sympathy, your help? At least it would be worth a try."

"They have," said Roz. "I'm to have tea with Florence tomorrow at four. To discuss something of importance. That was in the envelope you found on the floor of the Refectory."

"Hmm," said Alan. "That makes the warning even more peculiar. Hardly what you'd call a coordinated effort."

"You do think it's more than one person? They could make better use of their time if they got together. Not to mention mine," she said irritably. "I wonder what Giles will have to say about this."

"I can imagine. But never mind that now." Alan straightened up alongside her and shrugged his jacket back into place. "The first thing to do is block up that blasted trick door, and the next is to get all the locks changed. Our friend has obviously achieved the run of the place, but we don't have to make it easy for him. Or them."

"I'm going to clear up as much as I can tonight," Roz announced.

"I'm coming, too."

Roz studied Alan's face, reluctantly acknowledging the thought she had been suppressing for some time. What if Alan were in it, too? After all, who had seen to it she was safely off the premises this long while? What if this really were a conspiracy of the whole group to find out what was in the papers and to stop publication, in whatever ways might work? Behind Alan's quiet reserve, that sense she had of his keeping something back, could it be that he, too, was using her? Not only to gain access to the papers, but to find out how much she knew about what was in them? She was glad she had told him so little.

"You can't do it all yourself. Besides, I like even less, now, the idea of your being alone."

She stood uncertainly on the narrow step. As she watched Alan's face, his brow suddenly contracted. He looked away momentarily, then back, straight into her eyes. A mildly reproachful expression crossed his face. He knew that she suspected him. Then, with a slight shrug, he stuffed his hands in his pockets, still watching her with that level gaze of his.

"It's up to you, Roz," he said finally. "I can't make you trust me, if you don't already. But I'm here. And in spite of what you might think, I won't let anything happen to you."

Roz shut her eyes. She felt guilty and ashamed. Alan, of all people. Alan—thoughtful, calm, matter-of-fact Alan, who had run to her rescue, buoyed her spirits, reassured and comforted her. Alan, whose direct glance and warm physical presence were a constant distraction. No. It was the atmosphere of this place seeping in, corrupting her willingness to believe that everyone acted from the best of motives. She made an instantaneous decision.

"Come on, then."

And together they climbed the stairs to the Viola Room.

17

AS THEY WORKED TOGETHER FAR INTO THE night, straightening, picking up, sorting, refiling, Roz felt soothed and comforted, not just by Alan's presence, but by the work itself. They talked on and off, kneeling next to one another or crawling around in the litter of paper. At first, Alan had a number of questions about her methods of organization, how she had worked so far, but as they filed more and more letters—Roz had penciled in numbers when she was sure the sequence was complete—Alan grew quiet, even absorbed and thoughtful. Watching him, Roz could see he was not reading the letters; he worked too fast, and seemed to be a million miles away. She wondered what had made him so silent, and somewhat guiltily hoped it wasn't his feeling that she hadn't trusted him completely.

Tactfully, he had asked no questions about the letters themselves beyond the occasional "Where does this lot go?" Roz was grateful for that. After all, the intruder could still, objectively speaking, be any of them. But was that really true? She paused for a moment, sat back, and reflected. It had to be someone Viola knew and might have written to or about, not just once or twice, but over a period of time—and that time had to include several months of the year 1943, as well as the period 1965–1975. This ought to let Alan out, she reasoned, since he had come to the Abbey only a year or so ago and had not known Viola personally at all. Or so he said. But then, how many people who figured in the letters one way or another were, in fact, residents of the Abbey? Why not a good friend, a neighbor, or—and here was the reasoning behind her uncertainty about Alan—the son or nephew of a person perhaps long dead, but whose memory was green in his or her descendants? A chill ran up her back. Could this be what Alan was keeping from her? Still, he seemed so detached and unconcerned; why wouldn't he tell her? Because he knew it would compromise his position as detached observer and confidant? And that's what he wanted and needed to be, to find out . . .

Roz sighed. As much as she hated to admit it, she was justified in not taking him completely into her confidence. There was nothing she could do for the moment but keep her own counsel. And wait until Giles recovered so that she could tackle him. Reluctantly, she turned back to the papers.

She looked around the room. The mess was now almost completely cleared up, thanks to Alan's assiduousness. As far as Roz could tell, nothing was missing that hadn't been before, which made her suspect that the intruder had done little more than rummage around in the correspondence, write the warning, and hurl the books and files around more for effect than anything else. *And it had had its effect,* she thought, as she remembered the waves of dizziness that had momentarily overcome her when she read the warning.

YOU'RE NEXT. You, too, thought Roz. Throwing the room into chaos was evidence of growing anger, growing desperation, of someone getting closer to the breaking point, closer to irreversible and murderous violence, and suggested that anger and despair might at any moment overcome the methodical intelligence that had so far restrained the impulse to do anything and everything necessary to stop Giles from publishing the papers. There had been plenty of time for a leisurely, systematic, and unobtrusive search that would have left no trace. But the wreckage and the warning together suggested that if the person were pushed, sooner or later there would be a fatal incident. A chill came over Roz, and she tried to push the thought aside. Human beings—unlike plants—don't come back from the roots.

Still, why didn't the intruder destroy all the papers? she wondered. That would make the gesture more emphatic, and certainly more obstructive. It would hold her and Giles up for days, while they had new copies made. She sat on the floor, chin on hand, puzzling over it all, humming absently to herself. She had put a name to the shadowy figure, she realized suddenly. It all fit. Motive, opportunity, intelligence, expertise, and yes, restraint. It had to be Hugh.

She was startled by a snort of laughter from the other side of the room. She looked over at Alan. He was perched on the edge of Giles's desk, grinning at her.

"It doesn't necessarily have to be Hugh, you know," he said.

Roz's jaw dropped. "How did you know I was thinking that?"

"You've been muttering to yourself for quite some time, completely oblivious of my presence," he answered cheerfully, "and just now you were humming 'It had to be you, it had to be you.' Much as I might wish otherwise, I did not take the referent to be me. Really, Roz," he went on in mock reproach, "what a frightful pun." He paused. "But seriously, why didn't whoever it was just destroy the papers and be done with it?"

Roz thought for a moment. "Because they're just copies, of course," she answered finally. "What's the use of destroying the photograph if the negatives are still in the blackmailer's pocket? One of them might conceivably drive along to Duke's and say, 'Please might I see Mama's letters to Lady V,' but they'd never get permission to read so much as a line of Viola's, much less the whole collection. So why bother?

173

It will hold us up, but not for long. No, I think whoever it is hasn't eliminated the possibility that what he's looking for may still be here somewhere. And it's still easier to get at here than anywhere else. But I think it also means he doesn't know exactly where the danger lies, that it's just not all that cut and dried. He's afraid the papers will tell something awful, but he doesn't know just what, or where. Destroying the papers would only attract attention, give Giles more publicity to go on with and accomplish absolutely nothing."

Alan nodded. "So whoever it is is obviously not willing to risk everything—particularly public scrutiny—to keep you and Giles from going on until he *does* know. He doesn't want to be his own unwitting agent of the terrible revelation. I think that's the real reason he flung it all about so—to confuse you."

"So it wasn't just rage after all. It was much more calculated than that," Roz murmured.

"But that doesn't mean you can let down your guard," Alan replied. "As I said before, it could be anybody. Or everybody. Even me. You've got to go on thinking that for your own protection. For that matter, it could even be Giles himself. The symptoms of allothane poisoning are fairly easy to fake. Cross your eyes, stagger a bit, and slur your speech." Briefly, he assumed the demeanor of a drunken scarecrow. Roz laughed in spite of herself. "But never mind that now." He paused for a moment, gazing at her thoughtfully. "I don't expect you to believe me, but I'm not really involved. Though you of all people must admit I hardly had the opportunity to do this little lot."

Roz stared at him in mute apology. He grinned.

"If you'd spent more time keeping track of me instead of muttering to yourself while you sorted and filed like a bibliographical sorcerer's apprentice you'd have seen that I hardly even looked at the let-

174

ters themselves. Just the names and dates. Other people's mail bores me silly."

"Oh Alan. I'm sorry." She had a sudden impulse to tell him everything, the gaps, her doubts, her confusion. But she couldn't. Not yet.

Alan unpropped himself from Giles's desk, stretched, and yawned.

"Think nothing of it. But see here. I've had enough of this, and we've cleared up—or you have—quite a bit. Let's quit. You look all in."

"What time is it?"

Alan pulled out a large gold pocket watch. "Past two," he said.

Roz gestured limply in the direction of the bookcase behind which the secret entrance was once more hidden. "I don't suppose there's much point in locking up. Obviously they've got the key . . ." She stopped, suddenly recalling a fragment of overheard conversation. "I've got the key," Francesca had said to Florence. So Alan was right. It hadn't necessarily been Hugh.

"We can lug a few file cabinets in front of it, if you like," Alan was saying. "Make it a bit more difficult, anyway. Or . . ."

Roz looked dubiously at him.

"We could interpose our bodies between the intruder and the stairs. I'd volunteer, but since you are not sure even of me, that would not entirely suit. We could, seriously, lug mattresses out here and bed down on the premises. That way you could guard the papers, and I could guard you, which you, in your single-minded devotion to these orts, scraps, and fragments, seem to have forgotten the necessity of. Or, putting it another way, you could watch me while I guard the papers. But the question remains, how will we get any sleep, which is the second necessity that seems to have slipped your mind. Tie strings to our toes? Take turns? Stack ourselves on the steps like kippers in a pan and keep rearranging?"

175

Roz laughed, in spite of herself. Then she grew serious. "What's the point? As you said, whoever it is can get at the papers anytime they want. Why not just let them go ahead as a . . . a gesture of good faith?" *But what kind of good faith would it be,* she thought, *if the papers they want aren't even there?*

"You've put in a lot of work. Why let it all be undone again, if you can help it?"

"Oh, I don't know." Roz turned away and walked toward the door. "I just don't understand what would be so important to anyone that they would take such chances, make such elaborate schemes to make sure it wasn't revealed. It implies such a torment, such uncertainty. It makes me wonder if the project is worth it, if it's right to go on with this if even the thought of publication could cause such pain." In her mind she saw once more the appalled and horrified faces of the guests at Giles's luncheon. Florence's look of anguish. Hugh's pleading. Elsie. She shut her eyes, but the faces stayed.

"Aha, but that's not your responsibility, is it? You've got a job you were hired to do, and beyond that, it's your profession. Besides, we all choose our own obsessions, don't we? Whatever it is, it's in the past, and for the life of me I can't think what difference a few more letters are going to make to anyone. Let the dead past bury its dead."

"That's the mystery, isn't it?" Roz said. "No one ever does let the past alone. Sometimes I think we spend more time living in and taking care of the past than we do the present. Feeling, always, that the present can take care of itself, I suppose." She sighed. "But you're right. We just go round and round. Thank you so much for . . ."

She turned to face Alan and found him unexpectedly close. Before she could say anything, he reached out and pulled her to him. The Viola Room faded, and she was aware only of his mouth on hers, warm and searching, and the firm body so taut and muscular under those rumpled, disreputable, baggy clothes, the faint odor of turpentine . . . She slid her arms around his back underneath his jacket, felt the warmth of his skin under her hands. The papers, Giles, Hugh, all of it, dissolved in smoke.

Some time later Alan released his hold slightly and stood back, looking down at her. "That's another thing I've wanted to do for a long time—possibly forever," he said breathlessly. He gazed at her for a moment, then hugged her to him briefly and let her go, one hand still resting lightly on her shoulder.

"Now look here, fair Rosamund, I know you are very brave and self-reliant, but, simply put, neither because of this"—he bent and kissed her again, gently this time—"nor in spite of it, am I letting you stay alone tonight."

He stopped her from speaking with a finger on her lips. "Never mind, this is not what you think . . . at least, not yet. I'm spending the night in one of Giles's spare rooms. It's all right; don't look so bewildered! You really do need the sleep, and I know you have a great deal on your mind. After all, Giles is coming home bright and early tomorrow—in about six hours, actually—so you'll have him *and* the papers to contend with."

Roz gazed up at him, limp and confused. She did not know what she wanted. She still could feel the pressure of Alan's mouth on hers, the straight, firm length of his body.

She opened her mouth to protest. To her embarrassment she yawned right in his face. Alan hugged her to him, laughing.

"It's all right," he said. "You remind me of the girl in the fairy tale, having to spin roomfuls of straw into gold. But I'm not Rumplestiltskin, Roz. You have nothing to fear from me. Not ever." He looked at her for a moment. "Still, I want you to lock yourself in tonight. That way, when I go to fetch Giles, I won't have to worry about waking you up." He moved to the door and held it open. "But . . ." he

177

added enigmatically, "after tomorrow, you'll have to shift for yourself."

Giles, Roz thought. *Giles home tomorrow.* And that reminded her of something Alan had said earlier about Giles and the insecticide. As she walked toward the door, she murmured, "It can't be Giles, Alan. Why would he sabotage his own project? It doesn't make any sense."

"Search me." Alan shrugged. "Publicity, greater sales, scandal and violence, threats of repression. Sheer perversity. Or . . ." He looked down at her. "Maybe the whole project is nothing but an elaborate hoax. Wouldn't that be a surprise? Complete with bogus letters."

Roz stared at him, appalled.

"I admit it is a bit far-fetched, and for the life of me I can't imagine why Giles would bother. Still, the Montfort malefactor does not have a corner on Byzantine imaginings. You and I don't do badly ourselves. But listen here. I'm sorry I brought it up." He put a hand on her shoulder and gently propelled her down the stairs, followed her out, and slammed the door shut behind them. "Maybe we should have gone the other way. It's closer, and we wouldn't have had to go outside. I expect that was the original idea of whoever made the passage through. A private entrance, hidden from the public eye. An escape hatch, in fact. Are you going to lock up, after all, or wish the culprit joy of it?"

Roz locked the door and pocketed the keys. "Right now I don't care. But I have a feeling there'll be no more fishing around in the papers. What they need to know isn't there."

"I thought that might be the case. But it does exist? Somewhere?"

Now. Tell him. Tell him about the missing papers; take him into your trust completely. But once more she found herself instinctively, perversely holding back. She would tell him when she knew for sure, after she had talked to Giles. It didn't mean she didn't trust him. She ducked her head, unable to meet his eyes. "I don't know," she said. After all, it was the truth.

Alan smiled and draped one arm lightly across her shoulders. "I thought so. Giles said at lunch that the letters went to 1975. But there weren't any after 1965. So either he lied, or they are somewhere else." Roz turned to him, not sure whether to be upset or grateful that he knew. But she said nothing, only tucked her shoulder under his arm as they walked wearily down the stairs and across the Courtyard toward the Refectory—a long, dark shape with its lights still burning through the windows, shadowless and faceless—into the night.

18

ROZ WOKE THE NEXT MORNING AT A LITTLE AFter nine. She unlocked her door and went downstairs to the kitchen. There was a note from Alan propped against the sugar bowl. "Locksmith laid on for this afternoon. Hospital called, gone to get Giles. Take care. Love, Alan." She smiled as she folded the note and tucked it in her pocket.

The signs of Mrs. Farthing's presence were few but unmistakable—the uneven brick floor meticulously swept, even between the cracks, the cereal boxes lined up with their edges flush, the dishes and glasses put away in their cupboards. Roz pondered what Alan had told her about Giles's disgust at Elsie's deformity and the fact that she was Florence North's sister. Somehow Mrs. Farthing was involved in all this; her living quarters on the other side gave access to the blocked-up staircase that led to the Tower Room and to the other room over the gate. Whoever had been in with the papers had come through her apartment. Francesca? Elsie herself? But they both seemed to be on the periphery of things, with Francesca hardly in evidence since Roz had last seen her with Florence. There was only that barely overheard conversation to go on. And Elsie, so silent, so inconspicuous; who could say what corners she had been around, what conversations she had overheard?

Roz ate breakfast, then hurried across the Courtyard to the Tower Room to do as much as she could before Giles's return. She left the door to the Tower stair open so that she could hear what was going on below.

She had been at work about an hour when she heard a car pull up, various scufflings and slammings and scraps of talk, Alan's low, cheerful rumble and Giles's rather abrupt-sounding replies. She came down the stairs and through the arch just in time to see Alan supporting Giles's elbow as they disappeared through the door of the Refectory.

She followed them inside, upstairs, and stood in the doorway of Giles's room. Giles was seated on the edge of his bed looking pale and peaked, though his eyelids were evenly droopy, and his speech, if wan and feeble, was only mildly slurred.

"Oh, Rosamund," he said, looking up. "How nice to see you. Alan's just been telling me about the latest beastliness. How awful for you."

Alan came out of the bathroom, where he had deposited Giles's hospital belongings. He barely nodded at Roz. "I'll go along now," he said to Giles. "Roz can see that you have what you need." And without a word, he started for the door. Roz looked at him curiously. But as he passed by, he jostled her slightly more than was absolutely necessary by way

180

of greeting. Then he was gone. As he had said last night, she could shift for herself.

"It's much too dark in here," she said briskly as she moved across the room to fling back the heavy curtains that covered the windows on the Courtyard side. She glanced quickly at the tapestry covering the end wall. It looked undisturbed. Giles had swung his feet up and lay full-length on top of the covers, his hands behind his neck, staring at the ceiling. Roz sat down facing Giles in the knobby Jacobean chair near the bed. Her back was to the tapestry. She shifted uneasily. What if someone were listening?

"Yes, well, where are we now?" Giles said with an attempt at brightness. He seemed weary and strained. But beneath the languor Roz sensed something else, a restlessness, an excitement, an eagerness just barely repressed by his apparent limpness. She tried to dismiss the feeling, but Giles's eyes behind their half-closed lids glittered at her almost feverishly, and she found herself fidgeting in her chair. With an effort, she sat back and imitated Giles's quasi-relaxed pose of hands behind head so that she, too, could look at the ceiling instead of at him. The knobs poked her between the shoulder blades; she was not going to be able to keep this up for long. But she had made up her mind what to do next.

"I've been cleaning up the mess in the Viola Room, and I'm nearly done. Since I had catalogued most of the stuff already, it wasn't difficult for me to remember what went where. I've got it all pretty much in my head, anyway. I can go on as I have been by myself, if that's all right with you. Then when you feel up to it, we can go on together. Is that all right?"

"Perfectly," Giles said.

They both gazed at the ceiling for a while. Finally Roz sat forward, hands on her knees, fixed her eyes on Giles's averted face, and spoke.

"Giles, I really must talk to you about the situation here."

181

Slowly, Giles lowered his head. "Yes, of course, my dear."

She took a deep breath and began.

"I suppose the central question is, who wants to stop the publication of your mother's papers enough to wreck the garden, spray you with bug killer, threaten me, and go through the papers like a runaway windmill? It's clear enough that someone around here thinks there is something in those papers that will ruin his or somebody else's life. That's the why. But it doesn't answer what, or who. Or how we stop them."

"You sound exactly like a journalist. Who what why how. Oh yes, and when. You left that out."

"Giles," Roz said. "I know that there is absolutely nothing in the papers up in the Viola Room that could remotely be construed as harmful to anyone. So whatever it is must be in the ones that are missing."

Giles blinked once, then stared at her. She stared right back. "What's in those papers, Giles? You've read them all. What is the intolerably shocking revelation everyone's so worried about?"

"Why, Rosamund," he said in a surprised tone, "would I keep that from you?"

"Of course," she said simply. "You've kept the missing letters and diaries from me."

Giles did not reply.

"I want to see them now," she said. "I have to know what's in them, or I can't work." Roz held her breath. He could just dismiss her, here and now, and that would be the end of it. But things had gone far enough. She could not go on without knowing everything there was to know. She waited tensely for Giles's reaction.

"Well, my dear girl," he drawled, "it's all relative, isn't it?" He paused, giving the impression of deep consideration. "What is perfectly acceptable to someone like you or me might loom as some terrible transgression to, say, Elsie Farthing, or . . . or . . ." He paused again, as though he were searching for a name he could mention without giving everything away. "Or vice versa," he finished. "I really can't say."

Or won't, Roz added silently. Aloud she said, "I want you to show me the missing letters. Let me be the judge. If whoever it is won't believe you, perhaps they'll believe me. After all, I'm not really involved. We could even show them the letters in question to set their minds at ease. We can't go on like this, you know. It isn't professional, or even fair."

"Ah," said Giles, "fair. My dear Roz. You never expected anything like this, did you?"

He had never called her Roz before. And he sounded so sympathetic, so sincere.

"Giles, can't we just tell everyone there's nothing to worry about, and put an end to all this intrigue?"

There was a long silence while they stared at each other. Then Giles said, "No, I'm afraid we can't."

"Why not?"

"Because it would not be true. The missing papers are, in fact, terribly, frightfully shocking. That's one of the reasons I've kept them back even from you. I haven't been entirely sure what to do."

Giles sat up, arms around his knees, and regarded her with a concerned look in his face. "But look here," he said, "we can still do what you say. In a few days—when I'm feeling up to it—we'll have everyone in and announce that no one has anything to fear. Be reassuring. Then we'll have no more trouble—we can go on and keep to the terms of the contract."

Roz stared at him in disappointment. What he was proposing was an outright lie. She stood up.

"I can't do that, or let you do it. It isn't right. We have to bring everything out in the open—perhaps meet with the people who are involved. If the papers concern them, then they have a right to know what's there. And a say in what is done about publishing them. It's only just. And if you want me to go on with this . . ."

183

She paused, waiting for the words that would send her on her way. *Good-bye Giles, good-bye letters. Good-bye Alan.*

"All right," Giels said unexpectedly. "We'll try it your way. Of course you must go on." He paused. "I need your help now more than ever."

Roz stared at him, taken aback at the ease and swiftness of her victory. He was going to show her the papers just like that, and he was also going to agree to bring everything out into the open? She felt a sudden sense of exhilaration. She could hardly believe it. Giles needed her to stay on and do the papers; that was her trump card. Somehow she had become indispensable. And she felt at last as though she were close to finding out the whole truth. Only one more thing remained. She threw caution to the winds.

"I'd like to see the letters right away. And the diary entries. So we can get this cleared up as soon as possible."

Giles lay back on the pillows, breathing shallowly. "Yes, yes, of course. But I'm rather tired now; can it wait until this afternoon?" he said wearily.

"All right . . . no, wait. I'm supposed to have tea with Florence this afternoon. She sent me a note yesterday, saying it was urgent. What shall I tell her?"

"Florence?" Giles blinked his eyes. "Florence. Oh dear. I can't think. You must go, of course. Just let her talk—be reassuring, but tell her nothing, not until you've gone over the papers and we talk about what to do." Giles lifted his head, caught her eyes, and held them. "Promise me not to say a word to her, nor anyone else. Not yet." He sighed. "I'm very tired. Can't we leave it until tomorrow?"

"Of course." It was a small enough thing, now that she had almost everything she had asked for. She felt a bursting sense of her own power. Poor Giles. His pallor, his almost feverish look filled her with pity. "Well, that's that, then. I'm going back to the Viola Room. We can go over the papers after I have

184

tea with Florence. There's no hurry, really, now that we've agreed," she said gently. She smiled at him and turned to go. "See you later."

Giles nodded sleepily, then abruptly blinked his eyes open again. "I say, what time is your tea with Florence?"

"Four," she said over her shoulder. "Tea time."

"Of course," Giles said, closing his eyes. "Silly of me. Well, if you see anyone, tell them I don't want to be disturbed." He yawned. "Thanks ever so much."

Roz smiled again, waved, and went out of the room, pulling the door closed behind her.

Going across the Courtyard she met no one, which was just as well, since she would have been hard put to deny any of them the reassuring knowledge that things were going to be different now. It was going to be all right. And then she realized with a little pang that Giles had not said he wouldn't publish the papers in question, only that he would bring everything out in the open. Her reassurance might be false. She could not in good conscience say anything just yet. But it wouldn't be long.

As she settled down to work, she found herself speculating about what the missing papers contained, and how they would alter the picture she had in her mind of life at Montfort, of Viola, her laughing, wise, generous, kind presence spreading over all, informing everyone and everything with her own happy celebration of life and growth and freedom. But soon the other letters recaptured her attention, as they inevitably did. When she looked up some time later at the small alarm clock she had set on her desk, she saw that it was nearly four.

"Oh, do come in, come in. I'm so glad you were able to come," Florence said nervously, opening the door wide and standing back to let Roz inside. From somewhere close by came the crash of piano music, some sort of finale. Almost at once the music started again. Florence turned and beckoned her to follow,

185

finger to her lips, a small, tidy, fluttering presence, smelling faintly of lavender, one shoulder slightly raised to squeeze by Roz's taller figure. *Why, she looks exactly like Elsie Farthing,* Roz thought. *I should have known they were sisters.*

"Cedric's practicing," Florence said in a low voice. "I told him I didn't want him to have tea with us. We're nearly always together, and really, there are times . . ." She glanced wryly upward at Roz, then ducked her head sideways like a little bird. "Just ladies' talk, I said. I hope you don't mind." She led Roz into the sitting room.

The room was tastefully done in shades of celadon and gold. It looked rather new, and extremely tidy. The long windows in the west wall overlooking the Courtyard reflected sunlight upward onto the walls and ceiling so that the whole room had a golden aura, a warm, subdued but sunny look that contrasted, at least for the moment, with Florence's ghostly pallor. She was rubbing her hands together as though to warm them, and blinking her eyes. But then, she had not been particularly calm the other times Roz had seen her; perhaps this was just the way she was. She wondered if Florence knew about Giles's accident.

"Isn't it unfortunate about Giles? How is he?" Florence said as she sat down in the middle of a gold velvet Chippendale couch. In front of her was a large mahogany butler's tray full of tea things: thin, buttered slices of bread with the crusts cut off, cucumber slices, little cakes, sugar and creamer of plain Georgian silver, a tall, urn-shaped teapot, and a hot water jug. A full set, prominently monogramed FFN. Everything looked very nice, but not particularly substantial, and Roz found herself regretting that she had skipped lunch.

"Hugh called me this morning. I felt sure you wouldn't come, but I'm so glad . . . Hugh said he would be all right, though. Giles, that is."

Rox watched Florence's hands hovering indecisively over the tea tray. She wondered how Hugh had known that.

"He's all right, yes. In fact, he's back home. It wasn't nearly as bad as it could have been."

Florence sighed. With trembling fingers, she picked up the teapot and began to pour. "So many things happening lately, terrible things. This used to be such a peaceful place, in L . . . in Viola's time. Just Norths and Badgetts and Viola and Sir Herbert—Giles was at school, and then the service—but now, everything is so different. Oh dear." Florence looked down. A stream of plain hot water was pouring out of the teapot. Florence lifted up the lid and peered inside. "Oh, how silly of me. I've forgotten the tea."

She stood up quickly, beet-red and flustered. "Cedric made me give it up—bad for my nerves, he said, but I thought . . . a special occasion, company . . . Oh dear. I won't be a minute," she said as she hurried out.

Roz reached forward and picked up a cucumber sandwich so delicately cut she almost hated to bite into it. Then she stood up and began to move around the room, looking at the various objects that decorated it.

The whole north wall consisted of floor-to-ceiling bookshelves, filled partly with books and partly with trophies—silver presentation pieces, obviously prizes and gifts from Cedric's illustrious career. Shells, a bust of Chopin done in powdery-soft plaster, and a large, gold medallion in a black velvet case. But it was the last bookshelf that arrested Roz's attention; it held what must have been a fairly comprehensive collection of family photographs and enlarged snapshots. She walked toward them.

The music was louder here. The door was ajar and down the hall through another partly open door she could just see Cedric, his white hair flailing his forehead, his hands almost a blur on the keys, playing a baroque piece Roz recognized as by Scarlatti, very

rapid and complex. He was in a state of complete concentration, and she marveled at the strength and energy still possessed by his eighty-odd-year-old body.
She wondered how old Florence was. No more than
seventy, at a guess.

Roz moved quietly past the doorway to the bookcase and began to study the snapshots. More frozen
moments, these perhaps even more transfixed than
diaries or letters, but equally revealing. She looked
at the lower shelf.

Cedric and Florence, smiling, squinting in the
sun, ruins in the background. Gentlefolk in white
duck t˙ousers and lawn dresses, somewhere sub-
tropic, ˙lmost desertlike—probably Greece. A younger, still-smiling Cedric and another woman, tall,
angular, aristocratic, haughty. Florence, quite
young, an early forties pompadour and wide shoulders, with a rather dour-looking man and two blond
boys kneeling in front of her. Roz looked more
closely; this had to be Florence in her days as a
Badgett, the farmer and the farmer's wife. And the
farmer's son—one of the children had to be Hugh.
She peered more closely at the larger boy and
thought she discerned the lineaments of Hugh's
adult face, though this boy was relaxed and smiling.
How sad that life had changed so for him. And the
other child? A friend? Younger, too much so for
friendship, hardly more than a toddler, really. The
face looked vaguely familiar.

Roz stood looking thoughtfully at the photograph.
Had there been another child, some old tragedy of
loss no one had ever mentioned that might explain
the peculiarly sad look of Florence's face in repose,
her habitual anxiety and apparent lack of a firm grip
on daily life?

Roz moved up to the next row of pictures. A tiny
Cedric, birdlike in tails, seen from above seated at an
enormous grand piano, center stage in a great pil-
lared hall. Albert? Carnegie? Florence in the garden
with a grown-up Hugh and a woman—Beatrice, in

fact, though hardly recognizable without the scowl. She peered above at the next shelf, standing on tip-toe. A large cabinet photograph lay face down on the shelf, barely visible. Evidently it had fallen over some time ago; it was covered with dust. Roz took it down and recognized a portrait of the same little blond boy, grown larger, older, broad of face, quite handsome, even gay. She was just moving closer to the light to study it when she heard Florence come back in. She turned around.

Florence was standing by the couch, a distracted look on her face, dangling two bedraggled-looking tea bags from her hand. Without looking at Roz, she sat down in front of the tea tray, looked first at one bag, then the other, then plopped them both into the teapot. They plumped up immediately into little fat pillows, floating on the water.

"This is all I could find—isn't it odd?" she twittered as she stared intently at the bags. "I thought I had some loose tea left, but it's gone, and these were just lying out on the shelf. They look a little the worse for wear. I am sorry. Oh well, no matter," she chattered on. An odor of rotting leaves wafted through the room.

"As I was saying," Florence went on rapidly, her attention fixed on the tea she was pouring out, "things have changed so drastically in the last . . ." She looked up brightly and caught sight of Roz standing in front of the bookcase with the photo-graph in her hand. Her face turned dead white, and her mouth went slack.

"Oh. Oh my," she gasped. The tea tray rattled against her knees. "Whatever are you doing there?" Florence gagged, coughed, and quickly reached down, snatching up one of the cups and gulping down a huge mouthful of tea. Then, carefully, she put the teacup down, folded her hands tightly, and smiled apologetically at Roz. "I didn't mean to be rude. You startled me, standing in the shadows over there. Do come back and sit down. Those are just some old

189

snapshots—family things. I don't know why I even keep them out. So boring." She laughed nervously, then picked up the cup and swallowed the rest of the tea.

Roz set the photograph down and crossed back to her chair. Meanwhile, Cedric had started on the theme from Haydn's "Surprise" symphony. Thump-thump, thump-thump, thump-thump. Crash! Florence jumped. She rose shakily and closed the door, then sat down again and poured out another steaming cup of pale, greenish-brown tea. "I really don't want Cedric to know anything about this." She handed Roz her cup of tea. "Sugar? Cream?"

"No, thank you." Roz took a tiny sip of the boiling hot tea, and put the teacup down on the small side table next to her chair, her tongue scalded. Florence picked up the second cup of tea, still steaming, and drank it down thirstily. *She must have a gullet like a copper boiler,* Roz thought, watching her. *No wonder Cedric had made her stop. She was practically an addict.*

"My goodness, I'm thirsty," Florence said, looking oddly at her empty teacup. She licked her lips. "Well, where were we?" She cleared her throat. "There are letters—at least I think there are letters . . ." She paused, looking everywhere in the room but at Roz. ". . . . Letters from Viola to my ah . . . first husband, and . . . to others in my family . . ." Again Florence paused, seemed to swallow with difficulty, and, impossibly, poured herself another cup of tea.

Roz watched sympathetically, waiting for Florence to go on, wanting to hear her side of things. But Florence only sat looking quizzically at Roz, drinking her third cup of tea. If tea was courage, Florence was giving herself quite a jolt. Roz lifted her cup and sniffed it. She wished she had asked for coffee, even the instant boiled-bugs kind. This stuff smelled like stewed dead weeds. She put her cup down again.

"Giles threatens . . . no, I must try to be objective,

190

Hugh says . . . Giles *says* he is going to publish letters which I believe almost certainly contain an account of an episode very painful to me and the members of my family . . ." She jerked her head in the direction of the now-faint piano music. "And Giles simply refuses to see that it would cause so much pain and disruption . . . even though we've told him over and over . . ."

Her head jerked again, more violently this time, and, as Roz watched her face in horrified fascination, the pupils of her eyes began to jerk back and forth. Florence's mouth dropped open, and her eyes fixed momentarily on a point somewhere beyond Roz's left shoulder.

"Why, hello, dear," she said as though to someone just out of sight.

Roz glanced over her shoulder to see whom Florence was talking to. There was nothing but the wall, and the windows looking out over the Courtyard. " 'Twinkle, twinkle, little bat . . .' " Florence sang in a high, taut voice. Then she began to choke. Roz stared at her with alarm. Florence's eyes were glazed, and her hands—small, well-cared-for, delicate hands, not the rough hands of a farmer's wife—were plucking lightly, rhythmically, at the skirt of her dress, dancing across her knees, so that with the piano music in the background, it looked as though Florence were playing a child's pianoforte on her knees. Then her whole body began to jiggle and rock.

Oh my God, she's having a fit or a stroke, Roz thought as she reached toward Florence, who now appeared to be picking at something she saw next to her on the couch. Her fingers made desperate, scrabbling, chasing motions, her eyes glared, and then, as Roz watched, they crossed and uncrossed. Her face flushed, and she began to pant. Her legs jerked up convulsively, knocking the tea tray to the floor.

Roz stood up and grabbed her by the shoulder. Florence was red-hot, and she writhed in Roz's grasp

191

while the music from the other room seemed to reach an intolerable crescendo. Roz's head buzzed. She had to do something, but she was afraid to let Florence go.

"Help, help!" she shouted. "Mr. North! Somebody. Help!"

The piano music stopped. Cedric's white head appeared in the doorway, curious, his expression mildly annoyed. "Did I hear someone call?"

"Mr. North," Roz said as calmly as she could. "It's your wife. She's having a seizure of some kind. Please call an ambulance." With one hand she tried to grasp Florence's increasingly busy and senselessly picking, searching fingers, tightening the other arm around her shoulders. Florence's eyes rolled back in her head, the lids closing. Roz looked down at her, terrified. "Please call someone right now," she said desperately to Cedric. But Cedric rushed over to the couch, thrust Roz aside, and took the shaking Florence in his arms.

"Florrie, my God! What's wrong, Florrie? Florrie, stop it! Stop it this minute!" he shouted, clutching at her, holding her.

Roz stood up and looked around the room for a telephone, for anything to summon help with. But there was no time.

She stood in the middle of the room for a moment. Then she dashed over to the large windows overlooking the Courtyard, cranked open the bottom casement, and leaned out the window.

The Courtyard was empty, the shuttered buildings blank and strange in the late afternoon sun, the rays shining down obliquely, turning the moist, heavy air into the folds of a veil, smothering, choking. . . . With an odd sense of detachment, thinking, *But I never scream,* Roz took a deep breath, filled her lungs with the heavy, silent air—and screamed.

19

"I CAN'T BELIEVE IT," ROZ SAID, SHAKING HER head. She and Giles were sipping Duff Gordon in the slightly clammy sitting room of the Refectory, Giles sprawled on the couch, Roz perched uneasily in the chair nearest to him. She took a gulp of the sherry; it burned in her throat. She shook her head again, remembering the last hour. As soon as she screamed, the whole Courtyard had seemed to change shape like the scenery in a play, filling with people and the noise of doors slamming, feet running. Alan Stewart had come tearing out of the Moat House barefoot, with such a look of alarm on his face that Roz thought he was going to bolt right up the wall and through the window. When he saw her standing there apparently unharmed, he slid to a halt with a puzzled look.

But then he had taken charge, Nicander standing him in good stead, for it was clear that Florence had been poisoned. Stalks of jimsonweed stripped of their leaves had been found in the Poison Plant Garden. Giles had appeared briefly, declared himself *persona non grata*, and departed. Roz had waited with the rest of them until the ambulance arrived, and then come back alone to the Refectory to find Giles waiting for her with a tray of drinks.

"Why Florence? She seems so harmless," Roz asked.

"Tell me something," Giles answered. "Why didn't you drink the tea?"

Roz glanced quickly at him. The warm sherry hit a

193

cold lump in her stomach. "I don't generally drink tea. It reminds me of old boiled boots. With the feet left in."

"Not even on a social occasion, to please a dear old lady?"

"As a matter of fact I did take one sip, but it smelled disgusting, like stewed compost. And it was scalding hot." Roz stared at Giles, suddenly realizing his implication. Florence, in an irony of ineptitude, had gulped down the poison she had meant for Roz.

"Not Florence," she said in a quiet voice.

"I'm afraid so," Giles said. "It's quite obvious, really. She got the tea bags mixed. Poor Florence. Hoist by her own petard."

"Do you think she'll die?"

"I don't know. I rather expect she might. The next forty-eight hours will tell, I imagine." He reached over and patted her hand. "Come now, Rosamund, my dear. You would have had a better chance. Taller, heavier, younger. Florence is just a bit of a thing. I expect for you it would have been merely sick-making, not fatal. Another warning with teeth, just like mine. Oh Roz, do buck up! You look so pasty white you're worrying me."

Roz closed her eyes. The space inside her head whirled.

"Besides," Giles's voice whined from far away, coming nearer, like a mosquito in the dark, "it's she who stands to lose the most from the publication of the papers, isn't it?"

Roz opened her eyes. There he was, the same old Giles, sipping sherry and looking at her over the rim of the sherry glass tilted to his lips. How could he sound so cool and detached when Florence was in danger of dying?

"I want to see the missing papers," she said. "Now."

Giles blinked, then gazed at her as though he were appraising her resolve. She met his glance evenly.

194

They had agreed. And it was important not to lose any more time.

"All right, then," Giles said. He stood up and put his half-filled glass on the tray. "They're in the Abbot's Chapel, as you may have guessed. Now you know why I spent so much time there. I was going over and over them, trying to decide what to do. Whether the gift to posterity was worth the present distress." He sighed and held out his hand to her. "I suppose I should have told you sooner."

Roz turned away from his outstretched hand to set down her own glass. When she turned around, he was watching her impassively, hands in his pockets. "Shall we go?" he said politely.

Roz nodded.

The garden was quiet as they passed through the Courtyard. Only two parallel tracks of crushed grass across the lawn in front of the Granary reminded them that the ambulance had come and gone, bearing Florence and Cedric away. And who else? Had Alan gone, too?

She followed Giles into the Cloister, past the misshapen columnar lumps of stone that stood up in the field like so many rotting stumps of trees cut down and left to molder, down the long scarred wall into the Porcelain Garden.

The blue and white flowers, the different shapes and textures of foliage were translucent in the sharp rays of light slanting through the trees. But the formal effect of the garden was marred by the rough, weatherbeaten boards nailed every which way across the broken windows of the Chapel. Giles brought out his bunch of keys and unlocked the door, pushing it back for her to enter.

The inside of the chapel, dank and musty from being shut up, was dark, except for the light from the open door. Roz glanced around. Everything seemed so strange. Yet it was all just as she had last seen it.

She walked over to Giles's desk. The typewriter

was there, and a stack of typing paper. Each page was blank. What had Giles been working on when he was overcome? She stared down at the empty typewriter, remembering her desperate struggle to get Giles out of here. Had it been only yesterday? It hardly seemed possible. So much had happened since.

Giles said from behind her, "I'm just going to run upstairs and get the letters. I won't be a moment." Leaving her by the desk, he started up the miniature winding stair into the Chapel belfry. She heard his steps overhead as she stared thoughtfully at the desk.

Of course, everything had been tidied, the glass swept away. Without really thinking, she bent down to see if they'd gotten it all, a legacy of her own often-barefoot childhood wanderings as well as her mother's meticulous housekeeping. You broke a glass, you cleaned it up, every last sliver.

And then she saw, almost hidden under the foot of the desk, a triangle of white paper. She reached under and retrieved not one but two sheets of paper, one an unfinished letter to Giles's publisher, the other apparently blank. She was about to put both of them down on the desk when something about the backing sheet caught her eye. She stared down at the indentations. *That's odd,* she thought.

Just then she heard Giles's footsteps coming down the stairs. Quickly, she folded the blank sheet and put it in her pocket. She placed the partly typed letter on the stack of typing paper and turned just as Giles reappeared, ducking his head as he came down the last few steps. He walked straight over to her, holding out a stack of papers about two inches thick.

"Here," Giles said, "that's the lot. About two hundred letters, and as many diary leaves. Now you can fill in all the gaps and mysteries."

Roz took the stack of papers. They flopped limply in her hands. Of course they, too, were copies, but that didn't matter at this point. It was the story she was after.

"You'll find letters to Florence, to Humphrey Badgett, to Hugh and Fran . . . Francesca. They are, as you say in America, dynamite. They document to the last detail the terrible tragedy of the Badgett family, in which my mother played a small but crucial role." Giles paused, a bemused look on his face.

"Aren't you going to tell me what it is?"

"Shall I?" Giles said, a sudden gleam in his eye. "Or shall you find out for yourself as you go, like a mystery story?" He paused again. "I can't decide which would be more amusing for you."

Roz stared at him, appalled. He was talking about this as though it were a game. It didn't mean a thing to him.

"Giles! Miss Howard! Where are you?"

With a quick glance at Roz, Giles crossed to the door and looked out. Hugh and Francesca were walking toward the Chapel from the direction of the Rose Garden. Hugh was frowning, and Francesca swung along at his side, skirts floating, looking thin-lipped and determined. It was—finally—a delegation.

Giles walked out to meet them. Quietly, Roz followed and stood behind him.

Hugh spoke grimly. "We've just come from the hospital. It's touch and go with Mother. They may have to transfer her to London. Cedric's had a seizure."

"I'm sorry to hear that," Giles said politely.

Francesca stepped forward. "Are you satisfied now, Giles? It's you who've brought it all to this. You and your bloody papers!"

Giles looked at her coldly. "Why, Frankie . . . so sorry, Francesca. But isn't it rather more likely that you are the only begetter of all these revels?"

Francesca shrank back, her throat working, her face pale except for the garish spots of makeup that made her look like a clownish caricature of a woman.

"Giles, Frankie." Hugh tried to step between them. "Please, can't we—"

"Listen, Giles," Francesca said, "I've put up with your Hughie this and Frankie that and Lady Viola the Great all our lives. Well, times have changed."

"Why, Francesca," Giles said slowly, enunciating each syllable. "Whatever do you mean? Haven't we always done our best for you and your family? Don't you want things to go on just as they always have?"

Francesca's mouth pulled taut, and she flushed with anger. Roz shifted the papers onto one arm and stepped forward, but Francesca only went on talking in an ominously quiet voice.

"And now there's Mother, gone and nearly killed herself, all because of your threats. You have no right, no right—" Suddenly Francesca stopped, her mouth twisting, her eyes glittering. "I'm not going to let you get away with it. I have my rights, too. This is the end. I'm going to—"

Giles interrupted. "You can't stop me. I should think you'd have realized that by now," he said coldly. "Viola's life is important."

"Viola's life is over," Hugh said eloquently, hopelessly.

Francesca moved toward Giles, accidentally jostling Roz's arm. The papers slithered out of her grasp onto the ground. Both she and Francesca bent down automatically to pick them up. But Francesca stopped, half bent over, her eyes fixed on the pile of white sheets spread over the ground.

"What in the world are those?"

"They're some letters that Giles had been keeping back. Your letters, in fact. And some to Florence and Humphrey Badgett," Roz said calmly. She, at least, was not going to be evasive. "I'm not sure what's in them yet, but I'm going to find out."

"Letters to me?" Francesca said. "You've seen them? Real letters? In Viola's writing?"

"Some. Others are typed. These are copies of course, but Giles said . . ."

198

"Oh my God," Francesca whispered. She put a trembling hand to her rouged cheek. "But it can't be true. What has he done?" She straightened abruptly.

"It's even worse than we thought," she said to Hugh. She looked wildly from Giles to Hugh to Roz and back again. Then, as Roz and Hugh watched in horror, she drew back her head, sucked in her cheeks, and spat in Giles's face.

"Giles . . . Giles," Hugh said, drawing out a handkerchief and reaching toward Giles, who was standing, face livid, as though he had been turned to stone. "She didn't mean it. Surely we can . . ."

But Giles only slapped Hugh's hand away, and, with a look of supreme disgust, turned and stalked away toward the Cloister lawn. Hugh hurried after him. Roz gathered up the papers and started to follow them.

"No, wait," Francesca said clearly. "I've got to talk to you."

Roz turned and looked at the other woman.

"Meet me tonight, later. When he's gone to bed," Francesca begged. "Please." Her face was beseeching, pathetic, reminiscent of Florence's. What had happened to the proud, defiant Francesca?

"Where?"

Francesca didn't answer. A frightened look came over her face. Roz turned. Giles was walking back toward them with hard, deliberate steps echoing on the marble slabs, wiping his shirt sleeve across his face.

"Get out," he said to Francesca. "Get out of my sight."

There was time only for a word. "The Maze," Francesca whispered.

"All right," Roz whispered back.

Francesca gave Giles one angry, accusing look, then whirled and ran away down the path to the Rose Garden.

"Well," said Giles after a moment. "I'm sorry you

have to be exposed to all this. Clearly a matter of conflicting interests. They're being quite unreasonable, don't you think?"

Roz looked at his face; it was impassive. His voice was controlled, even cold. He didn't care about any of them.

Then, as if nothing had happened, Giles looked at his watch and said, "Past seven-thirty, and I'm famished. Don't suppose Farthing has made us anything to eat."

Casually, he reached toward Roz and detached her arm from its protective position across the papers and tucked it under one of his. "I think we should have something to eat, and then you can settle down with these papers and see what you think. The true story." He paused. "I'm quite counting on your support, you know. I feel we understand each other. I have an obligation now." He looked down at her. "Don't you agree?"

Roz stared at him, utterly speechless.

Smiling, Giles squeezed her arm, and then walked out of the Porcelain Garden in the direction of the Refectory. The great sheaf of words from the past dragged on Roz's arm like so many sheets of lead as she hurried after Giles through the fading light.

Giles hovered. For a man so recently in danger of his life, he seemed remarkably lively, rummaging around in the kitchen for a pick-up supper—Elsie Farthing was not there, for once—while Roz sat on the couch in the sitting room, papers spread out on either side. He popped his head in every few minutes, like a writer awaiting the verdict from his first reader. In the beginning he asked, "How are you coming?" but when he was answered only by increasingly short monosyllables, and finally not at all, he disappeared.

Roz was riveted on the papers, on the story they told. For there it was, the whole dramatic episode. The birth of a second son to Florence and Humphrey

Badgett in 1943, and the transformation, twenty-five years later, after much agonizing on all sides, of that boy into the woman Francesca. Dynamite, indeed. She could see why the Badgetts had wanted it suppressed; it was a lurid and complex tale of a terrible struggle among the poor, uneducated farmers and the worldly, aristocratic lords of the manor, with Frankie as the pawn. Finally, they had, as Florence said, lost her, or, as the case had been then, him.

The evening's work left no doubt in Roz's mind that the beautiful little boy in Florence's picture, the boy Frankie, and the statuesque, decidedly feminine Francesca were one and the same. That, not death, was the tragedy in Florence's face. Viola had paid for the operation, which had taken place in 1968. But in the events leading up to it—arguments with Florence, with Humphrey, with Hugh, threats, cajolings, encouragements, and comforting of Francesca—Viola emerged as reasonable, compassionate, fair, and slightly removed, while the Badgetts emerged as mean-spirited, frightened, narrowly and moralistically rigid, finally telling Francesca never to darken their door again. Only Elsie Farthing had remained loyal, but she was powerless. Nothing Viola said could alter their resolve to have no more to do with the changed Frankie. So of course Viola had taken her in.

Well, thought Roz. *No wonder Giles had thought it would sell books.* But he had hesitated; that showed his instincts were still those of a gentleman. The letters were certainly revelatory of Viola's character, of facets not seen in her books about the garden, in the rather abstract—intellectual but passionless—novels. It was a hitherto-unrevealed Lady Viola—more human, wiser, as well as sympathetic, strong, comforter of the torn, redeemer of the troubled. She was heroic in her efforts to help save the tormented Frankie. *If anything,* Roz thought, *it made her admire Viola more.* The Badgetts were another story. She could see why they would not want this made public; it was not a pretty picture of them, not at all, Frankie/Francesca aside. But it would certainly sell books.

She and Giles ate in the sitting room on trays. Only a faint sniffling from the kitchen, the rattle of pans, indicated the late return of Mrs. Farthing. The poor woman scuttled into the broom closet when Roz brought out her tray. Roz sighed, sorry for the woman who felt so self-conscious of her ugliness and had to bear as well her family's deformity, their shame, what they clearly felt was their degradation. Of course, they were all in it together. As she left the kitchen, Roz wondered briefly why Francesca had now been, if not exactly welcomed, at least taken back into the fold. After all these years, a kind of reconciliation and acceptance? Blood finally thicker than water? United in a common goal to keep the story private? And poor Florence, the most pathetic of all, feeling responsible, obscurely, for the creation of a monster, refusing to accept Viola's repeated assurances that nature sometimes erred, finally refusing to respond at all, retreating into the recesses of the Home Farm. And not emerging until after Humphrey's death in 1969, until her own marriage to Cedric in 1970.

After dinner Roz read on quietly, systematically, letting the story build. Finally Giles, who had been watching her, stretched, yawned, and said wearily, "I'm completely done in. I shall go to bed, I think. Don't stay up too late; you'll want to be fresh as a daisy tomorrow so we can talk about what to do."

He stood up and smiled at her. She looked up from the middle of a late diary entry—she was nearly finished—and smiled back at him. "I won't be much longer. I just want to get through what's here, to get an idea of the whole story, so we can fit it with the rest. I'll see you tomorrow."

Giles nodded and left the room. Roz considered briefly what to do. Alan had said she was not conscious enough of her own danger. First there had been the warning, then the accident with Flore. But was she really in danger now? Things h changed. Francesca was obviously shocked by th appearance of the letters, had asked her for help. They needed her, and they knew it. Roz shook her head, thinking about how desperate Francesca had looked in the Porcelain Garden. Wasn't it worth the risk—but, of course, there was no real risk, she could handle Francesca—to find out what Francesca had to say? Besides, she had promised. Of course she would go, and tell Giles in the morning.

She tiptoed upstairs, slid the papers between her mattress and box spring—a favorite hiding place of hers—then padded silently down the hall to Giles's door and listened intently for some time to his regular, heavy breathing. When she was sure he was asleep, she tunneled her way through the darkness of the house as surreptitiously as a mole, and let herself out into the night.

20

THE PALE, WATERY MOON WAS A MEDUSA'S FACE that transformed plants, leaves, flowers, grass, her own hands in front of her face, into the color and texture of stone. Layers of cloud were building up in the west as she walked across the Courtyard toward the entrance to the Cloister. She emerged into the Cloister lawn, facing the ruins of the old church.

She looked to her left toward the high hedges of the Maze, thinking that of all the different parts of the garden, this was the one she was the least familiar with. There was no one to be seen.

She took a deep breath, wondering if she should go back, after all. But no. They needed her. All of them were clearly at their wits' end. Somehow she had to get to the bottom of it all, put an end to the violence and ill-feeling. She walked forward slowly, feeling as though she were made of eyes and ears.

"Sst!" A piece of the hedge at the entrance to the Maze detached itself and beckoned to her. Roz squinted into the shadow. What in the world was Francesca wearing? Her figure was completely obscured by some flowing, rough-textured, hooded garment. Roz moved toward her, skin prickling, remembering the apparition she had seen her first day at the Abbey.

"Here." Francesca thrust something folded and blanketlike at her. "Put it on," she said in her husky voice. "You'll be less visible." She gestured impatiently at Roz's light-colored skirt and blouse.

Roz unfolded the cloth; it was a monk's heavy, cowled robe, just like the one she and Alan had seen in the room under the Viola Room in the Tower. Maybe it was the same one. Anyway, the hood—that was what Francesca was wearing—was draped low about her face, completely hiding her bright hair, obscuring the contours of her face. "Viola and I wore these when we used to meet here sometimes . . ." She stopped. Roz could not see her expression.

"But Francesca," she said gently, "why the Maze? Can't we just walk?"

The monk's hood swayed and shivered a *no*. "This is the best place. I know the garden inside out. There's only one way in, one way out. There's no one inside—I looked, and I've been standing right here since then. Once we're in the middle, no one can hear us, and no one can sneak in without our hearing, it's so overgrown. We'll be safe. I know my way around blindfolded. It's really simple, if you know the trick.

This is where we used to play." Francesca turned and went into the Maze.

Roz put on the monk's robe, feeling like a child playing an absurd game of dress-up. But it was chilly, and the robe was warm. She pulled the hood around her hair and followed Francesca.

It wasn't as bad as she had thought; the clay paths reflected palely whatever faint moonlight penetrated between the tall hedges. The hedges did rustle as they passed; a distinct plucking and snapping accompanied them as they walked along. Unkempt and overgrown, the Maze was no longer open to the public, its entrance blocked during the visiting hours by a discreet chain and a sign, because Giles could no longer afford to post someone on a ladder to help a trapped and panicky tourist out. Obviously not even the gardeners had been here in some time, for branches and fronds of yew stuck out every which way, leaving barely enough room to get by.

Francesca had not exaggerated when she said she knew the Maze by heart. They brushed up one alley, down the next, never hesitating, turning right here, left there, down one alley and up the next, Roz ducking and skimming past branches, soft fringes of yew brushing her face from either side. Francesca rustled on, a dark figure in the moonlight.

The sibilant drawing of their robes sounded loud in the silence, then suddenly they were at the center, in an area no more than six feet square, with one opening. Three small funerary stone benches stood against the tall hedges of boxwood, and stiff, pointed, lozenge-shaped leaves rose high above their hoods. Roz was finding it rather difficult to breathe inside the dusty material, so she threw her hood back, and sat on the bench across from Francesca. The hedge was as thick and impenetrable as a wall.

"Do you know?" Francesca said in a quiet voice.

"Yes. I read over the papers tonight. They tell the whole story."

Francesca's hood swayed; her face glared briefly. "And what is the story?"

Quickly Roz summarized the content of the letters and the substance of the diary. She was just about to describe the letters to Francesca herself when Francesca interrupted her.

"That's just it."

"What?"

"There are no letters to me. There can't be. Nor to my mother or father or any of us."

"What?" Roz stared at the hooded figure in disbelief.

"I saw her burn them. She promised me she would never let it come out, that I could start a new life. She took the letters and burned them right there in front of me in the Abbot's Chapel. After that, I went away."

Roz sat on the bench, cold even under the heavy monk's robe. How could this be? The letters existed; she had just read them.

"Couldn't she have copied them before she burned them?"

"Viola wouldn't have done that to me. She . . . loved me. We had a bargain, even though . . ." Francesca stopped and took a trembling breath. "That's the whole point. We had a bargain."

Roz wished she could see Francesca's face. She leaned forward.

"The letters don't seem so bad to me. In this day and age . . ."

"You don't understand," Francesca cried suddenly, her voice breaking. "The story in those letters isn't true. It's not the real story. Don't you see?"

Francesca threw off the hood, and her face shone in the shadow of the Maze, the cheeks varnished with tears. "You don't understand, can't understand. She made me. She made me become what I am today. I loved her, I loved her so much—she was everything none of the others were, and I would have done anything for her. But she said she had a son already, and I was a boy! . . . She wanted a daughter; someone just like her. She promised to leave me half of Montfort. I didn't know; it seemed possible, like a dream—to be her daughter. I was so much like her, almost a second self, except that I was a . . . a boy. And I really didn't want to be. Or thought I didn't. I was so young, so confused. Sometimes I felt I was a girl in a boy's body, but I just didn't know, wasn't sure. But she convinced me."

Roz sat speechless, watching Francesca's face, hearing the low, desperate voice. The face turned toward her, she saw now, was not a woman's at all, but the face of a beautiful adolescent boy, oddly unfinished. Involuntarily, Roz thought of the helpless young boys who once had made up the great cathedral choirs, the castrati, their manhood sacrificed to the preservation of their heavenly soprano voices, irrevocably mutilated in the name of . . . of what? Art? Francesca's face was the face of an arrested, almost-grown, doomed boy, a distraught caricature neither male nor female in its lineaments. No. That was not in the letters. Definitely not in the letters. So rudely forced? She stared at Francesca's tormented face.

Francesca pulled the hood back over her head and wiped a hand across her face. "The letters . . ." Then she straightened with an abrupt expulsion of breath, and slumped forward in an attitude of defeat. The hood fell over her face like a shroud.

What am I going to do? Roz thought desperately. *I've got to help her.*

Francesca did not move or speak. Roz sat silently across from her, struggling with her own confusion. Whom was she going to believe? The Viola as the letters showed her, not just these new ones, but all the letters and papers, gravely wise, loving, generous, the Viola everyone knew and loved already, but deeper, more human? Or was it this other Viola, the cynical exploiter, the forcer of souls, of bodies, the manipulator exerting power over Francesca and transforming her as she had her own garden? She found it hard to imagine Viola—the Viola she had built up in her mind over these years of reading her books, her poems, her letters, the Viola she thought she understood, and yes, the Viola enhanced by Roz's experience of living here where she had once lived— corrupt, imperious, monstrous? Viola of the gardens, the poet of the seasons, of nature, the life of the earth? Viola? She felt the vision slipping, fading into a chimera.

Roz rose from the bench, her mind made up. Frankie. How that very name must be a taunt, the act so irrevocable, so horribly irreparable. And now Francesca made no sound, not even the faint catch of muffled crying. Roz found her silent grief more heartsearing than hysterics.

"Listen, Francesca. I'm going to resolve this once and for all. There are ways to prove whether the letters are genuine."

Francesca sat silent, motionless, slumped over, the hood obscuring her face.

"It will take a little time, so you must tell the others to stop what they've been doing and let me get to the bottom of this. I promise I'll help you, but you must tell them to stop. Can you do that?"

Silence.

"Francesca?"

Roz reached over and pulled the hood back from Francesca's face. The blond hair tumbled out, pale against the dark hedge. Francesca's eyes were open, fixed. Roz prodded her shoulder, and, eerily, through what seemed like eons of slow revelation, Francesca tipped over and collapsed with no more substance than a robe falling off a peg, falling onto her side in a heap across the stone bench next to her. From the center of her back, just under her left shoulder blade, protruded the hard, worn, bone handle of a gardener's pruning knife.

* * *

Roz stood rigid, her breath coming in short gasps, her heart pounding painfully against her ribs. The Maze was absolutely silent; not even a faint rustle betrayed another presence. Francesca had been so certain of safety. They had heard nothing. The hand with the knife had struck silently through the dense-seeming hedge of boxwood that surrounded the small enclosure, and just as silently withdrawn. Whose hand, and where was the killer now?

Roz bent down to look closely at Francesca. Was she dead? Unconscious? Roz put a hand forward, trying to think what to do, and placed a finger on Francesca's throat, feeling for a pulse. There wasn't much blood that Roz could see. Not yet. Was that good or bad? Under her fingers, the vein fluttered—little more than a trembling of the skin. Then Francesca took a shallow, ragged breath.

Help, Roz thought, looking around wildly. *I must get help. She's not dead.* And with a numb sense of detachment, of having been through this before—but that had been with Florence, not Francesca—she thought again: *I've got to get help. And that means I've got to get out, find someone, find Giles. No, find Alan.*

Roz started for the opening of the enclosure, trying to remember the turnings they had taken coming in. Behind her, Francesca took another halting breath, long and shallow and even more ragged. The exhalation was long and labored, and there was no answering intake of breath. Roz stopped, listening intently, her eyes on the huddled form. Suddenly she was overwhelmed by the conviction that Francesca was dead. She groped blindly for the opening, went through, and turned the way they had come. She had to get help, even if it was too late.

Within a few steps she had already lost her way. Sharp left, or slanting right? She looked down at the clay path and tried to distinguish footprints going in one direction or the other. The scuffed-up path

209

blurred and faded in the dark; it was impossible to make out footprints.

But they had come in on a diagonal, with no more than three turns. Bearing right, she went ahead, ignored a left, and almost immediately found herself in a cul-de-sac. She backed up, took the left, walked a few steps, and bumped straight into a tall hedge of boxwood that formed one side of a long, straight avenue. She went along the track, the branches plucking and snapping at her, feeling her way along with both hands out to either side—on one side, the soft, flat, yielding fringes of yew; on the other, spearlike leaves of boxwood. She did not remember that coming in. Or did she? And then she found herself in another blind alley. Was it the same one? She couldn't be sure. Panic rose in her throat; she choked back a sob. She stopped, shut her eyes, and tried to get a picture in her mind, a bird's-eye view of the Maze. She had read about it, seen pictures—even an aerial view. There was something about crosses, the old devotional garden, much simpler than it appeared . . . some sort of key . . .

"Rosamund."

Roz jerked so hard she thought her bones would break. The voice had come from somewhere behind her. She whirled. The thicket rustled.

Roz stood rigid, holding her breath, afraid to move. She listened, ears straining. The monk's hood slid down her hair, as though a hand were slowly drawing it back. She whirled around again, forearms raised protectively in front of her face and neck. The monk's hood slipped down and bunched at the back of her neck in a protective cowl. There was no one there. The only thing in front of her was another impenetrable tangle of hedge.

"Rosamund," the voice hissed from somewhere in front of her, edged with malice. "You've been lucky so far, haven't you? Two near misses. Too bad about the other one, but I won't make any more mistakes now. You really are next."

210

Roz shrank back inside the monk's robe. Near misses? Mistakes? So Giles had been right, after all; the tea had been meant for her. And the knife, too? *You're next.* She stood frozen.

"Rosamund. I can see you, but you can't see me. You don't know where you are. You won't get out. Because I won't let you."

Roz took a deep breath. All around her, the Maze was quiet. *You can hear anybody moving,* Francesca had said. For the moment she was safe. The killer was not coming after her. Not yet.

All right, she thought. *You've got to get yourself out of here. If he—but who was to say it was a man?—if he moves, you can hear him. You mustn't let yourself be trapped. No screams. There's a hedge between you now, and—*she looked down the long avenue, the only way open to her at the moment, then searched the hedge, trying to see through—*if you can't see him, then he probably can't see you, whatever he says, and he can't get to you, either. The voice was bluffing. He's playing with you, trying to get you confused and in a panic. There's a thick hedge between you now; you've got to keep it that way.*

Roz took several deep breaths, trying to slow the wild hammering of her heart. She wrapped the monk's robe tightly around her, making herself as small and narrow and inconspicuous as possible, bent down into a crouch, and slid noiselessly away from where she had last heard the voice. Her eyes darted from side to side. She didn't think anyone could get at her through the yews; the hedge was thick and gnarled and much denser than the boxwood. She groped along the other side, her hand meeting the thick, knotted trunks of boxwood through its sparser foliage, trunks that writhed out of the ground like petrified snakes. How thick was it?

Her hand slipped through and met another hand—groping, strong fingers snatching at her, grabbing her fingers.

211

Leaping up, she yanked her hand back, barely feeling the scratches, strangling off into a moan the scream that rose in her throat. She crashed into the hedge in back of her before she stopped herself. *Stay calm. You must stay calm. He's on the other side. Waiting.* Her ears strained.

"Rosamund." The voice came again, low and sibilant, as if amused. There was a scrabbling in the bushes, and the branches to one side of her crackled and moved. Roz edged away, her eyes fixed on the swaying hedge. Would he come through? Or was he moving along the other side? Her breath came harsh and rasping, sawing faintly in her ears as though from far away; she sobbed, brought her hand up to her mouth . . .

And suddenly she was calm. A surge of warmth, a feeling of strength and confidence swept over her. She knew where the voice was, and if he were trying to get at her there, she would move away, silently as the ghosts of those long-dead monks who had perversely, sacrilegiously created this secular and labyrinthine entertainment, this sport of kings . . .

And that was it. She recalled the sense she had had, following Francesca, of how simple it all was. And something from Viola's book *The Making of Montfort.* There was a pattern. As in everything else, there was a pattern. Hidden sometimes, but still a pattern, revolving now up out of her subconscious like a child's pinwheel. Of course the monks had not created the Maze. This patch of garden had not originally been a maze at all; it, too, had once been consecrated to the greater glory of God—a hymn in evergreen. And then she saw the whole Maze as if from above, an aerial photograph colored red, white, and blue. The Union Jack. The diagonal X-shaped cross of St. Andrew imposed on the upright cross of St. George. The crosses had been planted in yew, centuries before Gilbert had replanted with boxwood, filling in to make his funhouse maze. She had felt yew on either side, coming in diagonally to

212

the center. Yew on either side. Right at the end, then out. All she had to do was find the alley that was yew on either side, slanting across the rest, and that was the way out.

Carefully, she put her arms out to either side, fingers barely touching the edges of the passage, and walked slowly, sweeping her hands ever so delicately along. The branches on the other side of the hedge crackled as if in answer. Slippery, stiff, lozenge leaves of boxwood on one side, softer fringes of yew on the left. With fingers newly sensitive, she crept along the path.

From the other side of the boxwood hedge came the sound of snapping branches, footsteps scuffling the clay. The killer was moving, too. In her concentration, she had almost forgotten. She felt momentarily disoriented, not sure where she was, the way she had once felt when, as a little girl, she had held up a mirror over her shoulder to look in her mother's dressing table mirror backward, and had seen the tunnel in the mirror, the one that stretched into infinity. The striped pinwheel began to revolve again, faster and faster, until it blurred into a circle, then hollowed out into the mirror tunnel. Then she was running, running next to a mirror image of herself, in parallel alleys of green bramble that stretched into infinity, on and on, running as fast as she could to stay in one place. To stay alive. Suffocating, the hedge pressing in, seeming to clutch at her, and still she was running, running down an endless spiral of branches, the sound of her own panting like the rasp of a saw . . .

And then she fell.

The clay was like velvet on her cheek, soft and cool. It smelled chalky, and the dust made her nose tickle. *I mustn't sneeze,* she thought clearly. Footsteps shuffled close to her head, then stopped. *If I just lie still a moment, maybe he'll think I've fainted.* She stifled an urge to scream, while her shoulder blades twitched in anticipation of the heavy blow, the . . .

It did not come. She held her breath, listening. The footsteps started again, seemed to pass by. She raised her head infinitesimally and turned her eyes to the path in the direction of the sound. No feet.

She looked around. The alley was empty; the footsteps had been in the next alley over. Through the ancient roots of yew she caught a flicker of movement. Searching. Her ears were mouse ears, huddled in a field of wheat, listening for the sound of the reaping, coming there, coming now, snick, snick, closer.

All right. He isn't here yet. He still had to walk the length of that long, straight, divided avenue, the long upright arm of St. George's cross, to get back to her; he was on one side, she on another, separated by Gilbert's boxwood hedge. There was no way through; that was the way she had come. The footsteps grew fainter.

Still, she didn't have much time. If she could just remember, keep the pinwheel from spinning. Hedges of yew on the diagonal went off to the left. She got up on her hands and knees. She wanted to be free to run. She shrugged off the monk's robe and left it in a heap in the middle of the path. *Maybe he'll think it's me lying there and stop to see, and that will give me more time.* Creeping forward, reaching out to either side, she felt the hedges, inched stealthily along.

At last, an opening to the left. Yews on the left corner, yews on the right corner. She peered around the hedge and saw a clear, straight path at right angles to the one she was in. In the feeble light, she could see another path going off at an angle at the far end. She slipped out of her shoes, feeling the clay path as soft as suede against her palms, her knees, her feet. *This may be the last pleasurable sensation I'll ever have,* she thought as she crawled silently down the avenue of yew toward the turning.

When the voice came again, even though she lurched painfully, she knew she was still safe, for the voice, tense with menace, now held a note of frustration, was querulous in its taunting. It came from far-ther away, and was not directed quite at her. "Rosa-mund," it called. "I'm right behind you. You can't get away. You won't get out."

But I will. Roz stopped just short of the end of the path, crept forward, looked cautiously to one side, then the other. The path ran diagonally away, one arm of St. Andrew. To her right, the path was blocked with boxwood, leaves glistening. Slightly to the right, across the alley, another path branched off.

But it was not diagonal, and it was edged with box-wood on the far side, the small, pointed leaves gleaming faintly. *So left it is.* Roz stood up and ran down the path of yew diagonally, her heart hammer-ing in her ears, pounding in her chest so hard she could barely hear the echoing footsteps behind her. The end of the diagonal. *Turn right, both sides still edged with yew, look for the last straight path.* As though she were in a film reversed, she saw herself and Francesca coming in. Her hand held out to the left side, like a child running a stick along a picket fence, she ran and ran.

And halfway down, the thicket suddenly dropped away; a gust of fresh air swept her skin. She flung herself through the opening. The hedges fell away, and she was in the open air, surrounded by acres and fields of space. She was running in grass, and she was free.

Suddenly she seemed almost to lift off the ground, running recklessly, headlong, as though she could run forever, feet barely touching the grass, flying from the smothering, airless thickets of the Maze, the voice, the terror, Francesca, death.

She ran until she was out of breath, then slowed to a walk, her arms and legs feeling oddly loose. She stood still and looked around her.

Where am I? she thought. She was in another en-closed garden, but she could not identify it either by the smell or by the dim shapes of plants and flowers.

It was as though the garden kept adding to itself, nightmarishly extending its dominion . . . She had no idea how far or in which direction she had run. She sniffed the air. There was a strange odor, acrid—almost a tobacco smell. Poison Plant? But no, this enclosure was bigger. Porcelain Garden? If only it were lighter . . . but she missed the tall, spiked delphinium, the great, blue feather globes of allium as big as a man's head, like giant dandelions gone to seed, swaying on their stalks. There were no pale whites gleaming, the darker shadows of blue absorbing light. It was too dark to see.

If only the moon would come out. Ears still pricked for any human noise, she bent down, felt around, scuffed her feet. She turned around and around, searching for some clue to where she was.

And there was the lumpy, irregular shape of the Abbot's Chapel, looming over her. Everything snapped into place; she was in the Porcelain Garden.

The moon broke through the enshrouding clouds, glowed briefly on her surroundings. The marble slab she was standing on gleamed coldly.

All around her, in Viola's elaborately figured beds, the forget-me-nots, the white roses, the pale leaves of silver mound, white phlox, dusty miller, cobalt-blue and china-white companula, veronica and pearlbush, all lay twisted and deformed across the marble slabs. The leaves were curled up in tortured shapes like wadded-up tissue paper, the flowers limp, wizened, and partially shorn of petals, like the nearly toothless mouths of ancient and bewrinkled crones. The odd smell was not natural; it was a chemical smell. Weed killer. Roz remembered the twisting rosettes of dandelions in her parents' lawn after her father had sprayed them. All around her, the blue and white patterns of the Porcelain Garden lay ruined, spotted, and wilted, grown to death. The elegant and pristine Blue Willow Pattern garden, Viola's horticultural tour-de-force, lay like a gnarled and wrinkled corpse, senile in decay. And sprawled across the center, like a pile of bones, its slender trunk sawn through, its branches scattered and broken, lay the blue willow tree.

Roz turned and ran blindly through the nearest opening in the wall, her heart thudding, crashing first this way and then that as she ran, not knowing where she was or where she was going.

Suddenly there loomed before her an amorphous shadow, a monk's cowled figure, huge and black, blocking her way.

Roz gasped, her brain signaling a frantic warning to stop and turn, but she was going too fast, and her body could not obey. Arms and legs flailing helplessly, she crashed straight into the monstrous shape. Great bat wings flapped out to envelop her. Letting out a half-strangled yelp of terror, she went completely limp, slipped out of the muffling arms, and collapsed face down upon the ground.

She was back in the Maze, cheek against the soft path. The clay was like velvet on her cheek, soft and warm. It smelled chalky, and of something else—something resinous, and soapy. It smelled of paint. And it prickled, coarsely, like grass or . . . The clay path rose and fell, rocking her head. It was damp, and warm, and . . . It was alive. She jerked away, struggling in terror.

"Roz, what's wrong? What's happened? Are you all right?" Alan's face bent close to hers, she was leaning against him, her cheek against his bare chest, supported in the crook of his arm. He was wearing a long robe of some sort, fallen open along his torso, loosely tied over a pair of beltless corduroy trousers. She looked up at him stupidly.

"I was sound asleep when I heard this frightful row outside my window, sobbing and crashing and scuffling, so I got up and came out. Are you all right? What's happened?"

Roz shook her head, unable to speak.

"What's that all over your face? All over you, in

217

point of fact." He turned her hand over and studied the palm, then reached up and brushed some of the clay dust off her cheeks, her hair. "Dust. And tear tracks, as my nanny used to call them. What have you been up to?"

Roz sat up. Her hands were moist and sticky; clay dust covered the palms like soft leather. She stared down at them.

Alan let her go. "You gave me quite a turn, barreling into me that way. Damn near knocked me over." He leaned forward, hands on his thighs, shoulders hunched, contemplating her. The long muscles of his forearms below the sleeve of the robe s\ od out in relief. *Of course you would need strong arms to stand there and paint all day,* Roz thought distractedly, *day in day out, strong arms and shoulders . . .*

She struggled to pull her dazed mind back to the present. Everything came out in a rush. "Francesca and I were talking in the Maze, and someone reached through the hedge and stabbed her and I'm afraid she's dead. She was telling me about the papers. And then the killer chased me, and threatened me, said it was meant for me, just like Florence's tea, and I ran, but I remembered the crosses and got out and then I just ran and ran." Roz stopped, gulped, barely conscious of the tears that began to roll down her cheeks. "But Francesca's . . . she's . . . she's . . ." Roz began to choke. "We've got to help her." But she knew in her heart it was too late.

Alan leaned over, put one arm behind her back, another under her knees, and stood up effortlessly, swinging her up in his arms. She leaned gratefully into his body, stifling her sobs in the hollow of his neck and shoulder. "All right, then," he murmured. "Never mind. You're not lost now. We'll go straight along to the Maze and see about Francesca." And he marched off down the path to the Rose Garden with Roz in his arms.

He carried her the length of the Rose Garden,

218

through the Herb Garden, all the way into the sitting room of the Moat House, carefully depositing her on the couch while he ran upstairs. In less than a minute he reappeared, pulling on a roll-neck jersey as he came through the door. He stood in front of her and extended his hand. "Can you walk?"

Roz nodded and stood up, her knees trembling. She could walk, barely. But she had to.

Roz stopped involuntarily as they came close to the tall hedges of the Maze. She shut her eyes, shaking her head. Alan turned to face her.

"Listen. You got out. Do you know the way back in? Because I don't."

Roz swallowed once, twice. Her insides churned at the idea of going back. But she nodded. "It's easy, once you know the secret."

"Are you sure?" He put his hands on her shoulders, looked down into her face, studying it. He took his hands away, and she walked forward toward the gap in the hedge.

Turn right and straight on, yews to either side, left on the diagonal, still the yews right and left, then straight along, straight until morning, yew on the left, boxwood on the right. She paused, Alan right behind her, and looked down along the path; her castoff monk's robe should be here somewhere. Yes, here were her shoes right where she'd left them; absently, she slipped them on. But beyond that the clay path stretched bare and undisturbed down the long divided avenue of the upright cross of St. George. Was she in the wrong place? No. One way out, and one way in. There was the little cul-de-sac, and there on her right was the opening to the little hedged-in chamber. She shut her eyes, seeing it all as she had left it, stone benches on three sides, a figure in a plain brown robe crumpled over, muffled and still. She stopped, let Alan pass her, waited for him to say something.

"Roz?"

She steeled herself, stepped forward, opened her eyes. The stone benches gleamed pristine and without stain, undisturbed in the faintly diffused glow of the moon. There was no sign of Francesca, of a body. No robe, no knife, no blood. Francesca was gone without a trace, as though she had never been.

21

ROZ AWOKE LATE NEXT MORNING WITH A HEADache. She felt as though a huge hand were ruthlessly pinching the back of her neck. She vaguely remembered sitting down on the bench in the Maze, then being carried out through the twists and turns into the Refectory, Giles's head poking sleepy-eyed out of his doorway, Alan gently lowering her into her bed, pulling the covers over her, then the sound of voices murmuring outside her door before she had fallen headlong into the mirror tunnel, winding down and down into a spiral of yew, a bottomless, sideless maze of sleep.

She studied herself in the mirror. There was a slight abrasion on her cheek from her fall onto the bricks in the Rose Garden. The flesh of her arms was crisscrossed with minute scratches, the palms of her hands threaded and latticed with deeper ones. She felt stiff all over. Slowly, she dressed herself in a long-sleeved shirt and soft chambray trousers to cover most of the bruises and scrapes. Then she went downstairs.

When she came into the kitchen, Giles was sitting at the table finishing his usual breakfast of cold cereal, milk, and instant coffee, engrossed in the morning paper, as though nothing had happened. He looked up and saw her.

"Oh, Rosamund, my dear. How *are* you?" he exclaimed, putting down the paper. He sounded sympathetic, but his eyes were cold.

"I'm all right, I guess," Roz said, sitting down at the pine table. She bent forward, head in her hands. Giles jumped up.

"Here now," he said, coming around to stand next to her. "Still feeling a bit dicey, I should imagine. Oh dear." He stood by her awkwardly, obviously at a loss as to what to do, what to say next. Roz kept her head in her hands. That was the whole of it, really. Giles in a nutshell. Whatever words he said, noises he made, Giles was incapable of imagining what other people in distress or pain might feel. She sighed and lifted her head away from her hands.

"How's Francesca? Did you find her?"

Just then Alan came in, looking even more rumpled than usual, as if he had actually slept in his clothes. Giles ignored him, turned away to stare out the window, and addressed Roz without looking at her.

"See here, Rosamund . . . Roz. It's all clearly been too much for you, really it has. I didn't realize until last night how it had affected you. I think you need to get away. I can work on the papers myself for a change," he went on. "I need to familiarize myself with them, anyway, after all this . . . trouble." He turned to her. "You go have an outing. Go for a drive, have lunch, look around. You've hardly been out of this place since you got here. Alan will take you. It's all arranged, isn't it, Alan?"

Alan moved closer and stood behind her chair, his hands resting lightly on her back, barely touching her—yet the whole of the room seemed suddenly to center on that light pressure of his fingers. Roz turned to him with a questioning look. He nodded.

"Fine with me. It's a nice day, as far as I could see from the sitting room." He bent, squinting past Giles out the kitchen window. "Whatever you like. Have a walk, drive around, visit Cambridge. You do need to get away."

"But what about Francesca?" she demanded, looking from one to the other. "Did you find her? Where was she?"

Giles ducked his head and rubbed the side of his nose with one finger, looking embarrassed. It was Alan who answered.

"We looked everywhere. There's not a trace. No sign of Francesca or anyone else. Giles and I searched the whole garden after we locked you in your room." Alan leaned back against the counter and folded his arms. Roz stared at both of them. She didn't know what to think. Could it have been her imagination—or worse, a hallucination? No, of course not, that was unthinkable. Her mind did not play tricks. She was right; she had to be. But Francesca gone without a trace?

Did Giles think *everything* had been a dream? Alan finding her in the Rose Garden, crying, frightened out of her wits? Did *he* think it had been a dream? Then she remembered the Porcelain Garden, the horribly, nightmarishly twisted, writhing plants, the broken willow tree.

"The Porcelain Garden?" she asked hesitantly.

Giles looked away. "Yes." And suddenly, without another word, he turned and flung himself out of the kitchen. Roz heard the hall door slam. She watched him stride past the window across the Courtyard toward the Cloister, rigid with . . . what? Anger, frustration, despair? She couldn't tell. She turned back slowly to find a bowl of cereal and a glass of orange juice on the table in front of her.

She looked up; Alan was sitting across the table, leaning on his elbows, watching her.

"So that part, at least, is true," she said.

"Yes. Cory says it couldn't have been done last night, though. It takes a day or two for the herbicide to work. Probably they only sawed down the willow last night. That wouldn't have taken long. Anyway, Viola's precious Porcelain Garden is a complete write-off. As you can see, Giles is more upset about that than about Francesca. To him that garden *is* his mother, I think. They've finally got him where he lives. I imagine that's why he wants us out of here, to be alone with his mother's papers. And what's left of the garden. But the fact is, to answer your question, we found absolutely nothing else. Not a trace. No Francesca, no knife, no blood, nothing."

Roz flushed, dropped her eyes, absently picked up her cereal spoon, and began to eat. Didn't anyone believe her? She didn't even want to look at Alan. But she knew she hadn't imagined it all. She had heard the sound of sawing, confusing it at the time with the sound of her own breath. That was real, the ruined willow. But then why hadn't Alan heard it? Because he had been asleep at the far end of the Moat House. Only the sound of her sobbing and crashing around under his window had awakened him. But the rest? All an hallucination? She stared miserably at her bowl of cereal.

Alan shifted in his seat; the chair creaked loudly. "But that is not to say you did not see what you saw, hear what you heard, you know. It's just that no one's found anything. Yet."

Roz looked up gratefully. He did believe her. At just that moment Giles swung back into the room, looking composed, even cheerful. "Ah, Roz, you're eating. Good. Must keep our strength up." He sat down at the end of the table, legs crossed, hands laced in back of his head as though the chair were a hammock, leaning back as far as possible in a cha-
· rade of relaxation.

"Now. About Francesca and the supposed stabbing. So melodramatic. Nevertheless, I've talked to Farthing, who says Francesca is not here now, but that when she made the bed up this morning, it did appear to be 'lain about in,' as she put it. But all Francesca's things are gone. It seems that she has departed." Giles paused and leaned back farther, his profile nearly parallel to the ceiling.

Abruptly, he thumped himself upright, and looked directly at Roz. "I'm quite sure you did see what you saw, Rosamund." He paused, then went on carefully. "Or rather thought you saw. You are neither hysterical nor mad. But I am also quite certain the whole incident was fabricated."

Roz spluttered in the middle of a mouthful of cereal.

"Think about it. Everything they've tried so far has failed. The ruining of the garden hasn't worked, personal appeals don't work, threats to me and you don't work. You are still here, in spite of the warnings. Under the guise of eliciting sympathy, telling you the 'true story,' Francesca gets you into the Maze, and then stages her own death, terrorizing you into thinking the knife was meant for you."

Roz stared at Giles, then at Alan, whose face across from her was for once unreadable.

Giles went on. "To what end; that is the question. You've been warned, and now frightened—if Alan is any witness—within an inch of your sanity. Though you did do remarkably well, by the way, to get out of the Maze yourself. Shows extraordinary presence of mind. Still, the question is *why.* And the answer, I think, is obvious: they want you out of here. They never meant to stab you, only to frighten you away. I imagine we won't be seeing Francesca around for some time, so no one will know for certain. But I'm convinced it was a put-up job. A desperate move to get you out of here, away from the letters. And from me. You know too much."

Roz swallowed again, dry-mouthed. "It seemed authentic enough to me," she said.

Giles reached over and patted her hand. "Of course. It would have to be, if they thought they were going to fool you. After all, you're so very clever. But remember, Francesca is an actress. What I don't think they bargained for is the hardiness of your

224

character." He gave her hand a squeeze. She withdrew it. They? They? She glanced sideways at Alan. He was watching Giles, frowning slightly.

Giles went on. "My dear, how else can you explain the lack of a body, blood, or any trace of violence? Or even removal? Did you hear anyone approach at any time?"

"No."

"Well then, I think that argues the point. Either Francesca faked it herself, or the supposed murderer was there already. In other words, a plant. Sorry. When they had sufficiently frightened you, they both simply walked out of the Maze and went about their business."

Roz looked curiously at Giles. He had a point. Two people, Hugh and Francesca, working together to frighten her. Or maybe Francesca and Elsie, in cahoots as they had always been. Elsie covering for Francesca even now. Roz sighed. Better, after all, to have herself fooled, played upon, taken in, than Francesca really dead. Florence's accident had been bad enough. She hoped Giles was right.

"Alan," she said, turning to him, "how long would you say it was from the time you found me in the Rose Garden until we got back to the Maze?"

"No more than three minutes."

"Time enough to drag a body out of the Maze? Pick up my robe and clear out, wipe away footprints, and everything?"

Alan considered. "Hardly. And, of course, there would be traces. To drag a body all around that Maze on those loose clay paths? No, I really don't think it would be possible. We would have seen or heard them at some point."

"Could they have hidden in another part?"

"I looked. Don't you remember? I sat you down on the bench and thrashed right around. Not a clue. And I made a beastly lot of noise in the bargain. Like an elephant in a field of dry bamboo. Giles is right

225

about that. No one could have got in without your knowing it."

Yes, she remembered. Sitting numbly on the bench, Alan shouting to her every few seconds to keep his bearings. The rustlings and crashings, mutterings and cursings. It had not been a quiet search. And then stumbling back out, ducking branches, swatted by fronds of yew. The only way to get around quietly in the Maze was to crawl. She had stumbled, and remembered Alan once again swinging her up into his arms, carrying her back to the Refectory, dazed and exhausted. Alan. It suddenly occurred to her that he had slept here, in his clothes. But they had left her alone to search the garden. She remembered voices in the hallway, raised in argument, the click of a key. Of course, they had locked her in. A precaution. Unnecessary, of course, in the face of what now looked very much like an elaborate charade played out for her benefit. But how were they to know at the time?

It was outlandish, unbelievable. That, and the destruction of the Porcelain Garden, made it seem clear that whoever was doing all this had come to the end of the line. Involuntarily, she shivered. What could be next? What was left? To kill Giles, kill her, burn Montfort to the ground—gardens, buildings, papers, and all?

She sighed, aware that Giles and Alan were both watching her expectantly. She was no closer to a solution to the mystery of the papers than she had been before talking to Francesca; in fact the mystery seemed to be developing new convolutions, blossoming out like one of Viola's impossibly baroque grandiflora roses. She had thought she could keep the garden and its inhabitants and Giles's personal relationships separate from her own work with the papers, her dialogue with Viola and the past, but that now seemed a distant and naive dream. Everything was connected, rooted together. If she only knew whom or what to believe. Roz recalled her promise to Francesca—but had she been tricked, played upon? Did it still hold? Was she still bound to find out which version of the story was the true one?

Giles stood up abruptly, tall and imposing in the low-beamed kitchen, interrupting her train of thought. He spoke brusquely.

"Well, there are things I must attend to. Cory and Stella are waiting for me, and then there are the papers. I shall have to catch up on all you've done. And also come to some final decision about the . . . ah"—he glanced at Alan—"random and fugitive bits I showed you." He looked at her inquiringly. "Anything else?"

"No, Giles." He was clearly anxious to be gone. "You go along. I'll be fine."

"We'll be off on our junket," Alan added, drumming his fingers on the table.

Giles smiled coldly, nodded, and then left the kitchen. Roz bent down to scoop up the last bits of cereal and milk. She had no idea what she had been eating all this while. She looked up to see Giles's shadow sliding across the glass. His expression, even in profile, was preoccupied and stern. Roz felt an abstract sort of sympathy for him. If he had only dealt directly and honestly from the very beginning . . .

"Look here," Alan said. "I'm just going to dash across and change. I spent the night on Giles's couch. Ordinarily I don't sleep in my clothes, even though I may often look that way." He stood up, balled his fists, and stretched, twisting his shoulders and arching his back. "Uncomfortable beast," he said.

"I thought I heard voices," Roz said, watching the flat muscles on his stomach, the strong line of his chest through the thin jersey.

"Oh yes. It was definitely over Giles's dead body, so to speak. He couldn't see why I was so determined not to leave you alone with him. It was his house, and I could bloody well sleep in my own. But as you can see, here I am." He relaxed and smiled reassuringly at her. "I can't really understand why he's so anxious to send us off together today. But he must have his reasons. Still, I couldn't be more delighted. So let's play along, shall we?"

Roz's head began to pound. The implications of Alan's actions had not escaped her, however light he made of them. He did not trust Giles, and he was not afraid to let him know it.

"I'd love to get away." She put her hand up over her face. "I need time to think. This place . . ."

"Say no more. I'll meet you outside the Gatehouse Tower in ten minutes. Or would you like to come with me right now?"

"No, it's all right," Roz said quickly. She stood up. "I'll meet you at the gate."

While Alan was still rattling dishes in the sink, she let herself out of the Refectory into the Courtyard, walked quickly across and through the arch to the other side. Behind her, the garden was quiet; overhead, the sky was a hazy blue with a few woolly clouds bumping each other along the horizon like reluctant, idiotic sheep.

She walked forward, looking out over the slight rise upon which the Abbey had been built, looking down to the hedge-enclosed meadows and the bluish fens beyond, trying to regain a sense of the permanence, the importance of the place, to dissipate her growing sense of the tenuousness of all these bits and pieces, these ruins and fragments, scraps of paper, fragments of stone—and people, too. The threat of violence, real or not, the atmosphere of corruption, destruction, of danger, had settled over Montfort like a pall, reaching backward even to Viola's life. Even the dead were vulnerable. Nothing made sense anymore, certainly not her work, not her assumptions about people, her judgments. If only she could get back to where she had begun, start over, sort things out afresh. But how many times could you go back over the same material, how many reevaluations could there be?

* * *

side in her seat. She was reminded of the taxi ride that had brought her to Montfort in the first place.

"I've got just the thing. We don't want to go through Newmarket, so I'm taking you along back roads to one of my favorite places. It's called the Devil's Ditch, and it's just the other side of Newmarket Heath toward Cambridge. It's a bit of a drive, but you can sit back and contemplate the scenery as we pass through such quaint villages as Iddingham, Gazeley, Woodditton, and Fenster Bottom. No, I'm serious—it's all true. And they *are* quaint. You'll see. Trust me." He glanced quickly at her. "Never mind. No need to talk."

Roz nodded and smiled gratefully at him. He knew; he understood that she had to work everything out for herself on the basis of what evidence she had. She might trust him—no, did trust him—but he couldn't help her work out what to do next. That was strictly up to her. She'd found her own way out of the Maze; she'd have to find her own way out of this.

After a moment Alan spoke quietly. "However clear the sky, it's always misty over the Fens. They breathe, the old men say. The Fens are live creatures living under the earth, and it's their breath that makes the haze. Those hills over there are called Gog and Magog, giants sleeping on their sides. Primitive notion, isn't it? Yet, who knows?"

Roz nodded dreamily. Still, the dikes, the roads, the canals meant that man had made his way even here; some of the low-lying land looked dry enough, and even farmed, the pointed spears of rush replaced by finer-textured fields of grain.

They passed a brightly painted gypsy wagon pulled off the road, and Alan began to sing "We're off to join the raggle-taggle gypsies oh!" in a pleasantly hoarse baritone. He went from that straight into "The Wild Colonial Boy," in an exaggerated Irish brogue, and then sang, more seriously, some folksongs that Roz recognized as Scots. Reluctantly

231

at first, then with more enthusiasm, she sang the ones she knew, and their voices rose louder and louder as Alan drove the Austin in and out of a labyrinth of lanes and alleys and tiny villages, until Roz felt she was very far indeed from Montfort Abbey. Out here, driving along the winding ways, she had the feeling that nothing much ever changed, that life with its simple expectations went on very much the same from generation to generation.

And wasn't that, after all, what Giles wanted? If only he hadn't so obviously put himself into conflict with the rest of them. And yet he bore responsibility for that, to a great extent. He was so rigid in his need to control. For the rest of them, it was leaving well enough alone, letting the dead past quietly bury its dead. For him, a matter of preservation—a gift to mankind. But of what? She contemplated Alan's profile, the recalcitrantly wavy hair, grayer at the temples and sides than she had first noticed, the jutting eyebrows and deep-set eyes, the rather blunt, almost upturned nose. A big, comfortable figure of a man, easy to underestimate until you saw the intelligence in those direct and level eyes. She sighed, leaned her head against the window, and let the vibrations dance her brain into a mindless jig of unrelated thoughts.

She was nearly asleep when Alan jerked the car to a stop. Roz looked up and realized that they had at some point come back on the main highway. Alan had pulled over onto the shoulder. In front of them, across a small ditch and bordered by deep gullies on either side, an earthen rampart shaped like a pyramid with the top lopped off reared up abruptly some twenty feet, one side steeper than the other and bare of all but the scruffiest vegetation. Thick, tangled brambles filled the gullies on either side. Up the side nearest them, a rough path was deeply hollowed out, ragged and worn, in the sandy, chamois-colored earth.

"Is this the Devil's Ditch?" she asked.

"None other. Want to walk? Or talk?"

"Let's walk."

Alan came around, opened the door, and offered his hand. Together they scrambled up the little eroded path to the top of the mound. Standing on top, Roz saw that it wasn't a mound at all, but a high and distinct ridge that stretched for miles across the heath, the scuffed, indented path meandering along the top like an undone zipper as the ridge dipped into a hollow and rose over the next rise and across the meadow. As far as Roz could see, the two darker rows of briar at the sides and bottom of the ridge clearly delineated it from the waving meadow grass on either side. On the other side of the road, a similar ridge disappeared into the horizon; obviously, the highway had been cut through in modern times. She had seen this before, from the road. The breeze swirled her hair, seeming to blow clear through her head.

"What is it, a Roman road?"

"No one knows. It's very ancient. It may be Roman; it may be even older than that. It goes for twenty miles across the heath, from below Newmarket almost to the Isle of Ely, just as you see it here—as straight as an arrow, or near as makes no difference. Twenty feet high and forty wide at the bottom, if you could see the bottom through the briars. But the best part, the part I like, is that it's a botanist's heaven. Species of plants grow here that grow nowhere else on the British Isles. Almost as though the dirt to make it came from somewhere else, fantastic as that sounds. One's always running into blokes like me crawling along with their noses in the dirt, squinting their eyes and scrabbling about, scribbling in their little notebooks. One rare little plant, the piebald cinquefoil, is a quarter-inch high. It was thought to be extinct, until it was discovered here."

"Who found it?" Roz asked, following Alan along the path. He was silent for a moment.

"Well, as a matter of fact, I did. But let's see what we can find. I love this sort of thing. It's a bona fide compulsive activity—completely absorbing. Takes your mind off things. You just go poking along in the hardscrabble, and you must pay complete attention, mind you, and let your intellect or your emotions or whatever run along on automatic pilot. And then when you're done, as often as not your subconscious has gone and solved the problem all by itself, just by being left alone and not chattered at and pushed on all the time. Amazing. Restful, too, sometimes, to just let things take care of themselves. I come here quite often."

Roz said nothing, but just followed him along, listening to the soft murmur of his voice. The path was too narrow for them to walk together without stumbling, so Alan went ahead, and Roz followed him along the top of the earthwork, watching him look intently from side to side, searching, studying the sparse ground cover.

"Why 'ditch,' Alan?" she said presently. "I mean, it's hardly a ditch. It's like walking along a battlement."

"I don't know, really. It's also known as the Devil's Dyke locally, so you can take your choice. I prefer Devil's Ditch myself, I expect because it's so perverse. I've always imagined that whoever named it must have thought what with the Devil being underground and everything topsy-turvy, as Milton tells us, that what would be a ditch to the Devil would be a mound to us. At least that's the only explanation I can think of."

"Makes perfect sense to me," Roz said contentedly, chewing on a pleasantly sour sorrel stem she had plucked from the edge of the path. She set her eyes and mind to seeking out small spots of color, unusual shapes in the knotted grass. As a child, she had been an inveterate finder of four-leaf clovers; she would walk along with her father and amaze him by looking down at her feet and finding one after another. "How do you do it, Rozzie?" he would say in astonishment, and she would reply, with a child's seriousness: "It just makes a different pattern in the grass."

She plucked a tiny, blue-purple blossom shaped like a miniature snapdragon, so small and perfect it reminded her that she had once believed in fairies. Alan identified it immediately as a kind of mint.

"Skullcap, they call it. Rather inappropriate, if you ask me—looks more like a dunce's hat. But maybe they meant numskull cap." Roz laughed. Alan grinned at her and shrugged ruefully. "Not rare," he said. "Their name is legion." And as they continued to walk along the rampart, Roz soon lost herself completely in the absorbing task of spying out minute and hidden patterns in the grass, all of which Alan quickly identified for her.

It wasn't until they had walked almost all the way back to the road and were standing not more than a hundred yards from the steep clifflike edge that Roz thought once again of Montfort Abbey. It no longer seemed so essential or important to know just where she stood, what the true story was; yet, she wanted to know what Alan thought. She realized suddenly that what he thought was very important to her.

"Alan?"

"Yes, love?" he said casually, turning to her, the wind rippling his hair, hands as always thrust casually into his rumpled trousers. Momentarily distracted by the "love," she blinked at him, then remembered the question she had been about to ask.

"Do you think everything has happened because of my coming here?"

He looked at her, and she knew that, like her, in some part of his mind he had been going over all the events at Montfort as they walked, trying to find some sense in what had gone on. Now he shook his head.

"No, I don't. I suppose you could be a kind of catalyst. But the situation existed before you came, and if you hadn't come, it would have been something or someone else. It was Giles's decision to bring out the papers, maybe even his finding of them, that started everything. It really has very little to do with you personally." He paused, regarding her. "But you know, Roz, speaking of all that—something has been bothering me. The ruining of the garden, the threats, the terrorizing, the attempted murders, if that's what they were—are obviously all related, that's clear enough. But there's something else. It's almost as though there were a contradiction somewhere." Alan stared off across the heath, considering. "I'm not sure the same person—or even the same group—is responsible for everything. There's the careful planning and execution of the garden sabotage, always falling just short of irrevocable disaster. But along with all that there's the violence against persons—first Giles, then Florence, now you and Francesca." Alan stood reflectively for a moment, then went on. "I just don't know. It's as though there were two different modes of thought at work. Two entirely different attitudes toward life and its value."

Roz stared at his profile. He was right. Not just two different people. Two different ways of seeing.

"But who?" she murmured speculatively. "My experience with Francesca last night, and then the Porcelain Garden—the odd thing is that, taken at face value, they both seem to be the ultimate action, the final step. Real destruction, and real murder. Two kinds of killing, two desperate last-ditch efforts, one against a place, the other against a person. But why both?"

Alan turned to face her. His face was serious. "I just don't know." He kicked at the ragged overhanging edge of the path and walked a few steps. "I just can't get at the pattern, the logic of it all . . ." He stopped, looking back at her. "But to answer your earlier question, No, I'm quite sure it's not because of you. It's all on Giles's head. He enjoys his power

236

over people—likes to be in charge, to play them up, manipulate their lives. I imagine he thinks, has always thought, that no one else is quite up to him, socially or intellectually. And there really isn't a straightforward bone in his body, as far as I can tell. And the rest seem almost to have caught it from him. Over the years, evasion and indirection have become a habit of life at Montfort, no one ever saying quite what he means. It's a taint, like a contamination or a blight. The garden's full of malice, but still so beautiful it turns everyone inside out and backward, throws us all off guard."

Roz nodded. "Sometimes I feel as though I'm stuck inside the looking glass, with everything the opposite of what I think. A game of chess where the rules are always changing. Change lobsters and dance."

"You, of course, are Alice. And who am I? The White Knight?"

Roz laughed. "You do always seem to run to the rescue. Or I run to you. But no, I don't think you're the White Knight. You're hardly ineffectual." She looked down, suddenly embarrassed.

"But I have no answers," he said gently.

"Maybe we're asking the wrong questions," Roz replied. "Oh, I don't know; I just don't know. I'm not used to being so confused."

"Never mind," Alan said. "You're safe with me." He reached out and took her hand, pulled her arm across his chest until she faced him, and slid his other arm around her back. Then he kissed her, quite gently at first, then more strongly, until Roz felt herself spiraling away, losing herself, far above the tiny figures embracing on the earthen rampart that stretched away to either side.

A car whooshed down the highway, honking appreciatively. Startled, Roz stepped back from Alan, caught her heel in a small dip in the path, and fell toward the side slope. Alan grabbed at her, caught her arm, and jerked her back. His face was white. He pulled her into his arms again.

"Here now, don't do that to me. I thought I'd lost you. If you'd fallen down into those briars I'd have had the devil's own time getting you back out. I'd have to send for the rescue unit and a set of extricators. They're centuries old, strong as barbed wire, and as complicated as the inside of Giles's head. And every bit as dangerous." He hugged her to him, studying her face, her eyes. "Phew, that's better. You frightened me." Roz buried her face in the soft tweed of his jacket. *The smell of paint thinner will never be the same,* she thought. She did not feel so bewildered nor isolated now; Alan, at least, was of a piece, was what he seemed. She clung to him, letting her head rest just for a little while against his chest.

Presently she drew back. Alan let her go, and they stood side by side, looking past the road across the flat meadows. Below them, cows now meandered with stupid unconcern across the highway along a smeared and muddy track, a slippery, medieval cowpath that completely obliterated the modern pavement. The cowpath had probably been there for centuries before the highway. Beyond, just along the horizon to the north and west, Roz made out a shape shimmering in the haze, a faded outline of blue with towers as faint and elusive as a ship far at sea. She stared, blinked, stared again, not sure that it was real. A single central tower, impossibly massive, square—no, not really square . . . She nudged Alan and pointed.

"Is that Ely?"

Alan stooped slightly to squint along the line of her pointing finger, then stood up.

"You're right. It is indeed Ely. We're in luck. You can't always see it from here; it's fifteen miles away as the crow flies. But it's one of my favorite sights in all the world. Would you like to go there? It's well worth the trip. We can get there for tea, or a late lunch."

Roz nodded, her eyes still on the massive cathedral

238

rising out of the flat land, so far away. She had seen it before, driving toward Montfort that first innocent day. The shape of a fist, one finger pointing upward.

"Come along, then," Alan said, grabbing her hand, and together they slid and scuffled down the steep path to the car.

23

WHEN THEY DROVE INTO THE TOWN OF ELY THE breeze had dropped completely, so that earth and sky seemed to be waiting for some anticipated revelation. The crooked houses and the bumpy streets resembled a picturesque landscape jigsaw puzzle done on someone's unmade bed, and, above it all, in massive disproportion, reared the great cathedral, shadowing and sheltering everything beneath. A great bell tolled at intervals, the sound dropping like a huge, round stone into the silence.

They had a lunch of thick cheese slabs with country bread and tomatoes and pints of bitter in a small pub off the cathedral green. Then they walked out into the still, suspended air. Time lagged and expanded around the ancient confines of the great cathedral as they walked silently in and out of its precincts, always aware of the great tower rising heavy and improbable out of the center of the simple, cross-shaped structure.

Roz had visited other cathedrals, but she had never seen anything like Ely, its ramparts soaring straight up to the single octagon, columns and arches of honey-colored stone dwarfing the rows of houses, also of the same honey-colored stone, along the streets of the little town. The houses seemed to huddle to one side, leaving the huge cathedral alone, its arches, lancets, turrets, and battlements completely dominating the sky.

They went inside, walked down the nave to stand at the crossing, and looked up the dizzying eight stories to the wooden vaults of the lantern. The vaulted interior lifted and soared like frozen fountains of stone, like fireworks arrested at the burst. Roz stood quietly staring up past the high clover-shaped clerestory windows along the high arches of gray stone, and found herself suddenly and sharply reminded of the great, vase-shaped elm trees, leafless as in winter, that had once lined the streets of home.

After a while Alan spoke. "This is the second longest nave in England—still standing, that is. Both Glastonbury and St. Edmund's were far longer, but, of course they've been destroyed. The one at Montfort was the fourth." They walked back down the length of the nave, their footsteps echoing in the vaulted interior. "The original tower fell in, you know. Almost a thousand years ago. They built this one afterward, and it stayed." Alan stopped at the end of the nave and looked around. "Of all English cathedrals, this is the one I love the best." He paused again. "Would you like to walk outside?"

Roz nodded, and Alan led her toward a cavelike door partway down the nave. A black-gowned verger stood red-faced and beaming, his hands folded behind him. Alan slipped a coin into the alms box beside him.

"This is the prior's door. There was a Benedictine Abbey here at one time. Abbot Simeon began it in 1083, and for a while this Abbey and the one at Montfort vied for the position of cathedral church. Ely won, and became the cathedral for this area in 1109. I suppose it must have been a bitter disappointment for the Abbot of Montfort. It took one hundred years for the nave and transepts to be built, another four hundred for the rest. The church at Montfort was never finished, and later, of course, Gilbert tore it down."

He waited for Roz to catch up; she had been staring upward, almost hypnotized by the great tower, an octagonal tunnel into the sky. They walked out into the Cloister Garth, two sides and a low wall, the stonework ruined now, but the lawn still mown, as though the enclosure had not fallen. Roz felt momentarily disoriented; this ruined cloister and the one at Montfort might have been the same.

It was so quiet here. Simple and secure. Ely, cathedral for eight hundred years. *There* was a past for you. She looked away from the remaining arches tucked against the wall of the church, out across the close-clipped lawns of the cathedral precincts. What looked like a farm road ran, rutted and stone-cobbled, down a slight hill beside a pasture; there were long, low cross-timbered buildings beyond, still within the walls of the park. A thin line of wire blocked off the end of the pasture from the buildings, and several fat, gray sheep meandered nonchalantly over the grass, nipping and crunching.

"And sheep may safely graze," Roz thought. She murmured the words from the old hymn over and over as they walked down toward the nearest building. Constable had painted scenes like this two hundred years ago, perhaps in this very place. And Montfort had once been like this.

But no longer. What Ely had become—surviving the centuries, belonging to no one family, not part of an estate, not invested with a persona—Montfort might once have been. Instead, it had become, as Alan said, a garden of malice.

"Come along, we'll have a look at the King's School," Alan was saying. He took her arm, and together they continued down a rough path along one side of the road. "It will give you an odd sense of *déjà vu;* many of the buildings are very like what's left of

241

Montfort." He stopped suddenly and grinned his triangular smile at her. "See here, I'm feeling rather tiresomely like a tour guide. I'll just keep still for a while; if you have any questions, you'll ask, won't you?"

And so they walked, not speaking, toward the long, low buildings of the King's School, peered companionably into the dining hall, the ruins of the Infirmary, the Prior's House, the tiny, exquisite Prior Crauden's Chapel; together, but thinking their own thoughts.

On the way back up the road, late sun sent their shadows fleeing over their shoulders onto the grassy verge, and Roz found to her dismay that tears were running down her cheeks. Alan glanced at her.

"Can I help?" he asked gently.

"Oh, Alan," she said, turning to him. "I keep asking myself, Why can't Montfort be what it seemed? I think of going back to Montfort, and driving down the drive, and there it is—the same amber stone, the arches and the towers, and you look and you think you see one building. But that's only what you think you see, because it's all an illusion, bits and pieces put together by a trick of perspective, and none of it, *none* of it is true. Just tricks and lies. I wanted it to be true; I wanted Giles to be what he seemed, and Viola, and the papers, and the garden. But what I wanted has nothing to do with what really is."

Alan had stopped walking, and deliberately now he reached for her, grasped her around the waist, lifted her off her feet, and set her on the low stone wall that ran along the road toward the cathedral. Then he took his handkerchief from a back pocket, handed it to her without a word, and lightly hoisted himself up next to her. Roz sat there sniffling into his handkerchief while Alan, leaning back slightly, stared up at the cathedral, his hands on the edge of the wall, his long legs swinging back and forth. Finally, he began to talk in a low, matter-of-fact voice.

"There are basically two kinds of people in the

world, you know; those who want to believe the best of people, and those who always believe the worst. The first risks appearing naive, the second cynical. The first—I'll call them the yea-sayers"—and here he nodded at her—"tend to let people go their own way, perhaps too easily assuming that the world will wag along well enough on its own, much as it always has. Take Ely, for instance—always changing hands, Abbot this and Bishop that, this bit left undone, the first tower falling in and wrecking the whole middle of the nave, no one ever really taking charge—yet, here it is after all these years, incomplete, but still magnificent. All because people believed that things would work out in the end, that other people much like themselves would take care of everything. Negligent, sometimes naive—perhaps. Still, people of a benign and well-seeking disposition, no doubt responsible through negligence and naivete for some of the world's ills, but much more for its good." Alan paused. Roz listened intently, no longer sniffling. He looked at her briefly, smiled, and then went on.

"But it's the second type that can be peculiarly evil and, in fact, corrupting; I suppose because finally the attitude of mind arises out of an extreme excess of ego—an individual and not a collective ego such as built this place." Alan waved a hand upward at the cathedral. "That person—the ill-thinker, the cynic—can never bring himself to believe that anyone is smarter, or more capable, or more deep-seeing, more in possession of the truth than he. The rest of the world is gullible, open to manipulation. The person doesn't see a mirror image of himself in everyone he meets, as the first one does; he sees a diminished version—smaller, weaker, less intelligent, a face deformed, and all too often beneath his contempt. That person, in fact, fancies himself more powerful, more intelligent than God. Think of Milton's Satan and his supreme arrogance, assuming that God would think and act as he does. Or Iago, believing Othello and Cassio guilty of his own vile passions, turning

243

their virtues hideously against them, all because the daily beauty in their lives made him ugly. Or the Pardoner. Or Gentleman Brown. Or Hitler. It's hubris, of course, purely and simply putting oneself above all, taking other people and twisting them into the shape of whatever suits one's fancy. Finally, what it comes to is forcing souls. Is there any greater evil than that, really?"

Alan stopped to gaze over the field of sheep. Roz felt her own mind beginning to spin around, absorbing what Alan had said. Forcing souls. Twisting lives. No one as smart—so much in possession of the truth, either as it was or as it ought to be. Naive. Easy to fool, innocent, young. A picture shimmered in the shadows of her mind. The great cathedral rose, persisted through centuries, straight and true. Francesca's face: pale, arrested, unfinished, a perpetual possibility. Lines from Eliot came to her: "Time present and time past/Are both perhaps present in time future/And time future contained in time past/ . . . Into the rosegarden." There was the truth about Giles and the Lady Viola papers and the past. Not contained, but constrained.

Roz turned slowly toward Alan. His eyes had a faraway, abstracted look. He was frowning now, but his hands still rested lightly on his knees. She watched him as the silence lengthened. "What that leads to, I suppose," she said after a while, "is the conviction that everyone but yourself is laughably, absurdly easy to fool—deserving, even, as we all stand innocently eager and ready to have the wool pulled over our eyes. The wolf says, 'Baa, baa black sheep, have you any wool?' and the black sheep grins and says, 'Yes sir, yes sir, three bags full' and hands them over."

Alan nodded. "The wolf may wear sheep's clothing, but he is still very much a wolf."

"Don't you think these yea-sayers of yours can be just as persistent in their efforts—when they're finally convinced that evil has in fact been done?" she asked speculatively.

Alan's profile was stern; he stared intently at the cathedral. Slowly he turned to her, reached up, and with one finger gently pushed back a lock of hair. "I certainly hope so, because there is no escaping the fact that you and I, fair Rosamund, my very fair Rosamund, are of the first persuasion. We like to think the best of everyone, to think everyone acts from the best of motives. It's so much easier, really; there's so much less responsibility." He sighed. "But however attractive that view of the world may be, I think there is no evading the fact that our friend Giles is clearly of the latter. A soul-forcer of the first magnitude. Who must be stopped, at whatever cost."

Roz sat bolt upright, staring across the field toward Ely. In a moment of insight, all the sharp-edged, glittering fragments shuffled, shook, and, with one final click, shuddered still. And there it was.

She knew why Giles had hired her out of all the others, knew what he had wanted her for, knew finally and without a doubt the extent of his manipulation of the past, the present, and the future, and the depth of his corruption. The reason for her presence, her part in the events at Montfort was all too clear. He had chosen her precisely for her innocence, her inexperience, her naivete. And her need. She was perfect, and he had made her his prod, his stalking horse, his cover. She had believed everything with her own peculiar kind of blindness. He had been certain she would do exactly what he wanted, agree with him and support him, no questions asked. And to a large extent, she had. For all he cared about was his mother's garden, frozen in time, a monument to Viola the kind, the just.

But what of the other Viola, who, according to Francesca, had corrupted her, forced her body—and, even worse, her soul—into a mold she hadn't fit, would never fit? A version of herself that had not

245

been true. It was a horrible, monstrous vision. And now Giles, trying to do the same—forcing the others to accept his version of the past.

But it was too late. She knew what he had done. Words across a page, almost invisible, engraved in white on white. A date—March 23, 1968. A salutation—Dear Frankie. She had tucked the paper away, meaning to ask Giles when she got the chance why he had been transcribing these letters. It had seemed odd, but not important; in all the confusion about Francesca in the Maze, she had forgotten. Until now. For of course he had not been transcribing them at all. He had been creating them. Giles, in seeking to preserve his mother's image for himself and for posterity, had not recovered but rewritten the past.

The destruction of the garden had not been the real evil, the true malice. The real evil was in Giles. Forcing souls, forcing lives. Even dead ones. She sat up straight, staring up at the tower of the Cathedral.

"Alan," she said. "I think the papers are a fraud."

Alan jumped down from the stone wall, stood in front of her, his hard muscular chest pressing against her knees, his hands on either side of her.

"Why?" he said.

She told him briefly about the backing sheet. "But it may not be enough to stop him. He could claim he was just transcribing. That's why I've got to see the originals," she said quietly. "He's kept them from me all this time; he must suspect there are ways to tell if the letters are fakes. But he doesn't know how much I know. I have to force his hand, make him give me access to the papers so I can prove the so-called originals are the ones he's just written. But I can't let him see that I know; I may have come too close already." Then, in a sudden paroxysm of regret, she cried, "I just can't believe that all the papers are fakes."

Alan's arms slid around her. He pressed closer,

holding her. In a moment she had recovered. "Maybe they're not, not all," she said. "But I'll find out."

Alan smiled at her. "That's the spirit. When do you start?"

"As soon as we get back."

Alan regarded her for a moment. "It's getting rather late," he said, looking back over his shoulder. The spiked blue shadow of Ely lay full-length across the grass, blanketing the Cloister, reaching long, probing fingers toward them. "I thought we might not go back tonight. There's a little inn here in Ely, called of all things the Sheep and Goats," he said. "I thought we might stay the night and go back in the morning."

He watched her gravely, patiently. The longing for him, both physical and emotional, rose up strongly in her. To extend the interlude, not just for a few more hours, but for a day, a night. . . .

As she looked at him, unable to decide, he moved his hands to her waist and lifted her down slowly, so that she slid the whole length of his body and stood for a moment pinned close between the wall and him. Her whole body flooded with warmth. He bent and kissed her, his arms a wreath enfolding her, until she broke away, almost in tears.

"I just can't stop thinking . . . what I really want . . ."

"It will all come right," he interrupted cheerfully. He let her go and stepped backward. "Everything, that is." He grinned. "I told you I was of the first persuasion, didn't I? Incurably hopeful for the best. And so are you, or you wouldn't even bother."

He reached down, took her hand, and they started up the little hill, past the sheepfold. The sheep piled up against the fence, jostled each other impatiently, and hooted their hoarse, expectant bleats. Roz and Alan walked up the rutted road, past the partially intact Cloister, along the great west front of Ely. Expectations. Trusting the future to contain the past. Those of the first persuasion. It would all come right.

When they reached the car, Alan stopped and turned to her. "Well, what do you think? Shall we stay?" His voice was casual. In his eyes she read neither a demand nor an entreaty, purely and simply an invitation. She was free to choose.

"Yes," she said. "Oh yes."

"I suppose," Roz murmured lazily, hours later in their room at the Sheep and Goats, which was lit by firelight for the cool June night, "we should have let someone at the Abbey know we weren't coming back tonight."

There was a muffled snort somewhere near her left ear. Alan propped himself up on his elbows and looked down at her. "I think it's quite probable that one or another of them has tumbled to it by now," he said gravely as he bent to kiss her. "Besides, who cares?"

24

THEY RETURNED TO MONTFORT ABBEY ABOUT ten o'clock the next morning. Roz was surprised to find that Ely was less than an hour away by straight road; she had had the sense during her brief interlude with Alan of being far removed in time and space from Montfort and everything connected with it. The time away had given her a better sense of where she stood in relation to all that had happened, and what she had to do. She was returning to Montfort determined not to let Giles use her and the papers any longer as a flail to make the others do his bidding; if he had in fact forged the letters about Francesca, as it seemed certain he had, then she would prove it and see that they were suppressed. The Badgetts would no longer have to go to such desperate lengths to protect themselves. And the rest of the papers? Roz hoped—on the whole, believed—they were authentic. In fact, she was counting on this. When she finished what she had to do, there would still be letters and diaries, even if she herself did not edit them. Viola would not be lost entirely.

They pulled up in front of the gatehouse. There was not a soul to be seen. Alan stopped the car and turned to her.

"Here we are, my love. As the walrus did in fact say . . ."

Roz nodded. "The time has come."

Alan leaned over and kissed her at some length, then moved to open his car door.

"No, don't get out," Roz said quickly. "I want to find Giles and talk to him alone. He's not going to like what I have to say. If you or someone else were there . . ."

He looked at her for several moments. "I understand," he said finally. "But see here, you'll call me if you need me? Shout or scream or ring me up?" He looked mildly worried.

She smiled. "Thank you, Alan. But really, you know, I *can* take care of myself."

He nodded. "All right, then. I'll just go along and put the car away, then go across to my place for a wash and brush-up. One loud hail out any window, you know . . ."

Roz kissed him quickly and got out of the car. "Yes, I do know," she said through the window. "See you later."

She walked quickly away from the car as it pulled away down the drive, and went into the Gatehouse Arch.

The little ticket window was closed and blank. The Courtyard buildings were as silent and empty as a mausoleum. *Giles is probably with the papers,* Roz thought, as she went up the turret stairs. The door to the Viola Room was ajar. She pushed it open and peered inside, expecting to see Giles at his desk.

No Giles.

And odder still, no papers.

There was not a file folder, not a box, not a volume of diary to be seen. The whole place had been cleaned out.

Roz turned and hurried back down the stairs, through the Courtyard to the Refectory. She went inside.

"Giles?" she called. No answer. No sounds from the kitchen indicating Mrs. Farthing might be in attendance. *They can't* all *be gone,* she thought as she dashed up the stairs to her room. She had to make sure that the backing sheet was safe. She had put it in the pocket of the skirt she'd been wearing the afternoon Florence . . .

Her hand found the skirt hanging in the clothes press; she felt the pockets—yes, the right one crackled reassuringly.

"Rosamund?"

She whirled, yanking her hand out of the pocket as though it had caught fire.

Giles was standing in the doorway of her room, a grim look on his face. Instinctively folding her hands behind her back like a naughty child, she took a step away from the press.

"You startled me."

"So I see. I'm terribly sorry; I didn't realize you were so absorbed." He moved forward a few steps into her room, and Roz had to stop herself from falling back before his advance. She glanced over her shoulder; both windows were closed. But why was she so apprehensive? There was nothing to be afraid of.

"I was rather worried about you when you didn't return last night."

"Yes, well . . ." Roz stammered. *Damn it,* she

250

thought, *where's my firm resolve and sense of control now?*

"But of course I knew you were in good hands," Giles said without irony. In fact, he seemed quite preoccupied. After a moment, he went on. "But I'm afraid your absence was rather overshadowed by the latest disaster."

Roz blinked. What now?

"Evidently Francesca staged a return appearance yesterday afternoon while I was sleeping—I still haven't got my strength back, you know—and absconded with all the papers we've worked so hard on. I needn't tell you it puts us right back where we started. Even further, since there are no other copies."

Giles sat down wearily on Roz's bed, the picture of dejection. "I'm afraid I can't allow this to go on. *I* can't go on. I can't stand up to the lot of them any longer, Rosamund." He looked up at Roz, a beleaguered expression on his face. "I'm giving up."

Roz stared at him in disbelief. Could it be true? Before she could even confront him with her charges and her evidence? She felt a stab of disappointment. Now she would never know the truth.

"I've talked to Hugh, and we've come to an agreement. I'm going to show him all the papers. He's to go through them and delete any that he believes are detrimental to his family's well-being. I don't see any other way." Giles sighed. "Do you?"

Roz shook her head, giddy with relief. There would still be a chance.

"And all because of that silly fellow, Hugh's brother. Frankie that was. Grotesque, isn't it? A terrible tragedy, so hard on the family. Elsie Farthing simply idolized that boy—her nephew, you know. He was like a son . . . I don't know what they would have done without my mother. She was so sympathetic, so supporting. Anything they wanted, any help . . ."

251

Roz watched as Giles stood up, walked over to the window, and gazed out over the garden.

"When she died . . . when she died, she left . . ." His voice trailed off. He cleared his throat. Roz wished she could see his face.

"She left . . ." he went on abruptly, almost angrily, as if struggling for control, "she left . . . a frightful mess." He turned around, smiling oddly. Roz was certain that he had not finished the sentence as he meant to when he started. She also did not like his smile.

"How fortunate I am to have you here," he said. "How fortunate we both are to be able to make a new start."

"I see you're uncertain," Giles said, as Roz looked at him blankly. "I think I can guess why. But consider, my dear Rosamund. If I agree to hand over the papers in question, mightn't it put an end to all the controversy? Then you and I can go on as we were." He regarded her with a disconcertingly ingenuous look. Roz studied his face, assessing his sincerity. Could it be that she had misjudged him? That he had seen the error of his ways and was about to make amends? It was almost too much to hope for. Or— even too much more to hope for—that his version, after all, was the true one? But no, it couldn't be; the others . . .

"At any rate," he said briskly, "I've made arrangements with Hugh to go to Duke's Library this morning. I can't show him the copies now, since Francesca has spirited them away, and he wants to see the originals, anyway. I'm so glad you've come back, because I need you with me. As a witness, and as a . . ." He waved his hand, leaving the word somewhere in the air.

It fitted so perfectly with her plans. A chance to see the originals without having to resort to threats or ultimatums after all. She pictured the whole scene in her mind: the drive to Cambridge, the trivial conversation, and then the actual papers. Hugh there as a witness . . . It was perfect.

"Of course, Giles," she said. "If you'll just give me a chance to wash and change, I'll be right with you."

"Oh, surely," Giles said. He nodded briefly, then turned and walked out of the room. "I'll meet you in the drive by the Gatehouse," he said, his voice floating hollowly down the empty hall. "In ten minutes' time."

She heard his steps going slowly down the stairs. The Refectory door slammed. Then she quickly washed, brushed out her hair, changed into the skirt that held the folded backing sheet, and hurried downstairs after Giles.

"Miss Howard," said Hugh Badgett, nodding at her from beside a maroon touring car. Giles was already sitting in the back seat. He leaned forward. Roz found herself looking straight into his eyes. Their glances met and locked. Giles's eyes were hard and opaque as marbles, but there was a gleam in them. A gleam of what? Fear? Excitement? Roz took a step backward. It had been almost a challenge, almost as if he knew what she knew. She hesitated.

"I'm not allowed to drive as yet, so Hugh has kindly consented to drive us in his car. Do get in, Rosamund."

"Miss Howard?" Hugh had opened the door for her and stood waiting politely.

"Just a moment," she said. "I'll just run across and tell Alan . . ."

"Oh, bother Alan," Giles said crossly. "I've told the librarians we'd be there by half past eleven and it's nearly quarter to. Must you?"

Remembering her last words to Alan, Roz decided not. This was one situation she could handle on her own.

"All right, Hugh," Giles said, as though talking to a chauffeur.

Without a word, Hugh yanked off the brake, let in

253

the clutch. With an angry spurt of gravel, the car shot forward along the drive, taking the three of them to Duke's Library, Cambridge, and the original Lady Viola papers, one of which should correspond exactly to the impression on the paper Roz carried with her, the letter she was almost certain had been typed by Giles himself not more than a week ago.

25

OVER THE NEXT SEVERAL HOURS IT SEEMED TO Roz that time stretched and folded like an accordian, the duration of some events seen as though on edge, narrow, oblique, and sharp; others drawn-out, flat, mundane. One moment she was watching the buildings of Montfort slide together behind the trees, the next moment they were at the outskirts of Cambridge, speeding by rows of dark, gray stone townhouses, shabby Georgian villas blurring at the margins, buildings closing in canyonlike as Hugh drove along the busy main road. Hugh was going quite fast; Roz wondered with a chill of apprehension if he might solve all their problems once and for all by running the three of them into a wall at high speed. But no. That didn't happen in real life, and it wouldn't be in character—not in his. In his forays into the garden Hugh—at least, she assumed it was Hugh—had always avoided finality.

They stopped at a traffic light; then Hugh went ahead to the left. Beside them, the rows of grimy houses opened out onto a large green. Beyond it, Roz made out the first tall Jacobean gates of the University.

"Slow down, Hugh," Giles said from the back. "We're almost there. That's Jesus along there. Just turn right on King's Parade, and Duke's Way is the third turning to your right past Market Square."

"I know," Hugh said wearily.

They bumped along past the ornate twin-towered gate of King's College, the massive lace oblong of King's College Chapel with its four oddly small towers poking up like the stiff decorated legs of a four-legged beast on its back, past the examination halls, the market, and down a little alley so narrow one door handle scraped the wall and Roz had to snatch her hand back quickly from where it rested on the windowsill to keep from grazing her knuckles.

They stopped in a chasmlike medieval court. Here the stone was blackened with coal smoke, pitted, moss-gilded. The ancient buildings wavered over them, institutional, scholastic, safe. Duke's College Library and the original papers at last.

They walked single file through an arch built for medieval people—barely high enough to clear Roz's and Hugh's heads; Giles had to duck. Up stone steps hollowed out like bowls, so that for a moment Roz felt the sense of being back at Montfort, where it had all begun. The steps rose up steeply like a wall and ended at a very unmedieval glass and golden oak door that read in plain painted letters on the glass: THE LIBRARY.

They stood inside a long, vaulted chamber, very dark in spite of the high, stone casement windows that lined the walls. The window light was deflected and absorbed by rank upon rank of amber varnished bookshelves set at right angles to the walls, crammed with books of every size, leaning drunkenly against each other, new and old, frayed and crumbling, smooth calf worn to suede, shiny fabric bright as ribbons. Books were piled on desks, on chairs, waiting to be replaced. The place smelled of neatsfoot oil, dust, and dry, old wood. It was as quiet as a tomb.

A rather small woman with a round face and a fringe of white hair standing out around it like a sunbonnet appeared, holding a handful of stapled-together sheets. She peered uncertainly through round spectacles, as if surprised to see them.

"Mr. Montfort-Snow? What an unexpected pleasure so soon after your last visit."

"Mrs. Felp," Giles said. He stopped, as though uncertain what to do next.

Roz looked at the little woman curiously. Hadn't Giles said something about an appointment? But clearly they were not expected. And why had he been here recently? She turned to look at Giles and was startled to see him standing pale, shaken-looking in front of Hugh, as though something awful were about to happen. He cleared his throat. "Yes. I've . . . we've . . ." He turned slightly toward Hugh, then back. "We've come to see my mother's papers. If you could just get them?" He gulped, his eyes darting back and forth.

Roz stared. What in the world was wrong with him? He acted like a man on the verge of collapse. Or someone in terrible danger.

"Ah, all of them, Mr. Montfort-Snow?" Mrs. Felp inquired with raised eyebrows. Giles stood silent, as though he were in a trance.

Looking at him oddly, Hugh stepped forward and said apologetically, "Yes, if you would. All of them."

"Well, then, Mr. Montfort-Snow, certainly, if you'll just sign here, uh . . . will you wait or . . . dear me, sounds like leaving off the laundry, so sorry. Or?" She stopped and peered over the round glasses at Giles.

Inexplicably, Giles said nothing. Finally Hugh cleared his throat. "Mr. Montfort-Snow would like to have the originals brought out right now," he said briskly. "We have some things to go over." *Ah, good,* Roz thought. *Hugh taking charge at last.*

Mrs. Felp looked suspiciously at Hugh, then at Roz. "And you are?"

Giles jumped as though he had been poked, and said in a distracted voice, "Oh yes. So rude of me. Miss Howard and Mr. Badgett, my ah . . . concerned associates."

Mrs. Felp's eyes rolled like billiard balls from one face to the next. "Both of them?" Obviously she didn't approve.

Giles nodded.

"Then you'll want the conference room, won't you? It would be the most private, and comfortable for . . . ? The sunbonnet face hesitated, looking from Giles to Hugh to Roz. "The three of you?"

"The three of us," Roz said quickly, wanting to get this over with.

"Ah yes, the three of you." Mrs. Felp picked up some forms from a nearby desk and held them out to Giles. "If you would just fill these in for the documents you require."

Giles hurriedly scribbled on the forms and handed them back to the librarian.

"Please come this way," she said.

They followed Mrs. Felp down the hall toward another door. Inside were a long wooden conference table, much scarred, and several heavy wooden chairs.

"Thank you very much," Giles said nervously. Mrs. Felp looked at them and went out. They all sat down at the table, waiting.

Several tense and silent minutes later, she shuffled back into the room, her head hidden behind two large document boxes. Carefully, she placed them on the table in front of Giles.

"These are the first of the documents you requested, Mr. Montfort-Snow. Please call me when you require more. We don't like to take too many out at once, as you know." And with a disapproving look at Hugh and Roz, Mrs. Felp hastened away, shutting the door quietly behind her.

Giles slid the boxes across to Hugh without a word, crossing his legs to make himself comfortable. Neither man said a word. The room was very quiet, the tension palpable.

Hugh swallowed, blinked his eyes, and pushed the boxes toward Roz. "I can't," he said. "You do it."

Roz opened the first box. The letters were arranged alphabetically by correspondent's last name. Letters to Frankie Badgett, 1965–1967, 1968–1975. Ten manila file folders. It was in one of these that she would find what she was looking for.

She took out a small stack of green stationery, noting the lavender ink, the spidery hand. It must have taken Giles a while to be able to learn how to counterfeit his mother's hand. She wondered how long he had been at this. The lavender ink ran uniform and pristine across the pages. The pages were creased, a little smudged here and there, but otherwise in good condition. They looked authentic. She put them to one side and lifted out the larger stack of typed letters. They, too, were on old paper, and also looked authentic, identical to the copies she had read.

The only sound in the room was the rustle of paper, the hollow thump of the stack on the wooden table. Hugh sat facing her. He leaned forward.

"Do you know what they say about us? About my family, about my . . . brother?"

Roz nodded, passing the earlier letters to Hugh. He held them away at arm's length, as though they might burst into flames. As briefly as she could, Roz summarized the contents of the letters on the table in front of them.

Hugh covered his face with his hands. "Just as we suspected," he said. "It's all lies." Then he turned to face Giles. "Did you do it, or did she?"

Giles stared back at him coldly.

And that's precisely what I mean to find out, Roz thought as she began surreptitiously to leaf through the stack of typed letters, praying that Giles would keep his eyes on Hugh.

"It was you, of course," Hugh went on. "You've perverted the truth to make us look bad, and Viola look marvelous. Oh, it would have sold all right . . ." Hugh stopped and leaned against the table. "I'll tell you how it really was, Miss Howard. Frankie was my mother's favorite—golden curls, so handsome, beautiful, really. He was clever, but delicate, with this odd quirk. We always believed he would come out of it, without . . ." Hugh swallowed. *Oh God,* thought Roz, *don't let him break down now.* Hugh shook his head and continued.

"Viola took a liking to him, and began to invite him to her rooms for private audiences; he was so young, so vulnerable. She told him how beautiful he was, how smart, how she would do anything for him. She wanted to adopt him. But she didn't care for sons. She already had a son, and she had wanted a girl. It was so flattering, so romantic. She would give him money for things, and she promised . . . She told him she and Herbert had only slept together once, to have Giles, and never again, but she wanted Frankie for a daughter. She wanted Frankie to be made in her image. He was so young, so impressionable, and he loved her; she had a hold over him. He was confused about himself, but he would have outgrown it. We tried to stop him, but he loved her. Then he went away, and before we knew it, it was too late. But she kept her promise . . ."

"Never mind that," Giles interrupted. "That's not the way it was at all, of course," he said, glancing back at Roz.

". . . and now you want to use it, rake it all up again, but not the truth," Hugh said, turning on Giles. "You want to make it seem as though that's what Frankie really wanted, that we stood in his way—poor, dumb, unenlightened peasants, your damned salt of the earth . . ."

Giles laughed, a single sharp, dismissive snort.

"Really, Hugh. How could you suggest my mother would do a thing like that? It's unthinkable. All her readers know that. It simply wasn't in her character."

Roz looked down at the letters in front of her. Oh yes, the tone, the reasonable implication, the kindness, they were in character, totally in the character created by Viola for herself, in her published works, now perpetuated by Giles. Who had created whom? Had Viola begun what Giles had tried to finish? Or had she merely destroyed, not substituted? Yet there were the handwritten letters, so authentic-looking. Had Viola begun the revision herself? Or was it Giles alone? And which story was true?

Giles droned on in his defense of Viola, while Roz carefully lifted out one letter after another.

And suddenly, there it was. The exact duplicate of the letter compressed on the white backing sheet Roz carried now in her pocket, the sheet with a clearly dated watermark, showing that the letter with its backing sheet had been written no earlier than this year. The typing was partly superimposed on a letter clearly dated only last week. She had her proof. Giles was passing off as originals the letters he had written himself. Roz pulled the letter off the stack and hid it in her lap. Neither Hugh nor Giles noticed; they were intent on one another. Then Hugh spoke.

"But don't you understand? Viola is dead. She can't be hurt, and we can. That's why we did it, Francesca and I, why we took down the signs, pulled up the plants, cut down the roses." Hugh took a breath. "There are only two things that matter to you in all this world—your mother's memory, and that garden. And only one of them's alive. I thought if we could hurt it, hurt you through it, make you see something you loved hurt, then you would realize how it felt, to have something important to you ruined and destroyed. We've come to terms with what happened to Frankie, but we couldn't let you bring it all back again. Don't you understand? I didn't want to kill

260

the garden, but you wouldn't pay attention. You and she"—he gestured vaguely at Roz—"just kept on, not caring, until my mother . . ."

Hugh broke off, looking from Roz to Giles and back again. "Don't you understand? Your mother is dead, and Frankie and my mother are alive."

Giles stared coldly at him. "Not for long, I take it. That will certainly solve one problem. And as for Frankie, that remains to be seen, doesn't it?"

Hugh shook his head, unable to speak.

"But the fact is, Hugh, all your efforts, ingenious as they were, are to no avail. There are the original letters." He gestured at the pile on the table. "They prove the version Roz has summarized so clearly to you. My mother behaved exactly as a reader of her books, her poems, her garden essays would expect her to—as a lady, a generous benefactress, a wise and intelligent and sympathetic woman of the world. Incorruptible, and uncorrupting. That is the version the world has now, that is the version it will keep, and the version that will reveal you for what you are, all of you—peasants with petty minds. Not to mention your abominable transsexual sibling."

Roz stared at Giles, appalled. She had been wrong, too hopeful to the last. It had all been a ruse. Whatever he had had in mind, bringing Hugh here, insisting that she come, it was not a change of heart. But he no longer had any power over her, over any of them.

"No, Giles," she said clearly. "That's not the way it's going to be." She reached into her pocket, drew out the backing sheet, smoothed it out, and placed it on the table along with the matching original letter.

And stared in disbelief.

The paper was as smooth and flat and white and unmarked as the day it had been made. It had never been used as a backing sheet or anything else.

"Is this what you were looking for, my dear Rosamund?"

As she watched in horror, Giles held up a folded

sheet of paper. He smiled at her and Hugh. Then he brought his other hand up from underneath the table. In it was a small bottle of clear fluid. Still holding the paper, Giles reached over with his other hand and carefully removed the stopper with a little pop. A gray vapor wound serpentlike out into the air and caught the edge of the paper, withering it back on itself. Roz watched the paper shrivel away. Then Giles leaned toward them, smiling his glittering, sardonic grin.

"Fuming sulfuric acid, my friends. Oleum, they called it in the old days. Just the vapor can make a man's skin peel. A drop of it will burn through your clothes and your skin, right to the bone. A splash of this can melt your face, just as it has melted this piece of paper. I shall use it without hesitation if the two of you don't do exactly as I say."

26

THE BELLOWS OF TIME CONTRACTED AND expanded. For Roz, the next few minutes—hours?—had an almost hallucinatory quality. Stiff as a broomstick with her outrage, the librarian handed Giles a release to sign, and then the four of them, loaded down with document boxes, marched single file down the stairs and out into the little courtyard to the car. Mrs. Felp and Hugh continued to shuffle back and forth, carrying boxes, while Giles and Roz stood by. Back and forth, back and forth, bringing box after box of documents, bobbing and weaving down the steps, faster and faster, like automatons. They loaded the trunk until it was filled, then piled boxes in the back seat. Where had it all come from? The boxes from the conference room came last, piled on top of the rest in the back seat, leaving just enough room for a passenger.

Hugh stood behind Giles, rigid, his hands in his pockets. *Why doesn't he do something,* Roz thought desperately, *jump up and down, call for help, tell the librarian what's really happening, instead of standing there just doing what Giles wants?*

And then the shaking, bobbing broomsticks stopped. Mrs. Felp retired to her domain. A fine rain, little more than mist, had started.

"You drive," Giles said to her.

"I can't drive . . . I . . ."

"You drive," Giles repeated, almost imperceptibly bringing his hand up.

Roz got into the driver's seat and looked at the unfamiliar controls. Her heart sank. Thinking *what have I got to lose,* she fastened her seat belt. She was an experienced driver at home, but here everything was transposed. She fumbled with the key, looked up into the rear view mirror, and caught sight of her own eyes, wide and frightened.

"Hugh, you sit in front." Giles climbed into the back and sat in the middle, shoving boxes out of the way. As Hugh slid in next to her without a word, Giles leaned forward and held the bottle of acid between them, close to their necks.

"No talking," he said.

Roz looked at his face in the rear view mirror. *He's insane,* she thought. *I should have known.*

"Drive," Giles said.

"Where to?" she asked idiotically, staring in fascination at his reversed image in the mirror.

"Back the way we came, for now," Giles said. "Turn right here."

Roz obeyed, edging the unfamiliar car out into the busy street. Unexpectedly, cars whizzed by from the right, inches from the front bumper. She pulled backward instinctively in her seat. The car stalled.

Whatever had Giles had in mind, making her drive? She had little control over anything except her own reflexes, and those could betray her so easily, make her go left instead of right. She could think of very little besides not getting hit. That was why he had wanted her to drive, of course. It was impossible for her to think what to do next, how to stop him. Her mind was whirling, but she had to concentrate on driving, or they would all be killed right now.

Right, out, and around; close to the curb going left. Her stomach clenched, but she gritted her teeth and drove. Passing down the canyon streets, her own image came and went in the windshield, distracting her from the road ahead. Viola's face, smiling, wise, kind, sympathetic, the blond hair wound about her head, the tall forehead, the face of an angel, and behind it another face: smirking, ironic, cynical, corrupt. Giles's face in the rear view mirror. And another face: Francesca's, the Botticelli face, peering out behind the face of a tortured adolescent boy. What in the world had made her think that it all would ever make sense, that she could make it right?

She shut her eyes briefly, trying to rid herself of the terrible images coming at her in the glass. And suddenly she was in the reflection, not looking at it, but trapped inside. She was spinning down the wrong side of the road, a mirror image of herself; everything was reversed and topsy-turvy, so that for one terrifying instant, in which the panic spread like cold lightning from the frozen pit of her stomach out to every extremity, her brain clouded and her vision dimmed. Dizzy, she took a hard grip on the wheel and forced her eyes to see the road ahead. But ahead the road ran straight, a narrow ribbon winding down the mirror tunnel, out of time on into infinity, and they were all trapped inside a tube of unreality, where nothing was what it seemed. She felt oddly removed, abstracted, and there was a strange humming noise in her ears.

The humming rose to an intolerable shriek.

"You can shift now," Giles said behind her left ear. Of course. She shifted the gear lever, and the shriek subsided.

They were almost out of town, the traffic thinning, moving faster. There were fewer distractions, fewer reflections. The road was just a road. She shifted into fourth. Where were they going?

"Of course you realize what must happen now," Giles said in a conversational tone. "I'm going to have to arrange to kill you both. An accident while Hugh was desperately trying to make off with the papers, having forced me to give them to him in the library. Mrs. Felp can attest to my obvious anxiety." He held up a tire iron he had removed from the trunk.

Silence. Of course. Roz stared at the road ahead. That explained his odd behavior at the library. But kill them both?

"Giles, why?" she said, not really expecting an answer. Somehow, though, she still wanted it all to make sense.

"That should be obvious, my dear. These letters and diaries are of great importance. My mother's life is important. My mother's image, her garden, her public. I can't let you ruin that—either of you. All my work, all Mother's work . . . Oh, what's the use." Giles gave a snort of disgust. "You'll never understand," he said petulantly. "It's too late."

"Giles . . ." Hugh began. "Can't we come to some agreement . . ."

"No," Giles snapped. "You've had your chance. I asked you to reason with Frankie, get him to sell his share . . ."

It was true, then. Viola had left Frankie half of Montfort. A bribe, and she had kept her dreadful bargain. And suddenly the fragment of conversation she had heard that first night came back to her. Frankie, coming home to force Giles to sell. Refusing to sell Giles her interest. Even Montfort had not really belonged to Giles. Francesca had the key. Viola's key. That had begun it all.

"You're the only one left now," Giles said. "I've taken care of Frankie, and Florence won't last long. It's only you, Hugh. You're the last."

Hugh turned fixed, anxious, horror-stricken eyes on Giles. "You don't mean . . ."

The acid bottle shook, a drop flew toward them. Involuntarily, Roz flinched sideways. The car swerved over into the other lane. They were going too fast, the car like a rocket. The acid sizzled on the seat, filling the car with acrid fumes. She began to cough. Next to her, Hugh choked, leaned forward, and rolled the window down. The wind boomed in like the report of a gun. They were going too fast. Too fast for what? In her distraction, she had pressed the accelerator nearly to the floor.

The car shot down the road, past flat fenlands crisscrossed with dikes filled with bristling cattails, past the low land, the swamp, the heath. Where were they? How far from help? *Alan,* she thought. *Where are you?* But she was going another way, in the mirror—going to, not from. Alan was not here. She clutched the wheel, listening, doomed to drive forever. Behind her, Giles was coughing now . . .

And suddenly Hugh wrenched himself around, reached back, and caught Giles's wrist. The two men writhed together, bumping against her seat, while Roz sat forward, trying to get out of the way, trying to keep the car on the road. In the rear view mirror she saw the bottle of acid fly up and fall out of sight among the boxes. Fumes started to rise, filling the car. The breath choked in her throat, and she heard the sound of whimpering. It was all around her, coming from her. If only she had a weapon, something to bash them with. In helpless frustration, she banged her hands on the wheel. The car lurched and wobbled, throwing the wrestling bodies to one side. Des-

266

perately, she leaned forward, fixing her eyes on the road.

And suddenly she realized where she was. Driving not the other way in the mirror, but the other way on a road she had already traveled—with Alan, just yesterday. She clenched her hands on the wheel, trying to disengage her attention from the grunting struggle next to her, the car's speed crescendoing with her thoughts. In the distance on the right, almost like a mirage, she saw the long, clifflike shape of the Devil's Ditch rising high and sinuous, shimmering in the fine rain along the road. As though she were watching a movie, she saw herself and Alan, standing on the top and looking down across the road. The muddy cowpath. "Rather dangerous, that," Alan's voice came back to her. Wet black mud, spread by misting rain into an oily swath some twenty feet wide. The car screamed toward the muddy slick, the Devil's Ditch. She could hardly breathe. She had to get out of the car. Roz fought the urge to slam on the brake. If she hit the brakes going through that slick, they would skid . . .

And that was it. She gripped the wheel hard with both hands and tensed her body. Ahead the Ditch loomed. The car entered the slick and began to fishtail slightly. Slowly, through eons of mirror time, Roz picked up her foot from the accelerator and brought it down hard on the brake.

The car spun in a lazy swirl, throwing Hugh and Giles and the boxes of papers, the acid bottle and the tire iron against the sides of the car. As the car began to swing sideways, she lifted her foot off the brake and slammed the gas pedal to the floor, spinning the wheel the other way.

The back of the car whipped around like a scorpion's tail, then snapped straight, and the car ran headlong over the righthand verge, bumped on the slight depression at the edge of the Devil's Ditch, and slammed into the side of the chamois-colored cliff.

27

GILES PITCHED SIDEWAYS, BURIED IN DOCUMENT boxes. The windows shattered in a cascade of glass; the vapors began to dissipate. Papers flew out, floating in air. Hugh fell backward, whacking his head on the dashboard; he slumped, apparently unconscious. Roz felt herself forced sharply against the seat belt, then snapped back against the seat.

As soon as she thumped back, she turned the ignition off and yanked the car keys out of the lock. Her fingers found the seat belt release. Behind her, Giles was retching. She stepped onto the gravel shoulder and ran to the edge of the road. She looked both ways. The road was so low between the cattails that she couldn't see far in either direction. She ran around the back of the car and started up the little indented path to the top of the Ditch. She and Alan had been able to see a long distance from there. She would see a car and wave to it for help. Or see the nearest farmhouse.

She clambered to the top and looked around. Down the road, beyond the cattle slick perhaps a half mile, was a farmhouse. To get to it, she would have to scramble back down, past the car, past Giles and the unconscious Hugh. No. She had to stay away from the car.

She turned and looked back along the length of the Ditch. About five hundred yards from where she stood a little path led downward, cutting through the thick brambles and winding across the heath toward the house. She started down the track that ran along the top of the Ditch.

"Miss Howard!" a voice called. She stopped. Miss Howard. Only Hugh called her that. "It's Giles! He's unconscious. He's horribly burned with the acid. Please come back. I can't get him out."

Roz started back. There was a noise of pebbles dropping, a scrabbling sound near the path at the end of the Ditch.

The top of a head appeared. She stood paralyzed on the little path, clutching the ring of keys. Then her eyes met Giles's, not twenty feet away, raised over the edge of the Devil's Ditch. Their glances locked.

"Rosamund!" he called, lifting head and shoulders above the scrubby undergrowth of the Ditch. "Do come back. I won't hurt you, you know that. I have no quarrel with you. Come back to Montfort, and you can pack your bags and go. No more need be said. We'll call the contract void." As he spoke, his torso rose, higher and higher, until he put one foot on the path. His face was bland, his tone reasonable, forgiving, apologetic.

"I can't do that, Giles," she said, backing away.

"Hugh is unconscious, Rosamund. Aren't you going to help him?" Slowly, Giles moved toward her, his eyes dark pools reflecting nothing, growing larger. There was a shadow behind his eyes.

"What have you done to Hugh, Giles?" Roz asked, taking a step backward. "Is he dead, like the others?"

"Oh, Rosamund, my dear," Giles said with a sigh. "You're not nearly so naive as I thought, are you? That's precisely the trouble . . ." Holding her in his gaze, he stood tall and straight, silhouetted against the sky.

Giles took a firm step forward. "I saw you take that letter, you know. While you were gone, I came into your room and took it back."

Paralyzed, Roz watched him walk toward her, slowly, holding her in his cobra's gaze. Then he smiled. His right hand came up, holding the heavy tire iron.

And like a hare, suddenly free, Roz turned and flung herself headlong down the long, raised strip that stretched before her. Twenty miles across the heath it ran. Giles was running, too; she could hear his feet thumping the hard clay. Running as hard as she could, she heard the slap of feet coming closer and glanced quickly back over her shoulder. He was running effortlessly, swiftly, the iron swinging loosely in his hand. Her legs turned to lead, churning up and down helplessly, in slow motion. Her breath came ragged in her ears, rasped in her chest. The little path. Could she make the little path? Keep ahead enough to scramble down? She tried to remember, tearing along the narrow way, how far she and Alan had walked and what had been in the path. No hiding place. But she had tripped and stumbled, almost fallen down the side into the brambles. Only Alan's hand had stopped her.

She forced her eyes ahead, straining to make out the features of the path that ran like a raveled string along the rampart. Not far ahead, the path dipped and folded, the small depression barely noticeable if you weren't looking for it, fading into the uniform line of the Ditch's progress across the heath. There.

She flew along, clutching the car keys in her hand. He would think she was heading for the other path leading down. Forty yards, thirty—twenty. Leaping lightly over the little crevice, she stopped and turned to face him.

Giles was running hard now, eyes on the ground. He had seen her run by the downward path. She could go nowhere except ahead. He would surely run her down. But he was watching the path, looking down at the broken, unfamiliar ground. She had to get his eyes up off the path, distract his attention long enough to keep him from seeing the small crevice. Closer, closer. Twenty yards, fifteen, ten.

270

"Giles!" she shouted. At the same time, she raised the keys, held them poised in her right hand.

Giles jerked his head up, startled to see her so much closer than he had expected. He tried to slow down; he flung his arms out in a desperate attempt to stop before he crashed right into her. His surprised eyes moved from her face to the uplifted keys.

Then his foot caught in the furrow and slipped. He stumbled, and at the same time Roz flung the keys straight in his face. They caught him hard across the bridge of his nose. His mouth opening, he brought his hands up in a silent pantomime of pain. He fell toward Roz headlong, his momentum pitching him face first into her. She braced herself, lifted her knee, and caught his shoulder as he fell, simultaneously pushing with all her strength, deflecting him, and sending him rolling over the edge, spinning down until he crashed heavily into the barbed wire thicket of brambles. The brambles swallowed him up, closed over him, and held him fast, while Roz stood, covering her ears, staring down from the top of the Devil's Ditch.

Roz sat down, trembling, on the edge of the small crevice and closed her eyes. After a while she opened them. She heard the sounds of struggling, the rending and tearing of cloth. Then Giles lay still, his pale face gleaming through the dense, thorny branches of the bramble thicket. As she watched, he struggled feebly, gasping as the thorns tore at his flesh.

"Don't move, Giles," she said. "You'll tear yourself to pieces. Lie still." Giles struggled more fiercely this time; thorns as sharp as nails scratched the skin of one upraised hand. "Listen to me," Roz said firmly. "You're already bleeding. I don't know how long it will take me to get help. If you struggle anymore you may hit an artery, and bleed to death in five minutes, whether I go for help or not. But I'm not going until you tell me everything."

Giles writhed in the briars, but didn't speak. His eyes were fixed on her face.

"Giles, you can't fool me anymore. If you don't answer my questions, I'll walk away and leave you here. What did you do with Hugh? Is he dead?"

"No, no. I left him in the car. He's just unconscious."

"Did you kill Francesca?"

The brambles twitched, shuddered.

"Yes. I stabbed him in the Maze. You were right all the time. You saw just what you thought you saw. He was going to make me sell Montfort. Sell everything."

"How did you get in without our hearing you? And out again before Alan and I came back?"

"There's a door hidden in the yews against the wall on the Refectory. It swings back, and the yews swing with it. It leads from the closet next to the fireplace in the sitting room. There's a path straight into the center. Gilbert designed it, and my mother . . . used it. I'm the only one who knows about it. Frankie didn't know everything, even though Mother . . ." Giles moved painfully and seemed to sink deeper into the briars. "I hid his body in the closet while you and Alan were out searching."

"Where is Francesca now?"

"I drove him away in his car, with the copies, and put him into the Silchurch fen. You'll never find them. Anyway, they were only copies."

"And Florence?"

"I left the tea bags in her kitchen and took everything else away. I had to get rid of her; she was in my way. They were all in my way. Silly Badgetts. Without them . . ."

"What if I had drunk it?"

Giles said nothing. Trembling now with anger, Roz started to walk away.

"No, wait," Giles gasped. "Even if you drank one whole cup, you're young . . . I had to take the chance.

272

Florence had to go. But I wouldn't have let you die," he said plaintively. Roz felt sick.

"Did you tell Hugh the truth? Is Florence dead?"

"No . . . yes . . . I don't know. She may still be alive. Roz, get me out of here." His eyes, glittering through the brambles, pleaded with her. The blood ran in trickles over his face and the exposed flesh of his arms.

"You faked the insecticide, too, didn't you? To make people think it was you they were after."

"Yes." The acquiescence was barely audible. Then the words tumbled out, the sudden, querulous justification. "I thought if I seemed to be a target then no one would suspect. It was Hugh and Frankie who made me do it. Wrecking Mother's garden that way, threatening me . . . I had to get rid of all of them once and for all. Frankie didn't care about the Abbey, about Mother, the garden, any of it. She would have sold out just to spite me. And Mother. People would have thought badly of Mother . . . I had to protect her . . ." Giles slumped back, exhausted. His eyes closed.

Roz stood watching him, wondering if, in fact, his life were in danger. On the whole, she thought not. And on the whole, she didn't really care. One life snuffed out, three others endangered, all for a plot of ground, a mess of paper, and a dead woman's face.

"I'll go for help, Giles. But I have one more question. Which version of the Frankie story is true? Yours or theirs? The one that's in the letters you wrote, or the one Francesca and Hugh told me? Which Viola is true?"

Silence. Then grudgingly, carefully, Giles opened his eyes. He shook his head slightly. Roz waited. But he said nothing.

Roz turned, picked up the keys from the side of the path where they had fallen, and began to walk down the path toward the car.

And then she saw in front of her, inexplicably, a dark, smoky cloud spiral up from beyond the cliff edge. As she watched, the smoke ballooned silently into a ball of flames. Before she could put her hands over her ears the explosion came, loud and abrupt, as though some great breath had been expelled, in one giant outburst of disgust.

28

Roz sat on the stone bench in the Herb Garden. It was the only part of the Abbey Garden not somehow tainted by either the fact or memory of malice. Her bags were packed; she had come here one last time before leaving the Abbey for good.

Alan stood looking down at her, his hands in his pockets. "Still mourning the letters?" he murmured gently.

Roz nodded. All the letters, the real ones as well as the ones Giles had faked, had burned in the fire set by Hugh after he had come to. All Viola's diaries and letters, sent off on the wind by the explosion like so many bits of soot. The ones that had been found in the car with Francesca's body were useless, obliterated by the dark fen water. So that was the end of that. Giles had lied, too, about there being other copies.

"I shall never forget the sight of you standing there next to the Ditch, hardly a hair out of place, holding the keys in one hand and supporting Hugh in the other, your expression mildly quizzical. Waiting for the White Knight to show up, late as always. I couldn't tell whether you were frightened or relieved to have it finally over. Of course, we didn't know then that you'd taken care of Giles. The police and I broke all the speed limits on our way to Cambridge after I found the three of you gone without so much as a by-your-leave."

"I'm glad you came when you did," Roz said. "The rest doesn't matter." But it did. She could not keep the regret out of her voice. Alan reached out and touched her cheek.

"When you went away without saying anything, I knew I had to come after you straightaway. Cory had seen you leave, but we weren't sure when. Hugh was a surprise, but that was exactly Giles's plan. Get the two of you away at once. After all, you knew too much. What did I say about your never missing a thing?"

"But I *did* miss a lot, and if I hadn't been so gullible, if I hadn't wanted to trust Giles and believed him as long as I did, maybe Francesca would still be alive."

Alan looked down, picked up a pebble, and tossed it across the garden. "But Florence is all right. And the Badgetts will stay here. Now that Giles won't be around to lord it over Hugh, Beatrice will be glad enough to come back. They'll give it over to the Britannia Trust, with Elsie as caretaker. Elsie in charge at last—and of course Cory and Stella will be staying on to look after the garden. Everyone's agreed it's the best thing."

"And no one ever knew about the secret entrance into the Maze?"

"No. That's why Giles saw to it the Maze was let go and got so overgrown, I imagine. Far-seeing of him, wasn't it? Almost spooky, as though he had the dead whispering at him over his shoulder. Though Gilbert maintained it for less murderous and more sensual purposes, as did Viola. Open the closet, slide back the panel, and out you go to meet your lover. Viola, too, obviously treading the old man's footsteps. Even Cory had trouble finding where the latches were, they were so well hidden in the shrubs. Then straight on, and the hedges thinned out. He must have made the holes that evening, after he overheard Francesca telling you to meet her. That throaty actor's voice of hers—it carried right over to him. They'll have no trouble proving premeditation, not with those great holes whacked out, just waiting for someone to sit down and be stabbed through them. I'm glad it wasn't you."

Roz shivered slightly. Giles hadn't really cared. Florence, Francesca, herself—it had not mattered a great deal to him. There was something inhuman about Giles, something rooted and vegetable about his soul. Hugh had been right, the garden was Giles's closest—his only—relation.

And he had waited there, silently, unheard and unseen behind them. The hood fell back . . . Roz shook her head. That was going to take some getting over.

"It's not so much the letters," she said, picking at a tiny piece of thyme between her fingers. "It's more my idea of Viola. And Giles, and the whole place. Everyone's idea. It's such a shock, to have your sense of the past, the firm ground you thought you were standing on, heaved up and tossed aside. And you see it's all an illusion, strips of paper over the void . . . You wonder who created whom."

Alan nodded sympathetically.

"And now there will never be any letters," she went on. "We'll never really know why Giles did what he did. Giles won't tell. I'm sure Viola really did burn those letters, but whether it was for her sake or for Francesca's, we'll never know either. Leaving half of Montfort to Francesca, she must have felt some responsibility, some guilt. Only fair—she was Francesca's only begetter, you might say. Or was it just affection? And Giles, wanting it all to himself—the Garden, of course, the Abbey, but even more his mother. Wanting her all to himself. And so creating her the way she should have been, ought to

276

have been, maybe even was, in his mind. Was that what he thought he was doing?"

"It doesn't bear much looking into, does it?" Alan said.

Roz shook her head. No. It didn't bear much looking into. Not at all. She saw Giles's face looking out at her from underneath the brambles. Who had created whom? Still, Viola was Viola, and Roz would have to accept her as she was, wise and foolish, pure and corrupt—all of her.

"What will you do now?" Alan said.

Startled out of her reverie, Roz looked up at him. His goodhumored eyes, serious now, watched her carefully.

She shrugged. "I don't know. Go back, I suppose. I've got half a year's leave, and nothing to do."

Alan sat down next to her and reached inside his rumpled jacket. "I have something for you." He held out a flat, thick oblong package tied with ribbon.

"This is for you. Something to go on with. Whenever and wherever. If you like." He nudged it at her; she took it, and, with trembling fingers, opened the package. Lavender paper, rubbed and stained, crossed with spidery green ink. Unbelieving, slow to hope, she focused her eyes on the first sheet. In the middle of the top margin, a tiny rosette of green ink. Letters. Viola's letters.

Montfort Abbey, June 11, 1934

Dearest Grace (I shant call you Grumbles anymore, we're far too old, but shall you mind?)
Herbert and I took possession of this dear old heap of stone yesterday, and if you are willing, I propose to write you a letter a month by way of journal . . .

Roz read on, tears stinging her eyes. She came to the end of the first letter, then carefully leafed through the rest. Only then did she look at Alan.

"There are about two hundred of them. Nearly one a month for twenty years. All about the garden, the seasons, and how she loved Montfort. A bit about the writing, but mostly the garden. Nothing else. One version of Viola. The best one."

"But where . . . ?"

"Grace was an old friend, and far away in Scotland. She's still alive. You ought to meet her sometime."

Roz stared at Alan. Understanding and sympathy —she read both in his frank and unaffected gaze. And something more. He had kept these letters back. But was that all? She remembered the sense she had had of his keeping something back, of not quite telling all he knew. She had almost forgotten that feeling of reserve.

"Grace Godwin is my aunt. Her friendship with Viola was the reason I came here to live."

She looked at him accusingly. "You never told me."

"You never asked," he replied imperturbably. "But actually, that's not fair. I thought at first you knew, that Giles had said something to you. But then, when things started to go wrong, I thought I'd keep still a while longer. I didn't want to complicate matters between us. And after that, there wasn't really time. But does it matter?"

"No," Roz said. Oddly, she felt relieved. He had said it would be all right. "And these?" She gestured at the letters.

"My aunt gave them to me two years ago, after Giles started gathering the rest of the letters. She'd kept them back when Giles wrote asking for her correspondence. She never cared much for Giles, so she sent a few early letters, but not these. She thought I might like to do an edition, draw the pictures, make a garden book. I hadn't got up the courage to tackle Giles about it yet, and then all hell broke loose here and I thought, well, all the more reason to hold onto them, wait till things cleared up."

"But . . ." Roz stared at the stack of letters in her hands.

"They're yours. To go on with, if you like. Or to stay on with."

Suddenly restless, he stood up. Roz watched him, her attention arrested once again by the seeming compactness of his body unfolding all at once, surprising her once again with its sudden tallness, air of authority, of stillness and repose beneath the surface.

"I thought we might do it together. Sometime."

Roz blinked back tears.

"Come to Scotland with me, Roz," he said softly. His voice, the quiet timbre of his voice, caught and stopped at her name. His eyes, watching her, blinked quickly, then steadied. It was neither a demand nor an entreaty; it was purely and simply an invitation. Roz wasn't sure about the garden book; she would have to think about that. But she didn't have to decide right now. She stood up, leaving the letters on the stone bench, and walked into his arms. They closed around her.

"I'd love to, Alan," she said. "And I've got lots of time."

About the Author

Susan Kenney attended Northwestern and Cornell universities and teaches English at Colby College. She received a creative writing grant from the National Endowment for the Arts and won the 1982 O. Henry Award for one of her short stories. IN ANOTHER COUNTRY is her most recent novel. GARDEN OF MALICE is her first mystery. She lives in China, Maine.

MURDER...
MAYHEM...
MYSTERY...

From Ballantine

TA-43